BY WILLIAM LANDAY

Mission Flats
The Strangler

Defending JACOB

a novel

William Landay

**Doubleday Large Print
Home Library Edition**

DELACORTE BOOKS

NEW YORK

Published in the United States by Delacorte Press, an imprint of The Random House Publishing Group, a division of Random House, Inc., New York.

DELACORTE PRESS is a registered trademark of
Random House, Inc., and the colophon is a trademark
of Random House, Inc.

ISBN 978-1-61793-462-9

Printed in the United States of America

**This Large Print Book carries the
Seal of Approval of N.A.V.H.**

Part
ONE

"Let us be practical in our expectations of the Criminal Law. . . . [For] we have merely to imagine, by some trick of time travel, meeting our earliest hominid ancestor, Adam, a proto-man, short of stature, luxuriantly furred, newly bipedal, foraging about on the African savannah three million or so years ago. Now, let us agree that we may pronounce whatever laws we like for this clever little creature, still it would be unwise to pet him."

—REYNARD THOMPSON,
A General Theory of Human Violence (1921)

1 | In the Grand Jury

Mr. Logiudice: State your name, please.

Witness: Andrew Barber.

Mr. Logiudice: What do you do for work, Mr. Barber?

Witness: I was an assistant district attorney in this county for 22 years.

Mr. Logiudice: "Was." What do you do for work now?

Witness: I suppose you'd say I'm unemployed.

In April 2008, Neal Logiudice finally subpoenaed me to appear before the
grand jury. By then it was too late. Too late
for his case, certainly, but also too late for
Logiudice. His reputation was already damaged beyond repair, and his career along
with it. A prosecutor can limp along with a
damaged reputation for a while, but his
colleagues will watch him like wolves and
eventually he will be forced out, for the
good of the pack. I have seen it many
times: an ADA is irreplaceable one day,
forgotten the next.

I have always had a soft spot for Neal
Logiudice (pronounced *la-JOO-dis*). He
came to the DA's office a dozen years before this, right out of law school. He was
twenty-nine then, short, with thinning hair
and a little potbelly. His mouth was over-
stuffed with teeth; he had to force it shut,
like a full suitcase, which left him with a
sour, pucker-mouthed expression. I used
to get after him not to make this face in
front of juries—nobody likes a scold—but
he did it unconsciously. He would get up
in front of the jury box shaking his head
and pursing his lips like a schoolmarm or
a priest, and in every juror there stirred a

secret desire to vote against him. Inside the office, Logiudice was a bit of an operator and a kiss-ass. He got a lot of teasing. Other ADAs tooled on him endlessly, but he got it from everyone, even people who worked with the office at arm's length—cops, clerks, secretaries, people who did not usually make their contempt for a prosecutor quite so obvious. They called him Milhouse, after a dweeby character on *The Simpsons,* and they came up with a thousand variations on his name: LoFoolish, LoDoofus, Sid Vicious, Judicious, on and on. But to me, Logiudice was okay. He was just innocent. With the best intentions, he smashed people's lives and never lost a minute of sleep over it. He only went after bad guys, after all. That is the Prosecutor's Fallacy—*They are bad guys because I am prosecuting them*—and Logiudice was not the first to be fooled by it, so I forgave him for being righteous. I even liked him. I rooted for him precisely because of his oddities, the unpronounceable name, the snaggled teeth—which any of his peers would have had straightened with expensive braces, paid for by Mummy and Daddy—even his naked ambition. I saw something in the guy. An air of sturdiness in the way he bore up under so much rejection, how he just took it and took it. He was obviously a working-class kid determined to get for himself what so many others had simply been handed. In that way, and *only* in that way, I suppose, he was just like me.

Now, a dozen years after he arrived in the office, despite all his quirks, he had made it, or nearly made it. Neal Logiudice was First Assistant, the number two man in the Middlesex District Attorney's Office, the DA's right hand and chief trial attorney. He took over the job from me—this kid who once said to me, "Andy, you're *exactly* what I want to be someday." I should have seen it coming.

In the grand jury room that morning, the jurors were in a sullen, defeated mood. They sat, thirty-odd men and women who had not been clever enough to find a way out of serving, all crammed into those school chairs with teardrop-shaped desks for chair arms. They understood their jobs well enough by now. Grand juries serve for months, and they figure out pretty quickly what the gig is all about: accuse, point your finger, name the wicked one.

A grand jury proceeding is not a trial. There is no judge in the room and no defense lawyer. The prosecutor runs the show. It is an investigation and in theory a check on the prosecutor's power, since the grand jury decides whether the prosecutor has enough evidence to haul a suspect into court for trial. If there is enough evidence, the grand jury grants the prosecutor an indictment, his ticket to Superior Court. If not, they return a "no bill" and the case is over before it begins. In practice, no bills are rare. Most grand juries indict. Why not? They only see one side of the case.

But in this case, I suspect the jurors knew Logiudice did not have a case. Not today. The truth was not going to be found, not with evidence this stale and tainted, not after everything that had happened. It had been over a year already—over twelve months since the body of a fourteen-year-old boy was found in the woods with three stab wounds arranged in a line across the chest as if he'd been forked with a trident. But it was not the time, so much. It was everything else. Too late, and the grand jury knew it.

I knew it too.

Only Logiudice was undeterred. He pursed his lips in that odd way of his. He reviewed his notes on a yellow legal pad, considered his next question. He was doing just what I'd taught him. The voice in his head was mine: Never mind how weak your case is. Stick to the system. Play the game the same way it's been played the last five-hundred-odd years, use the same gutter tactic that has always governed cross-examination—lure, trap, fuck.

He said, "Do you recall when you first heard about the Rifkin boy's murder?"

"Yes."

"Describe it."

"I got a call, I think, first from CPAC—that's the state police. Then two more came in right away, one from the Newton police, one from the duty DA. I may have the order wrong, but basically the phone started ringing off the hook."

"When was this?"

"Thursday, April 12, 2007, around nine A.M., right after the body was discovered."

"Why were you called?"

"I was the First Assistant. I was notified of every murder in the county. It was standard procedure."

"But you did not keep every case, did you? You did not personally investigate and try every homicide that came in?"

"No, of course not. I didn't have that kind of time. I kept very few homicides. Most I assigned to other ADAs."

"But this one you kept."

"Yes."

"Did you decide immediately that you were going to keep it for yourself, or did you only decide that later?"

"I decided almost immediately."

"Why? Why did you want this case in particular?"

"I had an understanding with the district attorney, Lynn Canavan: certain cases I would try personally."

"What sort of cases?"

"High-priority cases."

"Why you?"

"I was the senior trial lawyer in the office. She wanted to be sure that important cases were handled properly."

"Who decided if a case was high priority?"

"Me, in the first instance. In consultation with the district attorney, of course, but things tend to move pretty fast at the beginning. There isn't usually time for a meeting."

"So *you* decided the Rifkin murder was a high-priority case?"

"Of course."

"Why?"

"Because it involved the murder of a child. I think we also had an idea it might blow up, catch the media's attention. It was that kind of case. It happened in a wealthy town, with a wealthy victim. We'd already had a few cases like that. At the beginning we did not know exactly what it was, either. In some ways it looked like a schoolhouse killing, a Columbine thing. Basically, we didn't know what the hell it was, but it smelled like a big case. If it had turned out to be a smaller thing, I would have passed it off later, but in those first few hours I had to be sure everything was done right."

"Did you inform the district attorney that you had a conflict of interest?"

"No."

"Why not?"

"Because I didn't have one."

"Wasn't your son, Jacob, a classmate of the dead boy?"

"Yes, but I didn't know the victim. Jacob didn't know him either, as far as I was aware. I'd never even heard the dead boy's name."

"You did not know the kid. All right. But you did know that he and your son were in the same grade at the same middle school in the same town?"

"Yes."

"And you still didn't think you were conflicted out? You didn't think your objectivity might be called into question?"

"No. Of course not."

"Even in hindsight? You insist, you— Even in hindsight, you *still* don't feel the circumstances gave even the *appearance* of a conflict?"

"No, there was nothing improper about it. There was nothing even unusual about it. The fact that I lived in the town where the murder happened? That was a *good* thing. In smaller counties, the prosecutor often lives in the community where a crime happens, he often knows the people affected by it. So what? So he wants to catch the murderer *even more*? That's not a conflict of interest. Look, the bottom line is, I have a conflict with all murderers. That's my job. This was a horrible, horrible crime; it was my job to do something about it. I was determined to do just that."

"Okay." Logiudice lowered his eyes to his pad. No sense attacking the witness so early in his testimony. He would come back to this point later in the day, no doubt, when I was tired. For now, best to keep the temperature down.

"You understand your Fifth Amendment rights?"

"Of course."

"And you have waived them?"

"Apparently. I'm here. I'm talking."

Titters from the grand jury.

Logiudice laid down his pad, and with it he seemed to set aside his game plan for a moment. "Mr. Barber—Andy—could I just ask you something: why not invoke them? Why not remain silent?" The next sentence he left unsaid: *That's what I would do.*

I thought for a moment that this was a tactic, a bit of playacting. But Logiudice seemed to mean it. He was worried I was up to something. He did not want to be tricked, to look like a fool.

I said, "I have no desire to remain silent. I want the truth to come out."

"No matter what?"

"I believe in the system, same as you, same as everyone here."

Now, this was not exactly true. I do not believe in the court system, at least I do not think it is especially good at finding the truth. No lawyer does. We have all seen too many mistakes, too many bad results. A jury verdict is just a guess—a well-intentioned guess, generally, but you simply cannot tell fact from fiction by taking a vote. And yet, despite all that, I do believe in the power of the ritual. I believe in the religious symbolism, the black robes, the marble-columned courthouses like Greek temples. When we hold a trial, we are saying a mass. We are praying together to do what is right and to be protected from danger, and that is worth doing whether or not our prayers are actually heard.

Of course, Logiudice did not go in for that sort of solemn bullshit. He lived in the lawyer's binary world, guilty or not guilty, and he was determined to keep me pinned there.

"You believe in the system, do you?" he

sniffed. "All right, Andy, let's get back to it, then. We'll let the system do its work." He gave the jury a knowing, smart-ass look.

Attaboy, Neal. Don't let the witness jump into bed with the jury—*you* jump into bed with the jury. Jump in there and snuggle right up beside them under the blanket and leave the witness out in the cold. I smirked. I would have stood up and applauded if I'd been allowed to, because I taught him to do precisely this. Why deny myself a little fatherly pride? I must not have been all bad—I turned Neal Logiudice into a half-decent lawyer, after all.

"So go on already," I said, nuzzling the jury's neck. "Stop screwing around and get on with it, Neal."

He gave me a look, then picked up his yellow pad again and scanned it, looking for his place. I could practically read the thought spelled out across his forehead: *lure, trap, fuck.* "Okay," he said, "let's pick it up at the aftermath of the murder."

2 | Our Crowd

April 2007: twelve months earlier.

When the Rifkins opened their home for the shiva, the Jewish period of mourning, it seemed the whole town came. The family would not be allowed to mourn in private. The boy's murder was a public event; the grieving would be as well. The house was so full that when the murmur of conversation occasionally swelled, the whole thing began to feel awkwardly like a party, until the crowd lowered its voice as one, as if an invisible volume knob were being turned.

I made apologetic faces as I moved through this crowd, repeating "Excuse me," turning this way and that to shuffle by.

People stared with curious expressions. Someone said, "That's him, that's Andy Barber," but I did not stop. We were four days past the murder now, and everyone knew I was handling the case. They wanted to ask about it, naturally, about suspects and clues and all that, but they did not dare. For the moment, the details of the investigation did not matter, only the raw fact that an innocent kid was dead.

Murdered! The news sucker-punched them. Newton had no crime to speak of. What the locals knew about violence necessarily came from news reports and TV shows. They had supposed that violent crime was limited to the city, to an underclass of urban hillbillies. They were wrong about that, of course, but they were not fools and they would not have been so shocked by the murder of an adult. What made the Rifkin murder so profane was that it involved one of the town's children. It was a violation of Newton's self-image. For a while a sign had stood in Newton Centre declaring the place "A Community of Families, A Family of Communities," and you often heard it repeated that Newton was "a good place to raise kids." Which indeed it was. It brimmed with test-prep centers and after-school tutors, karate dojos and Saturday soccer leagues. The town's young parents especially prized this idea of Newton as a child's paradise. Many of them had left the hip, sophisticated city to move here. They had accepted massive expenses, stultifying monotony, and the queasy disappointment of settling for a conventional life. To these ambivalent residents, the whole suburban project made sense only because it was "a good place to raise kids." They had staked everything on it.

Moving from room to room, I passed one tribe after another. The kids, the dead boy's friends, had crowded into a small den at the front of the house. They talked softly, stared. One girl's mascara was smeared with tears. My own son, Jacob, sat in a low chair, lank and gangly, apart from the others. He gazed into his cell phone screen, uninterested in the conversations around him.

The grief-stunned family was next door in the living room, old grandmas, baby cousins.

In the kitchen, finally, were the parents of the kids who'd gone through the Newton schools with Ben Rifkin. This was our crowd. We had known one another since our kids showed up for the first day of kindergarten eight years earlier. We had stood together at a thousand morning drop-offs and afternoon pickups, endless soccer games and school fund-raisers and one memorable production of *Twelve Angry Men.* Still, a few close friendships aside, we did not know one another all that well. There was a camaraderie among us, certainly, but no real connection. Most of these acquaintanceships would not survive our kids' graduation from high school. But in those first few days after Ben Rifkin's murder, we felt an illusion of closeness. It was as if we had all suddenly been revealed to one another.

In the Rifkins' vast kitchen—Wolf cooktop, Sub-Zero fridge, granite counters, English-white cabinets—the school parents huddled in clusters of three or four and made intimate confessions about insomnia, sadness, unshakeable dread. They talked over and over about Columbine and 9/11 and how Ben's death made them cling to their own children while they could. The extravagant emotions of that evening were heightened by the warm light in the kitchen, cast by hanging fixtures with burnt-orange globes. In that firelight, as I entered the room, the parents were indulging one another in the luxury of confessing secrets.

At the kitchen island one of the moms, Toby Lanzman, was arranging hors d'oeuvres on a serving platter as I came into the room. A dish towel was slung over her shoulder. The sinews in her forearms stood out as she worked. Toby was my wife Laurie's best friend, one of the few enduring connections we had made here. She saw me searching for my wife, and she pointed across the room.

"She's mothering the mothers," Toby said.

"I see that."

"Well, we can all use a little mothering at the moment."

I grunted, gave her a puzzled look, and moved off. Toby was an incitement. My only defense against her was a tactical retreat.

Laurie stood with a small circle of moms. Her hair, which has always been thick and unruly, was swept up in a loose bun at the back of her head and held there by a big tortoiseshell hair clip. She rubbed a friend's upper arm in a consoling way. Her friend inclined toward Laurie visibly, like a cat being stroked.

When I reached her, Laurie put her left arm around my waist. "Hi, sweetie."

"It's time to go."

"Andy, you've been saying that since the second we got here."

"Not true. I've been thinking it, not saying it."

"Well, it's been written all over your face." She sighed. "I knew we should have come in separate cars."

She took a moment to appraise me. She did not want to go but understood that I was uneasy, that I felt spotlighted here, that I was not much of a talker to begin with—chitchat in crowded rooms always left me exhausted—and these things all had to be weighed. A family had to be managed, like any other organization.

"You go," she decided. "I'll get a ride home with Toby."

"Yeah?"

"Yeah. Why not? Take Jacob with you."

"You're sure?" I leaned down—Laurie is almost a foot shorter than me—to stage-whisper, "Because I'd *love* to stay."

She laughed. "Go. Before I change my mind."

The funereal women stared.

"Go on. Your coat's in the bedroom up-stairs."

I went upstairs and found myself in a long corridor. The noise was muted here, which came as a relief. The echo of the crowd still murmured in my ears. I began searching for the coats. In one bedroom, which apparently belonged to the dead boy's little sister, there was a pile of coats on the bed, but mine was not in the pile.

The door to the next room was closed. I knocked, opened it, poked my head in to peek around.

The room was gloomy. The only light came from a brass floor lamp in the far corner. The dead boy's father sat in a wing chair under this light. Dan Rifkin was small, trim, delicate. As always, his hair was sprayed in place. He wore an expensive-looking dark suit. There was a rough two-inch tear in his lapel to symbolize his broken heart—a waste of an expensive suit, I thought. In the dim light, his eyes were sunken, rimmed in bluish circles like a raccoon's eye-mask.

"Hello, Andy," he said.

"Sorry. Just looking for my coat. Didn't mean to bother you."

"No, come sit a minute."

"Nah. I don't want to intrude."

"Please, sit, sit. There's something I want to ask you."

My heart sank. I have seen the writhing of survivors of murder victims. My job forces me to watch it. Parents of murdered children have it worst, and to me the fathers have it even worse than the mothers because they are taught to be stoic, to "act like a man." Studies have shown that fathers of murdered children often die within a few years of the murder, often of heart failure. Really, they die of grief. At some point a prosecutor realizes he cannot survive that kind of heartbreak either. He cannot follow the fathers down. So he focuses instead on the technical aspects of the job. He turns it into a craft like any other. The trick is to keep the suffering at a distance.

But Dan Rifkin insisted. He waved his arm like a cop directing cars to move ahead, and seeing there was no choice, I closed the door gently and took the chair next to his.

"Drink?" He held up a tumbler of coppery whiskey, neat.

"No."

"Is there any news, Andy?"

"No. Afraid not."

He nodded, looked off toward the corner of the room, disappointed. "I've always loved this room. This is where I come to think. When something like this happens, you spend a lot of time thinking." He made a tight little smile: *Don't worry, I'm all right.*

"I'm sure that's true."

"The thing I can't get past is: why did this guy do it?"

"Dan, you really shouldn't—"

"No, hear me out. Just—I don't—I don't need hand-holding. I'm a rational person, that's all. I have questions. Not about the details. When we've talked, you and I, it's always about the details: the evidence, the

court procedures. But I'm a rational person, okay? I'm a rational person and I have
questions. Other questions."

I sank in my seat, felt my shoulders
relax, acquiescing.

"Okay. So here it is: Ben was so *good.*
That's the first thing. Of course no kid deserves this, anyway. I know that. But Ben
really was a good boy. He was *so* good.
And just a kid. He was fourteen years old,
for God's sake! Never made any trouble.
Never. Never, never, never. So why? What
was the motive? I don't mean anger, greed,
jealousy, that kind of motive, because
there *can't* be an ordinary motive in this
case, there can't, it just doesn't make
sense. Who could feel that kind of, of *rage*
against Ben, against any little kid? It just
doesn't make sense. It just doesn't make
sense." Rifkin put the four fingertips of his
right hand on his forehead and worked the
skin in slow circles. "What I mean is: what
separates these people? Because I've felt
those things, of course, those *motives*—
angry, greedy, jealous—you've felt them,
everybody's felt them. But we've never
killed anyone. You see? We never *could*

kill anyone. But some people do, some people *can.* Why is that?"

"I don't know."

"You must have some sense of these things."

"No. I don't, really."

"But you talk to them, you meet them. What do they say, the killers?"

"They don't talk much, most of them."

"Do you ever ask? Not why they did it, but what makes them capable of it in the first place."

"No."

"Why not?"

"Because they wouldn't answer. Their lawyers wouldn't let them answer."

"Lawyers!" He tossed his hand.

"They wouldn't know how to answer, anyway, most of them. These philosophical murderers—Chianti and fava beans and all that stuff—it's bullshit. It's just the movies. Anyway, they're full of shit, these guys. If they had to answer, they'd probably tell you about their rough childhoods or something. They'd make themselves the victims. That's the usual story."

He nodded once, to urge me on.

"Dan, the thing is, you can't torture your-self looking for reasons. There are none. It's not logical. Not the part you're talking about."

Rifkin slid down in his chair a little, con-centrating, as if he would need to give the whole thing more thought. His eyes glis-tened but his voice was even, controlled. "Do other parents ask these sorts of things?"

"They ask all kinds of things."

"Do you see them after the case is over? The parents?"

"Sometimes."

"I mean long after, years."

"Sometimes."

"And do they—how do they seem? Are they all right?"

"Some of them are all right."

"But some of them aren't."

"Some of them aren't."

"What do they do, the ones who make it? What are the key things? There must be a pattern. What's the strategy, what are the best practices? What's worked for them?"

"They get help. They rely on their fami-lies, the people around them. There are groups out there for survivors; they use those. We can put you in touch. You should talk to the victim advocate. She'll set you up with a support group. It's very helpful. You can't do it alone, that's the thing. You have to remember there are other people out there who have gone through it, who know what you're going through."

"And the other ones, the parents who don't make it, what happens to them? The ones who never recover?"

"You're not going to be one of those."

"But if I am? What happens to me, to us?"

"We're not going to let that happen. We're not even going to think that way."

"But it does happen. It does happen, doesn't it? It does."

"Not to you. Ben wouldn't want it to happen to you."

Silence.

"I know your son," Rifkin said. "Jacob."

"Yes."

"I've seen him around the school. He seems like a good kid. Big handsome boy. You must be proud."

"I am."

"He looks like you, I think."

"Yeah, I've been told."

He took a deep breath. "You know, I find

myself thinking about these kids from Ben's class. I feel attached. I want to see them succeed, you know? I've watched them grow up, I feel close to them. Is that unusual? Am I feeling that because it makes me feel closer to Ben? Is that why I'm latching onto these other kids? Because that's what it sounds like, doesn't it? It looks weird."

"Dan, don't worry about how things look. People are going to think whatever they think. The hell with 'em. You can't worry about it."

He massaged his forehead some more. His agony could not have been more obvious if he had been bleeding on the floor. I wanted to help him. At the same time, I wanted to get away from him.

"It would help me if I *knew,* if, if the case was resolved. It will help me when you resolve the case. Because the uncertainty—it's draining. It'll help when the case is resolved, won't it? In other cases you've seen, that helps the parents, doesn't it?"

"Yes, I think so."

"I don't mean to pressure you. I don't mean to sound that way. It's just, I think it will help me when the case is resolved and

I know this guy is—when he's *locked up* and *put away.* I know you'll do that. I have faith in you, of course. I mean, *of course.* I'm not doubting you, Andy. I'm just saying it will help me. Me, my wife, everyone. That's what we need, I think. Closure. That's what we're looking to you for."

That night Laurie and I lay in bed reading.

"I still think they're making a mistake opening the school so soon."

"Laurie, we've been all through this." My voice had a bored tone. *Been there, done that.* "Jacob will be perfectly safe. We'll take him there ourselves, we'll walk him right up to the door. There'll be cops all over. He'll be safer in school than anywhere else."

"Safer. You can't know that. How could you know that? Nobody has any idea who this guy is or where he is or what he intends to do next."

"They have to open the school sometime. Life goes on."

"You're wrong, Andy."

"How long do you want them to wait?"

"Until they catch the guy."

"That could take a while."

"So? What's the worst that could happen? The kids miss a few days of school. So what? At least they'd be safe."

"You can't make them totally safe. It's a big world out there. Big, dangerous world."

"Okay, safer."

I laid my book down on my belly, where it formed a little roof. "Laurie, if you keep the school closed, you send these kids the wrong message. School isn't supposed to be dangerous. It's not a place they should be afraid of. It's their second home. It's where they spend most of their waking hours. They *want* to be there. They want to be with their friends, not stuck at home, hiding under the bed so the bogeyman doesn't get them."

"The bogeyman already got one of them. That makes him not a bogeyman."

"Okay, but you see what I'm saying."

"Oh, I see what you're saying, Andy. I'm just telling you you're wrong. The number one priority is keeping the kids safe, physically. Then they can go be with their friends or whatever. Until they catch the guy, you can't promise me the kids'll be safe."

"You need a guarantee?"

"Yes."

"We'll catch the guy," I said. "I guarantee it."

"When?"

"Soon."

"You know this?"

"I expect it. We always catch 'em."

"Not always. Remember the guy who killed his wife and wrapped her in a blanket in the back of the Saab?"

"We *did* catch that guy. We just couldn't—all right, *almost* always. We almost always catch 'em. This guy we'll catch, I promise you."

"What if you're wrong?"

"If I'm wrong, I'm sure you'll tell me all about it."

"No, I mean if you're wrong and some poor kid gets hurt?"

"That won't happen, Laurie."

She frowned, giving up. "There's no arguing with you. It's like running into a wall over and over again."

"We're not arguing. We're discussing."

"You're a lawyer; you don't know the difference. *I'm* arguing."

"Look, what do you want me to say, Laurie?"

"I don't want you to say anything. I want you to listen. You know, being confident isn't the same as being right. Think. We might be putting our son in danger." She pressed her fingertip to my temple and shoved it, a gesture half playful, half pissed off. "Think."

She turned away, laid her book atop a wobbly pile of others on her night table, and lay down with her back to me, curled up, a kid in an adult body.

"Here," I said, "scootch over."

With a series of body hops, she moved backward until her back was against me. Until she could feel some warmth or sturdiness or whatever she needed from me at that moment. I rubbed her upper arm.

"It's going to be all right."

She grunted.

I said, "I suppose make-up sex is out of the question?"

"I thought we weren't arguing."

"I wasn't, but you were. And I want you to know: it's okay, I forgive you."

"Ha, ha. Maybe if you say you're sorry."

"I'm sorry."

"You don't sound sorry."

"I am truly, deeply sorry. Truly."

"Now say you're wrong."

"Wrong?"

"Say you're wrong. Do you want it or not?"

"Hm. So, just to be clear: all I have to do is say I'm wrong and a beautiful woman will make passionate love to me."

"I didn't say passionate. Just regular."

"Okay, so: say I'm wrong and a beautiful woman will make love to me, completely without passion but with pretty good technique. That's the situation?"

"Pretty good technique?"

"Astounding technique."

"Yes, Counselor, that's the situation."

I put away my book, McCullough's biography of Truman, atop a slippery pile of slick magazines on my own night table, and turned off the light. "Forget it. I'm not wrong."

"Doesn't matter. You already said I'm beautiful. I win."

3 | Back to School

Early the next morning there was a voice in the dark, in Jacob's room, a groan—and I woke up to find my body already moving, swinging up onto its feet, shuffling around the foot of the bed. Still dense with sleep, I passed out of the gloom of the bedroom, through the gray light of dawn in the hallway, then back into darkness again in my son's bedroom.

I turned on the wall switch and adjusted the dimmer. Jacob's room was cluttered with huge oafish sneakers, a MacBook covered with stickers, an iPod, schoolbooks, paperback novels, shoe boxes filled with old baseball cards and comic books. In a corner, an Xbox was hooked up to an old TV. The Xbox disks and their cases were piled nearby, mostly combat role-play games. There was dirty laundry, of course, but also two stacks of clean laundry neatly folded and delivered by Laurie, which Jacob had declined to put away in his bureau because it was easier to pluck clean clothes right from the piles. On top of a low bookcase was a group of trophies Jacob had won when he was a kid playing youth soccer. He had not been much of an athlete, but back then every kid got a trophy, and in the years since he had simply never moved them. The little statues sat there like religious relics, ignored, virtually invisible to him. There was a vintage movie poster for a 1970s chop-socky picture, *Five Fingers of Death,* which featured a man in a karate outfit smashing his well-manicured fist through a brick wall. ("The Martial Arts Masterpiece! SEE one incredible onslaught after another! PALE before the forbidden ritual of the steel palm! CHEER the young warrior who alone takes on the evil warlords of martial arts!") The clutter in here was so deep and permanent, Laurie and I had long since stopped fighting with Jacob to clean it up. For that matter, we had stopped even noticing it. Laurie had a theory that the mess was a projection of Jacob's inner life—that stepping into his bedroom was like stepping into his chaotic teenage mind—so it was silly to nag him about it. Believe me, this is what you get when you marry a shrink's daughter. To me, it was just a messy room and it drove me crazy every time I came into it.

Jacob lay on his side at the edge of his bed, not moving. His head was arched back and his mouth hung open, like a howling wolf. He was not snoring but his breathing had a clotted sound; he had been fighting a little cold. Between sliffy breaths, he whimpered, "N—, n—": *No, no.*

"Jacob," I whispered. I reached out to soothe his head. "Jake!"

He cried again. His eyes fluttered behind the eyelids.

Outside, a trolley clattered by, the first train into Boston on the Riverside line, which passed every morning at 6:05.

"It's just a dream," I told him.

I felt a little gush of pleasure at comforting my son this way. The situation triggered one of those nostalgic pangs that parents are subject to, a dim memory of Jake as a three- or four-year-old boy when we had a bedtime routine: I would ask, "Who loves Jacob?" and he would answer, "Daddy does." It was the last thing we said to each other before he went to sleep each night. But Jake never needed reassuring. It never occurred to him that daddies might disappear, not his daddy at any rate. It was me that needed our little call-and-response. When I was a kid, my father was not around. I barely knew him. So I resolved that my own children would never feel that; they would never know what it is to be fatherless. How strange that in just a few years Jake would leave *me.* He would go off to college, and my time as an everyday, active-duty father would be over. I would see him less and less, eventually our relationship would wither to a few visits a year on holidays and summer weekends. I could not quite imagine it. What was I if not Jacob's father?

Then another thought, unavoidable in the circumstances: no doubt Dan Rifkin meant to keep his son from harm too, no less than I did, and no doubt he was as unprepared as I was to say good-bye to his son. But Ben Rifkin lay in a refrigerated drawer in the M.E.'s office while my son lay in his warm bed, with nothing but luck to separate the one from the other. I am ashamed to admit that I thought, *Thank God. Thank God it was his kid that got taken, not mine.* I did not think I could survive the loss.

I knelt beside the bed and circled my arms around Jacob and laid my head on his. I remembered again: when he was a little kid, the moment he woke up every morning Jake used to pad sleepily across the hall to our bed to snuggle. Now, under my arms he was impossibly big and bony and coltish. Handsome, with dark curly hair and a ruddy complexion. He was fourteen. Certainly he would never allow me to hold him this way if he was awake. In the last few years he had become a little surly and reclusive and a pain in the ass. At times it was like having a stranger living in the house—a vaguely hostile stranger. Typical adolescent behavior, Laurie said. He was trying out different personas, getting ready to leave childhood behind for good.

I was surprised when my touch actually

settled Jacob down, stopped whatever bad dream he had been having. He drew in a single deep breath and rolled over. His breathing relaxed into a comfortable stride, and he settled into a deep sleep, deeper than I was capable of. (At fifty-one years old, I seemed to have forgotten how to sleep. I woke up several times a night and rarely got more than four or five hours of sleep.) It pleased me to think I had soothed him, but who knows? Maybe he did not even know I was there.

That morning the three of us were all skittish. The reopening of the McCormick School just five days after the murder had us all a little rattled. We followed our normal routine—showers, coffee and bagels, glance at the Net for email and sports scores and news—but we were tense and awkward. We were all up by six-thirty but we dawdled and found ourselves running late, which only added to the anxiety.

    Laurie in particular was nervous. She was not only afraid for Jacob, I think. She was unnerved by the murder, still, as healthy people are surprised when they become seriously ill for the first time. You might expect that living with a prosecutor all those years would have prepared Laurie better than her neighbors. She ought to have known by then that—though I was hard-hearted and tone-deaf to point it out the night before—life *does* go on. Even the wettest violence, in the end, is cooked down to the stuff of court cases: a ream of paper, a few exhibits, a dozen sweating and stammering witnesses. The world looks away, and why not? People die, some by violence—it is tragic, yes, but at some point it ceases to be shocking, at least to an old prosecutor. Laurie had seen the cycle many times, watching over my shoulder, yet she was still thrown by the irruption of violence in her own life. It showed in her every movement, in the arthritic way she held herself, in the subdued tone of her voice. She was working to maintain her composure and not having an easy time of it.

Jacob stared into his MacBook and chewed his rubbery microwaved frozen bagel in silence. Laurie tried to draw him out, as she always does, but he was not having any of it.

"How are you feeling about going back, Jacob?"

"I don't know."

"Are you nervous? Worried? What?"

"I don't know."

"How can you not know? Who else would know?"

"Mom, I don't feel like talking now."

This was the polite phrase we had instructed him to use instead of just ignoring his parents. But by this point he had repeated "I don't feel like talking now" so often and so robotically, the politeness had drained out of it.

"Jacob, can you just tell me if you're feeling all right so I don't have to worry?"

"I just *said.* I don't feel like talking."

Laurie gave me an exasperated look.

"Jake, your mother asked you a question. It wouldn't kill you to answer."

"I'm *fine.*"

"I think your mother was looking for a bit more detail than that."

"Dad, just—" His attention drifted back to his computer.

I shrugged at Laurie. "The child says he's fine."

"I got that. Thanks."

"No worries, mother. Hunky-dory, end of story."

"How about you, husband?"

"I'm *fine.* I don't feel like talking now."

Jacob shot me a sour look.

Laurie smiled reluctantly. "I need a daughter to even things up around here, give me someone to talk to. It's like living with a couple of tombstones."

"What you need is a wife."

"The thought has occurred to me."

We both accompanied Jacob to school. Most of the other parents did the same, and at eight o'clock the school looked like a carnival. There was a little traffic jam out front, heavy with Honda minivans and family sedans and SUVs. A few news vans were parked nearby, barnacled with dishes, boxes, antennae. Police sawhorses blocked either end of the circular driveway. A Newton cop stood guard near the school entrance. Another waited in a cruiser parked out front. Students wended their way through these obstacles toward the door, their backs bent under heavy packs. Parents loitered on the sidewalk or escorted their kids all the way to the front door.

I parked our minivan on the street almost a block away and we sat gawking.

"Whoa," Jacob murmured.

"Whoa," Laurie agreed.

"This is wild." Jacob.

Laurie looked stricken. Her left hand dangled from the armrest, her long fingers and beautiful clear nails. She always had lovely, elegant hands; my own mother's fat-fingered scrubwoman hands looked like dog's paws beside Laurie's. I reached across to take her hand, lacing my fingers in hers so that our two hands made one fist. The sight of her hand in mine made me briefly sentimental. I gave her an encouraging look and jostled our knotted hands. This was, for me, a hysterical burst of emotion, and Laurie squeezed my hand to thank me for it. She turned to gaze through the windshield again. Her dark hair was threaded with gray. Faint wrinkles branched from the corners of her eyes and mouth. But, looking across, I seemed to see her younger, unlined face too, somehow.

"What?"

"Nothing."

"You're staring."

"You're my wife. I'm allowed to stare."

"Is that the rule?"

"Yes. Stare, leer, ogle, anything I want. Trust me. I'm a lawyer."

A good marriage drags a long tail of memory behind it. A single word or gesture, a tone of voice can conjure up so many remembrances. Laurie and I had been flirting like this for thirty-odd years, since the day we met in college and we both went a little love-crazy. Things were different now, of course. At fifty-one, love was a quieter experience. We drifted through the days together. But we both remembered how it all started, and even now, in the middle of my middle age, when I think of that shining young girl, I still feel a little thrill of first love, still there, still burning like a pilot light.

We walked toward the school, climbing the little mound the building is set on.

Jacob sloped along between us. He wore a faded brown hoodie, droopy jeans, and Adidas Superstar throwbacks. His backpack was slung over his right shoulder. His hair was a little long. It hung down over his ears, with a wing across his forehead nearly covering his eyebrows. A braver boy would have taken this look further and flaunted himself as a goth or a hipster or some other flavor of rebel, but that was not Jacob. A hint of nonconformity was all he would risk. There was a wondering little smile on his face. He seemed to be enjoying all the excitement, which, among other things, undeniably broke up the tedium of eighth grade.

When we reached the sidewalk in front of the school, we were absorbed into a group of three young mothers, all of whom had kids in Jacob's class. The strongest and most outgoing of them, the implicit leader, was Toby Lanzman, the woman I'd seen at the Rifkins' shiva the night before. She wore shimmery black workout pants, a fitted T-shirt, and a baseball cap with her ponytail threaded through a hole in the back. Toby was a fitness addict. She had a runner's lean body and fatless face. Among the school fathers, her muscularity was both exciting and intimidating, but electric either way. Me, I thought she was worth a dozen of the other parents here. She was the type of friend you'd want in a crisis. The type who would stand by you.

But if Toby was the captain of this group of mothers, Laurie was its real emotional center—its heart and probably its brain too. Laurie was everyone's confidante. When something went wrong, when one of them lost a job or a husband strayed or a child struggled in school, it was Laurie she called. They were attracted to the same quality in Laurie that I was, no doubt: she had a thoughtful, cerebral warmth. I had a vague sense, at emotional moments, that these women were my romantic rivals, that they wanted some of the same things from Laurie that I did (approval, love). So, when I saw them gathered together in their shadow family, with Toby in the role of stern father and Laurie the warmhearted mother, it was impossible not to feel a little jealous and excluded.

Toby gathered us into the little circle on the sidewalk, welcoming each of us with a distinct protocol that I never got quite right: a hug for Laurie, a kiss on the cheek for me—*mwah,* she said in my ear—a simple hello for Jacob. "Isn't this all just terrible?" She sighed.

"I'm in shock," Laurie confessed, relieved to be among her friends. "I just can't process this. I don't know what to think." Her expression was more puzzled than distressed. She could not make any logic of what had happened.

"How about you, Jacob?" Toby trained her eyes on Jacob, determined to ignore the age difference between them. "How are you doing?"

Jacob shrugged. "I'm good."

"Ready to get back to school?"

He dismissed the question with another, bigger shrug—he jacked his shoulders up high then dropped them—to show he knew he was being patronized.

I said, "Better get going, Jake, you're going to be late. You have to go through a security check, remember."

"Yeah, okay." Jacob rolled his eyes, as if all this concern for the kids' security was yet another confirmation of the eternal stupidity of adults. Didn't they realize it was all too late?

"Just get going," I said, smiling at him.

"No weapons, no sharp objects?" Toby said with a smirk. She was quoting a directive that had gone out from the school principal via email, which spelled out various new security measures for the school.

Jacob thumb-lifted his backpack a few inches off his shoulder. "Just books."

"All right, then. Get going. Go learn something."

Jacob offered a wave to the adults, who smiled their benevolence, and he shambled off past the police sawhorses, joining the tide of students headed for the school door.

When he was gone, the group abandoned their pretense of cheerfulness. The full weight of worry descended on them.

Even Toby sounded beleaguered. "Has anyone reached out to Dan and Joan Rifkin?"

"I don't think so," Laurie said.

"We really should. I mean, we have to."

"Those poor people. I can't even imagine."

"I don't think anyone knows what to say to them." This was Susan Frank, the only woman in the group dressed in work clothes, the gray wool skirt-suit of a lawyer. "I mean, what *can* you say? Really, what on earth can you say to someone after that? It's just so—I don't know, overwhelming."

"Nothing," Laurie agreed. "There's absolutely nothing you can say to make it right.

But it doesn't matter what you say; the point is just to reach out to them."

"Just let them know you're thinking of them," Toby echoed. "That's all anyone can do, let them know you're thinking of them."

The last of the women present, Wendy Seligman, asked me, "What do you think, Andy? You have to do this all the time, don't you? Talk to families after something like this."

"I don't say anything, mostly. I just stick to the case. I don't talk about anything else. The other stuff, there's not a lot I can do."

Wendy nodded, disappointed. She considered me a bore, one of those husbands who must be tolerated, the lesser half of a married couple. But she revered Laurie, who seemed to excel in each of the three distinct roles these women juggled, as wife, mother, and only lastly as herself. If I was interesting to Laurie, Wendy presumed, then I must have a hidden side that I did not bother to share—which meant, perhaps, that *I* considered *her* dull, not worth the effort that real conversation required. Wendy was divorced, the only divorcée or single mom in their little group, and she was prone to imagine that others studied her for defects.

Toby tried to lighten the mood. "You know, we spent all those years keeping these kids away from toy guns and violent TV shows and video games. Bob and I didn't even let our kids have water guns, for God's sake, unless they looked like something else. And even then we did not call them 'guns'; we called them 'squirters' or whatever, you know, like the kids wouldn't *know.* Now this. It's like—" She threw up her hands in comic exasperation.

But the joke fell flat.

"It's ironic," Wendy agreed somberly, to make Toby feel heard.

"It's true." Susan sighed, again for Toby's benefit.

Laurie said, "I think we overestimate what we can do as parents. Your kid is your kid. You get what you get."

"So I could have given the kids the damn water guns?"

"Probably. With Jacob—I don't know. I just wonder sometimes if it ever really mattered, all the things we did, all the things we worried about. He was always what he is now, just smaller. It's the same with all our kids. None of them are really all that different from what they were when they were little."

"Yes, but our parenting styles haven't changed either. So maybe we're just teaching them the same things."

Wendy: "I don't have a parenting style. I'm just making it up as I go."

Susan: "Me too. We all are. Except Laurie. Laurie, you probably have a parenting style. Toby, you too."

"I do not!"

"Oh, yes, you do! You probably read books about it."

"Not me." Laurie put up her hands: *I'm innocent.* "Anyway, the point is, I just think we flatter ourselves when we say we can engineer our kids to be this way or that way. It's mostly just hardwired."

The women eyed one another. Maybe Jacob was hardwired, not their kids. Not like Jacob, anyway.

Wendy said, "Did any of you know Ben?" She meant Ben Rifkin, the murder victim. They had not known him. Calling him by his first name was just a way of adopting him.

Toby: "No. Dylan never was friends with

him. And Ben never played sports or anything."

Susan: "He was in Max's class a few
times. I used to see him. He seemed like a
good kid, I guess, but who ever knows?"

Toby: "They have lives of their own, these
kids. I'm sure they have their secrets."

Laurie: "Just like us. Just like us at their
age, for that matter."

Toby: "I was a good girl. At their age, I
never gave my parents a thing to worry
about."

Laurie: "I was a good girl too."

I said, intruding, "You weren't *that* good."

"I was until I met you. You corrupted me."

"Did I? Well, I'm quite proud of that. I'll
have to put it on my résumé."

But the kidding felt inappropriate so
soon after the mention of the dead child's
name, and I felt crude and embarrassed
before the women, whose emotional sen-
sibilities were so much finer than mine.

There was a moment's silence then
Wendy blurted, "Oh my God, those poor,
poor people. That mother! And here we are,
just 'Life goes on, back to school,' and her
little boy will never, never come back." Wen-

dy's eyes became watery. *The horror of it: one day, through no fault of your own—*

Toby came forward to hug her friend, and Laurie and Susan rubbed Wendy's back.

Excluded, I stood there a moment with a dumb, well-meaning expression—a tight smile, a softening around the eyes—then I excused myself to go check on the security station at the school entrance before things devolved into more weepiness. I did not quite understand the depth of Wendy's grief for a child she did not know; I took it as yet another sign of the woman's emotional vulnerability. Also, that Wendy had echoed my own words from the night before, "Life goes on," seemed to align her with Laurie in a tiff that had only just been resolved. All in all, an opportune moment to take off.

I made my way to the security station that had been set up in the school foyer. It consisted of a long table where coats and backpacks were inspected by hand and an area where Newton cops, two male, two female, swept the kids with metal-detecting wands. Jake was right: the whole thing was ridiculous. There was no reason to think anyone would bring a weapon into the school or that the murderer had any connection to the school at all. The body had not even been found on school grounds. It made sense only as a show for the anxious parents.

As I arrived, the Kabuki ritual of searching each student had come to a stop. In a rising voice, a young girl negotiated with one of the cops while a second cop looked on, his wand held across his chest at port arms as if he might be called upon to club her with it. The trouble, it became clear, was her sweatshirt, which read "F-C-U-K." The cop had deemed this message "inciteful" and thus, according to the school's improvised security rules, forbidden. The girl explained to him that the initials stood for a brand of clothing that you could find at any mall, and even if it did suggest a "bad word" how could anyone be *incited* by it? and she was not giving up her sweatshirt which was very expensive and why should she let some cop throw an expensive sweatshirt in a Dumpster for no good reason? They were at an impasse.

Her adversary, the cop, had a stooped posture. His neck craned forward so that his head rode out in front of his body, giving him a vulturous look. But he straightened when he saw me approach, drawing his head back, causing the skin under his chin to fold over itself.

"Everything okay?" I asked the cop.

"Yes, *sir.*"

Yes, *sir.* I hated the military mannerisms adopted by police departments, the bogus military ranks and chain of command and all that. "At ease," I said, intending it as a joke, but the cop looked down at his feet, abashed.

"Hi," I said to the girl, who looked like she was in seventh or eighth grade. I did not recognize her as one of Jacob's classmates, but she might have been.

"Hi."

"What's the problem here? Maybe I can help."

"You're Jacob Barber's dad, aren't you?"

"That's right."

"Aren't you like a cop or something?"

"Just a DA. And who are you?"

"Sarah."

"Sarah. Okay, Sarah. What's the trouble?"

The girl paused, uncertain. Then another gush: "It's just, I'm trying to tell this officer he doesn't have to take away my sweatshirt, I'll put it in my locker or I'll turn it inside out, what*ever.* Only he doesn't like what it says, even though no one will even *see* it, and there's nothing wrong with it anyway, it's just a *word.* This is all so totally—" She left off the last word: *stupid.*

"I don't make the rules," the cop explained simply.

"It doesn't *say* anything! That's, like, my whole thing! It doesn't say what he says it says! Anyway, I already told him I'll put it *away.* I *told* him! I told him like a million times but he won't listen. It's not fair."

The girl was about to cry, which reminded me of the grown woman I had just left on the sidewalk also near tears. Jesus, there was no escaping them.

"Well," I suggested to the cop, "I think it'll be okay if she just leaves it in her locker, don't you? I can't imagine what harm could come of it. I'll take responsibility."

"Hey, you're the boss. Whatever you want."

"And tomorrow," I said to the girl, to make it up to this cop, "maybe you'll leave that sweatshirt at home."

I winked at her, and she gathered up

her things and quick-marched away down the hall.

I took a position shoulder to shoulder with the affronted cop and together we looked out through the school doors toward the street.

A beat.

"You did the right thing," I said. "Probably should have kept my nose out of it."

It was bullshit, of course, both sentences. No doubt the cop knew it was bullshit too. But what could he do? The same chain of command that compelled him to enforce a stupid rule now compelled him to defer to some hulking dumb-ass lawyer in a cheap suit who did not know how hard it was to be a cop and how little of the cops' work ever made it into the police reports that found their way to the clueless virginal DAs all sealed up in their courthouses like nuns in a convent. *Pfft.*

"It's nothing," the cop told me.

And it was nothing. But I stood there awhile, anyway, presenting a united front with him, to be sure he knew whose team I was on.

4 | Mindfuck

The Middlesex County Courthouse, where the DA's office was headquartered, was an unrelievedly ugly building. A sixteen-story tower built in the 1960s, the exterior façades were molded concrete in various rectangular shapes: flat slabs, egg-crate grids, arrow-slit windows. It was as if the architect had banned curved lines and warm building materials in an effort to make the place as grim as possible. Things did not get much better inside. The interior spaces were airless, yellowed, grimy. Most offices had no windows; the solid block shape of the building entombed them. The modern-style court-rooms were windowless too. It is a common architectural strategy to build courtrooms without windows, to enhance the effect of a chamber isolated from the everyday world, a theater for the great and timeless work of the law. Here they need not have bothered: you could spend whole days in this building and never see sun or sky. Worse, the courthouse was known to be a "sick building." The elevator shafts were lined with asbestos, and every time an elevator door rattled open, the building coughed out a cloud of toxic particulate into the air. Soon enough the whole ram-shackle thing would have to be shut down. But for now, for the lawyers and detectives inside, the shabbiness did not matter much. It is in seedy places like this that the real work of local government so often gets done. After a while, you stop noticing.

Most days I was at my desk by seven-thirty or eight, before the phones really got going, before first call at nine-thirty. But with Jacob's school reopening that morn-ing, I did not get in till after nine. Anxious to see the Rifkin file, I immediately closed my office door, sat down, and arrayed the murder scene photos across my desk. I propped one foot on an open drawer and leaned back, staring at them.

At the corners of my desk, the photo-wood laminate had begun to peel away from the pressboard desk. I had a nervous habit of picking at these corners unconsciously, prying up the flexy laminate surface with my finger like a scab. I was sometimes surprised to hear the rhythmic clicking sound it made as I lifted and snapped it. It was a sound I associated with deep thought. That morning, I'm sure, I was ticking like a bomb.

The investigation felt wrong. Strange. Too quiet, even after five long days of digging. It is a cliché but it is true: most cases break quickly, in the frantic hours and days right after a murder, when the noise is everywhere, evidence, theories, ideas, witnesses, accusations—possibilities. Other cases take a little longer to sort out, to pick out the right signal in that noisy environment, the true story among many plausible ones. A very few cases never get solved. The signal never does emerge from the static. Possibilities abound, all plausible, none confirmable, none provable, and that is how the case ends. But in every case there is always noise. There are always suspects, theories, possibilities to consider. Not in the Rifkin murder. Five days of silence. Somebody stitched three holes in a line across that boy's chest and left nothing to indicate who or why.

The tantalizing anxiety this caused—in me, in the detectives working the case, even in the town—was beginning to grate. I felt like I was being toyed with, purposely manipulated. A secret was being kept from me. Jacob and his friends have a slang term, *mindfuck,* which describes tormenting someone by misleading him, usually by withholding a crucial fact. A girl pretends to like a boy—that is a mindfuck. A movie reveals an essential fact only at the end, which changes or explains everything that went before—*The Sixth Sense* and *The Usual Suspects,* for example, are what Jake calls *mindfuck movies.* The Rifkin case was beginning to feel like a mindfuck. The only way to explain the complete dead silence in the aftermath of the murder was that someone had orchestrated all this. Someone out there was watching, enjoying our ignorance, our foolishness. In the investigation phase of a violent crime, the detective often conceives a righteous hate for the criminal before he has any idea who the criminal is. I did not usually feel that sort of passion about any case, but I disliked this murderer already. For murdering, yes, but also for fucking with us. For refusing to submit. For controlling the situation. When I did finally learn his name and face, I would merely adjust my contempt to fit him.

In the murder scene photos spread out before me, the body lay in the brown leaves, twisted, face up toward the sky, eyes open. The images themselves were not especially grisly—a boy lying in the leaves. Anyway, gore itself did not usually faze me. Like many people who have been exposed to violence, I confined my emotions within a narrow range. Never too high, never too low. Since I was a kid, I have always made sure of that. My emotions ran on steel rails.

Benjamin Rifkin was fourteen years old, in eighth grade at the McCormick School. Jacob was a classmate but barely knew him. He told me Ben had a reputation at school as "kind of a slacker," smart but not much of a student, never in the advanced classes that filled Jacob's schedule. He was handsome, even a little flashy. He often wore his short hair swept up in front with something called hair wax. Girls liked him, according to Jacob. Ben liked sports and was a decent athlete, but he was more into skateboarding and skiing than team sports. "I didn't hang out with him," Jacob said. "He had his own crew. They were all a little too cool." He added, with the casual acid of adolescence, "Everybody's all into him now, but before, it was like nobody even noticed him."

The body was found on April 12, 2007, in Cold Spring Park, sixty-five acres of pine woods that bordered the school grounds. The woods were veined with jogging paths. They crisscrossed one another and led, through many branchings, to a main trail that ringed the perimeter of the park. I knew these trails pretty well; I jogged there most mornings. It was along one of the smaller trails that Ben's body had been flung facedown into a little gully. It slid to a stop at the foot of a tree. A woman named Paula Giannetto discovered the body as she jogged past. The time of discovery was precise; she switched off her jogging watch as

she paused to investigate at 9:07 A.M.—
less than an hour after the boy had left his
home for the short walk to school. There
was no blood visible. The body lay with
its head downhill, arms extended, legs
together, like a graceful diver. Giannetto reported that the boy was not obviously dead,
so she rolled him over hoping to revive him.
"I thought he was sick, maybe he passed
out or something. I didn't think—" The medical examiner would later note that the
body's inverted position on sloping ground,
feet above head, may have accounted for
the unnatural flush of the face. Blood had
drained into the head, causing "lividity."
When she rolled the boy over, the witness
saw the front of his T-shirt was sopped in
red blood. Gasping, she stumbled and fell
backward, crabbed a few feet away on her
palms and heels, then got up and ran. The
position of the body in the murder scene
photos—twisted, face up—therefore was
not accurate.

The boy had been stabbed three times
in the chest. One strike punctured the heart
and would by itself have been fatal. The
knife was driven straight in and jerked
straight out again, one-two-three, like a

bayonet. The weapon had a jagged edge, evidenced by shredding at the left edge of each wound and in the torn shirt fabric. The angle of entry suggested an attacker about Ben's size, five foot ten or so, although the sloping ground in the park made this projection unreliable. The weapon had not been found. There were no defensive wounds: the victim's arms and hands were unmarked. The best clue, perhaps, was a single pristine fingerprint, stamped in the victim's own blood, cleanly preserved on a plastic tag on the inside of the victim's un-zipped sweatshirt, where his murderer might have grabbed him by the lapels and tossed him down the slope into the gully. The print did not match either the victim or Paula Giannetto.

The bare facts of the crime had developed very little in the five days since the murder. Detectives had canvassed the neighborhood and twice swept the park, immediately after the discovery and again twenty-four hours later to find witnesses who frequented the park at that hour of the day. The sweeps had yielded nothing. To the newspapers and, increasingly, to the terrified parents at the McCormick School, the murder looked like a random strike. As the days passed with no news, the silence from the cops and the DA's office seemed to confirm parents' worst fears: a predator lurked in the woods of Cold Spring Park. Since then, the park lay abandoned, though a Newton Police cruiser idled in the parking lot all day to reassure the joggers and power-walkers. Only the dog owners continued to come, to let their dogs off the leash on a meadow designated for this purpose.

A state trooper in plain clothes named Paul Duffy slipped into my office with a familiar perfunctory knock and sat down opposite my desk, evidently excited.

Lieutenant Detective Paul Duffy was a policeman by birth, a third-generation cop, son of a former Boston P. D. homicide chief. But he did not look the part. Soft-spoken, with a receding hairline and fine features, he might have been in some gentler profession than policing. Duffy headed a state police unit detailed to the DA's office. The unit was known by its acronym, CPAC (pronounced *sea pack*). The initials stood for Crime Prevention and Control, but the title was essentially meaningless ("crime prevention and control" is ostensibly what all cops do) and hardly anyone knew what the letters actually meant. In practice, CPAC's charge was simple: they were the district attorney's detectives. They worked cases that were unusually complex, long term, or high profile. Most important, they handled all the county's murders. In homicide cases, CPAC detectives worked alongside the local cops, who for the most part welcomed the assistance. Outside Boston itself, homicides were rare enough that the locals could not develop the necessary expertise, particularly in the smaller towns where murders were rare as comets. Still, it was a politically delicate situation when the staties swept in to take over a local investigation. A light touch like Paul Duffy's was required. To lead the CPAC unit, it was not enough to be a smart investigator; you had to be supple enough to satisfy the different constituencies whose toes it was CPAC's job to step on.

I loved Duffy without reservation. Virtually alone among the cops I worked with, he was a personal friend. We often worked cases together, the DA's top lawyer and top detective. We socialized together too.

Our families knew each other. Paul had named me godfather to the middle of his three sons, Owen, and if only I had believed in God or fathers, I would have done the same for him. He was more outgoing than I, more gregarious and sentimental, but good friendships require complementary personalities, not identical ones.

"Tell me you have something or get out of my office."

"I have something."

"It's about time."

"That doesn't sound very grateful."

He flipped a file folder onto my desk.

"Leonard Patz," I read aloud from a Board of Probation record. *"Indecent A&B on a minor; lewd and lascivious; lewd and lascivious; trespass; indecent A&B, dismissed; indecent A&B on a minor, pending.* Lovely. The neighborhood pedophile."

Duffy said, "He's twenty-six years old. Lives near the park in that condo place, the Windsor or whatever they call it."

A mug shot paper-clipped to the folder showed a large man with a pudgy face, close-cropped hair, Cupid's-bow lips. I slipped it out from under the paper clip and studied it.

"Handsome fella. Why didn't we know about him?"

"He wasn't in the sex offender registry. He moved to Newton in the last year and never registered."

"So how'd you find him?"

"One of the ADAs in the Child Abuse Unit flagged him. That's the pending indecent A&B in Newton District Court, top of the page there."

"What's the bail?"

"Personal."

"What'd he do?"

"Grabbed some kid's package in the public library. The kid was fourteen, same as Ben Rifkin."

"Really? That fits, doesn't it?"

"It's a start."

"Wait, he grabs a kid's balls and he gets out on personal?"

"Apparently there's some question whether the kid wants to testify."

"Still. *I* go to that library."

"Might want to wear a cup."

"I never leave home without one."

I studied the mug shot. I had a feeling about Patz right from the start. Of course, I was desperate—I *wanted* to feel that feeling, I badly needed a suspect, I needed to produce something finally—so I distrusted my suspicion. But I could not ignore it altogether. You have to follow your intuition. That is what expertise is: all the experience, the cases won and lost, the painful mistakes, all the technical details you learn by rote repetition, over time these things leave you with an instinctive sense of your craft. A "gut" for it. And from this first encounter, my gut told me Patz might be the one.

"It's worth giving him a shake, at least," I said.

"There's just one thing: there's no violence on Patz's record. No weapons, nothing. That's the only thing."

"I see two indecent A&Bs. That's violent enough for me."

"Grabbing a kid by the nuts isn't the same as murder."

"You got to start somewhere."

"Maybe. I don't know, Andy. I mean, I see where you're going, but to me he sounds like more of a wanker than a killer. Anyway, the sex angle—the Rifkin kid had no signs of sexual assault."

I shrugged. "Maybe he never got that

far. He could have been interrupted. Maybe he propositions the kid or tries to force him into the forest at knifepoint, and the kid resists. Or maybe the kid laughs at him, ridicules him, and Patz flies into a rage."

"That's a lot of maybes."

"Well, let's see what he has to say. Go bring him in."

"Can't bring him in. We've got nothing to hold him on. There's nothing tying him to this case."

"So tell him you want him to come look through the mug books and see if he can identify anyone he might have seen in Cold Spring Park."

"He's already got a Committee lawyer for the pending case. He's not going to come in voluntarily."

"Then tell him you'll violate him for not registering his new address with the sex offender registry. You've already got him jammed up on that. Tell him the kiddy porn on his computer is a federal offense. Tell him anything, it doesn't matter. Just get him in and give a little squeeze."

Duffy smirked and raised his eyebrows. Ball-grabbing jokes never get old.

"Just go pick him up."

Duffy hesitated. "I don't know. It feels like we're jumping the gun. Why not just show Patz's picture around, see if anyone can put him in the park that morning? Talk to his neighbors. Maybe knock on his door, low-key it, don't spook him, get him talking that way." Duffy formed his fingers into a beak and flapped it open and shut: *talk, talk.* "You never know. If you pick him up, he'll just call his lawyer. You might lose your only chance to talk to him."

"No, it's better we pick him up. After that, you can sweet-talk him, Duff. That's what you're good at."

"You sure?"

"We can't have people saying we didn't push hard enough on this guy."

The comment was off key, and a doubtful expression crossed Duffy's face. We had always made it a rule not to give a shit how things looked or what people thought. A prosecutor's judgment is supposed to be insulated from politics.

"You know what I mean, Paul. This is the first credible suspect we've found. I don't want to lose him because we didn't do enough."

"Okay," he said with a sour little frown. "I'll bring him in."

"Good."

Duffy leaned back in his chair, the work conversation over, eager now to smooth the slight friction between us.

"How'd it go with Jacob at school this morning?"

"Oh, he's okay. Nothing bothers Jake. Now, Laurie, on the other hand . . ."

"She a little shook up?"

"A little? You remember in *Jaws* when Roy Scheider has to send his kids into the ocean to show everyone it's safe to swim?"

"Your wife looked like Roy Scheider? That's what you're saying?"

"The expression on her face."

"You weren't worried? Come on, I'll bet you looked like Roy Scheider too."

"Listen, pal, I was all Robert Shaw, I promise you."

"Things didn't end well for Robert Shaw, as I recall."

"For the shark either. That's all that matters, Duff. Now go get Patz."

"Andy, I'm a little uncomfortable with this," Lynn Canavan said.

For a moment I did not know what she was talking about. It actually crossed my mind she might be kidding. When we were younger, she used to like putting people on. More than once I got sucked in, taking seriously a comment that, a moment later, was revealed as a joke. But I saw, in the next moment, that she was quite serious. Or seemed to be. She had become a little hard to read lately.

There were three of us that morning in Canavan's big corner office, District Attorney Canavan, Neal Logiudice, and me. We were seated at a round conference table, at the center of which was an empty box from Dunkin' Donuts, left over from a meeting earlier that morning. The room had a dressy finish, with wood paneling and windows overlooking East Cambridge. But it still had the same chill as the rest of the courthouse. Same thin plum-purple industrial carpet over a concrete slab floor. Same dingy flecked acoustic tiles overhead. Same stale, twice-breathed air. As power offices go, it was not much.

Canavan fiddled with a pen, tapping the tip on a yellow pad, head tilted as if she was thinking it over. "I don't know. You handling this case, I don't know as I like it. Your son goes to that school. It's a close thing. I'm a little uncomfortable."

"*You're* uncomfortable, Lynn, or Rasputin here is?" I gestured toward Logiudice.

"Oh, that's funny, Andy—"

"I am," Canavan asserted.

"Let me guess: Neal wants the case."

"Neal thinks there might be an issue. I do too, frankly. There's an appearance of a conflict. That does matter, Andy."

Indeed, appearances did matter. Lynn Canavan was a rising political star. From the moment she was elected district attorney, two years earlier, there were rumors about which office she would run for next: governor, Massachusetts attorney general, even U.S. senator. She was in her forties, attractive, smart, serious, ambitious. I had known and worked alongside her for fifteen years, since we were both young lawyers. We were allies. She appointed me First Assistant the day she was elected DA, but I knew from the start it was a short-term gig. A courtroom mucker like me is of no value out in the political world. Wherever Canavan was headed, I would not be going along. But that was all still in the future. In the meantime, she was biding her time, polishing her public persona, her "brand": the no-nonsense law-and-order professional. On camera she rarely smiled, rarely joked. She wore little makeup or jewelry and kept her hair short and sensible. The older people in the office remembered a different Lynn Canavan—fun, charismatic, one of the boys, who could swear like a sailor and drink like she had a hollow leg. But the voters never saw any of that, and at this point maybe the old, more natural Lynn did not exist anymore. I suppose she had no choice but to transform herself. Her life was now an endless candidacy; you could hardly blame her for becoming what she pretended to be for so long. Anyway, we all do have to grow up, put childish things aside and all that. But something was lost too. In the course of Lynn's transformation from butterfly to moth, our long friendship had suffered. Neither of us felt the old intimacy, the sense of trust and connection we'd once had. Maybe she would make me a judge someday, for old times' sake, to pay the whole thing off. But we both knew, I think, that our friendship had run its course. We both felt vaguely awkward and mournful around each other because of it, like lovers on the downside of an unwinding affair.

In any event, Lynn Canavan's likely ascent created a vacuum behind her, and politics abhors a vacuum. That Neal Logiudice might actually fill it would have seemed absurd, once upon a time. Now, who knew? Clearly Logiudice did not see me as an obstacle. I had said over and over that I had no interest in the job, and I meant it. The last thing I wanted was to live an exposed, public life. Still, he would need more than bureaucratic infighting to get there. If Neal wanted to be DA, he would need a real accomplishment to show the voters. A splashy signature win in the courtroom. He needed a skin. Whose skin, I was just beginning to understand.

"Are you pulling me off the case, Lynn?"

"Right now I'm just asking what you think."

"We've been through this. I'm keeping the case. There's no issue."

"It hits pretty close to home, Andy. Your son might be in danger. If he'd been unlucky enough to be walking through that park at the wrong time . . ."

Logiudice said, "Maybe your judgment

is clouded, just a little. I mean, if you're being fair, if you stop and think about it objectively."

"Clouded how?"

"Does it make you emotional?"

"No."

"Are you angry, Andy?"

"Do I look angry?" I counted out the words one by one.

"Yeah, you do, a little. Or maybe just defensive. But you shouldn't be; we're all on the same side here. Hey, it's perfectly natural to be emotional. If my son was involved—"

"Neal, are you actually questioning my integrity? Or just my competence?"

"Neither. I'm questioning your objectivity."

"Lynn, does he speak for you? Are you believing this bullshit?"

She frowned. "My antennae are up, to be honest."

"Your antennae? Come on, what does that mean?"

"I'm uneasy."

Logiudice: "It's the appearance, Andy. The *appearance* of objectivity. Nobody's saying you actually—"

"Look, just fuck off, Neal, okay? This doesn't concern you."

"Excuse me?"

"Just let me run my case. I don't give a rat's ass about the appearance. The case is going slow because that's the way it's going, not because I'm dragging my feet. I'm not going to be stampeded into indicting someone just to make it look good. I thought I taught you better than that."

"You taught me I should push every case as hard as I could."

"I *am* pushing as hard as I can."

"Why haven't you interviewed the kids? It's been five days already."

"You know damn well why. Because this isn't Boston, Neal, it's Newton. Every frickin' detail has to be negotiated: which kids we can talk to, where we talk to them, what we can ask, who has to be present. This isn't Dorchester High. Half the parents in this school are lawyers."

"Relax, Andy. No one's accusing you of anything. The problem is how it will be perceived. From the outside, it might look like you're ignoring the obvious."

"Meaning what?"

"The students. Have you considered that

the killer might be a student? You've told me a thousand times, haven't you: follow the evidence wherever it leads."

"There's no evidence to suggest it's a student. None. If there were, I'd follow it."

"You can't follow it if you won't look for it."

This was an *aha!* moment. I finally got it. The time had come, as I always knew it would. I was the one immediately above Neal on the ladder. Now he would target me the way he had so many others.

I made a wry smile. "Neal, what is it you're after? Is it the case? You want it? You can have it. Or is it my job? What the hell, you can have that too. But it'd be easier for everyone if you'd just come out and say it."

"I don't want anything, Andy. I just want to see things come out right."

"Lynn, are you taking me off the case or are you going to back me?"

She gave me a warm look but an indirect answer. "When have I ever not backed you?"

I nodded, accepting the truth of this. I put on a resolute mask and declared a fresh start. "Look, the school just reopened today, the kids are all back. We have the student interviews this afternoon. Something good is gonna happen soon."

"Good," Canavan said. "Let's hope so."

But Logiudice chipped in, "Who's going to interview your son?"

"I don't know."

"Not you, I hope."

"Not me. Paul Duffy probably."

"Who decided that?"

"Me. That's the way it works, Neal. I decide. And if there's a mistake, it'll be me standing in front of the jury to take the hit."

He gave Canavan a look—*See? I told you, he won't listen*—which she met with a neutral expression.

5 | Everyone Knows You Did It

The student interviews began right after school. For the kids, it had been a long day filled with class meetings and grief counseling. CPAC detectives in plain clothes had gone from classroom to classroom encouraging kids to share tips with the investigators, anonymously if necessary. The kids stared back dully.

The McCormick was a middle school, which in this town meant it covered grades six through eight. The building was an arrangement of plain rectangular boxes. Inside, the walls were painted thick with many layers of teal. Laurie grew up in Newton and went to the McCormick in the 1970s; she said the school had hardly changed except for the illusion, as she walked down the halls, that the whole structure had shrunk.

As I had told Canavan, these interviews were a contentious subject. At first, the school principal flatly refused to allow us to "storm in" and talk to any kid we pleased. Had the crime happened in another place—in the urb rather than the sub-urb—we would not have bothered to ask permission. Here, the school board and even the mayor intervened directly with Lynn Canavan to slow us down. In the end, we were allowed to talk to the kids on school grounds but only on certain conditions. Kids who were not in Ben Rifkin's homeroom were off limits unless we had a specific reason to believe they might know something. Any student could have a parent and/or a lawyer present and could end the interview at any time, for any reason or no reason. Most of this was easy to concede. They were entitled to a lot of it anyway. The real point of stipulating so many rules was to send the cops a message: treat these kids with kid gloves. Which was fine, but precious time was lost while we diddled around negotiating.

At two o'clock, Paul and I commandeered the principal's office and together we interviewed the highest-priority witnesses: the victim's close friends, a few kids who were known to walk to school through Cold Spring Park, and those who specifically requested to speak with the investigators. Two dozen interviews were scheduled for the two of us. Other CPAC detectives would conduct interviews at the same time. Most we expected to be brief and yield nothing. We were trawling, dragging our net along the sea bottom, hoping.

But something odd happened. After just three or four interviews, Paul and I had the distinct impression we were being stonewalled. At first we thought we were seeing the usual repertoire of adolescent tics and evasions, the shrugs and *y'know*s and *whatever*s, the wandering eyes. We were both fathers. We knew that walling out adults was what all teenagers did; it was the whole point of these behaviors. In itself, there was nothing suspicious about it. But as the interviews went on, we realized something more brazen and purposeful was going on. The kids' answers went too far. They were not content to say they knew nothing about the murder; they denied even knowing the victim. Ben Rifkin seemed to have had no friends at all, only acquaintances. Other kids never spoke to him, had no idea who did. These were transparent lies. Ben had not been unpopular. We already knew who most of Ben's friends were. It was a betrayal, I thought, for his buddies to disown him so quickly and completely.

Worse, the eighth-graders at the Mc-Cormick were not especially competent liars. Some of them, the more shameless ones, seemed to believe that the way to pass off a lie convincingly was to oversell it. So, when they got ready to tell a particularly tall one, they would stop all the foot-shuffling and *y'know*s, and deliver the lie with maximum conviction. It was as if they had read a manual on behaviors associated with honesty—eye contact! firm voice!—and were determined to display them all at once, like peacocks fanning their tail feathers. The effect was to reverse the behavior patterns you might expect to see in adults—the teens seemed evasive when honest and direct when lying—but their shifting manner set off alarm bells just the same. The other kids, the majority, were too self-conscious to begin with and lying only made them more so. They were tentative. The truth inside them made them squirm. This obviously did not work either. I could have told them, of course, that a virtuoso liar slips the false statement in among the true ones without a flutter of any kind, like a magician slipping the bent card into the middle of the deck. I have had an education in virtuosic lying, believe me.

Paul and I began to exchange suspicious glances. The pace of the interviews slowed as we challenged some of the more obvious lies. Between interviews, Paul joked about a code of silence. "These kids are like Sicilians," he said. Neither of us said what we were truly thinking. There is a plummeting feeling, as if the floor has fallen away beneath you. It is the happy vertigo you feel when a case opens up and lets you in.

Apparently we had been wrong—there was no other way to say it. We had considered the possibility that a fellow student was involved, but we had discounted it. There was no evidence pointing that way. No sullen outcasts among the students, no sloppy schoolboy trail of evidence to follow. Nor was there an apparent motive: no grandiose adolescent fantasies of outlaw glory, no damaged, bullied kids out for revenge, no petty classroom feud. Nothing. Now, neither of us had to say it. That vertiginous feeling was the thought: these kids knew something.

A girl sloped into the office and dropped into the chair opposite us, then, with great effort, she refused to acknowledge us.

"Sarah Groehl?" Paul said.

"Yes."

"I'm Lieutenant Detective Paul Duffy. I'm with the state police. This here is Andrew Barber. He's the assistant district attorney in charge of this case."

"I know." She looked up at me finally. "You're Jacob Barber's dad."

"Yes. You're the sweatshirt girl. From this morning."

She smiled shyly.

"Sorry, I should have remembered you. I'm having a tough day, Sarah."

"Yeah, why's that?"

"Nobody wants to talk to us. Now, why is that, you have any idea?"

"You're cops."

"That's it?"

"Sure." She made a face: *Duh!*

I waited a moment, hoping for more. The girl returned a look of exquisite boredom.

"Are you a friend of Jacob's?"

She looked down, considered, shrugged. "I guess so."

"How come I haven't heard your name?"

"Ask Jacob."

"He doesn't tell me anything. I have to ask you."

"We know each other. We're not, like, friends, Jacob and me. We just know each other."

"How about Ben Rifkin? Did you know him?"

"Same. I knew him but I didn't really *know* him."

"Did you like him?"

"He was okay."

"Just okay?"

"He was a good kid, I guess. Like I said, we weren't really close."

"Okay. So I'll stop asking stupid questions. Why don't you just tell us, Sarah?

Anything at all that might help us, anything you think we ought to know."

She shifted in her seat. "I don't really know what you—I don't know what to tell you."

"Well, tell me about this place, this school. Start with that. Tell me something about McCormick that I don't know. What's it like to go to school here? What's funny about this place? What's strange about it?"

No response.

"Sarah, we want to help, you know, but we need some of you kids to help *us.*"

She shifted around in her seat.

"You owe that much to Ben, don't you think? If he was your friend?"

"I don't know. I don't have anything to say, I guess. I don't know anything."

"Sarah, whoever did this, he's still out there. You know that, don't you? If you can help, then you have a responsibility. A real responsibility. Otherwise this same thing is going to happen again to some other kid. Then it would be on you. If you didn't do everything—absolutely everything you could—to make it stop, then the next one would be on you, wouldn't it? How would that make you feel?"

"You're trying to guilt me. It won't work. My mom does that too."

"I'm not trying to guilt you. I'm just telling you the truth."

No response.

Bang! Duffy smacked the table with his open palm. Some papers drifted with the breeze he created. "Jesus! This is bullshit, Andy. Just put a subpoena on these kids already, would you? Put 'em in the grand jury, swear 'em in, and if they don't want to say anything, just lock 'em up for contempt. This is a waste of time. For Christ's sake!"

The girl's eyes dilated.

Duffy took his cell phone from a holster on his belt and looked at it, though it had not rung. "I have to make a call," he announced. "I'll be right back," and out he marched.

The kid said, "Is he supposed to be the bad cop?"

"Yeah."

"He's not very good at it."

"You jumped. I saw you."

"Only 'cause he startled me. He banged the table."

"He's right, you know. If you kids don't start helping us out, we'll have to do this another way."

"I thought we didn't have to say anything if we didn't want to."

"That's true today. Tomorrow, maybe not."

She thought it over.

"Sarah, it's true, what you said before. I'm a DA. But I'm also a dad, okay? So I'm not going to just let this thing go. Because I keep thinking of Ben Rifkin's dad. I keep thinking of how he must be feeling. Can you even imagine how your mom or dad would feel if this happened to you? How devastated they'd be?"

"They're split up. My dad's out of the picture. I live with my mom."

"Oh. I'm sorry to hear that."

"It's no big deal."

"Well, Sarah, look, you're all our kids, you know. All you kids in Jacob's class, even the ones I don't know, I care about. All of us parents feel that way."

She rolled her eyes.

"You don't believe that?"

"No. You don't even know me."

"That's true. Still, I care what happens

to you just the same. I care about this school, this town. I'm not going to just let this happen. This isn't going away. You understand that?"

"Is anyone talking to Jacob?"

"You mean my son Jacob?"

"Yeah."

"Of course."

"Okay."

"Why do you say that?"

"No reason."

"There must be a reason. What is it, Sarah?"

The girl studied her lap. "The cop who came to our class said we could tell you things anonymously?"

"That's right. There's a tip line."

"How do we know you won't try to, like, figure out who gave a tip? I mean, that's something you'd want to know, right? Who said something?"

"Sarah, come on. What is it you want to say?"

"How do we know it will stay anonymous?"

"You just have to trust us, I guess."

"Trust who? You?"

"Me. Detective Duffy. There's a lot of people working on this case."

"What if I just . . ." She looked up.

"Look, I'm not going to lie to you, Sarah. If you tell me something here, it's not anonymous. My job is to catch the guy who did this, but it's also to try him in court and for that I'll need witnesses. I'd be lying if I told you any different. I'm trying to be honest with you here."

"Okay." She considered. "I really don't know anything."

"You sure about that?"

"Yes."

I looked her in the eye just a moment to let her know I wasn't fooled, then I accepted her lie. I pulled a business card from my wallet. "This is my card. I'm going to write my cell phone number on the back. My personal email too." I slid the card across the desk. "You can contact me anytime, okay? Anytime. And I'll do what I can to look out for you."

"Okay."

She took the card and stood up. She looked down at her hands, at her fingers. Her fingertips were stained with black ink, imperfectly wiped off. All the students at the school were being fingerprinted that day, "voluntarily," though there were jokes about the implications of refusing. Sarah frowned at the ink stains, then crossed her arms to hide them and in that awkward posture she said, "Hey, can I ask you something, Mr. Barber? Are you ever the bad cop?"

"No, never."

"Why not?"

"It's just not me, I guess."

"So how do you do your job, then?"

"I have a mean streak, deep down. Trust me."

"You just hide it?"

"I just hide it."

That night, a little before eleven, I was alone in the kitchen, using my laptop computer which I had set up on the kitchen counter. I was cleaning up some odd bits of work, answering emails mostly. A new message arrived in my inbox. The subject line read—shouted—"RE: BEN RIFKIN >>> README." It was from a Gmail address, tyler durden982@gmail.com. The time stamp read 10:54:27 PM. The message contained a single line, a hyperlink: "Look here." I clicked the link.

The link took me to a Facebook group called "♥ Friends of Ben Rifkin ♥." The

Facebook group was new. It could not have been established more than four days before; the day of the murder, CPAC had looked at Facebook and it was not there.

We had found the dead boy's personal Facebook page (almost every kid at the McCormick was on Facebook), but Ben's page contained no hints about the murder. For what it was worth, in his profile he had been keen to present himself as a free spirit.

Ben Rifkin
is out boarding

Networks:	McCormick Middle School '07 Newton, MA
Sex:	Male
Interested in:	Women
Relationship Status:	Single
Birthday:	December 3, 1992
Political Views:	Vulcan
Religious Views:	Heathen

The rest was the usual clutter of digital junk: YouTube videos, games, pictures, a stream of vapid, gossipy messages. Relatively speaking, though, Ben had not been an especially heavy user of Facebook.

Much of the activity on his page happened after he was murdered, when messages from Ben's classmates continued to accumulate in a ghostly way until the page was removed at his parents' request.

The new "tribute" page apparently was opened in response, to give kids a place to go on posting messages about the murder. The title, "♥ Friends of Ben Rifkin ♥," seemed to use *friends* in the Facebook sense: it was open to anyone in the Mc-Cormick class of 2007, whether or not they had actually been Ben's friend.

At the top of the page was a small photo of Ben, the same one he had used on his personal page. Presumably it had been cut-and-pasted from the dead boy's old page by whoever launched this group. The picture showed Ben smiling, shirtless, apparently on a beach (the sand and ocean were visible behind him). He was making a "hang loose" gesture with his right hand. Down the right side of the page there was a panel called the Wall, filled with messages in reverse chronological order.

Jenna Linde (McCormick Middle School) wrote at 9:02pm on April 17th, 2007

I miss you ben. I remember our talks. i love you forever i love you I love you

Christa Dufresne (McCormick Middle School) wrote at 8:43pm on April 17th, 2007

this is the cruelest thing whoever did this. I will never forget you Ben. I think about you every day. ♥♥♥♥♥♥

It is important to note that in 2007 Facebook was still largely a kids' paradise. Its explosive growth among adults happened in the following couple of years. That was the case in our circle, at least. Most of the parents at the McCormick School looked at Facebook now and then to monitor what their kids were up to, but that was about it. A few of our friends joined, but they rarely used it. There were not enough other parents there yet to make it worthwhile. Personally I had no idea what Jacob and his friends saw in Facebook. I could not grasp why all this information-churning was so compelling. The only explanation, it seemed to me, was that Facebook was where kids went to be away from adults, their secret place where they strutted and flirted and goofed around with the bravado they could never muster in person in the school cafeteria. Jacob, certainly, was much more clever and assertive online than in person, as many shy kids are. Laurie and I saw the danger in allowing Jacob to carry on like this in secret. We insisted he give us his password so we could check up on him, but honestly, Laurie was the only one who ever looked at Jacob's Facebook page. To me, the kids' online conversation was even less interesting than the offline version. If I ever looked at Facebook back then, it was because the face in question was in one of my case files. Was I a neglectful parent? In hindsight, obviously yes. But then we all were, all the parents at Jacob's school. We did not know the stakes were so high.

There were already several hundred messages on the "♥ Friends of Ben Rifkin ♥" page.

Emily Salzman (McCormick Middle School) wrote at 10:12pm on April 16th, 2007

I am still totally wigged. who did this?
why did you do it? why? what was the
point? what did u get out of it? this is just
so sick

Alex Kurzon (McCormick Middle School)
wrote at 1:14pm on April 16th, 2007

at cold sprg pk now. yellow tape still up.
nthng to see though. no cops.

The messages went on like this, un-
guarded, confessional. The Web created
an illusion of intimacy, a byproduct of the
kids' dazed immersion in the "virtual"
world. Alas, they were about to learn the
Web belonged to grown-ups: I was already
thinking of the subpoena *duces tecum*—
the order to produce documents and
records—that I would send to Facebook
to preserve all these online conversations.
In the meantime, avid as an eavesdrop-
per, I went on reading.

Dylan Feldman (McCormick Middle
School) wrote at 9:07pm on April 15th,
2007

Jacob STFU. if you dont want to read it, go someplace else. you of all people. f*ck off. he considered you a friend. dickhead

Mike Canin (McCormick Middle School) wrote at 9:01pm on April 15th, 2007

Have to call you out on that Jake. You're not the FB police, esp the way things went down. you shd keep your head down & be quiet.

John Marolla (McCormick Middle School) wrote at 8:51pm on April 15th, 2007

WTF? JB what are you mouthing off here for? go die. the world would be a better place. go f*ck off & die.

Julie Kerschner (McCormick Middle School) wrote at 8:48pm on April 15th, 2007

Not cool, Jacob.

Jacob Barber (McCormick Middle School) wrote at 7:30pm on April 15th, 2007

Maybe you all haven't heard—Ben is dead.
Why are we still writing him messages?
And why are some people acting like his
best friend when you never were? Can we
just be real here?

I stopped at Jacob's name—at the realization that these last venomous messages were aimed at *my* Jacob. I was not prepared for the reality of Jacob's life, the complexity of his relationships, the trials he went through, the brutality of the world he inhabited. *Go die. The world would be a better place.* How could my son have been told such a thing and never shared it with his family? Never even let on? I was disappointed not in Jacob but in myself. How could I have left my son with the impression I did not care about such things? Or was I being a wimp, overreacting to the exaggerated, hopped-up tone of the Internet?

I also felt like a fool, honestly. I ought to have known about all this. Laurie and I had talked with Jacob only in the most general way about what he did on the Internet. We knew that when he went off to his room at night, he was able to go online. But we had some software installed on his computer to prevent him from looking at certain websites, porn sites mostly, and we felt that was enough. Facebook never seemed particularly dangerous, certainly. Also, neither of us wanted to spy on him. As a couple, we believed that you raise a child with good values and then you give him space, you trust him to behave responsibly, at least until he gives you reason not to. Modern, enlightened parents, we had not wanted to be Jake's adversaries, quizzing him about every move, hectoring him. It was a philosophy shared by most of the McCormick parents. What choice did we have? No parent can monitor his kid's every moment, online or off. In the end, every child leads his own life, largely out of his parents' sight. Still, when I saw the words *Go die,* I realized how naive and stupid we had been. Jacob did not need our trust or our respect as much as he needed our protection, and that we had not given him.

I scrolled through the messages more quickly. There were hundreds, each just a line or two. I could not possibly read them all, and I had no idea what Sarah Groehl wanted me to find. Jacob disappeared from the conversation for a long stretch as the messages got older. The kids consoled one another in maudlin messages (*we will never evr be the same*) and hard-boiled ones (*die young, stay pretty*). Over and over they expressed their shock. The girls protested their love and loyalty, the boys their anger. I scoured these endless repetitive messages for some worthwhile detail: *i cant believe this . . . we have to stick together . . . there are cops everywhere in school . . .*

Finally, I clicked over to Jacob's own Facebook page, where a hotter conversation was still simmering, this one from the immediate aftermath of the murder. Again, the messages were displayed in reverse chronological order.

Marlie Kunitz (McCormick Middle School) wrote at 3:29pm on April 15th, 2007

D.Y.: Do NOT say things like that here. That is GOSSIP and it could get people HURT. Even if it's a joke, it's stupid. Jake, just ignore him.

Joe O'Connor (McCormick Middle School) wrote at 3:16pm on April 15th, 2007

Everyone shd all just keep their mouths SHUT if we dont know what we're talking abt. that means you derek, you tool. this is SERIOUS SHIT here. NFW you shd be talking out of your ass like that.

Mark Spicer (McCormick Middle School) wrote at 3:07pm on April 15th, 2007

ANYbody could say ANYthing about ANYbody. maybe YOU have a knife derek? how does it feel when somebody starts a rumor about YOU?

Then this:

Derek Yoo (McCormick Middle School) wrote at 2:25pm on April 15th, 2007

Jake, everyone knows you did it. You have a knife. I've seen it.

I could not move. Could not budge my eyes from the message. I stared at it until the letters broke down into pixels. Derek Yoo was a friend of Jacob's, a good friend. He had been to our house a hundred times. The two boys had been in kindergarten together. Derek was a good kid.

I've seen it.

The next morning I let Laurie and Jacob both leave before me. I told them I had a meeting at the Newton police station and did not want to drive back and forth to Cambridge. When they were safely gone, I went up to Jacob's room and searched.

The search did not take long. In the top drawer of the bureau, I found something hard, lazily hidden in an old white T-shirt. I unrolled the T-shirt until it spilled onto the bureau a folding knife with a black rubberized handle. I picked it up daintily, tweezed the blade between my thumb and index finger, and pulled it open.

"Oh my God," I murmured.

It might have been a military knife or a hunting knife, but then it seemed too small for that. Unfolded, it was about ten inches long. The handle was black, grippy, shaped to accept four fingers. The blade was hook-shaped, with an intricately serrated cutting edge—a ripping blade—and it came to a lethal gothic point. The flat sides of the blade had been drilled out, presumably to save weight. The knife was sinister and beautiful, the shape of the blade, its curve and taper. It was like one of those lovely deadly things in nature, a lick of flame or the claw of an enormous cat.

6 | Descent

One year later.

TRANSCRIPT OF GRAND JURY INVESTIGATION.

Mr. Logiudice: When you discovered the knife, what did you do? I presume you reported it immediately.

Witness: No, I did not.

Mr. Logiudice: No? You discovered the murder weapon in an ongoing murder investigation and you did not tell anyone? Why not? You made such a pretty speech earlier this morning about how you believed in the system.

Witness: I did not report it because I did not believe that it was the murder weapon. I certainly did not know it for a fact.

Mr. Logiudice: You didn't know it for a fact? Well, how could you? You kept it hidden! You didn't submit the knife for forensic testing, for blood, fingerprints, comparison with the wound, and so forth. That would be the ordinary procedure, wouldn't it?

Witness: It would be if you genuinely suspected it was the weapon.

Mr. Logiudice: Ah. So you didn't even suspect it was the weapon?

Witness: No.

Mr. Logiudice: The thought never crossed your mind?

Witness: This was my son. A father does not think, can't even imagine his child in those terms.

Mr. Logiudice: Really? Can't even imagine it?

Witness: That's right.

Mr. Logiudice: The boy had no history of violence? No juvenile criminal record?

Witness: No. None.

Mr. Logiudice: No behavioral problems? No psychological problems?

Witness: No.

Mr. Logiudice: He had never hurt a fly, is that fair to say?

Witness: Something like that.

Mr. Logiudice: And yet when you found the knife, you covered it up. You behaved exactly as if you thought he was guilty.

Witness: That is not accurate.

Mr. Logiudice: Well, you didn't report it.

Witness: I was slow to realize—in hindsight, I admit—

Mr. Logiudice: Mr. Barber, how could you be slow to realize when, in fact, you'd been waiting for this moment for fourteen years, from the day your son was born?

[The witness did not respond.]

Mr. Logiudice: You'd been waiting for this moment. Fearing it, dreading it. But expecting it.

Witness: That's not true.

Mr. Logiudice: Isn't it? Mr. Barber, isn't it fair to say that violence runs in your family?

Witness: I object. That is a completely improper question.

Mr. Logiudice: Your objection is noted for the record.

Witness: You are trying to mislead this jury. You are suggesting that Jacob could inherit a tendency to violence, as if violence were the same as red hair or hairy ears. That's wrong on the biology and wrong on the law. In a word, it's bullshit. And you know it.

Mr. Logiudice: But I'm not talking about biology at all. I'm talking about your state of mind, what you believed at the moment you found that knife. Now, if you choose to believe in bullshit, that's your business. But what you believed is perfectly relevant and perfectly admissible as evidence. And you know it. But, out of respect, I'll withdraw the question. We'll approach it another way. Have you ever heard the phrase "the murder gene"?

Witness: Yes.

Mr. Logiudice: You've heard it where?

Witness: Just in conversation. I've used it
                  in conversation with my wife.
                  It's a figure of speech, nothing
                  more.

Mr. Logiudice: A figure of speech.

Witness: It is not a scientific term. I'm not
                  a scientist.

Mr. Logiudice: Of course. We're all non-
                  experts here. Now, when you
                  used this, this figure of speech,
                  "the murder gene," what were
                  you referring to?

[The witness did not respond.]

Mr. Logiudice: Oh, come on, Andy, there's no
                  reason to be shy about it. It's all
                  a matter of public record now.
                  You've felt a lot of anxiety,
                  haven't you, in your life?

Witness: A long time ago. When I was a
                  kid. Not now.

Mr. Logiudice: A long time ago, okay. You
                  were worried—a long time ago,
                  when you were a kid—about
                  your own history, your own
                  family, weren't you?

[The witness did not respond.]

Mr. Logiudice: It's fair to say you're descended from a long line of violent men, aren't you, Mr. Barber?

[The witness did not respond.]

Mr. Logiudice: It's fair to say that, isn't it?

Witness: [Inaudible.]

Mr. Logiudice: I'm sorry, I didn't hear you. You're descended from a long line of violent men, aren't you? Mr. Barber?

Violence did run in my family. You could follow it like a red thread back through three generations. Probably there were more. Probably the red thread ran right the way back to Cain, but I never had any desire to trace it. A few stories, lurid, mostly unverifiable, and a few photographs had come down to me; that was affliction enough. When I was a kid, I wanted to forget these stories entirely. I used to wonder what it would be like if a magical amnesia descended and erased my mind completely, leaving only a body and some sort of blank self, all potential, all soft clay. But of course, no matter how I tried to forget, the story of my ancestors was always stored in deep memory, always ready to poke up into awareness. I learned to manage with it. Later, for Jacob's sake, I learned to drink it down entirely, leaving nothing for anyone to see, nothing to "share." Laurie was a great believer in sharing, in the talking cure, but I never meant to cure myself. I never believed such a thing was possible. That is what Laurie never understood. She knew that my father's ghost troubled me, but not why. She presumed the issue was that I never knew him and there would forever be a daddy-shaped hole in my life. I never told her anything else, though she tried to pry me open like an oyster. Laurie's own dad was a shrink, and before Jacob was born she was a teacher at the Gavin Middle School in South Boston, fifth- and sixth-grade English. She believed, based on these experiences, that she had some understanding of under-fathered young boys. "You'll never be able to deal with it," she would tell me, "if you won't talk about it." Oh, Laurie, you never got it! I never intended to "deal with it." I intended to stop it cold. I meant to stop the whole sordid criminal line of descent by absorbing it all inside me. I would stand there and stop it like a bullet. I would simply refuse to pass it along to Jake. So I chose not to learn much. Not to research my history or analyze it for causes and effects. I purposely orphaned myself from the whole brawling lot of them. As far as I knew—as far as I chose to know—the red thread went back to my great-grandfather, a slit-eyed thug named James Burkett, who came east from North Dakota carrying in his bones some feral, wicked instinct for violence that would manifest itself over and over, in Burkett himself, in his son, and most spectacularly in his grandson, my father.

James Burkett was born near Minot, North Dakota, sometime around 1890. The circumstances of his childhood, his parents, whether he had any education—I knew nothing about these things. Only that he grew up on the High Plains of Dakota in the years after Little Big Horn, at the closing of the frontier. The first real evidence I had of the man was a sepia photograph on thick card stock, taken in New York City at the H.W. Harrison Photographic Studio on Fulton Street on Wednesday, August 23, 1911. The day and date were carefully noted in pencil on the back of the photo

along with his new name, "James Barber."
The story behind this journey was also
murky. The way I heard it—from my mother,
who got it from my father's father—was
that Burkett lit out of North Dakota to escape an armed robbery charge. He lay low
awhile on the southern shore of Lake Superior, clamming and working on fishing
boats, then made his way to New York under a new name. Why he changed his
name—whether it was to avoid an arrest
warrant or just to make a new start with a
new identity out east, or for some other
reason—no one knew for sure. Nor could
anyone explain why my great-grandfather
chose Barber as his new surname. The
only solid evidence I had of this period was
the photo itself. It was the only image of
James Burkett-Barber I ever saw. He would
have been about twenty or twenty-one
when it was taken. He is shown full figure.
Slim and taut, bandy-legged, in a borrowed
coat, with a bowler held in the crook of his
arm. He squints into the camera with a
Bowery smirk, one corner of his mouth
curling up like smoke.

I surmised that the charge in North Dakota was probably more serious than

armed robbery. Not only did Burkett-Barber go to great lengths to escape it—a low-rent stickup man on the lam did not have to travel so far or transform himself so completely—but upon arriving in New York he displayed an aptitude for violence almost immediately. There was no apprenticeship. He did not work his way up from petty assaults, as novice criminals do; he stepped onstage a hoodlum in full flower. His criminal record in New York included arrests for ABDW, assault with intent to rob, assault with intent to murder, mayhem, possession of an infernal device, possession of an unlicensed firearm, rape, and attempted murder. Between his first arrest in New York state in 1912 and his death in 1941, James Barber spent nearly half his days in prison or in custody awaiting trial. On two charges of rape and attempted murder alone, he served fourteen years combined.

It was the record of a professional criminal, and the one description of him that surfaced in the casebooks bore that out. The case was an attempted murder in 1916. It generated a perfunctory appeal and was therefore written up in the New York case reports in 1918. The summary of the facts of the case, as reported by Judge Barton in his decision, is just a few sentences long:

The defendant became embroiled in an argument with the victim, a man named Payton, at a Brooklyn bar. The argument had to do with a debt Payton owed either to the defendant himself (according to the defendant) or to another for whom the defendant worked as a "stalker," or debt-collector (according to the State). In the course of this argument, the defendant, in a transport of rage, attacked the victim with a bottle. He persisted in the attack even after the bottle had broken, after the affray had spilled from the bar out onto the street, and after the victim's left eye was badly damaged and his left ear shorn nearly off. The attack finally ended when several bystanders, to whom the victim was known, intervened to overwhelm the defendant and hold him forcibly, with great effort, until police arrived.

One other detail from that court decision stood out. The judge noted, "The defendant's reputation for violence was well known to Payton, as indeed it was well known generally."

James Barber left at least one son, my grandfather Russell, who was called Rusty. Rusty Barber lived until 1971. I knew him only briefly, when I was a very little kid. Most of what I know about him comes from stories he told my mother, who later passed them on to me.

Rusty never met his father and therefore never missed him. Didn't waste a hell of a lot of thought on him. Rusty was raised in Meriden, Connecticut, where his mother had people and where she returned from New York City, pregnant, to raise him up. She told the boy about his father, including his crimes. She did not mince words, but neither she nor the boy made a big deal about it or felt especially burdened. Lots of folks had it worse in those days. It did not occur to anyone that Rusty's father might affect the boy's future in any way. On the contrary, Rusty was raised with essentially the same expectations his neighbors were. He was a mediocre student and a little wild, but he did graduate from Meriden High School. He entered West Point in 1933 but left after his plebe year, much of which he spent in special confinement and walking disciplinary tours. He came back to Meriden, worked odd jobs, drifted. He married a local girl, my grandmother, and seven months later had a son, whom he called William. Once, Rusty was involved in a minor scuffle and wound up getting arrested for assaulting a police officer, though he had not done any such thing, really. Just did not like the way the man laid hands on him.

It was the war that turned things around for Rusty Barber. He joined the Army as a private and took part in the D-day invasion with the First Infantry Division. By the time the war was over, he was a lieutenant in the Third Army, a winner of the Medal of Honor and two Silver Stars, and a certified hero. During the battle for Nuremberg in April 1945, he single-handedly stormed a German machine-gun emplacement, killing six Germans, the last two using his bayonet. There was a parade for him back in Meriden. He rode on the back of an open convertible and waved to the girls.

After the war, he had two more kids, bought his own little wood-frame house in Meriden. But he was not nearly as well suited to peacetime. He flopped in a series of businesses—insurance, real estate, a restaurant. He did finally find a place as a traveling salesman. He repped a number of clothing and shoe lines, and he spent most of his working life driving around southern New England with boxes of samples in his car trunk, which he displayed to storekeepers in one cramped office after another. Looking back on this period in my grandfather's life, he must have been laboring mightily to stay straight. Rusty Barber had his father's genius for violence, which the war encouraged and rewarded, but he was not exceptionally talented in any other respect. Still, he might have made it. He might have got through life peacefully, in a left-handed way. But it was a precarious thing, and events conspired against him.

On May 11, 1950, he was in Lowell, Massachusetts, calling on Birke's clothing store to show the new line of Mighty Mac parkas for the fall. He stopped for lunch at a hot dog place he liked called Elliot's. As he left

Elliot's, there was an accident. A car swiped the front of Rusty's Buick Special as he crept out of the parking lot. There was an argument. A shove. The other man produced a knife. When it was over, the man lay on the street, and Rusty walked away as if nothing had happened. The man stood up with his hands pressed to his belly. Blood seeped through his fingers. He opened his shirt but held his hands over his stomach a moment, as if he had a bellyache. When the man finally pulled his hands away, a slick coiled snake of intestines drooped out of him. A vertical incision split his stomach from the pelvis to the bottom of the chestbone. With his own hands, the man lifted his intestines back into his own body, held them there, and walked inside to call the police.

They threw the book at Rusty: assault with intent to murder, mayhem, ABDW. At trial, he argued self-defense but he confessed, fatally, that he did not recall any of the things he was accused of, including taking the man's knife and gutting him with it. His memory failed at the moment the man came at him with the knife. He was sentenced to seven to ten years; he served three. By the time he got back to Meriden, his eldest son, William—my father, Billy Barber—was eighteen and already too wild for any father to control, even one as formidable as Rusty.

And here we reach the part of the story where the fabric frays and runs out. For I have no real memories of my own father back then, just fragments—

an unfocused blue-green tattoo on the inside of his right wrist, in the shape of a cross or a dagger, which he picked up in prison somewhere—

his hands, pale red-knuckled bony talons, quite credible as instruments of murder—

his mouth full of long yellow teeth—

a curved pearl-handled knife, which he always carried in his belt at the small of his back, tucked there every morning automatically, the way other men slipped a wallet into a back pocket.

Beyond these glimpses, though, I just cannot remember him. And even these scraps I don't really trust; I have had years to embellish them. It was 1961 when I last saw my father. I was five, he was twenty-six. For a long time, as a little kid, I tried to preserve my memories of him to keep him from disappearing. That was before I really understood what he was. Over the years, he dematerialized anyway. By the time I was ten or so, I had no real memory of him except these few stray puzzle pieces. A little while after that I quit thinking of him altogether. For convenience, I lived as if I had no father, as if I had come into the world unfathered, and this attitude I never questioned because nothing any good could ever come of it.

One memory did stick, if imperfectly. Sometime in that last summer, 1961, my mom took me to visit him in the Whalley Avenue jail in New Haven. We sat at one of the pitted wood tables in the crowded visiting room. The prisoners in their boxy prison dungarees and pajama tops all looked like the crayon drawings of flat, square-shaped men that my friends and I used to draw. I must have been shy that day—you had to be careful around him—because my father had to coax me. "Come here, let me look at you." He clamped his fist around my tiny upper arm and drew me forward. "Come here. You come all this way to visit, get over here." Years later, I can still feel his grip on my arm, twisting it slightly, the way you would twist a chicken leg to tear it away.

He had done a terrible thing. I knew that. No adult would tell me what it was exactly. It involved a girl and one of the empty boarded-up row houses on Congress Avenue. And the pearl-handled knife. That was the part that made grown-ups go quiet.

My childhood ended that summer. I learned the word *murder.* But it is not enough to be told a word as big as that. You have to live with it, carry it around with you. You have to pace around and around it, see it from different angles, at different times of day, in different light, until you understand, until it enters you. You have to hold it inside yourself in secret for years, like the hideous stone inside a peach.

How much of this did Laurie know? None of it. I knew the moment I laid eyes on her that she was a Nice Jewish Girl from a Nice Jewish Family and she would not consider me if she knew the truth. So I told her in vague and romantic terms that my father had a raffish reputation but I had never known him. I was the product of a short, unhappy love affair. For the next thirty-five years that was how things stood. To Laurie, I was essentially fatherless. I never told her any different because in my own mind I *was* essentially fatherless. Certainly I was not Bloody Billy Barber's son. There was nothing very dramatic in all this. When I told my girlfriend, who became my wife, that I did not know who my father was, I was simply saying out loud what I had been repeating to myself for years. I was not misleading her at all. If I had once been Billy Barber's son, by the time I met Laurie I had long ceased to be, except in strict biological terms. What I told Laurie was nearer the truth than the actual facts were. You will say, *Okay, but surely in all those years there must have come a time when you could have told her.* But the truth is, as time went by, what I had told Laurie became more and more true. As a grown man, I was even less Billy's boy. It was all just a story, some old myth that had nothing to do with who I actually was. I did not even think about it much, honestly. At some point as adults we cease to be our parents' children and we become our children's parents instead. What was more, I had the girl. I had Laurie, and we were happy. Our marriage settled into a rhythm, we believed we knew each other, and we were each happy with our conception of our partner. Why spoil that? Why risk the rare happy marriage— rarer still, a love marriage that endures— for something as common and as toxic as complete, unthinking, transparent honesty? Who would be helped by my telling? Me? Not at all. I was made of steel, I promise you. There is a more mundane explanation too: it just never came up. It turns out there is no good time in the average day to announce to your wife that you are the son of a murderer.

7 | Denial

Logiudice was half right: by this point I did suspect Jacob, but not of murder. The scenario Logiudice was trying to sell to the grand jury—that, because of my family history and because of the knife, I immediately knew Jacob was a psychopath and covered for him—was pure bullshit. I don't blame Logiudice for overselling the case that way. Juries are hard of hearing by nature, the more so in this case where circumstances essentially forced them to stick their fingers in their ears. Logiudice had no choice but to shout. But the fact is, nothing so dramatic had happened. The suggestion that Jacob might be a murderer was just crazy; I did not seriously consider it. What I thought, rather, was that something was up. Jacob knew more than he was telling. Lord knows, that was unsettling enough. Suspicion, once it started to corkscrew itself into my thoughts, made me experience everything twice: as questing prosecutor and as anxious father, one after the truth, the other terrified of it. And if I did not exactly confess all that to the grand jury, well, I knew enough to oversell my case too.

The day I discovered the knife, Jacob got home from school around two-thirty. From the kitchen, Laurie and I listened to him clatter into the front hall and back-heel the door shut, then slip off his backpack and coat in the mudroom. We exchanged nervous glances as, like sonar operators, we interpreted these sounds.

"Jacob," Laurie called, "can you come in here, please?"

There was a moment's stillness, a catch, before he said, "Okay."

Laurie made a positive face to reassure me.

Jacob shambled into the kitchen apprehensively. From my perspective, looking up at him, it struck me how big he had gotten, this man-sized boy.

"Dad. What are you doing home?"

"There's something we need to talk about, Jake."

He came in a little farther and saw the knife on the table between us. With the blade folded into the handle, the knife had lost its menace. It was just a tool.

I said, in as neutral a tone as I could manage, "You want to tell us what this is?"

"Um, a knife?"

"Don't fool around, Jacob."

"Sit down, Jacob," his mother encouraged. "Sit down."

He sat. "You looked through my room?"

"I did, not your mother."

"You searched it?"

"Yup."

"Ever heard of privacy?"

"Jacob," Laurie said, "your father was worried about you."

He rolled his eyes.

Laurie continued, "We're both worried. Why don't you just tell us what this is all about."

"Jacob, you put me in a difficult position,

you know. Half the state police are looking for this knife."

"For *this* knife?"

"Not *this* knife; *a* knife. You know what I mean. For a knife like this. I just don't understand what a kid like you is doing with a knife like this. Why do you need it, Jake?"

"I don't need it. It's just something I got."

"Why?"

"I don't know."

"You got it but you don't know why?"

"It's just, I don't know, something I did. For no reason. It doesn't mean anything. Why does everything have to mean something?"

"Then why did you hide it?"

"Probably because I knew you'd freak out."

"Well, you got that right, at least. Why do you need a knife?"

"I just told you, I don't need it. I just thought it was kinda cool. I liked it. I just wanted it."

"Are you having problems with other kids?"

"No."

"Is there someone you're afraid of?"

"No. Like I said, I just saw it and I thought it was cool so I bought it." He shrugged.

"Where?"

"This army-navy store in town. They're not hard to find."

"Is there a record of the sale? Did you use a credit card?"

"No, cash."

My eyes narrowed.

"It's not that unusual, Jesus, Dad. People do use cash, you know."

"What do you do with it?"

"Nothing. I just look at it, hold it, see how it feels."

"Do you carry it with you?"

"No. Not usually."

"But sometimes?"

"No. Well, rarely."

"Do you bring it to school?"

"No. Except once. I showed it to some kids."

"Who?"

"Derek, Dylan. Couple others maybe."

"Why?"

"'Cause I thought it was cool. It was like, Hey, check this out."

"Have you ever used it for anything?"

"Like what?"

"I don't know, whatever you'd use a knife for: to cut."

"You mean have I ever stabbed anyone with it in Cold Spring Park?"

"No, I mean, have you ever used it at all?"

"No, never. Of course not."

"So you just got it and stuck it in your drawer?"

"Pretty much, yeah."

"That doesn't make sense."

"Well, it's the truth."

"Why would you—"

"Andy," his mother cut in, "he's a teenager. That's why."

"Laurie, he doesn't need help."

Laurie explained, "Teenagers do stupid things sometimes." She turned to Jacob. "Even *smart* teenagers do stupid things."

"Jacob, I need to ask you, for my own peace of mind: is this the knife they're looking for?"

"No! Are you crazy?"

"Do you know anything about what happened to Ben Rifkin? Anything you heard from your friends? Anything at all you can tell me?"

"No. Of course not." He looked at me evenly, meeting my gaze with his own. It only lasted a moment but it was unmistakably a challenge—the sort of eye-fuck a defiant witness will flip you on the stand. Once he had outfaced me, his point made, he became a petulant kid again: "I can't believe you're asking me this stuff, Dad. It's like, I get home from school and suddenly I get all these questions. I just can't believe this. I can't believe you actually think these things about me."

"I don't think anything about you, Jacob. All I know is you brought that knife into my house and I'd like to know why."

"Who told you to look for it?"

"Never mind who told me."

"One of the kids at school, obviously. Someone you interviewed yesterday. Just tell me who."

"It doesn't matter who. This isn't about what other kids did. You're not the victim here."

"Andy," Laurie warned. She had told me not to confront or cross-examine him, not to accuse. *Just talk to him, Andy. This is a family. We talk to each other.*

I looked away. Deep breath. "Jacob, if I

submit that knife for testing, for blood or any other evidence, would you object?"

"No. Go ahead, do whatever tests you want. I don't care."

I considered for a moment. "Okay. I believe you. I believe you."

"Do I get my knife back?"

"Absolutely not."

"It's my knife. You have no right to take it."

"I'm your father. That gives me the right."

"You're also with the cops."

"Are you worried about the cops for some reason, Jake?"

"No."

"Then what are you talking about your rights for?"

"What if I don't let you take it?"

"Try."

He stood there looking at the knife on the table and at me, weighing the risk and reward. "This is *so* wrong," he said, and he frowned at the injustice.

"Jake, your father's just doing what he thinks is best because he loves you."

"What about what *I* think is best? That doesn't matter, I suppose."

"No," I said. "It doesn't."

By the time I got to the Newton police station that same afternoon, they had Patz in the interview room, where he sat as still as an Easter Island head, staring into a camera that was hidden in the face of a schoolhouse clock. Patz knew the camera was there. The detectives were required to inform him and get his consent to record the interview. The camera was hidden anyway in the hope that suspects would stop thinking about it.

Patz's image was piped to a small computer screen in the detective bureau, right outside the interview room, where a half dozen Newton and CPAC detectives stood watching. So far it had not been much of a show, apparently. The cops wore flat expressions, not seeing much, not expecting to see much.

I came into the detective bureau and joined them. "He say anything?"

"Nothing. He's Sergeant Schultz."

Onscreen, Patz's image filled the frame. He sat at the head of a long wood table. Behind him was a bare white wall. Patz was a big man. According to his probation officer he was six foot three and two hundred sixty pounds. Even seated behind a table, he looked massive. But his body was soft. His sides, belly, and tits all sagged against his black polo shirt, as if he had been poured and bagged up inside this black sack cinched shut at the neck.

"Jesus," I said, "this guy could use a little exercise."

One of the CPAC guys said, "How about jerking off to kiddie porn?"

We all sniggered.

In the interview room, on one side of Patz was Paul Duffy from CPAC, on the other a Newton detective, Nils Peterson. The cops were visible onscreen only now and then, when they leaned forward into the camera frame.

Duffy was leading the Q&A. "Okay, take me through it one more time. Tell me what you remember from that morning."

"I already told you."

"One more time. You'd be surprised the things that come back to people when they go back over the story."

"I don't want to talk anymore. I'm getting tired."

"Hey, Lenny, do yourself a favor, all right?

I'm trying to exclude you here. I already told you: I'm trying to rule you *out.* This is in your interest."

"It's Leonard."

"A witness puts you in Cold Spring Park that morning."

That was a fib.

Onscreen, Duffy said, "You know I have to check that out. With your record, that's just the way it is. I wouldn't be doing my job if I didn't."

Patz sighed.

"Just one more time, Lenny. I don't want to get the wrong guy."

"It's Leonard." He rubbed his eyes. "All right. I was in the park. I walk there every morning. But I was nowhere near where the kid got killed. I never go that way, I never walk in that part. I didn't see any-thing, I didn't hear anything"—he began to count these points on his fingers—"I don't know the kid, I never saw the kid, I never heard of the kid."

"All right, calm down, Lenny."

"I am calm." A glance into the camera.

"And you didn't see anyone that morn-ing?"

"No."

"No one saw you leave your apartment or come back?"

"How should I know?"

"You didn't see anyone in the park who looked suspicious, anyone who didn't be-long there, who we should know about?"

"No."

"All right, let's take a quick break, okay? You stay here. We'll be back in a few min-utes. We'll just have a few more questions and then that'll be it."

"What about my lawyer?"

"Haven't heard from him yet."

"You'll tell me when he gets here?"

"Sure, Lenny."

The two detectives got up to leave.

"I've never hurt anyone," Patz said. "You remember that. I never hurt anyone. Ever."

"Okay," Duffy reassured him, "I believe you."

The detectives crossed in front of the camera and stepped through the door di-rectly into the room where they had been only distant images in the computer moni-tor.

Duffy shook his head. "I've got nothing. He's used to dealing with cops. I just don't have anything to challenge him with. I'd like to let him sit there awhile and cool off, but I don't think we'll have time. His lawyer's on the way. What do you want to do, Andy?"

"You've been going like this for how long?"

"A couple hours maybe. Something like that."

"Just like this? Deny, deny, deny?"

"Yeah. It's useless."

"Do it again."

"Do it again? Are you kidding? How long have you been watching?"

"I just got here, Duff, but what else can we do? He's our only real suspect. A little boy is dead; this guy likes little boys. He's already given you the fact he was in the park that morning. He knows the area. He's there every morning, so he knows the routine, he knows kids walk through those woods every morning. He's certainly big enough to overpower the victim. That's motive, means, and opportunity. So I say stay with it till he gives you something."

Duffy's eyes flicked to the other cops in the room then back to me. "His lawyer's about to shut it down anyway, Andy."

"Then there's no time to waste, is there?

Get back in there. Get me a confession and I'll take it to the grand jury this afternoon."

"Just get you a confession? Just like that?"

"That's why you get the big bucks, pal."

"What about the kids at the school? I thought that's where we were headed."

"We'll keep looking at it, Duff, but what do we have, really? A bunch of freaked-out kids running their mouths on Facebook? So what? Look at this guy. Just look at him. Name me a better suspect. We don't have one."

"You really believe that, Andy? This is the guy, you think?"

"Yes. Maybe. *Maybe.* But we need something real to prove it. Get me a confession, Duff. Get me the knife. Get me anything. We need something."

"Okay, then." Duffy looked resolutely at the Newton detective who was his partner on this case. "We do it again. Like the man says."

The cop hesitated, appealing to Duffy with his eyes. *Why waste time?*

"We do it again," Duffy repeated. "Like the man says."

Mr. Logiudice: They never got the chance, did they? The detectives never got back into the interrogation room with Leonard Patz that day.

Witness: No, they did not. Not that day or any other day.

Mr. Logiudice: How did you feel about that?

Witness: I thought it was a mistake. Based on what we knew at the time, it was a mistake to turn away from Patz as a suspect so early in the investigation. He was our best suspect by far.

Mr. Logiudice: You still believe that?

Witness: Without a doubt. We should have stayed on Patz.

Mr. Logiudice: Why?

Witness: Because that's where the evidence was pointing.

Mr. Logiudice: Not all the evidence.

Witness: All? You never have all the evidence pointing in one direction, not in a tough case like this one. That's precisely the problem. You don't have enough information, the data is incomplete. There is no clear pattern, no obvious answer. So detectives do what all people do: they form a narrative in their head, a theory, and then they go looking in the data for evidence to support it. They pick a suspect first, then they look for the evidence to convict him. And they stop noticing evidence that points at other suspects.

Mr. Logiudice: Like Leonard Patz.

Witness: Like Leonard Patz.

Mr. Logiudice: Are you suggesting that's what happened here?

Witness: I'm suggesting mistakes were made, yes, certainly.

Mr. Logiudice: So what is a detective supposed to do in this situation?

Witness: He has to be wary of locking onto one suspect too soon. Because if he guesses wrong, he will miss evidence pointing him toward the right answer. He'll miss even obvious things.

Mr. Logiudice: But a detective has to form theories. He has to focus on

	suspects, usually before he has clear evidence against them. What else can he do?
Witness:	That's the dilemma. You always start with a guess. And sometimes you guess wrong.
Mr. Logiudice:	Did anyone guess wrong in this case?
Witness:	We didn't know. We just didn't know.
Mr. Logiudice:	All right, go on with your story. Why didn't the detectives go on interrogating Patz?

An older man with a battered lawyer's bag came into the detective bureau. His name was Jonathan Klein. He was short, slight, a little stooped. He wore a gray suit with a black turtleneck. His hair was long and strikingly white. He swept it straight back over his head where it hung over the back of his collar. He had a white goatee as well. He said in a soft voice, "Hello, Andy."

"Jonathan."

We shook hands with real warmth. I always liked and respected Jonathan Klein. Bookish and vaguely bohemian, he was unlike me. (I am as conventional as white toast.) But he did not lecture or lie, which set him apart from his brethren in the defense bar, who had only a casual regard for the truth, and he was genuinely smart and knew the law. He was—there is no other word for it—wise. Also, it must be said, I had a childish attraction to men of my father's generation, as if I still harbored a faint hope of being unorphaned, even at this late date.

Klein said, "I'd like to see my client now." His voice was soft—it was naturally soft, this was not an affectation or a tactic—so that the room tended to grow quiet around him. You found yourself leaning in close to make out what he was saying.

"I didn't know you were representing this guy, Jonathan. Kind of a low-rent case for you, isn't it? Some crummy pedophile ball-grabber? It's bad for your reputation."

"Reputation? We're lawyers! Anyway, he's not here because he's a pedophile. We both know that. This is a lot of cops to put on a case about ball-grabbing."

I stepped aside. "All right. He's right in there. Go on in."

"You'll turn off the camera and the microphone?"

"Yeah. You want to use another room instead?"

"No, of course not." He smiled gently. "I trust you, Andy."

"Enough to let your man keep talking?"

"No, no. I trust you too much for that."

And that was the end of Patz's Q&A.

Nine-thirty P.M.

Laurie lay on the couch gazing at me, her book tented on her belly. She wore a brown V-neck shirt with a wreath of chunky embroidery around the neck, and her tortoiseshell reading glasses. Over the years she had found a way to carry her younger style into middle age; she had upgraded the embroidered peasant blouses and ripped jeans of her brainy funkster teens for a more elegant, tailored version of the same look.

She said, "Do you want to talk about it?"

"Talk about what?"

"Jacob."

"We already did."

"I know, but you're brooding."

"I'm not brooding. I'm watching TV."

"The Cooking Channel?" She smiled, warmly skeptical.

"There's nothing else on. Anyway, I like cooking."

"No, you don't."

"I like *watching* cooking."

"It's okay, Andy. You don't have to if you're not ready."

"It's not that. It's just there's nothing to say."

"Can I ask you one question?"

I rolled my eyes: *Does it matter if I say no?*

She picked up the remote from the coffee table and switched off the TV. "When we talked to Jacob today, you said you didn't think he did anything, but then you turned around and cross-examined him."

"No, I didn't."

"You did. You never accused him of anything, exactly, but your tone was . . . prosecutorial."

"It was?"

"A little."

"I didn't mean for it to be. I'll apologize to him later."

"You don't have to apologize."

"I do, if that's how I came off."

"I'm just asking why. Is there anything you're not telling me?"

"Like what?"

"Whatever made you go after him that way."

"I didn't go after him. Anyway, no, I was just upset about the knife. And what Derek wrote on Facebook."

"Because Jacob's had some behavioral—"

"Jesus, Laurie, come on. Be serious. This is just some kids gossiping. If I could get my hands on Derek. That was incredibly stupid, what he wrote. Honestly, sometimes I think that kid isn't all there."

"Derek's not a bad kid."

"Will you still say that when Jacob gets a knock on the door one day?"

"Is that a real possibility?"

"No. Of course not."

"Do we have any responsibility here?"

"You mean, is it our fault somehow?"

"Fault? No. I mean, do we have to report it?"

"No. God, no. There's nothing to report. It's not a crime to have a knife. It's not a crime to be a stupid teenager either— thank God, or we'd have to throw half of 'em in the can."

Laurie nodded neutrally. "It's just, he's

been accused, and now you know about it. And it's not like the cops aren't going to find it anyway; it's right there on Facebook."

"It's not a credible accusation, Laurie. There's no reason to bring the whole world down on Jake's head. The whole thing is ridiculous."

"Is that what you really think, Andy?"

"Yes! Of course. Don't you?"

She searched my face. "Okay. So this isn't what's bothering you?"

"I already told you: nothing's bothering me."

"Really?"

"Really."

"What did you do with the knife?"

"I got rid of it."

"Got rid of it where?"

"I threw it away. Not here. In a Dumpster somewhere."

"You covered for him."

"No. I just wanted that knife out of my house. And I didn't want anyone using it to make Jacob look guilty when he's not. That's all."

"How is that different from covering for him?"

"You can't *cover* for someone who didn't do anything wrong."

She gave me a searching look. "Okay. I'm going up to bed. You coming?"

"In a little while."

She got up, came over to plow her fingers through my hair and kiss my forehead. "Don't stay up too late, sweetheart. You won't be able to get up in the morning."

"Laurie, you didn't answer my question. I asked you what *you* think? Do you agree it's ridiculous to think Jacob did this?"

"I think it's very hard to imagine, yes."

"But you *can* imagine it?"

"I don't know. You mean you can't, Andy? You can't even imagine it?"

"No, I can't. This is our son we're talking about."

She pulled back from me visibly, cautiously. "I don't know. I guess I can't imagine it either. But then I think: when I woke up this morning, I could not have imagined that knife."

8 | The End

**Sunday, April 22, 2007, ten days
after the murder.**

On a raw, drizzly morning, hundreds of volunteers turned out to sweep
Cold Spring Park for the missing knife. They
were a cross-section of the town. Kids from
the McCormick, some who had been
friends with Ben Rifkin, some who were
clearly from other school tribes—jocks,
geeks, kittenish good girls. There were lots
of young mothers and fathers. A few of the
activist *macher*s who were constantly or-
ganizing community efforts of one kind or

another. All these assembled in the morning damp, listened to instructions from Paul Duffy about how the search would proceed, then in teams they tromped off across the spongy wet ground to search their assigned quadrants of the woods for the knife. There was a determined mood to the whole adventure. It was a relief for everyone to do something finally, to be admitted into the investigation. Soon, they were sure, the whole thing would be resolved. It was the waiting, the uncertainty that was wearing them down. The knife would end all that. It would bear fingerprints or blood or some other morsel that would unlock the mystery, and the town would finally be able to exhale.

Mr. Logiudice: You didn't take part in the search, did you?

Witness: No, I did not.

Mr. Logiudice: Because you knew it was a fool's errand. The knife they were looking for had already been found in Jacob's dresser drawer. And you had already dumped it for him.

Witness: No. I knew that was not the

knife they were looking for. There was no doubt in my mind. Zero.

Mr. Logiudice: Then why didn't you join the search?

Witness: A prosecutor never takes part in his own searches. I couldn't risk becoming a witness in my own case. Think about it: if I were the one to find the murder weapon, I'd have become an essential witness. I'd be forced to cross the courtroom and take the stand. I'd have to give up the case. That's why a good prosecutor always hangs back. He waits at the police station or out on the street while a search warrant is executed, he watches from the next room while a detective conducts an interrogation. That is Prosecution 101, Neal. It's standard procedure. It's exactly what I taught you, once upon a time. Maybe you weren't listening.

Mr. Logiudice: So it was for technical reasons?

Witness: Neal, no one wanted the search to succeed as much as I did. I wanted my son to be proven innocent. Finding the real knife would have accomplished that.

Mr. Logiudice: You're not the least bit troubled by the way you disposed of Jacob's knife? Even now, knowing what happened?

Witness: I did what I thought was right. Jake was innocent. It was the wrong knife.

Mr. Logiudice: Of course you weren't willing to test that theory, were you? You didn't submit the knife for forensic testing, for fingerprints or blood or fiber traces, as you threatened Jacob you might?

Witness: It was the wrong knife. I did not need a test to confirm that for me.

Mr. Logiudice: You already knew.

Witness: I already knew.

Mr. Logiudice: What was it—what made you so sure?

Witness:	I knew my son.
Mr. Logiudice:	That's it? You knew your son?
Witness:	I did what any father would do. I tried to protect him from his own stupidity.
Mr. Logiudice:	Okay. We'll leave it. All right, so while the others searched in Cold Spring Park that morning, you waited where?
Witness:	In the parking lot at the entrance to the park.
Mr. Logiudice:	And at some point Mr. Rifkin, the victim's father, appeared?
Witness:	Yes. When I first saw him, he was coming from the direction of the woods. There are playing fields at the front of the park there, soccer fields, baseball. That morning the fields were empty. It was just a huge flat open grassy expanse. And he was making his way across it toward me.

This will always be my lasting image of Dan Rifkin alone in his misery: a small figure meandering across this massive green

space, head bowed, arms thrust down into his coat pockets. The wind kept blustering him off course. He zigzagged like a little boat tacking upwind.

I went out onto the fields to meet him, but we were some distance apart and the crossing took time. For an awkward interval we watched each other approach. What must we have looked like from above? Two tiny forms inching across an empty green field toward a meeting somewhere in the center.

As he drew close, I waved. But Rifkin did not return the gesture. Thinking he was upset by accidentally running across the search, I made a churlish note to ream out the victim advocate who had forgotten to warn Rifkin away from the park that day.

"Hey, Dan," I said in a wary tone.

He wore aviator sunglasses, though the weather was gray, and his eyes showed dimly through the lenses. He stared up at me, his eyes behind those lenses as huge and inexpressive as a fly's. Angry, apparently.

"Are you okay, Dan? What are you doing here?"

"I'm surprised to see *you* here."

"Yeah? Why is that? Where else would I be?"

He snorted.

"What is it, Dan?"

"You know"—his tone going philosophical—"I've had the strangest feeling lately, like I'm onstage and all the people around me are actors. Everyone in the world, every single person rushing around me on the sidewalk, they march around with their noses up in the air pretending like nothing has happened, and I'm the only one who knows the truth. I'm the only one who knows Everything Has Changed."

I nodded, benign, indulging him.

"They're *false.* You know what I mean, Andy? They're pretending."

"I can only imagine how you must feel, Dan."

"I think maybe you're an actor too."

"Why do you say that?"

"I think you're false." Rifkin took off his sunglasses, folded them carefully, and stowed them in an inside pocket of his jacket. The bags under his eyes had darkened since I saw him last. His olive skin had taken on a grayish pallor. "I hear you're being taken off the case."

"What? You heard that from who?"

"Doesn't matter who. I just want you to know: I want another DA."

"Okay, well, that's something we can talk about, certainly."

"There's nothing to talk about. It's already done. Go call your boss. You need to talk to your own people. I told you, I want another DA. Someone who won't just sit on the case. And that's going to happen now."

"Sit on the case? Dan, what the hell are you talking about?"

"You said everything was being done. What was being done, exactly?"

"Look, it's been a hard case, I acknowledge—"

"No, no, it's more than that and you know it. Why haven't you pressed those kids? Still, to this day? I mean, really put the screws to them? That's what I want to know."

"I *have* talked to them."

"Including your own kid, Andy?"

My mouth fell open. I extended my hand toward him, to touch his arm, to connect, but he raised his arm as if to backhand it away.

"You've been lying to me, Andy. All along you've been lying."

He looked off toward the trees. "Do you know what bothers me, Andy? About being here, in this place? It's that for a while—for a few minutes, maybe just a few seconds, I don't know how long—but for some amount of time my son was alive here. He was out there lying in some *fucking* wet leaves, bleeding to death. And I wasn't here with him. I was supposed to be here to help him. That's what a father does. But I didn't know. I was off somewhere, in the car, in my office, talking on the phone, whatever it was I was doing. Do you understand that, Andy? Do you have any idea how that feels? Can you even imagine it? I saw him get born, I saw him take his first steps and . . . and learn to ride a bike. I took him to his first day of school. But I wasn't here to help him when he died. Can you imagine how that feels?"

"Dan," I said weakly, "why don't I get a cruiser down here to drive you home? I don't think it's good for you to be here. You should be with your family."

"I can't be with my family, Andy, that's the fucking point! My family is dead."

"Okay." I looked down at the ground, at his white sneakers spattered with mud and pine needles.

"I'll tell you something," Rifkin added. "It doesn't matter what happens to me now. I could become a . . . a drug addict or a thief or a bum. It just doesn't matter what happens to me from here. Why should it? Why should I care?"

He said this with a bitter snarl.

"Call your office, Andy." A beat. "Go on, call. It's over. You're out."

I took out my cell phone and called Lynn Canavan directly on her cell. It rang three times. I could imagine her reading the caller ID window, preparing herself to answer.

"I'm at the office," she said. "Why don't you come down here right away."

I told her, as Rifkin looked on with satisfaction, that if she had something to say, she could say it right then and save me the trip.

"No," she insisted. "Come to the office, Andy. I want to talk to you face-to-face."

I snapped the phone shut. I wanted to say something to Rifkin, good-bye or good luck or some valedictory bullshit, who knew what? Something told me he was right and this was good-bye. But he did not want to hear it. His posture announced as much. He had already assigned me a villain's role. Probably he knew more than I did, anyway.

I left him on that green field and drove across the river to Cambridge in a defeated reverie. I was resigned to the fact that I would be removed from the case; it simply did not make sense that Rifkin would have come up with that on his own. Somebody had tipped him off, probably Logiudice, whose Iago whispers in the district attorney's ear had finally won the day. Okay, then. I would be removed for a conflict of interest, a technicality. I had been outmaneuvered, that was all. It was office politics, and I was an apolitical guy, always had been. So Logiudice would have his high-profile case, and I would move on to the next file, the next body, the next case to enter the funnel. I still believed all this, foolish or delusional or rationalizing as I was. I still did not see what was coming. There was so little evidence pointing to Jacob—a schoolgirl with a secret, some kids gossiping on Facebook, even the knife. As evidence these were nothing. Any semicompetent defense lawyer would swipe them aside like cobwebs.

At the courthouse, there were no fewer than four plainclothes troopers waiting at the front door to meet me. I recognized them all as CPAC guys but I knew only one very well, a detective named Moynihan. They escorted me like a Praetorian guard through the courthouse lobby to the district attorney's office, then through cubicles and hallways abandoned on a Sunday morning, to Lynn Canavan's corner office.

There were three people there, seated at the conference table, Canavan, Logiudice, and a press guy named Larry Siff, whose constant presence at Canavan's side for the past year or so had been a discouraging sign of the permanent campaign. I had no beef with Siff personally, but I despised his intrusion into a sacred process to which I had devoted my life. Most of the time he did not even have to speak; his mere presence ensured that political implications would be considered.

District Attorney Canavan said, "Sit down, Andy."

"Did you really think you needed all this, Lynn? What did you think I was going to do? Jump out the window?"

"It's for your own good. You know how it goes."

"How what goes? I feel like I'm under arrest."

"No. We just have to be careful. People get upset. They react unpredictably. We don't want any scenes. You'd have done the same thing."

"Not true." I sat down. "So what am I going to be upset about?"

"Andy," she said, "we have some bad news. On the Rifkin case? The print on the victim's sweatshirt? It's your son Jacob's." She slid a stapled report toward me.

I scanned the report. It was from the State Police Crime Lab. The report identified a dozen points of comparison between the latent found at the murder scene and one of the knowns on Jacob's print card, much more than the standard eight required for a positive match. It was the right thumb: Jacob had reached out and grabbed the victim by his unzipped sweatshirt, leaving the print on that inside tag.

I said, bewildered, "I'm sure there's some explanation."

"I'm sure there is."

"They go to the same school. Jacob is in his class. They knew each other."

"Yes."

"It doesn't mean—"

"We know, Andy."

They looked at me with pity. All except for the younger troopers, now standing by the window, who did not know me and could still despise me as they would any other bad guy.

"We're putting you on paid leave. It's partly my fault: it was a mistake to let you have the case in the first place. These guys"—she gestured toward the troopers—"will go to your office with you. You can take your personal belongings. No papers, no files. You're not to touch the computer. Your work product belongs to the office."

"Who's taking the case?"

"Neal is."

I smiled. *Of course he is.*

"Andy, do you object to Neal trying the case for some reason?"

"Does it matter what I think, Lynn?"

"Maybe, if you can make a case."

I shook my head. "No. Let him have it. I insist."

Logiudice looked away, avoiding my eyes.

"Have you arrested him?"

More eyes darting around the room, avoiding me.

"Lynn, have you arrested my son?"

"No."

"Are you going to?"

Logiudice cut in, "We don't have to tell you that."

Canavan put out her hand to still him. "Yes. We don't have much choice, in the circumstances."

"In the circumstances? What circumstances? You think he's going to take off for Costa Rica?"

She shrugged.

"You already have the warrant?"

"Yes."

"Lynn, you have my word: he'll turn himself in. You don't need to arrest him. He doesn't belong in a jail, even for one night. He's no flight risk, you know that. He's my son. He's my son, Lynn. I don't want to see him arrested."

"Andy," the district attorney advised, waving away my pleading like smoke, "it'd probably be best for everyone if you stayed away from the courthouse for a while. Let the dust settle. Okay?"

"Lynn, I'm asking you as a friend, as a personal favor: please, don't arrest him."

"It's not a close call, Andy."

"Why? I don't understand. Because of a fingerprint? One fucking fingerprint? That's all there is? You must have more. Tell me there's more."

"Andy, I suggest you go get a lawyer."

"Get a lawyer? I *am* a lawyer. Tell me why you're doing this to my son. You're destroying my family. I have a right to know why."

"I'm just reacting to the evidence, that's all."

"The evidence points to Patz. I've told you that."

"There's more than you're aware of, Andy. Much more."

It took me a moment to absorb the implications of that. Just a moment, though. I folded my cards and determined that from then on, I would show them nothing.

I stood up. "Okay. Let's get moving."

"Just like that?"

"Was there anything else you wanted to say to me? You, Neal?"

Canavan said, "You know, we're still concerned about you. Whatever your son . . . may have done, he's not you. You and I go back a ways, Andy. I don't forget that."

I felt my face go hard, as if I was peering through the eye-holes of a stone mask. I looked only at Canavan, my old friend whom I still loved and still, despite everything, trusted. I did not dare glance at Logiudice. There was a wild energy rushing into my right arm. In that moment I felt that if I so much as looked at him, my hand would flash out, snatch up his throat, and crush it.

"Are we done here?"

"Yes."

"Good. I have to go. I have to find my family right away."

District Attorney Canavan's face was wary. "You okay to drive, Andy?"

"I'm fine."

"All right. These guys will go with you to your office."

In my office I tossed a few things into a cardboard box, papers and desk-debris, pictures plucked off the wall, the little souvenirs of years of work. An axe handle, evidence from a case I had never been able to push through the grand jury. It all fit into one cardboard box, all the years, the work, the friendships, the respect I had accumulated by little spoonfuls in case after case. All gone now, no matter how Jacob's case turned out. For even if Jacob was cleared, I would never escape the stain of the accusation. A jury could only declare my son "not guilty," never "innocent." The stink would never leave us. I doubted I would ever walk into a courtroom again as a lawyer. But things were racing too fast to linger over the past or future. There was only now.

I was not panicked, oddly. I never did lose my nerve. Jacob's homicide charge was a grenade—we would all inevitably be destroyed by it; only the details remained to be worked out—but a strange, calm urgency came over me. Surely a search warrant team was already on its way to my home. That may even have been why the DA had brought me all the way down here: to keep me out of that house before it could be searched. It was exactly what I would have done.

I bolted out of the office.

I called Laurie's cell from the car. No answer. "Laurie, it's very, very important. Call me back right away, the second you get this message."

I called Jacob's cell phone too. No answer.

I got home too late: four Newton cruisers were already parked outside, watching, freezing the house while they waited for the warrant to arrive. I continued around the block and parked.

My house is adjacent to a train stop on the suburban commuter-train line. An eight-foot fence separates the platform from my backyard. I spidered over it easily. There was so much adrenaline in me, I could have clambered up Mount Rushmore.

In my yard, I pushed through the arbor vitae at the edge of the lawn. The leaves flicked and needled across me as I bodied through the bushes.

I ran across my backyard. My neighbor was in his backyard, gardening. He waved to me, and out of neighborly reflex I waved back as I sprinted by.

Inside, I called out quietly for Jacob. To prepare him for what was coming. No one was home.

I bolted up the stairs, into Jacob's room, where I yanked open drawers, the closet, tossed up the laundry piles on the floor, desperate to find anything remotely incriminating and get rid of it.

Does that sound awful to you? I hear the little voice in your head: *Destruction of evidence! Obstruction of justice!* You are naive. You imagine the courts are reliable, that wrong results are rare, and therefore I ought to have trusted the system. *If he truly believed Jacob was innocent,* you are thinking, *he would have simply let the police sweep in and take whatever they liked.* Here is the dirty little secret: the error rate in criminal verdicts is much higher than anyone imagines. Not just false negatives, the guilty criminals who get off scot-free—those "errors" we recognize and accept. They are the predictable result of stacking the deck in defendants' favor as we do. The real surprise is the frequency of false positives, the innocent men found guilty. That error rate we do not acknowledge—do not even think about—because it calls so much into question. The fact is, what we call proof is as fallible as the witnesses who produce it, human beings all.

Memories fail, eyewitness identifications are notoriously unreliable, even the best-intentioned cops are subject to failures of judgment and recall. The human element in any system is always prone to error. Why should the courts be any different? They are not. Our blind trust in the system is the product of ignorance and magical thinking, and there was no way in hell I was going to trust my son's fate to it. Not because I believed he was guilty, I assure you, but precisely because he was innocent. I was doing what little I could to ensure the right result, the just result. If you do not believe me, go spend a few hours in the nearest criminal court, then ask yourself if you really believe it is error-free. Ask yourself if you would trust *your* child to it.

In any event, I did not find anything even remotely worrisome in Jake's room, just the usual teenage junk, dirty laundry, sneakers molded to the shape of his enormous feet, schoolbooks, video-gamer mags, charging cables for his various electronics. I don't know what I expected to find, really. The trouble was that I did not know what the DA had yet, what made them so anxious to charge Jacob, and it made me crazy wondering what that missing piece could be.

I was still tossing the room when my cell phone rang. It was Laurie. I told her to get home right away—she was visiting a friend in Brookline, twenty minutes away—but I did not tell her anything more. She was too emotional. I did not know how she would react and I did not have time to deal with her. *Help Jacob now, fix Laurie later.* "Where's Jacob?" I asked. She did not know. I hung up on her.

I took a last glance around the room. I was tempted to hide Jacob's laptop. God only knew what was on his hard drive. But I worried that stashing the computer would hurt him either way: if the computer went missing, that would be suspicious, given his online presence; on the other hand, if found it might contain devastating evidence. In the end I left it—unwisely, maybe, but there was no time to consider. Jacob knew he had been publicly accused on Facebook; presumably he had been wily enough to scrub his hard drive if need be.

The doorbell rang. Game over. I was still breathing heavily.

At the door, none other than Paul Duffy was there to hand me the search warrant. "Sorry, Andy," he said.

I stared. The troopers in their blue windbreakers, the cruisers with their flashers on, my old friend extending the trifolded warrant toward me—I simply did not know how to react, so I barely reacted at all. I stood there, mute, as he pressed the paper into my hand.

"Andy, I have to ask you to wait outside. You know the drill."

It took a few seconds to rouse myself, to come back into the moment and accept that this was really happening. But I was determined not to make the amateur's mistake, not to stumble and give them anything. No dumb statements blurted out under pressure in the critical early moments of the case. That is the mistake that puts people in Walpole.

"Is Jacob here, Andy?"

"No."

"Do you know where he is?"

"No idea."

"Okay, come on, buddy, step out, please." He put his hand gently on my upper arm to encourage me, but he did not pull me out of the house. He seemed willing to wait till I was ready. He leaned in and said confidentially, "Let's do this the right way."

"It's okay, Paul."

"I'm sorry."

"Just do your job, okay? Don't fuck it up."

"Okay."

"You dot those *i*'s and cross those *t*'s, or Logiudice'll throw you under the bus. He'll make you look like Barney Fife at the trial, mark my words. He'll do what he has to do. He won't protect you like I would."

"Okay, Andy. It's all right. Come on out."

I waited on the sidewalk in front of the house. Gawkers accumulated across the street, drawn by the cruisers out front. I would have preferred to wait in the back-yard, out of view, but I had to be there when Laurie or Jacob got home, to com-fort them—and to coach them.

Laurie arrived just a few minutes into the search. She wobbled when she heard the news. I steadied her and whispered into her ear not to say anything, not even to show any emotion, not fear or sadness.

Give them nothing. She made a scornful sound, then she cried. Her sobbing was honest, uninhibited, as if no one was watching. She did not care what people thought, because no one had ever thought badly of her, not for one moment in her life. I knew better. We stood together in front of the house, I with my arm around her in a protective, possessive way.

When the search stretched into its second hour, we retreated to the back of the house and sat on the deck. There Laurie cried softly, gathered herself, cried again.

At some point Detective Duffy came around back and climbed the stairs to the deck. "Andy, just so you know, we found a knife this morning in the park. It was in the muck next to a lake."

"I knew it. I knew it would show up. Are there any prints, blood, anything on it?"

"Nothing obvious. It's at the lab. There was this dried algae all over it, like green powder."

"It's Patz's."

"I don't know. Maybe."

"What kind of knife was it?"

"Just, like, a regular kitchen knife."

Laurie said, "A *kitchen* knife?"

"Yeah. You guys got all yours?"

I said, "Come on, Duff, be serious. What are you asking a question like that for?"

"All right, sorry. It's my job to ask."

Laurie glared.

"You guys heard from Jacob yet, Andy?"

"No. We can't find him. We've been calling everyone."

Duffy stifled a skeptical look.

"He's a kid," I said, "he disappears sometimes. When he gets here, Paul, I don't want anyone talking to him. No questions. He's a minor. He has a right to have a parent or guardian present. Don't try and pull anything."

"Jesus, Andy, nobody's going to *pull anything.* We would like to talk to him, though, obviously."

"Forget it."

"Andy, it might help him."

"Forget it. He's got nothing to say. Not one word."

In the middle of the yard, something caught our eyes and all three of us turned. A rabbit, tree-bark gray, sniffed the air, twitched its head, alerted, relaxed. It hopped a few feet, stopped. Motionless, it blended into the grass and the gloomy light. I almost lost sight of it until it hopped a little more, a gray ripple.

Duffy turned back to Laurie. Only a few Saturdays before, we had all gone out to a restaurant for dinner, Duffy and his wife and Laurie and I. It seemed like another lifetime. "We're just about done here, Laurie. We'll be out of here soon."

She nodded, too pissed off and heartbroken and betrayed to tell him it was all right.

"Paul," I told him, "he did not do it. I want to say that to you in case I don't get another chance. You and I aren't going to talk for a while, probably, so I want you to hear it right from me, okay? He did not do it. He did not do it."

"Okay. I hear you." He turned to go.

"He's innocent. As innocent as your kid."

"Okay," he said, and he left.

Over by the arbor vitae, the rabbit hunched, jaws munching.

We waited until after dark for Jacob, until the cops and the voyeurs had all drifted away. He never came.

He had been hiding for hours, mostly in the woods of Cold Spring Park, in backyards, and in the play structure behind the elementary school he had once attended, which is where the cops found him at around eight o'clock.

He submitted to the handcuffs without complaint, the police report said. He did not run. He greeted the cop by saying "I'm the one you're looking for" and "I didn't do it." When the cop said dismissively, "Then how did your fingerprint get on the body?," Jacob blurted—foolishly or cannily, I am still not sure—"I found him. He was already lying there. I tried to pick him up so I could help him. Then I saw he was dead, and I got scared and ran." It was the only statement Jacob ever gave the police. He must have realized, belatedly, that it was risky to blurt out confessions like that one, and he never said another word. Jacob knew, as few boys do, the full value of the Fifth Amendment. Later, there would be speculation about why Jacob made this singular statement, how complete and self-serving it was. There were intimations he had crafted the statement beforehand and conveniently let it slip—he was gaming the case, launching his defense as early as possible. All I know for sure is that

Jacob was never as smart or as cunning as he was described in the media.

In any case, after that, the only thing Jacob told the cop, over and over, was "I want my dad."

He could not be bailed that night. He was held in the lockup in Newton, just a mile or two from our house.

Laurie and I were allowed to see him only briefly, in a little windowless visiting room.

Jacob was obviously shaken. His eyes were watery and red-rimmed. His face was flushed, a single horizontal slash of red across each cheek, like war paint. He was obviously scared shitless. At the same time he was trying to stay composed. His manner was clenched, rigid, mechanical. A boy imitating manliness, at least an adolescent's conception of manliness. That was the part that broke my heart, I think, the way he struggled to hold it together, to keep that storm of emotion—panic, anger, sorrow—all siloed up inside himself. He would not be able to do it much longer, I thought. He was burning fuel fast.

"Jacob," Laurie said in a wobbly voice, "are you all right?"

"No! Obviously *not.*" He gestured at the room around him, the situation he was in, and made a sardonic face. "I'm dead."

"Jake—"

"They're saying *I* killed Ben? No way. No *way.* I can't believe this is happening. I can't *believe* this."

I said, "Hey, Jake, it's a mistake. It's some kind of horrible misunderstanding. We'll work it out, okay? I don't want you to lose hope. This is just the beginning of the process. There's a long way to go."

"I can't believe it. I can't believe it. I'm just, like"—he made an exploding sound and with his hands he sculpted a mushroom cloud—"you know? It's like, it's like, who's that guy? In the story?"

"Kafka."

"No. The guy from, whatsit? The movie."

"I don't know, Jake."

"Where the guy, like, finds out the world isn't really the world? It's just, like, a dream? Like a simulation? A computer made it all? And now he gets to see the real world. It's, like, an old movie."

"I'm not sure."

"*The Matrix*!"

"*The Matrix*? That's old?"

"Keanu Reeves, Dad? Please."

I looked at Laurie. "Keanu Reeves?"

She shrugged.

It was amazing that Jake could be goofy, even now. But he was. He was the same dorky kid that he had been a few hours before—had always been, for that matter.

"Dad, what am I supposed to do?"

"We're going to fight. We'll fight this every step of the way."

"No, I mean, like, not generally. *Now.* What happens next?"

"There'll be an arraignment tomorrow morning. They'll just read the charge and we'll set bail and you'll come home."

"How much is bail?"

"We'll find out tomorrow."

"What if we can't afford it? What happens to me?"

"We'll find it, don't worry. We have some money saved up. We have the house."

He sniffed. He'd heard me complain about money a thousand times. "I'm so sorry. I didn't do it, I swear. I know I'm not, like, a perfect kid, okay? But I didn't do this."

"I believe you."

Laurie added, "You *are* perfect, Jacob."

"I didn't even *know* Ben. He was just, like, this kid from school. Why would I do this? Huh? Why? Okay, why are they saying I did this?"

"I don't know, Jake."

"This is your case! What do you mean, you don't know?"

"I just don't know."

"You mean, you don't want to tell me."

"No. Don't say that. Jake, do you think I was investigating *you*? Really?"

He shook his head. "So just for no reason—for no reason—I killed Ben Rifkin? That's just—that's just—I don't know what it is. It's crazy. This whole thing is totally crazy."

"Jacob, you don't have to convince us. We're on your side. Always. No matter what happens."

"Jesus." He raked his fingers through his hair. "This is Derek's fault. He did this. I *know* it."

"Derek? Why Derek?"

"He's just—he's like—he gets freaked out by stuff, you know? Like, the littlest things and he freaks out about them. I swear, when I get out, I'm going to fuck him up. I swear it."

"Jake, I don't think Derek could have done this."

"He did. You watch. That kid."

Laurie and I exchanged a puzzled look.

"Jake, we're going to get you out of here. We'll put up the bail, whatever it is. We'll find the money. We're not going to let you sit in jail. But you're going to have to spend the night here, just until the arraignment in the morning. We'll meet you at the courthouse first thing. We'll have a lawyer with us. You'll be home for dinner tomorrow. Tomorrow you're going to sleep in your own bed, I promise."

"I don't want a lawyer. I want you. You be my lawyer. Who could be better?"

"I can't."

"Why not? I want you. You're my father. I need you now."

"It's a bad idea, Jacob. You need a defense lawyer. Anyway, it's all taken care of. I called my friend Jonathan Klein. He's very, very good, I promise you."

He frowned, disappointed. "You couldn't do it anyway. You're a DA."

"Not anymore."

"You got fired?"

"Not yet. I'm on leave. They'll fire me later, probably."

"'Cuz of me?"

"No, not 'cuz of you. *You* didn't do anything. It's just the way things go."

"So what are you going to do? Like, for money? You need a job."

"Don't worry about money. Let me worry about money."

A cop, some young kid I did not know, knocked and said, "Time."

Laurie told Jacob, "We love you. We love you *so much.*"

"Okay, Mom."

She wrapped her arms around him. For a moment he did not move at all, and Laurie stood there hugging him as if she had embraced a tree or a building column. Finally he relented and patted her back.

"Do you know it, Jake? Do you know how much we love you?"

Over her shoulder, he rolled his eyes. "Yes, Mom."

"Okay." She pulled herself away and swiped the tears from her eyes. "Okay, then."

Jacob seemed to tremble on the verge of crying as well.

I hugged him. I pulled him close, squeezed hard, then stepped back. I looked him over from head to toe. There was mud ground into the knees of his jeans from the hours he had spent hiding in Cold Spring Park, in a rainy April. "You be strong, okay?"

"You too," he said. He grinned, apparently catching the dopiness of his answer.

We left him there.

And still the night was not over.

At two A.M. I was in the living room, slumped on the couch. I felt marooned, unable to move my body up to the bedroom or to fall asleep where I was.

Laurie padded down the stairs barefoot, in pajama bottoms and a favorite turquoise T-shirt that was now too threadbare for anything but sleeping in. Her breasts drooped inside it, defeated by age, gravity. Her hair was a mess, her eyes half shut. The sight of her nearly brought me to tears. From the third step she said, "Andy, come to bed. There's nothing more we can do tonight."

"Soon."

"Not soon; now. Come."

"Laurie, come here. There's something we have to talk about."

She shuffled across the front hall to join me in the living room, and in those dozen steps she seemed to come fully awake. I was not the type to ask for help often. When I did, it alarmed her. "What is it, sweetheart?"

"Sit down. There's something I have to tell you. Something that's going to come out soon."

"About Jacob?"

"About me."

I told her everything, all that I knew about my bloodline. About James Burkett, the first bloody Barber, who came east from the frontier like a reverse pioneer bringing his wildness to New York. And Rusty Barber, my war-hero grandfather who wound up gutting a man in a fight over a traffic accident in Lowell, Massachusetts. And my own father, Bloody Billy Barber, whose shadowy climactic orgy of violence involved a young girl and a knife in an abandoned building. After thirty-four years of waiting, the whole story took only five or ten minutes to tell. Once it was out, it seemed like a puny thing to have found

so burdensome for so long, and I was confident, briefly, that Laurie would see it that
way too.

"That's what I come from."

She nodded, blank-faced, doped with
disappointment—in me, in my history, in
my dishonesty. "Andy, why didn't you ever
tell me?"

"Because it didn't matter. It was never
who I was. I'm not like them."

"But you didn't trust me to understand
that."

"No. Laurie, it's not about that."

"You just never got around to it?"

"No. At the beginning I didn't want you
to think of me that way. Then the longer it
went, the less it seemed to matter. We were
so . . . happy."

"Until now, when you *had* to tell me, you
had no choice."

"Laurie, I want you to know about it now
because it's probably going to come out—
not because it really has anything to do
with this, but because shit like this always
comes out. It has nothing to do with Jacob. Or me."

"You're sure of that?"

I died for a moment. Then: "Yes, I'm sure."

"So sure that you felt you had to hide it from me."

"No, that's not right."

"Anything else you haven't told me?"

"No."

"You're sure?"

"Yes."

She thought it over. "Okay, then."

"*Okay* meaning what? Do you have any questions? Do you want to talk?"

She gave me a reproachful look: *I* was asking *her* if she wanted to talk? At two in the morning? On *this* morning?

"Laurie, nothing is different. This doesn't change anything. I'm the same person you've known since we were seventeen."

"Okay." She looked down at her lap where her hands were wrestling. "You should have told me before, that's all I can say right now. I had a right to know. I had a right to know who I was marrying, who I was having a child with."

"You did know. You married *me.* All this other stuff is just history. It's got nothing to do with us."

"You should have told me, that's all. I had a right to know."

"If I'd told you, you wouldn't have married

me. You wouldn't have gone out with me in the first place."

"You don't know that. You never gave me the chance."

"Oh, come on. If I'd asked you out and you knew?"

"I don't know what I would have said."

"I do."

"Why?"

"Because girls like you don't . . . settle for boys like that. Look, let's just forget it."

"How do you know, Andy? How do you know what I'd choose?"

"You're right. You're right, I don't. I'm sorry."

There was a lull, and it could have been all right still. At that moment we could still have survived it and moved on.

I knelt in front of her, rested my arms on her lap, on her warm legs. "Laurie, I'm sorry. I'm truly sorry I didn't tell you. But I can't undo that now. The important thing is, I need to know you understand: my father, my grandfather—I'm not them. I need to know you believe that."

"I do. I mean, I guess I do—*of course* I do. I don't know, Andy, it's late. I have to get some sleep. I can't do this now. I'm too tired."

"Laurie, you know me. Look at me. You know me."

She studied my face.

From this close I was surprised to discover she looked rather old and exhausted, and I thought it had been selfish of me and a little cruel to unload this on her now, in the middle of the night after the worst day of her life, just to get it off my chest, to ease my own mind. And I remembered her. I remembered the girl with brown legs sitting on a beach towel on Old Campus freshman year, the girl so far out of my league that she was actually easy to talk to because there was nothing to lose. At seventeen, I knew: my entire childhood had been just a prelude to this girl. I had never felt anything like it, and still haven't. I felt changed by her, physically. Not sexually, though we had sex everywhere, like minks, in the library stacks, in an empty classroom, her car, her family's beach house, even a cemetery. It was more: I became a different person, myself, the person I am now. And everything that came after—my family, my home, our entire life together—was a gift she gave me. The spell lasted thirty-four years. Now, at fifty-one, I saw her as she actually was, finally. It came as a surprise: no longer the shining girl, she was just a woman after all.

Part
TWO

"That murder might be any business of the state is a relatively modern idea. For most of human history, homicide has been a purely private affair. In traditional societies, a killing was simply the occasion for a dispute between two clans. The killer's family or tribe was expected to resolve the dispute equitably by some sort of offering to the victim's family or tribe. The restitution varied from society to society. It might involve anything from a fine to the death of the murderer (or a stand-in). If the victim's kin was unsatisfied, a blood feud might ensue. This pattern endured across many centuries and many societies. . . . Current practice notwithstanding, by long tradition murder has been strictly a family matter."

—JOSEPH EISEN,
  Murder: A History (1949)

9 | Arraignment

The next morning, Jonathan Klein stood with Laurie and me in the gloom of the Thorndike Street garage as we armored ourselves against the reporters gathered at the courthouse door, just down the street. Klein wore a gray suit with his usual black turtleneck. No tie today, even for court. The suit, particularly the pants, hung loosely off him. He must have been a tailor's nightmare, with his thin, assless body. Reading glasses hung from an Indian-bead lanyard around his neck. He carried his ancient cowhide briefcase, worn slick as an old saddle. To an outsider, no doubt, Klein would have seemed inadequate to the job. Too small, too meek. But something about him was reassuring to me. With his backswept white hair, white goatee, and benevolent smile, I thought there was a magical quality about him. A sense of calm surrounded him. Lord knows, we needed it.

Klein peeked down the block at the reporters, who loafed and chatted, a wolf pack sniffing about for something to do. "All right," he said. "Andy, I know you've been through this before, but never from this side. Laurie, this will all be new to you. So I'm going to read you the catechism, both of you."

He extended his hand to touch Laurie's sleeve. She looked devastated by the double shocks of the day before, Jacob's arrest and the Barber curse. We had spoken very little in the morning as we ate, dressed, and got ready for court. It crossed my mind for the first time that we were headed for divorce. However the trial turned out, Laurie would leave me when it was over. I could tell she was eyeing me, making up her mind. What did it mean to find out that she had been tricked into marrying me? Should she feel betrayed? Or acknowledge that her uneasiness meant I was right all along: girls like her don't marry boys like me. In any event, Jonathan's touch seemed to comfort her. She manufactured a brief little smile for him, then a bleary look returned to her face.

Klein: "From this moment on, from the time we arrive at the courthouse until you get back home tonight and close the door of your house, I want you to show nothing. No emotion at all. Keep a poker face. Got it?"

Laurie did not respond. She seemed dazed.

"I'm a potted plant," I assured him.

"Good. Because every expression, every reaction, every flicker of emotion will be interpreted against you. Laugh, and they'll say you don't take the proceedings seriously. Scowl, and they'll say you're surly, you're not contrite, you resent being hauled into court. Cry, and you're faking."

He looked at Laurie.

"Okay," she said, less sure of herself, particularly of this last item.

"Don't answer any questions. You don't have to. On TV only the pictures matter; it is impossible to tell whether you heard a question that someone shouted at you. Most important—and I'll speak to Jacob about this when I get to the lockup—any sign of anger, from Jacob in particular, will confirm people's worst suspicions. You have to remember: in their eyes, in *everybody's* eyes, Jacob is guilty. You *all* are. They only want something to confirm what they already know. Any little scrap will do."

Laurie said, "It's a little late to be worried about our public image, isn't it?"

That morning the *Globe* had run a page-one headline: DA's TEEN SON CHARGED IN NEWTON KILLING. The *Herald* was sensational but, to its credit, forthright. Its tabloid cover showed a background photo of what appeared to be the murder scene, an empty slope in a forest, with a snapshot of Jacob that they must have culled from the Web, and the word MONSTER. There was a teaser at the bottom: "Prosecutor benched amid allegations of cover-up as his own teenage son is unmasked in Newton knife murder."

Laurie had a point: after that, maintaining a poker face as we walked into court did seem a little inadequate.

But Klein only shrugged. The rules were

beyond question. They might as well have been written on stone tablets by the finger of God. He said, in his quiet, commonsense way, "We'll do the most we can with what we have."

So we did as we were told. We kept our feet moving through the proxy mob of reporters waiting for us in front of the courthouse. We showed no emotion, answered no questions, pretended we did not hear the questions as they were yelled in our ears. They kept on shouting questions anyway. Microphones bristled and probed around us. "How are you doing?" "What do you say to all the people who trusted you?" "Anything to say to the victim's family?" "Did Jacob do it?" "We just want to hear your side." "Will he testify?" One, trying to provoke, said, "Mr. Barber, how does it feel to be on the other side?"

I held Laurie's hand and we pushed through into the lobby. Things were surprisingly quiet, even normal inside. Reporters were barred here. At the lobby security station, people stood back to let us pass. The sheriff's officers who used to wave me through with a smile now wanded me and inspected the change from my pocket.

We were alone again, briefly, in the elevator. As we rode to the sixth floor, where the first-session courtroom was, I reached for Laurie's hand, my fingers scrabbling against hers to find a fit. My wife was a good deal shorter than I, so in order to hold her hand I had to haul it up to the level of my hip. She was left with her elbow bent, as if she were checking her watch. A look of distaste crossed her face—her eyelids fluttered, her lips tightened. It was barely perceptible, a micromovement, but I noticed and released her hand. The elevator doors shivered as the box was lifted. Klein kept his eyes on the panel of ranked buttons, tactfully.

When the doors rattled open, we marched through the crowded lobby to courtroom 6B, there to wait on the front center bench until our case was called.

An awkward interval passed before the judge took the bench. We had been told our case would be called promptly at ten so the court could deal with us—and the circus of reporters and gawkers—then quickly get back to business. We arrived at the courtroom around quarter of. Time dragged while we waited. It felt like a lot more than fifteen minutes. The crowds of lawyers, most of whom I knew well, stood back as if there were a magnetic field around us.

Paul Duffy was there, standing against the far wall with Logiudice and a couple of the CPAC guys. Duffy—who was essentially an uncle to Jacob—glanced at me once as we sat down, then turned away. I was not offended. I did not feel shunned. There was an etiquette to these things, that's all. Duffy had to support the home team. That was his job. Maybe we would become friends again after Jacob was cleared, maybe we wouldn't. For now, the friendship was suspended. No hard feelings, but that was the way it had to be. I know that Laurie was not so bloodless about Duffy's snubs or anyone else's. To her, it was awful to see friendships snapped off this way. We were the same people *after* that we had been *before,* and because we had not changed, it was easy for her to forget that others saw us—all of us, not just Jacob—in a completely new way. At a minimum, Laurie felt, people ought to see that, whatever Jacob may have done, she and I were certainly innocent. It was a delusion I never shared.

Courtroom 6B had an extra jury box to accommodate large jury pools, and that morning in the empty extra jury box a TV camera was set up to provide a shared video feed to all the local stations. While we waited, the cameraman kept the lens pointed at us. We wore our defendants' blank masks, said nothing to each other, barely even blinked. It is not an easy thing to be watched for so long. I began to notice little things, as one does during extended downtimes. I studied my own hands, which were big and pale, with prominent scuffed knuckles. Not a lawyer's hands, I thought. Strange to see them appended to my own coat sleeves. That quarter hour of waiting and being stared at in the courtroom—a courtroom I once owned, a room as comfortable to me as my own kitchen—was even worse than what followed.

At ten, the first-session judge swept in wearing her black robe. Judge Rivera, a terrible judge but a good break for us. You must understand: Courtroom 6B, the first-session court, was a hardship post for judges; they rotated in and out of it every few months. It was the job of the first-session judge to make the trains run on time—to assign cases to the other courtrooms in such a way that the workload was spread evenly, to winnow the docket by cajoling plea bargains out of reluctant ADAs and defendants, and to sort through the remaining administrative busywork on the daily docket as efficiently as possible. It was a hectic job—delegate, dump, defer. Lourdes Rivera was fiftyish, with a frazzled demeanor, and magnificently miscast as the judge to make the trains run on time. It was all she could do to get herself to court on time with her robe zipped up and her cell phone turned off. The lawyers scorned her. They grumbled about how she got the job because of her good looks or her opportune marriage to a politically connected lawyer or to plump up the number of Latinos on the bench. They called her Lard-Ass Rivera. But we could hardly have picked a better judge that morning. Judge Rivera had been on the Superior Court bench less than five years but already she had a towering reputation in the district attorney's office as a defendant's judge. Most of the judges in Cambridge had the same reputation: soft, unrealistic, liberal. Now it seemed perfectly appropriate to load the dice that way. A liberal, it turns out, is a conservative who's been indicted.

When the clerk called Jacob's case— "Indictment number oh-eight-dash-four-four-oh-seven, Commonwealth v. Jacob Michael Barber, one count of murder in the first degree"—my son was ushered in by two court officers from the lockup and made to stand in the middle of the courtroom, in front of the jury box. He scanned the crowd, saw us, and immediately dropped his eyes to the floor. Embarrassed and awkward, he began to fuss with his suit and tie, which Laurie had picked out for him and Klein had delivered. Jacob was not used to wearing a suit and he seemed to feel both dapper and straitjacketed. He had already begun to outgrow the coat. Laurie used to joke that he was growing so fast that, at night when the house was quiet, she could hear his bones stretching. Now he fidgeted to make the coat sit properly on his shoulders but it would not stretch that far. From all this fidgeting, reporters would later say that Jacob was vain, that he even enjoyed his moment in the spotlight, a slur we would hear over and over when the trial actually began. The truth was, he was an awkward boy and so thoroughly terrified that he did not know where to put his hands. The wonder was that he managed to stand there with as much composure as he did.

Jonathan passed through the swinging gate in the bar, laid his briefcase on the defense table, and took a position beside Jacob. He put his hand on Jacob's back, not for Jacob's benefit but to make a point: *This boy is no monster, I am not afraid to touch him.* And more: *I am not simply a hired gun doing my professional duty for a distasteful client. I believe in this kid. I am his friend.*

"Commonwealth," Lard-Ass Rivera said, "I'll hear you."

Logiudice stood up at the prosecutor's table. He ran his palm down the length of his tie then reached around to give the back hem of his coat a little tug. "Your Honor," he began mournfully, "this is a heinous case." He pronounced the word *hay-eenus,* and I understood that the actual reason court-rooms often have no windows is to prevent the parties from heaving lawyers out of them. Logiudice recited the facts of the case, already familiar to everyone from the

last twenty-four hours of news reports, re-
told now with a minimum of embellishment
for the torches-and-pitchforks mob beyond
the camera. There was even a little sing-
song in his voice, as if we had all heard
these facts often enough to be bored by
them.

But when he reached his bail argument,
Logiudice's tone became somber. "Your
Honor, we all know and have fond feelings
for the defendant's father, who is in the
courtroom today. I personally have known
this man. Respected and admired him. I
have great affection for this man, and compassion, as we all do, I'm sure. Always the
smartest man in the room. Things came
so easily to him. But. But."

"Objection."

"Sustained."

Logiudice turned to look at me, not by
twisting his body but by snaking his neck
around his own shoulder.

Things came so easily to him. Could he
really have believed that?

"Mr. Logiudice," Lard-Ass said, "I presume you know *Andrew* Barber is not accused of anything."

Logiudice faced front again. "Yes, Your Honor."

"Let's get to the bail, then."

"Your Honor, the Commonwealth is seeking a very high bail: five hundred thousand cash, five million surety. The Commonwealth would argue that, because of the unusual circumstances of his family situation, this defendant poses a particular risk of flight in light of the savagery of the crime, the overwhelming likelihood of conviction, and the unusual sophistication of this defendant, who has grown up in a home where criminal law is the family business."

Logiudice went on with this horseshit for a few minutes. He seemed to have memorized his lines and was delivering them now without any particular feeling.

In my head the odd mention of me went right on playing like a countermelody. *I have great affection for this man, and compassion. Always the smartest man in the room. Things came so easily to him.* In the courtroom it seemed to have been received almost as a slip of the tongue, a sniffly little tribute blurted out on the spur of the moment. They were touched. They had watched this scene before: the disillusioned young apprentice sees his mentor revealed as an ordinary man or otherwise brought low, the scales fall from his eyes, etc., etc. Bullshit. Logiudice was not the type to make extemporaneous speeches, not with the camera running. I imagine he practiced this line before a mirror. The only question was what he expected to get out of it, how exactly he meant to sink the knife into Jacob.

In the end, Lard-Ass Rivera was unmoved by Logiudice's bail argument. She set the bail where it had been since the day he was arrested, at a measly ten grand, a token number reflecting the fact that Jacob had nowhere to run and, after all, his family was known to the court.

Logiudice shrugged off the defeat. His bail argument was nothing but grandstanding anyway. "Your Honor," he barreled on, "the Commonwealth would also raise an objection to the entry of an appearance by Mr. Klein as defense counsel in this case. Mr. Klein was previously engaged as attorney for another suspect in this homicide, a man whose name I will not mention in open court. To represent a second defendant in the same case creates a clear conflict of interest. Defense counsel would surely have been privy to confidential information from this other suspect that might impact the defense in this case. I can only imagine that the defendant is planting the seed for an appeal based on ineffective assistance if he is convicted."

The suggestion of a sneaky trick pulled Jonathan to his feet. It was exceptionally rare for one lawyer to attack another so openly. Even in the scrum of a bitter trial, in court a formal, clubby politeness was always maintained. Jonathan was genuinely insulted. "Your Honor, if the Commonwealth had taken the time to ascertain the actual facts, he would never have made that accusation. The fact is, I was never retained by the other suspect in this case nor did I ever have any conversation with him about it. This was a client I represented years ago on an unrelated matter who called me out of the blue to come to the Newton police station where he was being questioned. My sole involvement with him in this case was to advise that he not answer any questions. As he was never accused, I never spoke to him again. I was not privy to any information, confidential or otherwise, now or in any previous matter, that bears on this case even remotely. There is no conflict of interest at all."

"Your Honor," Logiudice said with an unctuous shrug, "as an officer of the court, it is my duty to report an issue like this. If Mr. Klein is offended . . ."

"Is it your duty to deny the defendant the counsel of his choosing? Or to call him a liar before the case even begins?"

"All right," Lard-Ass said, "both of you. Mr. Logiudice, the Commonwealth's objection to the entry of Mr. Klein's appearance as counsel is noted and overruled." She glanced up from her papers and eyed him over the top of the judge's bench. "Don't get carried away."

Logiudice limited his response to a pantomime of disagreement—a tip of the head, eyebrows raised—so as not to provoke the judge. But in the shadow trial of public opinion, he had probably scored a point. In the next day's papers, on talk radio, on the Internet chat boards that dissected the case, they would be discussing whether Jacob Barber was trying to pull a fast one. Anyway, it was never Logiudice's intention to be liked.

"I'm sending this case out to Judge French for trial," Lard-Ass Rivera said with finality. She flipped the file toward the clerk. "We'll recess for ten minutes." She frowned at the cameraman and the reporters in the back and—I may have imagined this—at Logiudice.

The bail was arranged quickly, and Jacob was released to us. Together we left the courthouse through a gauntlet of reporters that seemed to have grown since we arrived. Grown more aggressive too: out on Thorndike Street, they tried to stop us by standing in our path. Somebody—it may have been a reporter, though no one saw him—pushed Jacob in the chest, knocking him back a few steps, trying to elicit a response. Jacob gave none. His blank face never wavered. Even the more polite ones had a slippery tactic to get us to stop and talk: they asked, "Can you just tell us what happened in there?" as if they did not know, as if the whole thing had not been broadcast to them via the live video feed and text messages from their colleagues.

By the time we rounded the corner and drove up to our home, we were exhausted. Laurie in particular looked wrung out. Her hair was beginning to craze in the humidity. Her face looked drawn. Since the catastrophe, she had been losing weight steadily and her lovely heart-shaped face was becoming gaunt. As I began to turn the car into the driveway, Laurie gasped, "Oh my God," and clapped her hand over her mouth.

There was graffiti on the front of our house, drawn with a thick black marker.

MURDERER
WE HATE YOU
ROT IN HELL

The letters were big, blocky, and neat, written in no particular haste. Our house was faced with tan shingles, and the edges of these shingles caused the pen to skip as it crossed from one to the next. Otherwise it had been done carefully, in broad daylight, while we were gone. The graffiti had not been there when we left that morning, I am sure of that.

I looked up and down the street. The sidewalks were empty. Down the block a gardening crew had parked a truck, and their mowers and leaf blowers buzzed loudly. No sign of neighbors. No people at all. Just neat green lawns, rhododendrons blooming pink and purple, a cordon of big old maples running the length of the block, shading the street.

Laurie jumped out and ran into the house, leaving Jacob and me to stare at the graffiti.

"Don't let them get to you, Jake. They're just trying to scare you."

"I know."

"This is just one idiot. That's all it takes is one idiot. It's not everyone. It's not how people feel."

"Yes, it is."

"Not everyone."

"Of course it is. It's okay, Dad. I don't really care."

I twisted to look at him in the back seat. "Really? This doesn't bother you?"

"No." He sat with his arms crossed, eyes narrow, lips tight.

"If it did, you'd tell me, right?"

"I guess."

"Because it's okay to feel . . . hurt. You know that?"

He frowned disdainfully and shook his head, like an emperor declining to grant an indulgence. *They can't hurt me.*

"So tell me. What are you feeling inside, Jake, right now, this minute?"

"Nothing."

"Nothing? That's not possible."

"Like you said, it's just one asshole. One idiot, whatever. I mean, it's not like kids have never said anything bad about me, Dad. They do it to my face. What do you think school *is*? This"—he gestured with his chin toward the graffiti on the house—"this is just a different platform."

I gazed at him a moment. He did not move, except that his eyes traveled from me to the passenger window. I patted his knee, though it was awkward to reach and the best I could manage was to tap my fingertip against the hard bone of his knee-cap. It occurred to me that I had given him the wrong advice the night before, when I had told him to "be strong." I was telling him, in so many words, to be like me. But now that I saw he had taken my words to heart and swaddled himself in theatrical toughness, like an adolescent Clint Eastwood, I regretted the comment. I wanted the other Jacob, my goofy, awkward son, to show his face again. But it was too late. Anyway, his tough-guy act was oddly moving to me.

"You're a great kid, Jake. I'm proud of you. I mean, the way you stood up there today, now this. You're a good kid."

He snorted. "Yeah, okay, Dad."

Inside I found Laurie on her hands and knees rummaging through the cleaning supplies in the cabinet under the kitchen sink. She was still wearing the navy skirt she wore to court.

"Just leave it, Laurie. I'll take care of it. You go rest."

"You'll take care of it when?"

"Whenever you want."

"You say you'll take care of things and then you don't. I don't want that thing on my house. Not for one more minute. I'm not going to just leave it there."

"I said I'll take care of it. Please. Go rest."

"How can I rest, Andy, with that thing? Honestly. Did you see what they wrote?

On our home! On our *home,* Andy, and you want me to just go rest? Great. This is just great. They walk right up and write on our house and nobody says anything, nobody lifts a finger, not one of our fucking neighbors." She enunciated the expletive meticulously, right down to the final *G,* as people who are not used to swearing often do. "We should call the cops. It's a crime, isn't it? It *is* a crime, I know it is. It's vandalism. Should we call the cops?"

"No. We're not calling the cops."

"No. Of course not."

She came up with a bottle of Fantastik, then snatched up a dish towel and soaked it under the faucet.

"Laurie, please, let me do this. Let me help you, at least."

"Would you just stop? I said I'll do it."

She had taken off her shoes and she marched out like that, barefoot in her nylons, and she scrubbed and scrubbed and scrubbed.

I went out with her, but there was nothing for me to do except watch.

Her hair bounced to the vigorous movements of her arm. Her eyes were wet and her face flushed.

"Can I help, Laurie?"

"No. I'll do it."

At length, I gave up watching and went back in. I heard her scruffing against the side of the house for a long time. She succeeded in rubbing out the words, but the ink left a gray cloud on the paint. It is still there today.

10 | Leopards

Jonathan's office was a little warren of cluttered rooms in a century-old Victorian near Harvard Square. The practice was essentially a one-man operation. He did have an associate, a young woman named Ellen Curtice who was just out of Suffolk Law. But he used her only as a stand-in on days when he could not be in court himself (usually because he was held on trial elsewhere) and to handle basic legal research. It was understood, apparently, that Ellen would move on when she was ready to launch her own practice. For now, she was a vaguely disconcerting presence in the office, a mostly silent, dark-eyed observer of the clients who came and went, the murderers, rapists, thieves, child molesters, tax evaders, and all their cursed families. There was a bit of Northampton about her, a bit of the college kid's ortho-dox radicalism. I imagined she judged Ja-cob harshly—the suburban rich kid who pissed away all the advantages he had lucked into, something like that—but her behavior gave nothing away. Ellen treated us with elaborate politeness. She insisted on calling me Mister Barber and offered to take my coat whenever I showed up, as if any hint of intimacy would undermine her neutral pose.

The only other member of Jonathan's team was Mrs. Wurtz, who kept the books, answered the phone, and, when she could no longer stand the mess, reluctantly scrubbed the kitchen and bathroom while murmuring murder under her breath. She bore an uncanny resemblance to my mother.

The best room in the office was the li-brary. It had a red-brick fireplace and book-cases lined with familiar old law books: the honey bindings of the Massachusetts and federal case reports, the army-green Mass.

Appeals reports, the wine red of the old Mass. Practice series.

It was in this warm little den that we gathered just a few hours after Jacob's arraignment, in early afternoon, to discuss the case. We three Barbers sat around an old circular oak table with Jonathan. Ellen was there too, scribbling notes on a yellow legal pad.

Jacob wore a burgundy hoodie that had the logo of a clothing company on the chest, a silhouette of a rhino. As the meeting began, he slumped in his chair with the cavernous hood over his head like a druid. I told him, "Jacob, take your hood off. Don't be disrespectful." He slipped it off with a sulky flip and sat there with an absent expression, as if the meeting was a matter for grown-ups that held little interest for him.

Laurie, in her sexy schoolmarm glasses and a lightweight fleece pullover, looked like a thousand other suburban soccer moms, except for the shock-hammered look in her eyes. She asked for a legal pad of her own and gamely made ready to take notes along with Ellen. Laurie seemed determined to keep her head—to think her way out of the maze, to remain clear-headed and industrious even in this surreal dream. She might have had an easier time of it, honestly, if she had not been so engaged. The stupid and belligerent have it easy in these situations; they can simply stop thinking and gird for battle, trust to the experts and to fate, insisting that everything will turn out right in the end. Laurie was neither stupid nor belligerent, and in the end she paid an awful price—but I am getting ahead of the story. For the moment, seeing her with her pad and pen inevitably reminded me of our college days, when Laurie was a bit of a grind, at least compared to me. We rarely took classes together. Our interests were not the same—I was drawn to history, Laurie to psych, English, and film—and anyway we did not want to become one of those nauseating inseparable couples that mooned around campus side by side like Siamese twins. In four years, the one class we shared was Edmund Morgan's intro to early American history, which we took freshman year when we'd just started dating. I used to steal

Laurie's notebook before exams to catch up on the lectures I'd skipped. I remember gaping at her class notes, page after page of neat cursive. She captured long phrases from the lectures verbatim, broke the lectures down into branching concepts and subconcepts, added her own thoughts as she went. There were few of the cross-outs or scribbles or snaking arrows that filled my sloppy, frantic, clownish class notes. In fact, that notebook from Edmund Morgan's lectures was part of the revelation of meeting Laurie. What struck me was not just that she was probably smarter than me. Coming from a small town—Watertown, New York—I was prepared for that. I fully expected Yale to be swarming with brainy, worldly kids like Laurie Gold. I had studied up on them by reading Salinger stories and watching *Love Story* and *The Paper Chase.* No, the epiphany I had looking at Laurie's notebook was not that she was smart but that she was unknowable. She was every bit as complex as I was. As a kid, I had always believed there was a special drama about being Andy Barber, but the interior experience of being Laurie

Gold must have been just as fraught with secrets and sorrows. She would always be a mystery, as all other people are. Try as I might to penetrate her, by talking, kissing, stabbing myself into her, the best I would ever do was to know her just a little. It is a childish realization, I admit—no one worth knowing can be quite known, no one worth possessing can be quite possessed—but after all, we were children.

"Well," Jonathan said, looking up from his papers, "this is just the initial package from Neal Logiudice. All I have here is the indictment and some of the police reports, so obviously we don't have all the prosecution's evidence yet. But we have a general picture of the case against Jacob. We can begin talking, at least, and try to get a general picture of what the trial will look like. We can start to figure out what we need to do between now and then.

"Jacob, before we begin, I want to say a couple of things to you in particular."

"Okay."

"First, you're the client here. That means that, as far as possible, you are the decision maker. Not your parents, not me, not anyone else. This is *your* case. *You* are always in control. Nothing is going to happen here that *you* don't agree with. Okay?"

"Okay."

"To the extent you want to leave the decision-making up to your mom and dad or to me, that's perfectly understandable. But you should not feel like you don't have a say in your own case. The law is treating you as an adult. For better or worse, by law in Massachusetts every kid your age charged with first-degree murder is charged as an adult. So I'm going to do my best to treat you as an adult too. Okay?"

Jacob said, " 'Kay."

Not a wasted syllable. If Jonathan was expecting an outpouring of gratitude, he had the wrong kid.

"The other thing is, I don't want you to feel overwhelmed. I want to warn you: in every case like this, there's an 'oh shit' moment. That's when you look up at the case against you, you see all the evidence, all the people on the DA's team, you hear all the things the DA is saying in court, and you panic. You feel hopeless. Deep down, a little voice says, 'Oh shit!' I want you to understand, it happens every time. If it hasn't hit you yet, it will. And what I want you to remember, when that 'oh shit' feeling hits, is that we have enough resources right here in this room to win. There's no reason to panic. It does not matter how big the DA's team is, it doesn't matter how strong the DA's case looks, or how confident Logiudice seems. We are not outgunned. We do need to stay cool. And if we do, we have everything we need to win. Now, do you believe that?"

"I don't know. Not really, I guess."

"Well, I'm telling you it's true."

Jacob's eyes dropped to his lap.

A microexpression, a disappointed pucker, fluttered across Jonathan's face.

So much for the pep talk.

Giving up, he slipped on his half-moon glasses and paged through the papers in front of him, mostly photocopies of police reports and the "statement of the case" filed by Logiudice, which laid out the essentials of the government's evidence. Without his jacket, wearing the same black turtleneck he'd worn in court, Jonathan's shoulders looked slight and bony.

"The theory," he said, "seems to be that Ben Rifkin was bullying you, therefore you got a knife and, when the opportunity presented itself or perhaps when the victim bullied you one time too many, you took your revenge. There don't seem to be any direct witnesses. A woman who was walking in Cold Spring Park places you in the area that morning. Another walker in the park heard the victim cry out, 'Stop, you're hurting me,' but she didn't actually see anything. And a fellow student—that's Logiudice's phrase, *a fellow student*—alleges you had a knife. That fellow student is not named in the reports I have here. Jacob, any idea who that is?"

"It's Derek. Derek Yoo."

"Why do you say that?"

"He said the same thing on Facebook. He's been saying it for a while."

Jonathan nodded but did not ask the obvious question: *Is it true?*

"Well," he said, "it's a very circumstantial case. There's the thumbprint, which I want to talk about. But fingerprints are a very limited kind of evidence. There is no way to tell exactly when or how a fingerprint got there. There's often an innocent explanation."

He dropped this remark in an offhand way, without looking up.

I squirmed.

Laurie said, "There is something else."

A beat, a curious feeling in the room.

Laurie glanced around the table apprehensively. Her voice was momentarily husky, congested. "What if they say Jacob inherited something, like a disease?"

"I don't understand. Inherited what?"

"Violence."

Jacob: "What!?"

"I don't know if my husband has told you: there is a history of violence in our family. Apparently."

I noticed that she said *our family,* plural. I clung to that to prevent myself from falling off a cliff.

Jonathan sat back and slipped off his glasses, let them dangle from the lanyard. He looked at her with a puzzled expression.

"Not Andy and me," Laurie said. "Jacob's grandfather, his great-grandfather, great-great-grandfather. Et cetera."

Jacob: "Mom, what are you *talking* about?"

"I'm just wondering, could they say Jacob

has a . . . a tendency? A . . . genetic tendency?"

"What sort of tendency?"

"To violence."

"A *genetic* tendency to violence? No.
Of course not." Jonathan shook his head,
then his curiosity got the better of him.
"Whose father and grandfather are we
talking about?"

"Mine."

I felt myself redden, the warmth rising in
my cheeks, my ears. I was ashamed, then
ashamed at feeling ashamed, at my lack
of self-command. Then ashamed, again,
that Jonathan was watching my son learn
of this in real time, exposing me as a liar, a
bad father. Only last was I ashamed in my
son's eyes.

Jonathan looked away from me, point-
edly, allowing me to recover myself. "No,
Laurie, that sort of evidence would definitely not be admissible. Anyway, as far as
I know, there is no such thing as a genetic
tendency to violence. If Andy really does
have violence in his family background,
then his own good nature and his life prove
that the tendency doesn't exist." He glanced

at me to be sure I heard the confidence in his voice.

"It's not Andy that I doubt. It's the DA, Logiudice. What if he finds out? I Googled it this morning. There have been cases where this sort of DNA evidence has been used. They say it makes the defendant aggressive. They called it 'the murder gene.'"

"That's ridiculous. 'The murder gene'! You certainly did not find any cases like that in Massachusetts."

"No."

I volunteered, "Jonathan, she's upset. We just talked about this last night. It's my fault. I shouldn't have put all this on her right now."

Laurie held herself erect to demonstrate how wrong I was. She was in control, not reacting wildly out of emotion.

In a comforting tone, Jonathan said, "Laurie, all I can tell you is that if they do try to raise that as an issue, we'll fight it tooth and nail. It's insane." Jonathan snorted and shook his head, which for a soft-spoken guy like him was a rather violent outburst.

And even now, looking back on that moment when the idea of a "murder gene" was first raised, by Laurie of all people, I feel my back stiffen, I feel the anger ooze up my spine. The murder gene was not just a contemptible idea and a slander—though it absolutely was both of those things. It also offended me as a lawyer. I saw right away the backwardness of it, the way it warped the real science of DNA and the genetic component of behavior, and overlaid it with the junk science of sleazy lawyers, the cynical science-lite language whose actual purpose was to manipulate juries, to fool them with the sheen of scientific certainty. The murder gene was a lie. A lawyer's con game.

It was also a deeply subversive idea. It undercut the whole premise of the criminal law. In court, the thing we punish is the criminal intention—the *mens rea,* the guilty mind. There is an ancient rule: *actus non facit reum nisi mens sit rea*—"the act does not create guilt unless the mind is also guilty." That is why we do not convict children, drunks, and schizophrenics: they are incapable of *deciding* to commit their crimes with a true understanding of the significance of their actions. Free will is as important to the law as it is to religion or any other code of morality. We do not punish the leopard for its wildness. Would Logiudice have the balls to make the argument anyway? "Born bad"? I was sure he would try. Whether or not it was good science or good law, he would whisper it in the jury's ear like a gossip passing a secret. He would find a way.

In the end Laurie was right, of course: the murder gene would haunt us, if not quite the way she anticipated. But in that first meeting, Jonathan—and I—trained in the humanist tradition of the law, instinctively rejected it. We laughed it off. The idea had got ahold of Laurie's imagination, though, and Jacob's too.

My son's jaw literally hung open. "Is somebody going to tell me what you guys are talking about?"

"Jake," I began. But the words did not come.

"What? Somebody tell me!"

"My father is in prison. He has been for a long time."

"But you never knew your father."

"That's not entirely true."

"But you *said.* You've always said."

"I did, I *said.* I'm sorry for that. I never *really* knew him, that was true. But I knew who he was."

"You lied to me?"

"I didn't tell you the whole truth."

"You lied."

I shook my head. All the reasons, all the things I had felt as a kid, seemed ridiculous and inadequate now. "I don't know."

"Jeez. What did he do?"

Deep breath. "He killed a girl."

"How? Why? What happened?"

"I don't really want to talk about it."

"You don't want to talk about it? No shit you don't want to talk about it!"

"He was a bad guy, Jacob, that's all. Let's just leave it at that."

"How come you never told me?"

"Jacob," Laurie cut in softly, "I never knew either. I only found out last night." She laid her hand on Jacob's and rustled it. "It's okay. We're still kind of figuring out how to process all this. Try to stay calm, okay?"

"It's just—it can't be true. How come you never told me? This is my—what?— my grandfather? How could you keep that from me? Who do you think you are?"

"Jacob. Watch how you talk to your father."

"No, it's okay, Laurie. He's got a right to be upset."

"I *am* upset!"

"Jacob, I never told you—I never told anyone—because I was afraid people would look at me differently. And now I'm afraid it's how people are going to look at you too. I didn't want that to happen. Someday, maybe someday very soon, you'll understand."

He gawped at me, unsatisfied.

"I didn't mean for it to come to all this. I wanted—I wanted to move past it."

"But Dad, it's who I am."

"That's not how I looked at it."

"I had a right to know."

"That's not how I looked at it, Jake."

"I *didn't* have a right to know? About my own family?"

"You had a right to *not* know. You had a right to start with a blank slate, to be whatever you wanted to be, same as every other kid."

"But I *wasn't* the same as every other kid."

"Of course you were."

Laurie looked away.

Jacob tossed himself backward in his chair. He seemed more shocked than aggrieved. The questions, the complaints, were just a way to channel his emotion. He sat there awhile, deep in thought. "I don't be*lieve* it," he said, bewildered. "I just don't believe it. I don't believe you *did* that."

"Look, Jacob, if you want to be mad at me for lying, okay. But my intentions were good. I did this for you. Even before you were born, I did it for you."

"Oh, come *on*. You did it for yourself."

"I did it for myself, yes, and for my son, for the son I hoped I was going to have someday, to make things a little easier for him. For *you*."

"It didn't work out so great, did it?"

"I think it did. I think your life has been easier than it would have been. I certainly hope so. It's been easier than mine was, that's for sure."

"Dad, look where we are."

"So?"

He said nothing.

Laurie offered, in a honeyed voice, "Jacob, we need to be careful how we talk to each other, okay? Try to understand your father's position even if you disagree with it. Put yourself in his shoes."

"Mom, you're the one who said it: I have the murder gene."

"I did not say that, Jacob."

"You implied it. Of course you did!"

"Jacob, you know I didn't say that. I don't even think there is such a thing. I was talking about other trials I read about."

"Mom, it's okay. It's just a *fact.* If you weren't concerned about it, you wouldn't have Googled it."

"A fact? How do you know it's a fact, all of a sudden?"

"Mom, let me ask you something: why do people only want to talk about inheriting good things? When an athlete has a kid who's good at sports, nobody has any problem saying the kid inherited his talent. When a musician has a musical kid, when a professor has a smart kid, whatever. What's the difference?"

"I don't know, Jacob. It's just different."

Jonathan—who had not spoken in so long I had almost forgotten he was present—said calmly, "The difference is it's not a crime to be athletic or musical or smart.

We need to be very careful about locking people up for what they *are* rather than what they *do*. There is a very long ugly history of that sort of thing."

"So what do I do if this is what I *am*?"

Me: "Jacob, what are you saying, exactly?"

"What if I have this thing inside me and I can't help it?"

"There's nothing inside you."

He shook his head.

There was a very long silence, ten seconds or so that seemed to last much longer.

"Jacob," I said, "the 'murder gene' is just a phrase. It's a metaphor. You understand that, right?"

Shrug. "I don't know."

"Jake, you've just got it wrong, okay? Even if a murderer had a child who was also a murderer, you wouldn't need genetics to explain that."

"How do *you* know?"

"Oh, I've thought about it, Jacob, believe me, I've thought about it. But it just can't be. I think of it this way: if Yo-Yo Ma had a son, the kid wouldn't be born knowing how to play the cello. He'd have to learn to play the cello just like everyone else. The most you can inherit is talent, potential. What you do with it, what you become, all that is up to you."

"Did you inherit your father's talent?"

"No."

"How do you know?"

"Look at me. Look at my life, like Jonathan said. You know me. You've lived with me fourteen years now. Have I ever been violent, ever?"

He shrugged again, unimpressed. "Maybe you just never learned to play your cello. Doesn't mean you don't have the talent."

"Jacob, what do you want me to say? It's impossible to prove a thing like that."

"I know. That's my problem too. How do I know what's in me?"

"Nothing is in you."

"I'll tell you what, Dad: I think you know exactly how I'm feeling right now. I know exactly why you didn't tell anyone about this for so long. It wasn't because of what *they* might think you were."

Jacob leaned back and folded his hands on his belly, closing off the subject. He had clasped onto the idea of a murder gene and after that I don't think he ever let it go. I let the subject drop too. No sense preaching to him about the boundlessness of human potential. He had his generation's instinctive preference for scientific explanations over the old verities. He knew what happens when science comes up against magical thinking.

11 | Running

I am not a natural runner. Too heavy-legged, too big and bulky. I am built like a butcher. And honestly I derive little pleasure from running. I do it because I have to. If I don't, I get fat, an unhappy tendency I inherited from my mother's side, all stout-bodied peasant stock from eastern Europe, Scotland, and points unknown. So most mornings around six or six-thirty I galumphed through the streets and the jogging paths in Cold Spring Park until I had pounded out my daily three miles.

I was determined to keep on doing it even after Jacob was indicted. No doubt the neighbors would have preferred that we Barbers not show our faces, particularly in Cold Spring Park. I did accommodate them somewhat. I ran early in the morning, I kept my distance from others, I bowed my head like a fugitive when passing a jogger going the opposite direction. And of course I never ran near the murder site. But I decided from the start that, for my own sanity, I would hold on to this aspect of before-life.

The morning after our initial conference with Jonathan, I experienced that elusive, oxymoronic thing, a "good run." I felt light and fast. For once, running was not a series of leaps and thuds, but—and I don't mean to be too poetic about this—like flying. I felt my body rush forward with a kind of natural ease and predatory speed, as if I had always been meant to feel like this. I don't know why it happened, exactly, though I suspect the added anxiety of the case flooded my system with adrenaline. I moved quickly through Cold Spring Park in the damp chill, around the loop that follows the perimeter of the park, hopping over tree roots and rocks, leaping the little pools of rainwater and the squelching mud patches that dot the park in spring. I felt so good, in fact, that I ran past my usual park exit and went on through the woods a little farther, to the front of the park where, with only the vaguest intention or design in my head, but a conviction—fast growing into a certainty—that Leonard Patz was the one, I came out into the parking lot of the Windsor Apartments.

I padded around the parking lot a bit. I did not have the vaguest idea where Patz's apartment was. The buildings were plain blocks of red brick, three stories high.

I found Patz's car, a rusting plum-colored late-nineties Ford Probe whose description I remembered from Patz's file, among the details Paul Duffy had begun to gather. It was just the sort of car a child molester ought to drive. The vehicular embodiment of a pedophile is precisely a plum-colored late-nineties Ford Probe. Short of flying the NAMBLA flag from the antenna, the car could not have suited the man better. Patz had adorned his pedo-mobile with various disarming badges: a "Teach Children" Massachusetts vanity plate, bumper stickers for the Red Sox and the World Wildlife Fund, with its cuddly panda logo. Both doors were locked. I cupped my hands over the driver's window to peer inside. The interior was immaculate, if worn.

At the entrance to the nearest apartment building, I found the buzzer for his apartment, "PATZ, L."

The apartment complex was beginning to stir. A few residents straggled out to their cars or to make the short walk to Dunkin' Donuts just down the street. Most wore business clothes. One woman coming out of Patz's building held the door open for me politely—there is no better disguise for a stalker in the suburbs than to present oneself as a clean-shaven Caucasian in jogging clothes—but I declined with a thankful expression. What would I do inside the building? Knock on Patz's door? No. Not yet, at least.

The idea was only just forming in my head that Jonathan's approach was too timid. He was thinking too much like a defense lawyer, content to put the Commonwealth to its burden, win it on cross, poke a few holes in Logiudice's case then argue to the jury that, yes, there was some evidence against Jacob but it wasn't enough. I preferred to attack, always. To be fair, this was a misinterpretation of what Jonathan had said and badly underestimated him. But I knew—and Jonathan surely did as well—that the better strategy is to offer the jury an alternate narrative. The jurors would want to know, naturally, if Jacob did not do it, who did? We had to offer them a story to satisfy that craving. We humans are swayed more by stories than by abstract concepts like "burden of proof" or "presumed innocent." We are pattern-seeking, storytelling animals, and have been since we began drawing on cave walls. Patz would be our story. That sounds calculating and dishonest, I realize, as if the whole thing was a matter of trial tactics, so let me add that in this case the counternarrative happened to be true: Patz actually did do it. I knew it. It was only a matter of showing the jury the truth. That was all I ever wanted with respect to Patz: to follow the evidence, play it straight, as I always had. You will say I am protesting too much, making myself sound too virtuous—arguing my own case to a jury. Well, I acknowledge the illogic: Patz did it because Jacob did not. But the illogic was not apparent to me then. I was the boy's father. And the fact is, I was right to suspect Patz.

12 | Confessions

Bringing in a shrink was Jonathan's idea. It was standard procedure, he told us, to seek a "competency and criminal responsibility evaluation." But a quick Google search revealed that the shrink he chose was an authority on the role of genetic inheritance in behavior. Despite what he had said about the absurdity of a "murder gene," Jonathan was preparing to confront the issue if need be. I was convinced that, whatever the scientific merit of the theory, Logiudice would never be allowed to argue it to the jury. The argument was bogus, just a slicked-back, scienced-up version of an ancient courtroom trick, what lawyers call "propensity evidence": the defendant tends to do stuff like this, so he probably did it here too, even if the prosecution can't prove it. It's simple: the defendant is a bank robber; a bank has been robbed—we all know what happened here. It is a way for the prosecution to tempt the jury with a wink and a nudge to convict despite a weak case. No judge would let Logiudice get away with it. Equally important, the science of genetically influenced behavior simply had not matured enough to be admitted in court. It was a new field, and the law purposely lags behind science. The courts cannot afford to make mistakes by taking chances on cutting-edge theories that may not prove out. I did not blame Jonathan for preparing to challenge the murder gene theory. Good trial preparation is really over-preparation. Jonathan had to be prepared for everything, even the one-in-a-hundred chance the judge might admit murder gene evidence. What bothered me was that he did not confide in me what he was up to. He did not trust me. I had fooled myself that we would act as a team, fellow lawyers, colleagues. But to Jonathan,

I was just a client. Worse, I was a crazy, unreliable client, one who had to be misled.

Our meetings with the shrink took place on the campus of McLean Hospital, the mental hospital where Dr. Elizabeth Vogel practiced. We met in a bare, bookless room. It was sparsely furnished with a few chairs and low tables. African masks hung on the wall.

Dr. Vogel was a big woman. Not flabby; on the contrary, she had none of the pale softness of an academic, though she was one. (She taught and researched at Harvard Medical School as well as McLean.) Rather, Dr. Vogel had broad shoulders and a great square carved head. She was olive-skinned and, in May, already very tan. Her hair, mostly gray, was cut short. No makeup. A constellation of three diamond studs was arrayed on her brown earlobe. I imagined her hiking up sun-blasted mountain trails every weekend or bashing her way through the waves off Truro. She was big in the sense of prominent too, a big shot, which only enhanced her imposing quality. It was not clear to me why such a woman would choose the quiet, patient work of psychiatry. Her manner suggested a low tolerance for bullshit, of which she must have listened to quite a lot. She did not just sit there and nod, as shrinks are supposed to do. She leaned forward, tilted her head as if to hear you better, as if she was avid for good frank talk, for the real story.

Laurie confessed everything to her willingly, eagerly. In this Earth Mother she felt she had a natural ally, an expert who would explain Jacob's problems. As if the doctor was on our side. In long question-answer exchanges Laurie tried to draw on Dr. Vogel's expertise. She quizzed the doctor: How to understand Jacob? How to help him? Laurie did not have the vocabulary, the specific knowledge. She wanted to extract those things from Dr. Vogel. She seemed unaware, or maybe just unconcerned, that Dr. Vogel was extracting from her as well. To be clear, I do not blame Laurie. She loved her son and she believed in psychiatry, in the power of gab. And of course she was shaken. After a few weeks living with the fact of Jacob's indictment, the strain was beginning to tell; she was vulnerable to a sympathetic ear like Dr. Vogel's. But for all that, I could not just sit there and let it happen. Laurie was so determined to help Jacob, she nearly hung him.

In our first meeting with the shrink, Laurie offered this rather startling confession: "When Jacob was a baby I used to be able to tell from the sound of his crawl when he was in a scary mood. I know that sounds outrageous, but it's true. He would come storming down the hall on all fours, and I just knew."

"You knew what?"

"I knew I was in for it. He would go on rampages. He'd throw things, he'd scream. There was nothing I could do with him. I'd just put him in his crib or his Pack 'n Play and I'd walk away. I'd let him scream and thrash till he calmed down."

"Don't all babies scream and thrash, Laurie?"

"Not like this. Not like this."

I said, "That's ridiculous. He was a baby. Babies cry."

"Andy," the doctor purred, "let her speak. You'll have your turn. Go on, Laurie."

"Yes, go on, Laurie. Tell her how Jacob pulled the wings off flies."

"Doctor, you'll have to forgive him. He doesn't believe in this—in talking honestly about private things."

"That's not true. I do believe in it."

"Then why don't you ever do it?"

"It's a talent I don't possess."

"Talking?"

"Complaining."

"No, this is called talking, Andy, not complaining. And it's a skill, not a talent; you could learn it if you wanted to. You can talk for hours in court."

"That's different."

"Because a lawyer doesn't have to be honest?"

"No, it's just a different situation, Laurie. There's a time and a place for everything."

"My God, Andy, we're in a psychiatrist's office. If this isn't the time and place . . ."

"Yes, but we're here for Jacob, not us. Not you. You need to remember that."

"I think I remember why we're here, Andy. Don't worry. I know exactly why we're here."

"Do you? You're not talking like you know it."

"Don't lecture me, Andy."

Dr. Vogel said, "Hold on. I want to make

something clear. Andy, I was hired by the defense team. I work for you. There's no need to hide anything from me. I'm on Jacob's side. My findings here can only help your son. I'll submit my report to Jonathan, then you all can decide what to do with it. It's entirely your decision."

"And if we want to throw it in the trash?"

"You can. The point is, our conversation here is entirely confidential. There's no reason to hold back. You don't need to defend your son, not in this room. I only want the truth about him."

I made a sour face. The truth about Jacob. Who could say what that was? What was the truth about anyone?

"All right," Dr. Vogel said. "Laurie, you were describing Jacob as a baby. I'd like to hear more about that."

"From the time he was two, other kids started getting hurt around Jacob."

I gave Laurie a hard look. She seemed ethereally unaware of the danger of frankness.

But Laurie returned my glare with a fierce look of her own. I cannot say for certain what she was thinking; Laurie and

I did not talk as much or as easily since the night I confessed my secret history. A little curtain had come down between us. But clearly she was in no mood for lawyerly advice. She meant to have her say.

She said, "It happened several times. At day care once, Jacob was toddling on the top of a play structure when another boy fell off. The boy needed stitches. Another time, a little girl flew off the monkey bars and broke her arm. A boy down the street rode his tricycle down a steep hill. That boy needed stitches too. He said Jakey pushed him."

"How often did these things happen?"

"Every year or so. Jacob's day care teachers told us all the time that they could not take their eyes off him, he was too rough. I was scared to death he would get kicked out of day care. Then what would we do? I was still working at the time, teaching; we needed day care. There were long waiting lists at all the other day care centers. If Jacob got thrown out, I'd have to stop working. We actually put our name on the list at another day care, just in case."

"Oh my God, Laurie, he was four years

old! This is *years* ago! What are you talking about?"

"Andy, really, you have to let her speak or this just won't work."

"But the time she's talking about, Jacob was four—years—old."

"Andy, I understand where you're coming from. Just let her finish, then you'll have a turn, all right? All right. Laurie, I'm curious: what did the other kids at day care think of him?"

"Oh, the kids, I don't know. Jacob had very few playdates, so I imagine the other kids didn't like him especially."

"And the parents?"

"I'm sure they didn't want their kids to be alone with him. But none of the moms ever said anything to me about it. We were all too nice for that. We didn't criticize each other's kids. Nice people don't do that, except behind each other's backs."

"What about you, Laurie? What did you think about Jacob's behavior?"

"I knew I had a difficult child. I did. I knew he had some behavior problems. He was rambunctious, he was a little too rough, a little too aggressive."

"Was he a bully?"

"No. Not exactly. He just didn't think about other kids, how they would feel."

"Was he short-tempered?"

"No."

"Mean?"

"Mean. No, *mean* isn't the word for it either. It was more like—I don't know what to call it, exactly. He just couldn't seem to imagine how other kids would feel if he pushed them down, so he was . . . hard to control. I guess that's it: he was hard to control. But a lot of boys are like that. That's how we talked about it at the time: 'A lot of boys go through this. It's a phase. Jacob will outgrow it.' That was how we looked at it. I was horrified when other kids got hurt, of course, but what could I do? What could *we* do?"

"What *did* you do, Laurie? Did you ever try to get help?"

"Oh, we talked about it endlessly, Andy and I. Andy always told me not to worry. I asked the pediatrician about it, and he told me the same thing: 'Don't worry, Jake is still very little, it will pass.' They made me feel a little crazy, like I was one of those crazy, jumpy moms always hovering over their kids, freaking out about Band-Aids and . . . and peanut allergies. And here was Andy and the pediatrician saying, 'It will pass, it will pass.'"

"But it *did* pass, Laurie. You *were* over-reacting. The pediatrician was right."

"Was he? Honey, look where we are. You never want to face this."

"Face what?"

"That maybe Jacob needed help. Maybe it's our fault. We should have done something."

"Done what? Or else what?"

Her head drooped, hopeless. The memory of these early childhood incidents haunted her, as if she had seen a shark's fin that disappeared under water. It was lunacy.

"Laurie, what are you suggesting? This is our son we're talking about."

"I'm not suggesting anything, Andy. Don't make this a loyalty contest or a—a fight. I'm just wondering about what we did back then. I mean, I don't know what the answer was, I have no idea what we should have done. Maybe Jake needed medication. Or counseling. I don't know. I just can't help thinking we must have made mistakes. We must have. We tried so hard and we meant so well. We don't deserve all this. We were good, responsible people. You know? We did everything right. We weren't too young. We waited. In fact, we almost waited too long; I was thirty-six when I had Jacob. We weren't rich, but we both worked hard and we had enough money to give the baby everything he needed. We did everything right, and yet here we are. It isn't fair." She shook her head and murmured, "It isn't fair."

Beside me, Laurie's hand rested on the arm of her chair. I thought I might lay my hand on hers to soothe her, but in the moment it took to consider it, she withdrew her hand and knotted her arms down tight over her belly.

She said, "I look back on us then and I see we weren't ready at all. I mean, no one ever is, right? We were kids. I don't care how old we were; we were kids. And we were clueless and we were scared shitless, like all new parents. And I don't know, maybe we made mistakes."

"What mistakes, Laurie? Really. You're being dramatic. It just wasn't that bad. Jacob was a little boisterous and rough. Is that really such a big deal? He was a little boy! Some kids got hurt because four-year-olds get hurt. They totter around, and three-quarters of their body weight is in their enormous heads, so they fall down and crash into things. They fall off play struc-tures, they fall off bicycles. It happens. They're like drunks. Anyway, the pediatri-cian was right: Jacob did outgrow it. This stuff all stopped when he got older. You're beating yourself up, but there's nothing to feel guilty about, Laurie. We didn't do any-thing wrong."

"That's just what you always used to say. You never wanted to admit anything was out of place. Or maybe you just never saw it. I mean, I'm not blaming you. It wasn't your fault. I see that now. I understand what you were dealing with, what you must have been carrying around inside."

"Oh, don't put it on that."

"Andy, it must have been a burden."

"It wasn't. Ever. I promise you."

"All right, whatever you say. But you need to think about the possibility that you don't see Jacob objectively. You're not re-liable. Dr. Vogel needs to know that."

"*I'm* not reliable?"

"No, you're not."

Dr. Vogel was watching, saying nothing. She knew my backstory, of course. It was the reason we hired her, an expert on genetic wickedness. Still, the subject embarrassed me. I fell silent, ashamed.

The psychiatrist said, "Is that true, Laurie? Jacob's behavior got better as he got older?"

"Yes, in some ways. I mean, it was *better,* certainly. Kids weren't getting hurt around him anymore. But he still misbehaved."

"How?"

"Well, he stole. He always stole, his whole childhood. From stores, from CVS, even from the library. He would steal from me. He'd go right into my purse. I caught him shoplifting a couple of times when he was little. I talked to him about it but it never made any difference. What was I supposed to do? Cut off his hands?"

I said, "This is totally unfair. You're not being fair to Jacob."

"Why? I'm being honest."

"No, you're being honest about how you *feel,* because Jacob's in trouble and you feel responsible somehow, so you're reading back into his life all these terrible things that just weren't there. I mean, really: he stole from your purse? So what? You're just not giving the doctor an accurate picture. We're here to talk about Jacob's court case."

"So?"

"So what does shoplifting have to do with murder? What's the difference if he took a candy bar or a pen or something from CVS? What on earth does that have to do with Ben Rifkin being brutally stabbed to death? You're lumping these things together like shoplifting and bloody murder are the same thing. They're not."

Dr. Vogel said, "I think what Laurie is describing is a pattern of rule-breaking. She's suggesting that Jacob, for whatever reason, can't seem to stay within the bounds of accepted behavior."

"No. That's a sociopath."

"No."

"What you're describing—"

"No."

"—is a sociopath. Is that what you're saying? Jacob is a sociopath?"

"No." Dr. Vogel put up her hands. "I didn't say that, Andy. I did not use that word. I'm just trying to get a complete picture of Jacob. I haven't come to any conclusions about anything. My mind is wide open."

Laurie said, earnest and grave, "I think Jacob may have problems. He may need help."

I shook my head.

"He's our son, Andy. It's our responsibility to take care of him."

"That's what I'm trying to do."

Laurie's eyes glistened but no tears came. She had already done her crying. This was a thought she'd been holding inside awhile, working it through, arriving at this awful conclusion. *I think Jacob may have problems.*

Dr. Vogel said, with treacherous compassion, "Laurie, do you have doubts about Jacob's innocence?"

Laurie swiped her eyes dry and sat up stiff-backed. "No."

"It sounds like you might."

"No."

"You're sure?"

"Yes. He's not capable of this. A mother knows her child. Jacob's not capable of this."

The psychiatrist nodded, accepting the statement even if she did not quite believe it. Even, for that matter, if she did not believe that Laurie believed it.

"Doctor, do you mind if I ask you something? Do *you* think I made mistakes? Was there a pattern there that I missed? Was there something more I should have done, if I'd been a better mom?"

The doctor hesitated for just a moment. On the wall above her, two of the African masks howled. "No, Laurie. I don't think you did anything wrong at all. Honestly, I think you need to stop beating yourself up. If there was a pattern there, if there was a way to predict Jacob was heading for trouble, I don't see how any parent could have recognized it. Not based on what you've told me so far. A lot of kids have the sort of issues Jacob had and it means nothing at all."

"I did the best I could."

"You did fine, Laurie. Don't do that to yourself. Andy's not wrong: what you've described so far? You did what any mother would have done. You did the best you could for your child. That's all anyone can ask."

Laurie held her head up, but there was a brittleness about her. It was like watching tiny threadlike cracks begin to spread and craze over her. Dr. Vogel seemed to perceive this fragile quality too, but she could not have known how entirely new it was. How changed Laurie already was. You had to really know Laurie and cherish her to appreciate what was happening. Once, my wife read so constantly that she would hold a book in her left hand while she brushed her teeth with the right; now, she never picked up a book, she could not muster the concentration or even the interest. Before, she had this way of focusing on whomever she spoke to, so that you felt you were the most impossibly captivating person in the room; now, her eyes wandered and she seemed not to be in the room herself. Her clothes, her hair, her makeup all were a bit wrong, a bit mismatched and sloppy. The quality that had always made her shine—a youthful, eager optimism—had begun to fade. But of course you had to know her Before in order to see what Laurie had lost. I was the only one in the room who understood what was happening to her.

Still, she was nowhere near surrender. "I did the best I could," she announced with a sudden, unconvincing resolve.

"Laurie, tell me about Jacob now. What is he like?"

"Hm." She smiled at the thought of him. "He's very smart. Very funny, very charming. Handsome." She actually blushed a little at the word *handsome.* Mother-love is love, after all. "He's into computers, he loves gadgets, video games, music. He reads a lot."

"Any problems with temper or violence?"

"No."

"You've been telling us Jacob had issues with violence when he was a preschooler."

"It stopped as soon as he got to kindergarten."

"I'm just wondering if you still have any concerns about it. Does he still behave in any way that disturbs or worries you?"

"She already said no, Doctor."

"Well, I want to explore it a little further."

"It's okay, Andy. No, Jacob's never violent anymore. I almost wish he would act out *more.* He can be very hard to communicate with. He's hard to read. He doesn't talk a lot. He broods. He's very introverted. Not just shy; I mean he introverts his feelings, his energy is all directed inward. He's very remote, very guarded. He smolders. But no, he's not violent."

"Does he have other ways to express himself? Music, friends, sports, clubs, whatever?"

"No. He's not much of a joiner. And he only has a few friends. Derek, a couple of others."

"Girlfriends?"

"No, he's too young for that."

"Is he?"

"Isn't he?"

The doctor shrugged.

"Anyway, he's not mean. He can be very critical, caustic, sarcastic. He's cynical. Fourteen years old and he's already cynical! He hasn't experienced enough to be cynical, has he? He hasn't earned it. Maybe it's just a pose. It's how kids are today. Arch, ironic."

"Those sound like unpleasant qualities."

"Do they? I don't mean them to. Jacob's just complicated, I think. He's moody. You know, he likes to be the angry boy, the 'nobody fucking understands me' boy."

This was too much.

I snapped, "Laurie, come on, that's every

teenager, the angry boy, the 'nobody fucking understands me' boy. Come on! What
you've just described is every adolescent
on earth. It's not a kid; it's a bar code."

"Maybe." Laurie bowed her head. "I
don't know. I always thought maybe Jacob
should see a shrink."

"You've *never* said he should see a
shrink!"

"I didn't say I said it. I said I wondered if
it was the right thing to do, just so he would
have someone to talk to."

Dr. Vogel growled, "Andy."

"Well, I can't just sit here!"

"Try. We're here to listen to each other,
to support each other, not argue."

"Look," I said, exasperated, "enough is
enough. The whole presumption of this
conversation is that Jacob has something
to answer for, to explain. It's just not true.
A horrible thing happened, all right? Horrible. But it's not our fault. It's certainly not
Jake's fault. You know, I'm sitting here and
I'm listening, and I'm thinking, What the
hell are we talking about? Jacob had nothing to do with Ben Rifkin getting killed,
nothing, but we're all sitting here talking
about Jake as if he's some kind of freak or

monster or something. He's not. He's just an ordinary kid. He has his flaws like every other kid, but he had nothing to do with this. I'm sorry, but somebody has to stand up for Jacob here."

Dr. Vogel: "Andy, looking back, what do *you* think about all those kids who got hurt around Jacob? All the kids falling off playground structures and crashing bicycles? Was it all just bad luck? Coincidence? How do you think about it?"

"Jacob had a lot of energy; he played too rough. I acknowledge that. It's something we dealt with when he was a kid. But that's all it was. I mean, this all happened before Jake got to kindergarten. Kindergarten!"

"And the anger? You don't think Jacob has an issue with anger?"

"No, I don't. People get angry. It's not an *issue*."

"There's a report here from Jacob's file that he punched a hole in the wall in his bedroom. You had to call a plasterer. This was just last fall. Is that true?"

"Yes, but—how did you get that?"

"Jonathan."

"That was for Jacob's legal defense only!"

"That's what we're doing here, preparing his defense. Is it true? Did he punch a hole in the wall?"

"Yes. So what?"

"People don't generally punch holes in walls, do they?"

"Sometimes they do, actually."

"Do you?"

Deep breath. "No."

"Laurie thinks you may have a blind spot about the possibility of Jacob being . . . violent. What do you think of that?"

"She thinks I'm in denial."

"Are you?"

I shook my head in a stubborn, melancholy way, like a horse swaying its head in a narrow stall. "No. Just the opposite. I'm hyperalert to these things; I'm hyperaware. I mean, you know my background. My whole life—" Deep breath. "Lookit, you're always concerned when kids get hurt; even if it's an accident, you never want to see something like that. And you're always concerned when your own kid behaves in ways that are . . . disturbing. So yes, I was aware of these things, I was concerned. But I knew Jacob, I knew my kid, and I loved him and I believed in him. And I still do. I'm sticking with him."

"We're all sticking with him, Andy. That's completely unfair! I love him too. It's got nothing to do with that."

"I never said you didn't, Laurie. Did you hear me say you didn't love him?"

"No, but you always retreat to that: *I love him.* Of course you love him. We both love him. I'm just saying, you can love your child and still see his flaws. You *have* to see his flaws, otherwise how can you help him?"

"Laurie, did you or did you not hear me say you didn't love him?"

"Andy, that's not what I'm saying! You're not listening!"

"I am listening! I just don't agree with you. You're drawing this picture of Jacob as violent and moody and, and dangerous, based on nothing, and I just disagree. But if I disagree, you say I'm being dishonest. Or 'unreliable.' You're calling me a liar."

"I did *not* call you a liar! I've never called you a liar."

"You didn't use the word, no."

"Andy, no one's attacking you. There's

nothing wrong with admitting your son might need a little help. It doesn't say anything about you."

The comment bayoneted me. Because *of course* Laurie was talking about me. This whole thing was completely about me. I was the reason, the only reason, she thought our son might be dangerous. If he were not a Barber, no one would ever have parsed his childhood so closely for signs of trouble.

But I remained silent. What was the use? There was no defense to being a Barber.

Dr. Vogel said cautiously, "Okay, maybe we should just stop here. I'm not sure it would be productive to go on much longer. This isn't easy for anyone, I realize. We've made some progress. We can try again next week."

I looked down at my lap, avoiding Laurie's eyes, ashamed, though for what I was not exactly sure.

"Let me just ask you both one last question. Maybe we can leave on a happier note, okay? So let's assume for a moment that this case will go away. Assume that in a few months the case will be dismissed and Jacob will be free to go and do whatever he pleases. Just as if this case had never happened. No qualifications, no lingering shadows, nothing at all. Now, if that were to happen, where would you see your son in ten years? Laurie?"

"Wow. I can't think that way. I'm just getting through from one day to the next, you know? Ten years is just . . . too hard to imagine."

"Okay, I understand. But just as a thought exercise, try. Where do you see your son in ten years?"

Laurie considered. She shook her head. "I can't. I don't even like to think about it. I just can't envision anything good. I think about Jacob's situation constantly, Doctor, *constantly,* and I can't see how this story could end happily. Poor Jacob. I just *hope,* you know? That's all I can do. But if I think about when he's older and we're not around? I don't know, I just hope he's okay."

"That's all?"

"That's all."

"All right, how about you, Andy? If this case disappeared, where would you see Jacob in ten years?"

"If he walks on this case?"

"That's right."

"I see him happy."

"Happy, okay."

"Maybe with someone, a wife who makes him happy. Maybe a father. With a son."

Laurie shifted.

"But through with all this teenage crap. All the self-pity, the narcissism. If Jacob has a weakness, it's that he doesn't have the kind of discipline it takes. He's . . . self-indulgent. He doesn't have the . . . I don't know . . . the steel."

Dr. Vogel: "The steel to do what?"

Laurie looked at me across her shoulder, curious.

We all heard the answer in our heads, I think, even Dr. Vogel: *the steel to be a Barber.*

"To grow up," I said weakly. "To be an adult."

"Like you?"

"No. Not like me. Jake's got to do it his own way, I know that. I'm not one of those dads."

I pulled my elbows into my lap, as if trying to squeeze through a narrow passageway.

"Jacob doesn't have the kind of discipline you had as a kid?"

"No, he doesn't."

"Why does that matter, Andy? What is he steeling himself for? Or against?"

The two women shared a glance, the briefest eye-tap. They were studying me, together, understanding each other. Judging me *unreliable,* in Laurie's word.

"Life," I murmured. "Jacob's got to steel himself against life. Same as every other kid."

Laurie leaned forward, elbows on knees, and she took my hand.

13 | 179 Days

After the catastrophe of Jacob's arrest, every day had an unbearable urgency. A dull, constant anxiety set in. In some ways, the weeks that followed the arrest were worse than the event itself. We were all counting the days, I think. Jacob's trial was scheduled for October 17, and the date became an obsession. It was as if the future, which we had formerly measured by the length of our lives, as everyone does, now had a definite endpoint. Whatever lay beyond the trial, we could not imagine. Everything—the entire universe—ended on October 17. All we could do was count down the 179 days until then. This is something I did not understand when I was like you, when nothing had ever happened to me: how much easier it was to endure the big moments than the in-between times, the non-events, the waiting. The high drama of Jacob's arrest, his arraignment in court, and so on—bad as those were, they barreled past and were gone. The real suffering came when no one was looking, during those 179 long days. The unoccupied afternoons in a quiet house, when worry silently engulfed us. The intense awareness of time, the heaviness of the passing minutes, the dizzying, trippy sense that the days were both too few and too long. In the end, we were eager for the trial if only because we could not stand the waiting. It was like a deathwatch.

One night in May—28 days after the arrest, 151 still to go—the three of us were sitting at the dinner table.

Jacob was sullen. He rarely lifted his eyes from his plate. He chewed his food noisily, like a little kid, making wet, squishing sounds, a habit he had since he was a little kid. "I don't understand why we have to do this every night," he said in an offhand way.

"Do what?"

"Have, like, a big sit-down dinner, like it's a party or something. It's just the three of us."

Laurie explained, not for the first time, "It's pretty simple, really. That's what families do. They sit down and have a proper dinner together."

"But it's just us."

"So?"

"So it's like, every night you spend all this time cooking for *three people.* Then we sit down and eat for, like, fifteen minutes. Then we have to spend even more time after, doing all the dishes, which we wouldn't even *have* if you didn't make such a big deal about it every night."

"It's not so bad. I don't see you doing too many dishes, Jacob."

"That's not the point, Mom. It's just a waste. We could just have pizza or Chinese or whatever and the whole thing'd be over in like fifteen minutes."

"But I don't want the whole thing to be

over in fifteen minutes. I want to enjoy dinner with my family."

"You actually *want* it to take an hour every night?"

"I'd prefer two hours. I'll take what I can get." She smirked, sipped her water.

"We never made a big deal about dinner before."

"Well, we do now."

"I know why you're really doing it, Mom."

"Yeah? Why's that?"

"So I won't get all depressed. You think if I just have a nice family dinner every night, my case will just go away."

"Well, I certainly don't think that."

"Good, because it's not going away."

"I just want it to go away for a little while, Jacob. Just one hour a day. Is that really so awful?"

"Yes! Because it doesn't work. It makes things worse. It's like, the more you pretend everything is so normal, the more you remind me how *un*-normal it really is. I mean, look at this." He waggled his arms around, flummoxed by the old-fashioned, *haimish* dinner Laurie had made: chicken pot pie, fresh string beans, lemonade, with a cylindrical candle for a centerpiece. "It's *fake* normal."

"Like jumbo shrimp," I said.

"Andy, shush. Jacob, what do you want me to do? I've never been in this situation before. What should a mom do? Tell me and I'll do it."

"I don't know. If you want to keep me from getting depressed, give me drugs, not . . . chicken pot pie."

"I'm afraid I'm all out of drugs at the moment."

"Jake," I said between bites, "Derek could probably hook you up."

"That's very helpful, Andy. Jacob, has it ever occurred to you that the reason I make dinner every night, and the reason I don't let you eat in front of the TV, and the reason I don't let you stand around the kitchen eating your dinner out of Tupperware or skip dinner altogether and stay up in your room playing video games, is because of *me.* Maybe this is all for me, not you. This isn't easy for me either."

"Because you don't think I'm going to get off."

"No."

The phone rang.

"Yes! I mean, *obviously.* Otherwise you wouldn't need to count every dinner."

"No, Jacob. It's because I want to have my family around me. When times are tough, that's what families do. They gather around, they support each other. Everything isn't always about you, you know. *You* need to be there for *me* too."

There was a moment's silence. Jacob seemed unabashed at his adolescent self-absorbed narcissism; he just couldn't think of a suitably snappy comeback.

The phone rang again.

Laurie gave Jacob a so-there look—eyebrows raised, chin tucked—then she got up to answer the phone, hurrying a little to reach it before the fourth ring, when the answering machine would intercept the call.

Jacob looked wary. Why was Mom answering the phone? We had already learned not to respond to the ringing. Jacob knew, certainly, that the call was not for him. His friends had all dropped him cold. Anyway, he had never used the telephone much. He considered it intrusive, awkward, archaic, inefficient. Any friend who wanted to speak to Jake would just text him or log on to

Facebook to chat. These new technologies were more comfortable because less intimate. Jake preferred typing to talking.

I felt an instinctive urge to warn Laurie not to answer, but I held back. I did not want to spoil the evening. I wanted to support her. These family dinners were important to Laurie. Jacob was essentially right: she wanted to preserve as much normalcy as possible. Presumably that's why she let her guard down: we were laboring to behave like a normal family, and normal families are not afraid of the phone.

I said, in a coded reminder, "What does the caller ID say?"

"'Private caller.'"

She picked up the phone, which was in the kitchen, in clear view of the dining room table. Her back was to Jacob and me. She said, "Hello," then went silent. Over the next few seconds, her shoulders and back slumped by infinitesimal degrees. It was as if she was deflating slightly as she listened.

I said, "Laurie?"

In a shaky voice, she said to the caller, "Who is this? Where did you get this number?"

More listening.

"Don't call here again. Do you hear me? Don't you dare call here again."

I took the phone from her gently and hung it up.

"Oh my God, Andy."

"Are you okay?"

She nodded.

We went back to the table and sat quietly for a moment.

Laurie picked up her fork and scooped a token bit of chicken into her mouth. Her face was rigid, her body still wilted and round-shouldered.

"What did he say?" Jacob asked.

"Just eat your dinner, Jacob."

I could not reach her across the table. All I could offer was a concerned face.

"You could star-sixty-nine him," Jacob suggested.

"Let's just enjoy our dinner," Laurie said. She took another nibble and chewed busily, then sat absolutely stone still.

"Laurie?"

She cleared her throat, mumbled "Excuse me," and left the table.

There were still 151 days to go.

14 | Questioning

Jonathan: "Tell me about the knife."

Jacob: "What do you want to know?"

"Well, the DA is going to say you bought it because you were being bullied. They'll say that's your motive. But you told your folks you bought it for no reason."

"I didn't say I bought it for no reason. I said I bought it because I wanted it."

"Yes, but *why* did you want it?"

"Why did you want that necktie? Do you have a reason for everything you buy?"

"Jacob, a knife is a little different from a necktie, wouldn't you say?"

"No. It's all just stuff. That's how our society works: you spend all your time making money so you can trade it for stuff, then—"

"Now it's gone?"

"—then you go out and make *more* money so you can buy *more* stuff—"

"Jacob, the knife is gone?"

"Yeah. My dad took it."

"You have the knife, Andy?"

"No. It's gone."

"You got rid of it?"

"It was dangerous. It wasn't an appropriate knife for a kid to have. It wasn't a toy. Any father would have—"

"Andy, I'm not accusing you of anything. I'm just trying to confirm what happened."

"Sorry. Yes, I got rid of it."

Jonathan nodded but offered no comment. We were sitting at the round oak table in his office, the only room he had that was large enough to accommodate our entire family. The young associate, Ellen, was there too, assiduously scribbling notes. It occurred to me that she was there to witness the conversation in order to protect Jonathan, not to help us. He was creating a record just in case he ever fell out with his clients and there was a dispute about what he had been told.

Laurie watched with her hands folded in her lap. Her composure, once so natural, now required more effort to maintain. She spoke a little less, involved herself a little less in these legal strategy sessions. It was as if she was conserving her energy for the moment-to-moment effort of just holding herself together.

Jacob was sulking. He picked at the surface of the table with a fingernail, his goofy teenage pride wounded by Jonathan's lack of enthusiasm for his insights into the rudiments of capitalism.

Jonathan petted his short beard, absorbed in his own thoughts. "But you had the knife the day Ben Rifkin was killed?"

"Yes."

"Did you have it with you in the park that morning?"

"No."

"Did you have it with you when you left?"

"No."

"Where was it?"

"In a drawer in my room, same as always."

"You're sure?"

"Yeah."

"So when you left for school, was there anything unusual about the morning?"

"When I left? No."

"Did you follow your usual route to school? Through the park?"

"Yes."

"So the spot where Ben was killed was right on the path you normally follow through the park?"

"I guess so. I never really thought about it that way."

"Before you found the body, did you see or hear anything as you walked through the park?"

"No. I was just walking and then there he was, just lying there."

"Describe him. How was he lying when you first saw him?"

"He was just lying there. He was, like, lying on his stomach on this, like, little slope, in a bunch of leaves."

"Dry leaves or wet leaves?"

"Wet."

"You're sure?"

"I think."

"You think? Or you're guessing?"

"I don't really remember that part too well."

"So why did you answer the question?"

"I'm not really sure."

"From now on, you answer absolutely honestly, okay? If the accurate answer is *I don't remember,* then that's what you say, all right?"

"All right."

"So you see a body lying on the ground. Was there any blood?"

"I didn't see any right then."

"What did you do as you approached the body?"

"I kind of called his name. Like 'Ben, Ben. You okay?' Something like that."

"So you recognized him right away?"

"Yeah."

"How? I thought he was lying facedown with his head at the bottom of a slope, and you were looking down from above."

"I guess I just recognized, like, his clothes and, you know, his look."

"His look?"

"Yeah. Like, his appearance."

"All you could see was the bottom of Ben's sneakers."

"No, I could see more than that. You can just tell, you know?"

"All right, so you find the body and you say 'Ben, Ben.' What next?"

"Well, he didn't answer and he wasn't moving, so I figured he must be hurt pretty bad, so I kind of went down to him to see if he was okay."

"Did you call for help?"

"No."

"Why not? Did you have a cell phone?"

"Yeah."

"So you find a victim of a bloody murder and you have a phone in your pocket, but it never occurs to you to call nine-one-one?"

Jonathan was careful to ask all his questions in a curious tone, as if he was just trying to figure the whole thing out. It was an interrogation, but not a hostile one. Not obviously hostile.

"Do you know anything about first aid?"

"No, I just figured I should see if he was okay first."

"Did it occur to you that a crime had occurred?"

"It occurred to me, I guess, but I wasn't totally sure. It could have been an accident. Like if he just fell or something."

"Fell on what? Why?"

"Nothing. I'm just saying."

"So you had no reason to think he just fell?"

"No. You're twisting things."

"I'm just trying to understand, Jacob. Why didn't you call for help? Why didn't you call your father? He's a lawyer, he works for the DA—he would have known what to do."

"It just—I don't know, I didn't think of it. It was kind of an emergency. I wasn't, like, *prepared* for it. I didn't know what I was supposed to do."

"Okay, what happened next?"

"I kind of went down the hill and I got down beside him."

"Got down on your knees, you mean?"

"I guess so."

"In the wet leaves?"

"I don't know. Maybe I stayed standing."

"You stayed standing. So you were looking down over him, right?"

"No. I don't really remember. When you say it like that, I think maybe I must have been down on a knee."

"Derek saw you a few minutes later in

school and he did not say anything about your pants being wet or muddy."

"I guess I must have been standing, then."

"All right, standing. So you're standing over him, looking down at him. What next?"

"Like I said, I kind of rolled him over to check on him."

"Did you say anything to him first?"

"I don't think so."

"You see a classmate lying facedown, unconscious, and you just flip him over without a word?"

"No, I mean maybe I said something, I'm not completely sure."

"When you were standing over Ben at the bottom of the slope, did you see any evidence of a crime then?"

"No."

"There was a long smear of blood going all the way down the hill from Ben's wounds. You didn't notice it?"

"No. I mean, I was, like, freaking out, you know?"

"Freaking out how? What does that mean, exactly?"

"I don't know. Just, like, panicking."

"Panicking why? You said you didn't

know what happened, you did not think there'd been a crime. You thought it might be an accident."

"I know, but this kid was just lying there. It was just a freaky situation."

"When Derek saw you just a few minutes later, you weren't freaking out."

"No, I was. I just didn't show it. I was freaking out on the inside."

"All right. So you're standing over the body. Ben is already dead. He's bled out from three wounds in his chest and there's a trail of blood leading down the hill to the body, but you didn't see *any* blood and you didn't have any idea what happened. And you're freaking out but only on the inside. What next?"

"It sounds like you don't believe me."

"Jacob, let me tell you something: it doesn't matter if I believe you. I'm your lawyer, not your mom or dad."

"Yeah, but still. I don't really appreciate how you're making it sound. This is my story, okay? And you're making it sound like I'm lying."

Laurie, who had not spoken throughout this entire meeting, said, "Please stop, Jonathan. I'm sorry. Just please stop. You've made your point."

Jonathan was brought up short, chastened. "All right, Jacob, your mother's right. Maybe we'd better stop right here. I don't mean to upset you. But I want you to think about something. This whole story of yours might have sounded good when you told it in your head, when you were alone in your room. But things tend to sound different under cross-examination. And I promise you, what we're doing here is a walk in the park next to what Neal Logiudice will do to you if you take the stand. I'm on *your* side; Logiudice isn't. I'm also a nice guy; Logiudice—well, he has a job to do. Now, I think what you're about to tell me is that, faced with this body lying facedown with blood flooding out of three gaping chest wounds, you somehow managed to stick your arm underneath the body so that you could leave a single thumbprint *inside* Ben's sweatshirt—yet when you pulled your arm out again there was not a trace of blood on it, so that when you showed up at school a few minutes later no one thought anything was amiss. Now, if you were a juror, what would you think about that story?"

"But it's true. Not the details—you messed me up on the details. He wasn't lying, like, totally facedown, and it wasn't like blood was gushing all over. It just wasn't like that. That's just you, you know, playing games. I'm telling the truth."

"Jacob, I'm sorry I upset you. But I am not playing games."

"I swear to God, it's the truth."

"Okay. I understand."

"No. You're calling me a liar."

Jonathan did not respond. It is, of course, the last resort of a liar to challenge his inquisitor to call him a liar directly. Worse, there was an edge in Jacob's voice. It might have been the hint of a threat or it might have been a terrified boy near tears.

I said, "Jake, it's all right. Jonathan has a job to do."

"I know, but he doesn't believe me."

"It's okay. He'll be your lawyer whether he believes you or not. Defense lawyers are like that." I gave Jacob a wink.

"What about my trial? How am I going to get up there?"

"You're not," I said. "You're not going

anywhere near that witness stand. You're going to sit at the defense table and the only reason you're going to get up is to go home at night."

Jonathan slipped in, "I think that's wise."

"But how will I tell my story?"

"Jacob, I don't know if you've been listening to yourself the last few minutes. You cannot take the stand."

"Then what's my defense?"

Jonathan said, "We don't have to present a defense. We have no burden. The burden is entirely on the prosecution. We're going to attack their case at every turn, Jacob, until there's nothing left of it. That's our defense."

"Dad?"

I hesitated. "I'm not sure it's going to be enough, Jonathan. We can't just throw a few spitballs at Logiudice's case. He has the thumbprint, he has the witness who puts a knife in Jacob's hand. We're going to have to do more. We have to give those jurors *something*."

"So what do you suggest I do, Andy?"

"I just think maybe we need to consider presenting a real, affirmative defense."

"Love to. What do you have in mind? As

far as I can see, all the evidence points one way."

"What about Patz? The jury should at least *hear* about him. Give them the real killer."

"The real killer? Oh, my. How do we prove that?"

"We'll hire a detective to dig into it."

"Dig into what? Patz? There's nothing there. When you were in the DA's office, you had the state police, every local police department, the FBI, CIA, KGB, NASA."

"We always had less resources than you defense guys imagined."

"Maybe. But you had more than you have now, and you never found anything. What's a private detective going to do that a dozen state police detectives couldn't?"

I had no answer.

"Andy, look, I know *you* understand that the defense has no burden of proof. You know it, but I'm not entirely sure you believe it. This is how the game is played from the other side. We don't get to pick our clients, we don't get to just drop a case if the evidence isn't there. So this is our case." He gestured toward the papers in front of him. "We play the cards we're dealt. We have no choice."

"Then we have to find some new cards."

"Where?"

"I don't know. Up our sleeves."

"I note," Jonathan drawled, "that you are wearing a short-sleeve shirt."

15 | Playing Detective

At the Starbucks in Newton Centre, Sarah Groehl had plugged herself into a MacBook. Seeing me, she disengaged herself from the computer, canting her head left then right to remove her earphones, just as women do when they take off earrings. She looked at me sleepily, blinking, rousing herself from a Web-trance.

"Hi, Sarah. Am I disturbing you?"

"No, I was just . . . I don't know."

"Can I talk to you?"

"About what?

I gave her a look: *Come on.* "We can go somewhere else if you want."

She did not immediately answer. The tables were crowded together, and people pretended not to be listening, obeying the etiquette of coffee shops. But the ordinary awkwardness of having a conversation within others' hearing was multiplied by my family's infamy and by Sarah's own awkwardness. She was embarrassed to be seen with me. She may have been afraid of me too, after all she had heard. With so much to consider, she seemed unable to answer. I suggested we sit on the park bench across the street, where I figured she would feel safe in the sight of others yet out of hearing range, and she made a sweeping motion with her head to swing her bangs off her forehead, away from her eyes, and said okay.

"Can I buy you another coffee?"

"I don't drink coffee."

We sat side by side on the green-slatted bench across the street. Sarah held herself royally erect. She was not fat, but she was not thin enough for the tight T-shirt she wore. A little roll of flesh blossomed

over her shorts—a "muffin top," the kids
called it without embarrassment. I thought
she might be a nice girl for Jacob when all
this was over.

I held my Starbucks paper cup. I'd lost
interest in it but there was no place to
dump it now. I turned it in my hands.

"Sarah, I'm trying to find out what really
happened to Ben Rifkin. I need to find the
guy who really did this."

She gave me a skeptical sidelong gaze.
"What do you mean, 'the guy who really
did this'?"

"Jacob didn't do it. They have the wrong
guy."

"I thought that wasn't your job anymore.
You're playing detective?"

"It's my job as a father now."

"O-*kay.*" She smirked and shook her
head.

"Does that sound crazy, to say he's innocent?"

"No. I guess not."

"I think maybe you know Jacob is innocent too. The things you said . . ."

"I never said *that.*"

"Sarah, you know we adults don't really
have any idea what's going on in your lives.

How could we? But somebody has to open up to us a little bit. Some of you kids have to help."

"We have."

"Not enough. Don't you see, Sarah? A friend of yours is going to go to prison for a murder he didn't commit."

"How do I know he didn't commit it? Isn't that, like, the whole thing? It's like, how would anyone know that? Including you."

"Well, do you think he's guilty?"

"I don't know."

"So you have doubts."

"I just said, I don't know."

"I do know, Sarah. Okay? I've been doing this for a long time and I know: Jacob did not do it. I promise you. He didn't do it. He's completely innocent."

"Of course you think that. You're his father."

"I am, it's true. But I'm not just his father. There's evidence, Sarah. You haven't seen it but I have."

She looked at me with a beneficent little smile, and briefly she was the adult and I was a foolish child. "I don't know what you want me to say, Mr. Barber. What do I know? It's not like I was tight with either one of them, Jacob or Ben."

"Sarah, you were the one who told me to look on Facebook."

"I did not."

"Okay, well, let's just say if—*if* you were the one who told me to look on Facebook. Why did you do that? What did you want me to find?"

"Okay, I'm not saying it was me that told you anything, okay?"

"Okay."

"Because I don't want to be, like, involved, okay?"

"Okay."

"It was just, you know, there were these rumors going around and I thought you should know what kids were saying. 'Cause nobody seemed to know, you know? Like, nobody who was in charge. No offense, but you all seemed kind of clueless. Kids knew. Kids were saying Jacob had a knife, and Jake and Ben had a fight. But you guys were running around totally clueless. Actually Ben had been kind of a bully to Jake for a long time, you know? It wasn't like that makes anyone a murderer, all right? But it was just kind of something I thought you guys should know."

"What was Ben bullying Jake about?"

"Why don't you just ask Jake? He's your kid."

"I have. He never mentioned anything about Ben bullying him. All he tells me is everything was just fine, he had no problems with Ben or anyone else."

"Okay, then maybe—I don't know, I mean, maybe I'm just wrong."

"Come on, you don't think you're wrong, Sarah. What was Jake being bullied about?"

She shrugged. "Look, it's not like it's such a big deal. Everyone gets bullied. Well, not bullied—teased, okay? I see how your eyes light up when I say 'bullied,' like it's some big thing. Adults love to talk about bullying. We've had all these training classes in bullying and all that." She shook her head.

"Okay, so not bullied—teased. What about? What were they getting on him about?"

"The usual stuff: he's gay, he's a geek, he's a loser."

"Who was saying that?"

"Just kids. Everyone. It was not a big

thing. It happens for a while, then it moves on to the next kid."

"Was Ben teasing Jacob?"

"Yeah, but it wasn't, like, *only* Ben. Don't take this the wrong way, but Jacob isn't exactly in the cool crowd."

"No? What crowd is he in?"

"I don't know. He's not really in a crowd. He's just kind of nothing. It's hard to explain. Jacob's kind of like a cool geek, I'd say, only there kind of isn't really such a thing. Does that make sense?"

"No."

"Well, it's like there's jocks? He definitely isn't one of those. And there's smart kids? Only he isn't really smart enough to be one of them either. I mean, he's smart, okay?, but he isn't like *that* smart. It's like you need to have a *thing,* you know? You need to play an instrument or be on a team or be in a play or whatever, or like be ethnic or lesbian or retarded or something— not that there's anything wrong with those things. It's just, like, if you don't have any of those things then you're just kind of one of those kids, you know? Like just a regular kid, and nobody knows what to call you—you're nothing, but not in a *bad* way.

And that's kind of like what Jacob was, you know? He was just like a regular kid. Does *that* make sense?"

"Perfect sense."

"Really?"

"Yes. What are *you,* Sarah? What's your 'thing'?"

"I don't have one. Same as Jacob. I'm nothing."

"But not in a bad way."

"That's right."

"Well, I don't want to get all Cliff Huxtable here, but I don't think you're nothing."

"Who's Cliff Huxtable?"

"Never mind."

Across the street, people stole glances at us as they went in and out of Starbucks, though it was not clear if they recognized me. Maybe I was being paranoid.

"I just want to say, like"—she searched around for the words—"I think it's really cool what you're trying to do? Like trying to prove Jacob innocent and all? You seem like a really good dad. Only Jacob isn't like you. You know that, don't you?"

"No? Why?"

"Just, like, his manner? He's kind of quiet? He's really shy? I'm not saying he's

a bad kid. I mean, not at *all*. But he doesn't
have a lot of friends, y'know? He has, like,
his little circle? Like Derek and that kid
Josh? (That kid is totally weird, by the way.
I mean, like, totally random.) But Jacob
doesn't really have a lot of friends in, like,
his network. I mean, I guess he likes it that
way, y'know? Which is okay, it's *totally
fine.* I'm not saying anything. It's just like,
there must be a lot going on inside there,
in his—y'know, inside. I just, I don't know
if he's happy."

"Does he seem unhappy to you, Sarah?"

"Yeah, a little. But I mean, everyone's unhappy, right? I mean sometimes?"

I didn't answer.

"You need to talk to Derek. Derek Yoo?
He knows more about all this than I do."

"Right now I'm talking to you, Sarah."

"No, go talk to Derek. I don't want to get
in the middle of it, you know? Derek and
Jacob have been really tight, like, since they
were little kids. I'm sure Derek can tell you
more than I can. I mean, I'm sure he'll *want*
to help Jacob. He's like Jacob's best friend."

"Why don't *you* want to help Jacob,
Sarah?"

"I do want to. I just, I don't really know.

I don't know enough about it. But Derek does."

I wanted to pat her on the hand or the shoulder or something, but that sort of fatherly contact has been drummed out of us. So I tipped my paper cup toward her in a sort of toast, and I said, "There's something we always asked when we ended an interview in my old job: is there anything you think I ought to know that I didn't ask about? Anything at all?"

"No. Not that I can think of."

"You're sure?"

She held up her pinkie. "Promise."

"Okay, Sarah, thank you. I know Jacob's probably not the most popular kid right now, and I think it's very brave of you to talk to me like this."

"It's not brave. If it was brave, I wouldn't do it. I'm not a brave person. It's more like, I like Jake. I mean, I don't know about the case and all that? But I used to like Jake, you know, like *before.* He was a good kid."

"Is. Is a good kid."

"Is. Right."

"Thanks."

"You know what, Mr. Barber? I bet you had like a really good father. Because, you

know, you're like a really good father, so I
bet you had a good father who kind of taught
you. Am I right?"

Jesus, didn't this kid read the papers?

"Not exactly," I said.

"Not exactly but close?"

"I didn't have a father."

"Stepfather?"

I shook my head.

"Everybody has a father, Mr. Barber.
Except, like, God or something."

"Not me, Sarah."

"Oh. Well, then, maybe that's kind of a
good thing. Just, like, take fathers totally
out of the equation."

"Maybe. I'm probably not the best guy
to ask."

The Yoos lived on one of the mazy, shady
streets behind the library, near the elementary school where all these kids first met.
The house was a tidy little center-entrance
colonial on a small lot, white with black shutters. A previous owner had built a brick
shelter around the front door, which stood
out on the white face of the building like a
red-lipsticked mouth. I remembered crowd-
ing into this little compartment when Lau-

rie and I used to visit during the winter months. That was back when Jacob and Derek were in grade school. Our families had been friendly then. Those were the days when the parents of Jacob's friends tended to become our friends too. We used to line up other families like puzzle pieces, father to father, mother to mother, kid to kid, to see if we had a match. The Yoos were not a perfect fit for us—Derek had a little sister named Abigail, three years younger than the boys—but the friendship between our families had been convenient for a while. That we saw them less now was not the result of a breakup. The kids had simply outgrown us. They socialized among themselves now, and there had not been enough left of the family friendship to cause either of the parent couples to seek out the other. Still, I felt we were friends, even now. I was naive.

It was Derek who answered the door when I rang. He froze. Just gawped at me with his big dumb syrupy brown eyes until I finally said, "Hi, Derek."

"Hey, Andy."

The Yoo kids had always called Laurie and me by our first names, a permissive practice I never quite got used to and which, under the current circumstances, grated all the more.

"Can I talk to you a minute?"

Again, Derek seemed unable to formulate any answer at all. He stared at me.

From the kitchen, Derek's dad, David Yoo, called, "Derek, who is it?"

"It's all right, Derek," I reassured him. His panic seemed almost comical. Why on earth was he so rattled? He had seen me a thousand times.

"Derek, who is it?"

I heard a chair scrape along the kitchen floor. David Yoo came out into the front hall and, with a hand placed lightly around the back of Derek's neck, he drew his son back away from the door. "Hi, Andy."

"Hi, David."

"Was there something we can do for you?"

"I just wanted to talk to Derek."

"Talk about what?"

"About the case. What happened. I'm trying to find out who really did it. Jacob is innocent, you know. I'm helping prepare for the trial."

David nodded in an understanding way.

His wife, Karen, now came out of the kitchen and greeted me briefly, and they all stood together in the doorway like a family portrait.

"Can I come in, David?"

"I don't think that's a good idea."

"Why not?"

"We're on the witness list, Andy. I don't think we're supposed to talk to anyone."

"That's ridiculous. This is America—you can talk to whoever you want."

"The prosecutor told us not to talk to anyone."

"Logiudice?"

"That's right. He said, don't talk to anyone."

"Well, he meant reporters. He didn't want you running around making conflicting statements. He's just thinking about the cross-examination. I'm trying to find the tru—"

"That's not what he said, Andy. He said, don't talk to anyone."

"Yes, but he can't say that. Nobody can tell you not to talk to anyone."

"I'm sorry."

"David, this is my *son.* You know Jacob. You've known him since he was a kid."

"I'm sorry."

"Well, can I at least come in and we'll talk about it?"

"No."

"No?"

"No."

We locked eyes.

"Andy," he said, "this is our family time. I really don't appreciate you being here."

He went to close the door. His wife stopped him, holding the edge of the door, imploring him with her eyes.

"Please don't come back here," David Yoo told me. He added, weakly, "Good luck."

He removed Karen's hand from the door and gently closed it and, I could hear, he slid the chain into the lock.

16 | Witness

I was greeted at the Magraths' apartment door by a dumpy, pie-faced woman with a frizz of unsprung black hair. She wore black spandex leggings and an oversized T-shirt with an equally oversized message stamped across the front: *Don't Give Me Attitude, I Have One of My Own.* This witticism ran six full lines, drawing my eyes southward over her person from wavering bosom to detumescent belly, a journey I regret even now.

I said, "Is Matthew here?"

"Who wants to know?"

"I represent Jacob Barber."

A blank look.

"The murder in Cold Spring Park."

"Ah. You his lawyer?"

"Father, actually."

"It's about time. I was beginning to think that kid was all alone in the world."

"How's that?"

"It's just we been waiting for someone to show up here. It's been weeks. Where's the cops already?"

"Can I just—is Matthew Magrath here? That's your son, I assume?"

"You sure you're not a cop?"

"Pretty sure, yeah."

"Probation officer?"

"No."

She put a hand on her hip, tucking it under the little skirt of fat that circled her waist.

"I'd like to ask him about Leonard Patz."

"I know."

The woman's behavior was so strange—not just her cryptic answers but the oddball way she looked up at me—that I was slow to grasp what she was saying about Patz.

"Is Matt here?" I repeated, anxious to be rid of her.

"Yeah." She swung the door open. "Matt! There's someone here to see you."

She shuffled back into the apartment as if she had lost interest in the whole thing. The apartment was small and cluttered. Posh a suburb as Newton is, there are still corners that working people can afford. The Magraths lived in a small two-bedroom apartment in a white vinyl-sided house sub-divided into four units. It was early evening, and the light inside was dim. A Red Sox game played on an enormous, ancient rear-projection TV. Facing the TV was a mottled, mustard-colored plush armchair, into which Mrs. Magrath dropped herself.

"You like baseball?" she said over her shoulder. "'Cuz I do."

"Sure."

"You know who they're playing?"

"No."

"I thought you said you liked baseball."

"I've had some other things on my mind."

"It's the Blue Jays."

"Ah. The Blue Jays. How could I forget?"

"Matt!" she blasted. Then, to me: "He's in there with his girlfriend doing God knows what. Kristin, that's the girlfriend. Kid hasn't said two words to me all the times she's been over here. Treats me like I'm a piece of shit. Just wants to go running off with Matt like I don't even exist. Matt too. He only wants to be with Kristin. They got no time for me, the both of them."

I nodded. "Oh."

"How'd you get our name? I thought sex victims are supposed to be confidential."

"I used to be with the DA's office."

"Oh yeah, that's right, I knew that. You're the one. I read about you in the papers. So you seen the whole file?"

"Yeah."

"So you know about this guy Leonard Patz? What he did to Matt?"

"Yeah. Sounds like he groped him in the library."

"He groped him in the balls."

"Well, the—okay, there too."

"Matt!"

"If this is a bad time . . ."

"No. You're lucky he's here. Usually he goes off with the girlfriend and I don't even see him. His curfew's eight-thirty but he doesn't care. He just goes off. His probation officer knows all about it. I guess I can tell you that, can't I, he's got a probation officer? I don't know what to do with him. I don't know what to tell anyone anymore, you know? DYS had him for a while, then they sent him back. I moved here from Quincy so he wouldn't be around his friends, who were no good. So I came here 'cuz I thought it would help him, you know? You ever try to find a section-eight apartment in this town? *Pfft.* Me, I don't care where *I* live. It doesn't matter to me. So you know what? You know what he says to me now? After I do all this for him? He says, 'Oh, you've changed, Ma. Now you moved to Newton, you think you're fancy. You wear your fancy glasses, your fancy clothes, you think you're like these Newton people.' You know why I wear these glasses?" She picked up a pair of glasses from a table beside the armrest. "'Cuz I can't see! Only now he's got me so crazy I don't even wear them in my own house. I wore these same glasses in Quincy and he didn't say a thing. It's like, no matter what I do for him, it's never enough."

"It's not easy being a mother," I ventured.

"Oh, well, he says he doesn't want me to be his mother anymore. He says that all the time. You know why? I think it's because

I'm overweight, it's because I'm not attractive. I don't have a skinny body like Kristin
and I don't go to the gym and I don't have
nice hair. I can't help it! This is what I am!
I'm still his mother! You know what he calls
me when he gets mad? He calls me a fat
shit. Imagine saying something like that to
your mother, calling her a fat shit. I do everything for this kid, everything. Does he
ever thank me? Does he ever say, 'Oh, I
love you, Ma, thank you'? No. He just tells
me, 'I need money.' He asks me for money
and I tell him, 'I don't have any money to
give you, Matty.' And he says, 'Come on,
Ma, not even a couple a bucks?' And I tell
him I need that money to buy him all these
things he likes, like this Celtics jacket he
had to have, for a hundred fifty bucks, and
like a fool I go and buy it for him, just to
make him happy."

The bedroom door opened and Matt
Magrath came out, barefoot, wearing only
Adidas gym shorts and a T-shirt. "Ma, give
it a rest, would you? You're freaking the
guy out."

The police reports in Leonard Patz's
indecent A&B case described the victim
as fourteen years old, but Matt Magrath

seemed a few years older than that. He was handsome, square-jawed, with a slouchy, wised-up manner.

The girlfriend, Kristin, followed him out of the bedroom door. She was not as pretty as Matt. She had a thin face, small mouth, freckles, flat chest. She wore a wide-necked shirt that hung off one side, exposing a milky shoulder and a vampy lavender bra strap. I knew instantly that this boy did not care about her. He would break her heart, probably very soon. I felt sorry for her before she even got all the way out of the bedroom door. She looked about thirteen or fourteen. How many men would break her heart before she was through?

"*You're* Matthew Magrath?"

"Yeah. Why? Who are you?"

"How old are you, Matthew? What's your birth date?"

"August 17, 1992."

I was distracted momentarily by the thought of it: 1992. How recent it sounded, how far along in my life I was already. In 1992 I had already been a lawyer for eight years. Laurie and I were trying to conceive Jacob, in both senses.

"You're not even fifteen years old yet."

"So?"

"So nothing." I glanced at Kristin, who was watching me with a lidded expression like a proper bad girl. "I came to ask you about Leonard Patz."

"Len? What do you want to know?"

"'Len'? Is that what you call him?"

"Sometimes. Who are you again?"

"I'm Jacob Barber's father. The boy who's accused in the Cold Spring Park murder."

"Yeah." He nodded. "I figured you were something like that. I figured you might be a cop or something. The way you were looking at me. Like I done something wrong."

"Do *you* think you've done something wrong, Matt?"

"No."

"Then you've got nothing to worry about, do you? Doesn't matter if I'm a cop or not."

"What about her?" He inclined his head toward the girl.

"What about her?"

"Isn't it a crime if you have sex with a kid and she's, like, too young—so it's like, what do they call it?"

"Statutory rape."

"Right. Only it doesn't count if I'm too young too, does it? Like, if *two* kids have sex, you know, with each other, and they're *both* under the age and they're boning each other—"

His mother gasped, "Matt!"

"The age of consent in Massachusetts is sixteen. If two fourteen-year-olds have sex, they're both committing rape."

"You mean they're raping each other?"

"Technically, yes."

He gave Kristin a conspiratorial look. "How old are you, girl?"

"Sixteen," she said.

"My lucky day."

"I wouldn't go that far, son. The day's not over yet."

"You know what? I don't think I better talk to you, about Len or anything else."

"Matt, I'm not a cop. I don't care how old your girlfriend is, I don't care what you do. I'm only concerned with Leonard Patz."

"You're that kid's father?" Touch of a Boston accent: *fatha.*

"Yeah."

"Your kid didn't do it, you know."

I waited. My heart began to pound.

"Len did."

"How do you know that, Matt?"

"I just know."

"You know *how*? I thought you were the victim in an indecent A&B. I didn't think you knew . . . Len."

"Well, it's complicated."

"Is it?"

"Yeah. Lenny and me are friends, kind of."

"He's the kind of friend you report to the cops for indecent A&B?"

"I'll be honest with you. What I reported him for? Lenny never did that."

"No? So why'd you report him?"

A little grin. "Like I said, it's complicated."

"Did he grab you or not?"

"Yeah, he did."

"So what's complicated?"

"Hey, you know what? I'm not really comfortable with this. I don't think I should be talking to you. I have a right to remain silent. I think I'll go ahead and take that, a'ight?"

"You have a right to remain silent with the cops. I'm not a cop. The Fifth Amendment doesn't apply to me. In this room right now, there is no Fifth Amendment."

"I could get in trouble."

"Matt—son. Listen to me. I'm a very

patient man. But you're beginning to try my patience. I'm starting to feel"—deep breath—"angry, Matt, okay? That's not something I like to feel. So let's stop playing games here, all right?"

I felt the enormity of the body that houses me. How much bigger I was than this kid. I had the sense I was expanding, I was becoming too big for the room to hold me.

"If you know something about that murder in Cold Spring Park, Matt, you're going to give it to me. Because, son, you have no idea what I've been through."

"I don't want to talk in front of them."

"Fine."

I clamped my fist around the kid's right upper arm and twisted it—but not twisting it anywhere near the limits of my strength at that moment, because I felt how easily I could separate that arm from his body with just a little torque, how I could tear it off him, skin, muscle, and bone—and I led him into his mother's bedroom, which was furnished, memorably, with a night table comprised of two Hood milk crates stacked and turned upside down and a collage of photos of male movie stars carefully cut out of magazines and Scotch-taped to the wall. I closed the door and stood in front of it, arms crossed. As quickly as it had formed, the adrenaline was already receding from my arms and shoulders, as if my body sensed the crisis had passed its peak, the kid had already folded.

"Tell me about Leonard. How do you know him?"

"Leonard came up to me once at McDonald's, like all greasy and pathetic, and he asked me if I wanted anything, like a burger or anything. He said he'd buy me whatever I wanted if I'd just eat it with him, like just sit at the table with him. I knew he was a fag, but if he wanted to buy me a Big Mac, what did I care? I know *I'm* not gay, so what does it matter to me? So I said okay, and we're eating and he's trying to be all beast, like he's this cool dude, like he's my buddy, and he asks me if I want to come see his apartment. He says he's got a bunch of DVDs there and we can watch a movie or whatever. So I knew what he was after. So I told him straight up I wasn't going to do anything with him, but if he had some money maybe we could work something out. So he says he'll give me fifty bucks if he can, like, touch my package or whatever, like over my pants. I told him he could do it if he gave me a hundred bucks. So he did."

"He gave you a hundred bucks?"

"Yeah. Just, like, to touch my ass and stuff." The kid snorted at the price he had extorted for such a small thing.

"Go on."

"So after that he kept saying he wanted to keep doing it. So he'd give me a hundred bucks every time."

"And what did you do for him?"

"Nothing. I swear."

"Come on, Matt. A hundred bucks?"

"Really. Alls I ever did was let him touch my ass and, like . . . my front."

"Did you take anything off?"

"No. My clothes were on the whole time."

"Every time?"

"Every time."

"How many times were there?"

"Five."

"Five hundred bucks?"

"That's right." The kid sniggered again. Easy money.

"Did he reach inside your pants?"

Hesitation. "Once."

"Once?"

"Really. *Once.*"

"How long did this go on?"

"A few weeks. He said it was all he could afford."

"So what happened at the library?"

"Nothing. I've never even been to the library. I don't even know where it is."

"So why'd you report him?"

"He said he didn't want to pay me anymore. He said he didn't like paying, he shouldn't have to pay if we were, like, friends. I told him if he didn't pay me, I'd report him. I knew he was on probation, I knew he was on the sex offender list. If he got violated on his probation, he was going away. Even he knew that."

"And he wouldn't pay?"

"He paid some. He comes to me all like, 'I'll pay you half.' So I told him, 'You'll pay me *all.*' He had it. He's got lots of it. Anyway, it wasn't like I *wanted* to. But I need *money,* you know? I mean, look at this place. You know what it's like to have no money? It's like you can't *do* anything."

"So you were shaking him down for money. So what? What's this got to do with Cold Spring Park?"

"That was his whole reason, like, for dropping me. He said there was this other kid he liked, some kid who walked through the park in the morning near his apartment."

"What kid?"

"The one who got killed."

"How do you know it's the same kid?"

"'Cuz Leonard said he was going to try and meet him. He was, like, scouting him out. Like, walking through the park in the morning trying to meet him. He even knew the kid's name. He heard his friends say it. It was Ben. He said he was going to try to talk to him. This was all before it happened he's saying these things. I didn't even think anything about it until the kid got killed."

"What did Leonard say about him?"

"He said he was beautiful. That was the word he used, *beautiful.*"

"What makes you think he could be violent? Did he ever threaten you?"

"No. Are you kidding? I'd fuck him up. That's just it. Lenny's kind of a pussy. That's why he likes kids, I think, because he's a big guy but he figures kids are smaller."

"So why would he be violent with Ben Rifkin if he met him in the park?"

"I don't know. I wasn't there. But I know Lenny had a knife and he took it with him when he thought he might be meeting people, because he said sometimes, you know, if you're like a fag and you go up to the wrong guy, it can be bad."

"You saw the knife?"

"Yeah, he had it with him the day I met him."

"What did it look like?"

"Just, I don't know, it was a knife."

"Like a kitchen knife?"

"No, more like a fighting knife, I guess. It had, like, teeth. I almost took it from him. It was pretty cool."

"Why didn't you ever tell anyone about this? You knew that kid got murdered."

"I'm on probation too. I couldn't really tell anyone I was, like, getting money out of him or, like, that I lied about him grabbing me in the library. That's like a crime."

"Stop saying 'like.' It's not *like* a crime. It *is* a crime."

"Right. Exactly."

"Matt, how long were you going to go before you told anyone this? Were you going to let my son get convicted of a murder he didn't commit just so you wouldn't have to be embarrassed you were letting some guy grab your nuts every week? Were you going to just keep your mouth shut while they sent my son off to Walpole?"

The kid did not answer.

The anger I felt was of an old, familiar kind now. A simple, righteous, soothing anger I knew like an old friend. I was not angry at this smart-ass punk. Life tends to punish fools like Matt Magrath anyway, sooner or later. No, I was angry at Patz himself, because he was a murderer—and the worst kind of murderer, a child murderer, a category for which cops and prosecutors reserve a special contempt.

"I figured no one would believe me. 'Cuz my whole problem was, like, I couldn't tell about the kid that got killed because I already lied about the thing in the library. So if I told the truth, they were just going to say, 'Well, you already lied once. Why should we believe you now?' So what would be the point?"

He was right, of course. Matt Magrath

was about as bad a witness as you could dream up. An admitted liar, no jury would ever trust him. The only trouble was, like the boy who cried wolf, he happened to be telling the truth this time.

17 | Nothing's Wrong with Me!

Facebook froze Jacob's account, probably because of a subpoena compelling the production of everything he had ever posted. But with suicidal persistence, he opened a new Facebook account under the name "Marvin Glasscock" and began friending his inner circle again. He made no secret of this, and I roared about it. To my surprise, Laurie took Jacob's side. "He's all alone," she said. "He needs *people.*" Everything Laurie did—everything she ever did—was to help her son. She insisted that Jacob was completely isolated now and his "online life" was such a necessary, integral, "natural" part of how kids socialize that it would be cruel to deny him even this minimal human contact. I reminded her that the Commonwealth of Massachusetts intended to deprive him of a hell of a lot more than that, and we agreed at least to place some limits on the new account. Jacob was not to change the password, which would deny us access and the ability to edit him; he was not to post anything that touched on the case even remotely; and he was strictly forbidden to post photos or video, which were impossible to keep from squirting around the Internet once they got loose and which could easily be misconstrued. Thus began a cat-and-mouse game in which an otherwise intelligent child endeavored to make jokes about his own situation in terms just vague enough that his father would not censor what he wrote.

I made it a part of my morning rounds on the Internet to check what Marvin Glasscock had written on Facebook the night before. Every morning: first stop Gmail, second Facebook. Then Google "Jacob Barber" for news of the case. Then, if all was clear, I would disappear down the rabbit hole of the Internet for a few minutes to forget the raging shit-storm I was standing in.

What I found most amazing about my son's reincarnation on Facebook was that anyone was willing to "friend" him at all. In the real world, he had no friends. He was now utterly alone. No one ever called him or visited. He had been suspended from school and, come September, the town would be obliged to hire a tutor for him. The law required it. Laurie had been negotiating with the school department for weeks, haggling over how much in-home tutoring Jake was entitled to. In the meantime, he seemed to be utterly friendless. The same kids who were willing to link to Jacob online refused to acknowledge him in person. Granted, there were only a handful who accepted "Marvin Glasscock" into their online circle. Before the Rifkin murder, Jacob's Facebook network—the number of kids who read Jacob's dashed-off comments and whose comments Jacob followed in turn—numbered 474, mostly classmates, mostly kids I had never heard of. After the murder, he had only four, one of whom was Derek Yoo. I wonder if those four, or Jacob, ever quite understood that their every move online created a record, every keyboard click was recorded and stored on a server somewhere. Nothing they did on the Web—nothing—was private. And unlike a phone call, this was a written form of communication: they were generating a transcript of every conversation. The Web is a prosecutor's fantasy, a monitoring and recording device that hears the most intimate, lurid secrets, even those never spoken out loud. It is better than a wire. It is a wire planted inside everyone's head.

It was a matter of time, of course. Sooner or later, typing into his laptop late one night in the stoned-out bliss of Web surfing, Jacob would make a dumb-shit teenage slipup. It finally came in mid-August. Early on a Sunday morning I glanced at Marvin Glasscock's Facebook page to find an image of Anthony Perkins in *Psycho,* the famous silhouetted figure with a knife raised over his shoulder to stab Janet Leigh in the shower, now with Jacob's face Photoshopped onto it—Jacob as Norman Bates. The face was clipped from a snapshot of Jacob, apparently at a party. It showed Jacob grinning. Jacob had posted the mash-up photo with the caption "What people think of me." His friends responded with these comments: "Dude looks like a lady." "Awesome job. You should make this your new profile pic." "Wee-wee-wee [*Psycho* music]." "Marvin Glasscock! Dude comes in with the total facemelter!!!"

I did not immediately delete the photo. I wanted to confront Jacob with it. I carried the laptop upstairs with me, the machine humming in my hand.

He was in his room, still asleep. One of his young-adult novels lay open, pages down, on the night table. These were invariably futuristic science fiction or military fantasies about ultrasecret Army units with names like "Alpha Force." (No broody teen vampires for Jacob: not escapist *enough.*)

It was around seven. The shades were down, the light in the room was muted.

As I tromped barefoot to the side of his bed, Jacob woke up and twisted to look at me. No doubt I was scowling. I turned the computer around to show the screen to him, the evidence of his crime.

"What is this?"

He groaned, not quite awake.

"What is this?"

"What?"

"This!"

"I don't know. What are you talking about?"

"This picture on Facebook. From last night? Did you put this up?"

"It's a joke."

"A joke?"

"It's just a joke, Dad."

"A joke? What's wrong with you?"

"Do we have to make a big deal—"

"Jacob, do you know what they're going to do with this picture? They're going to wave it around in front of the jury and do you know what they're going to say? They're going to say it shows consciousness of guilt. That's just the phrase they'll use, *consciousness of guilt.* They'll say, 'This is how Jacob Barber sees himself. Psycho. When he looks in the mirror, this is the reflection he sees: Norman Bates.' They'll use the word *psycho* over and over, and they'll hold this picture up and the jury will stare at it. They'll stare at it and guess what? They'll never be able to forget it, they'll never be able to quite get it out of their minds. It'll stick in their heads. It'll affect them. It'll twist them, it'll stain them. Maybe not all of them, maybe not much. But it will move the needle just a little further against you. That's how it works. That's what you did with this: you gave them a gift. A gift. For no good reason. If Logiudice finds this, it will never go away. Don't you get that? Don't you know what's at stake, Jacob?"

"Yes!"

"Do you know what they want to do to you?"

"Of course I do."

"Then why? Tell me. Because it doesn't make any sense. Why would you do this?"

"I already told you, it was a joke. It means the opposite of what you're saying. It's how other people see me. It's not how I see myself. It's not even about me."

"Oh. Well, that's perfectly reasonable. You were just being clever and ironic. And of course the DA and the jury, they'll all understand that too. Jesus. Are you stupid?"

"I'm not stupid."

"Then what's wrong with you?"

Laurie's voice, behind me: "Andy! Enough." Her arms were crossed, eyes still sleepy.

Jacob said mournfully, "Nothing's wrong with me."

"Then what possessed you to—"

"Andy, stop."

"Why, Jacob? Just tell me why?" My anger had peaked. Still, I was feeling wild enough to spray a few bullets Laurie's way too. "Can I ask him that? Can I ask him why? Or is that too much?"

"It was just a joke, Dad. Can we just delete it?"

"No! We can't just delete it. That's the whole point! It doesn't go away, Jacob. We can delete it but it doesn't go away. When your buddy Derek goes to the DA and tells him you have a Facebook account named Melvin Glasscock or whatever and you put this picture up, all the DA has to do is send them a subpoena and he gets it. Facebook will just give it to him, all of it. This stuff sticks to you. It's like napalm. You can't do this. You can't do it."

"Okay."

"You can't do stuff like this. Not now."

"O-*kay,* I said. Sorry."

"Don't be sorry. Sorry won't fix the problem."

"Andy, stop already. You're scaring me. What do you want him to do? It's done. He said he's sorry. What do you keep haranguing him for?"

"I keep haranguing him because it's important!"

"It's done. He made a mistake. He's a kid. Please calm down, Andy. Please."

She came across the room, took the laptop from my hands—I was barely aware I was still holding it—and she examined the photo closely. She held the laptop with one hand on each edge, like a cafeteria tray.

"All right." She shrugged. "So let's just delete it and be done with it. How do I delete it? I don't see a button."

I took the laptop and searched the screen. "I don't see it either. Jacob, how do you delete this thing?"

He took the laptop and, now seated on the edge of his bed, he clicked it a few times. "There. Gone." He closed the lid, handed it to me, then lay down and rolled over, turning his back to me.

Laurie gave me a look, like *I* was the crazy one. "I'm going back to bed, Andy." She padded out of the room, then I heard our bed rustle as she climbed back into it. Laurie had always been an early riser, even on Sundays, until this happened to us.

I stood there a moment, the laptop by my side now, held at my hip like a closed book.

"I'm sorry I yelled."

Jacob sniffed. I could not tell what that sniff signaled, whether he was near tears or angry with me. But it struck something in me and made me sentimental. I remembered Baby Jake, our little precious beautiful blond wide-eyed baby. That this boy, this child-man, was one and the same person as that baby—it came to me like a new idea, something I had never known. The baby did not become the boy; the baby *was* the boy, the same creature, unchanged at the core. This was the very baby I had held in my arms.

I sat down on the bed beside him and laid my hand on his bare shoulder. "I'm sorry I yelled. I shouldn't lose my temper. I'm just trying to look out for you. You know that, don't you?"

"I'm going back to sleep."

"Okay."

"Just leave me alone."

"Okay."

"Okay, so go away."

I nodded, rubbed his shoulder a few times as if I could press the thought into him through his skin, *I love you,* but he lay there like a stone and I stood up to leave.

The shape in the bed said, "There's nothing wrong with me. And I know exactly what they're going to do to me. I don't need you to tell me."

"I know, Jake. I know."

And then, with the bravado and heedlessness of a child, he fell asleep.

18 | The Murder Gene, Redux

One Tuesday morning near summer's end, Laurie and I sat in Dr. Vogel's office for our weekly meeting under the eyes of those howling African masks. The session had not begun—we were still settling ourselves in our familiar chairs, making ritualistic comments about the warm weather outside, Laurie shivering a little in the air-conditioning—when the doctor announced, "Andy, I have to tell you, I think this is going to be a difficult hour for you."

"Yeah? Why is that?"

"We need to talk about some of the biological issues involved in this case, the genetics." She hesitated. Dr. Vogel studiously maintained an impassive expression during our sessions, presumably to keep her own emotions from influencing ours. But this time her mouth and jaw clenched visibly. "And I need to take a DNA sample from you. It's just a quick swab of your mouth. No needles, nothing intrusive. I just use a sterile Q-tip to wipe your gums and take a sample of your saliva."

"A DNA sample? You've got to be kidding me. I thought we were going to exclude all that."

"Andy, look, I'm a doctor, not a lawyer; I can't tell you what's going to be allowed into evidence or what will be excluded. That's between you and Jonathan. What I can tell you is that behavioral genetics— and by that I mean the science of how behavior is influenced by our genes—cuts two ways. The prosecution may want to introduce this sort of evidence to show that Jacob is violent by nature, a born killer, because obviously it makes it more likely that Jacob committed this murder. But we may want to introduce it too. If it gets to the point where the DA has likely proven Jacob actually killed this boy—I'm saying *if;* I'm not predicting, I'm not saying this is what I believe, just *if*—then we may want to bring in the genetic evidence as mitigation."

Laurie said, "Mitigation?"

I explained, "To reduce it from first-degree homicide to second or manslaughter."

Laurie winced. The technical terms were discouraging, a reminder of how efficiently the system worked. A courthouse is a factory, sorting violence into a taxonomy of crimes, processing suspects into criminals.

I was discouraged too. The lawyer in me knew, instantly, the calculation Jonathan was making. Like a general preparing for battle, he was planning his fallback positions, a controlled tactical retreat.

I told my son's mother in a gentle tone, "First-degree is life without parole. It's a mandatory sentence. The judge has no discretion. With second-degree Jake would be parole-eligible in twenty years. He'd only be thirty-four. He'd still have a whole life ahead of him."

"Jonathan has asked me to research the issue, to prepare for it, just in case. Laurie, I think the point, the easiest way to think of it, is this: the law punishes intentional crimes. It presumes every act is intentional, a product of free will. If you did it, it is assumed you meant to do it. The law is very unforgiving of 'yes but' defenses. *Yes, but I had a hard childhood. Yes, but I have a mental disease. Yes, but I was drunk. Yes, but I was carried away by anger.* If you commit a crime, the law will say you are guilty despite these things. But it *will* take them into account when it comes to the precise definition of the crime and when it comes to the sentence. At that point, anything that affects your free will— including a genetic predisposition to violence or low impulse control—at least theoretically can be taken into account."

"It's ridiculous," I scoffed. "No jury would ever buy it. You're going to tell them, 'I killed a fourteen-year-old boy but let me go anyway'? Forget it. Not gonna happen."

"We may not have a choice, Andy, *if.*"

"This is bullshit," I told Dr. Vogel. "You're gonna take a sample of *my* DNA? I've never hurt a fly."

The doctor nodded. No reaction. A perfect shrink, she just sat there and let the words break over her like waves on a jetty because that was the way to keep me talking. Somewhere she had learned that if an interviewer remains silent, the interviewee will rush to fill the silence.

"I've never hurt anyone. I don't have a temper. That's just not me. I never even played football. My mother never let me. She knew I wouldn't like it. She knew. There was no violence in our house. When I was a kid, do you know what I played? I played the clarinet. While all my friends were playing football, I played the clarinet."

Laurie slid her hand over mine to smother my growing agitation. These sorts of gestures between us were becoming more rare, and I was moved by it. It calmed me.

Dr. Vogel said, "Andy, I know you have a lot invested in this. In your identity, your reputation, in the man you've become, the man you've made yourself. We've talked about that, and I understand perfectly. But that's exactly the point. We are not just a product of our genes. We are all a product of many, many things: genes and environment, nature and nurture. The fact that you are who you are is the best example I know of the power of free will, of the individual. No matter what we find encoded in your genes, it will say nothing about who you are. Human behavior is much more complex than that. The same genetic sequence in one individual may produce a completely different result in different individuals and different environments. What we're talking about here is just a genetic predisposition. Predisposition is not predestination. We humans are much, much more than our DNA. The mistake people tend to make with a new science like this one is overdeterminism. We've discussed this before. We are not talking about the genes that code for blue eyes here. Human behavior has many, many more causes than simple physical traits."

"That's a lovely speech—and yet you still want to stick a Q-tip in my mouth. What if I don't want to know what's in my DNA? What if I don't like what I'm programmed for?"

"Andy, as hard as this is for you, it's not about you. It's about Jacob. The question is, how far will you go for Jacob? What will you do to protect your son?"

"That's not fair."

"It's the way it is. I didn't put you here."

"No. Jonathan did. He's the one who should be telling me these things, not you."

"Probably he doesn't want to fight with

you about it. He doesn't even know if he'll use it at trial. It's just something he wants to keep in his pocket, just in case. Also, he might think you'd say no to him."

"He's right. That's why he ought to be having this conversation himself."

"He's just doing his job. You of all people should understand that."

"His job is to do what his client wants."

"His job is to win, Andy, not to spare anyone's feelings. Anyway, you're not the client; Jacob is. The only thing that matters here is Jacob. That's why we're all here, to help Jacob."

"So Jonathan wants to argue in court that Jacob *does* have the murder gene?"

"If it comes down to it, if we get desperate, yes, we may have to argue that Jacob has certain specific gene variants that make him more likely to act in aggressive or antisocial ways."

"All those qualifications and nuances, to ordinary people it's mumbo jumbo. The newspapers will call it a murder gene. They'll say we're natural-born killers. Our whole family."

"All we can do is tell them the truth. If

they want to distort it, sensationalize it, what can we do?"

"Okay, say I go for it, I let you take your DNA sample. Tell me exactly what it is you're looking for."

"Do you know anything about biology?"

"Only what I got in high school."

"Were you any good in high school biology?"

"I was better at clarinet."

"Okay, in a nutshell? Bearing in mind that the causes of human behavior are infinitely complex and there is no simple genetic trigger for particular human behaviors; we are always talking about a gene-environment interaction; and anyway 'criminal' behavior is not a scientific term, it's a legal one, and certain behaviors that may be defined as criminal in one situation may not be criminal in another, like war—"

"Okay, okay, I get it. It's complicated. Dumb it down for me. Just tell me: what are you looking for in my spit?"

She smiled, relenting. "Okay. There are two specific gene variants that have been linked to male antisocial behavior, which might help account for multigenerational patterns of violence in families like yours. The first is an allele of a gene called MAOA. The MAOA gene is located on the X chromosome. It controls an enzyme that metabolizes certain neurotransmitters like serotonin, norepinephrine, and dopamine. It's been called 'the warrior gene' because of its association with aggressive behavior. The mutation is called *MAOA Knockout.* It has been argued in court as a trigger for violence before, but the argument was too simplistic and it was rejected. Our understanding of the gene-environment interplay has improved since then—the science is getting better and very quickly—and we may have better testimony now.

"The second mutation is located in what's called the serotonin transporter gene. The official name for the gene is SLC6A4. It's located on chromosome 17. It encodes a protein that facilitates the activity of the serotonin transporter system, which is what enables the re-uptake of serotonin from the synapse back into the neuron."

I held up my hand: *enough.*

She said, "The point is, the science is good and it's getting better every day. Just imagine: up till now, we've always asked,

What causes human behavior? Is it nature or nurture? And we've been very good at studying the nurture side of the equation. There's lots and lots of good studies on how environment affects behavior. But now, for the first time in human history, we can look at the nature side. This is cutting-edge stuff. The structure of DNA was only discovered in 1953. We're just beginning to understand. We're just beginning to look at what we are. Not as some abstraction like the 'soul' or metaphor like the 'human heart,' but the real mechanics of human beings, the nuts and bolts. This"—she pinched the skin of her own arm and pulled up a sample of her own flesh—"the human body is a machine. It is a system, a very complex system made of molecules and driven by chemical reactions and electrical impulses. Our minds are part of that system. People have no trouble accepting that nurture affects behavior. Why not nature?"

"Doctor, will this keep my kid out of prison?"

"It might."

"Then do it."

"There's more."

"Why does this not surprise me?"

"I need a swab from your father too."

"My father? You're joking. I haven't spoken to my father since I was five years old. I have no idea if he's even alive."

"He is alive. He's in Northern Prison in Somers, Connecticut."

A beat. "So go test him."

"I tried. He won't see me."

I blinked at her. I was wrong-footed both by the news my father was alive and by the fact that she had already got a message from him. She had an advantage over me. Not only did she know my history, she did not consider it history at all. It was no burden to her. To Dr. Vogel, trying to contact Billy Barber was no harder than picking up the phone.

"He says you have to ask."

"Me? He wouldn't know me if I stood up in his soup."

"Apparently he wants to change that."

"He does? Why?"

"A father gets old, he wants to know his son a little." She shrugged. "Who can understand the human heart?"

"So he knows about me?"

"Oh, he knows all about you."

I felt myself flush like a little kid with the

thrill of it: a father! Then, just as quickly, my mood plummeted, the thought of Bloody Billy Barber turned to acid.

"Tell him to fuck off."

"I can't tell him that. We need his help. We need a sample to argue that a genetic mutation is more than a one-off but a family trait passed down from father to son to son."

"We could get a court order."

"Not without giving away to the DA what we're up to."

I shook my head.

Laurie finally spoke. "Andy, you need to think about Jacob. How far would you go for him?"

"I'd go to hell and back."

"Okay, then. So you will."

19 | The Cutting Room

In the last week of August—that non-week, the week of Sundays when we all move a little slower and mourn the passing of summer and get ourselves ready for fall—the temperatures climbed and the air thickened until the heat was all anyone could talk about: when it would break, how high it would go, how unbearable the humidity was. It drove people indoors, as if it was winter. The sidewalks and shops were oddly quiet. To me the heat was not an affliction, it was merely a symptom, as a fever is a symptom of the flu. It was only the most obvious reason the world was fast becoming unbearable.

We were all a little heat-crazy by then, Laurie and Jacob and I. Looking back on it, it is hard to believe how self-absorbed I had become, how this whole story seemed to be about *me,* not Jacob, not our entire family. Jacob's guilt and mine were entangled in my mind, though no one had ever accused me of anything explicitly. I was coming apart, of course. I knew this. I distinctly remember exhorting myself to hold it together, to keep up appearances, not to crack.

But I did not share my feelings with Laurie, and I did not try to draw out hers either, because we were all coming apart. I discouraged any sort of frank emotional talk, and soon enough I stopped noticing my wife altogether. I never asked—never even asked!—what the experience was like for the mother of Jacob the murderer. I thought it was more important to be—at least to seem—a tower of strength and to encourage her to be strong as well. It was the only sensible approach: tough it out, get through the trial, do whatever it takes to keep Jacob safe, then repair the emotional damage later. After. It was as if there was a place called After, and if I could just push my family across to that shore, then everything would be all right. There would be time for all these "soft" problems in the land of After. I was wrong. I think about that now, how I should have seen Laurie then, should have paid more attention. She had saved my life, once. I came to her damaged and she had loved me anyway. And when she was damaged, I did not lift a finger to help her. I only noticed that her hair was getting grayer and sloppier, and her face was becoming crazed with lines like an old ceramic vase. She had lost so much weight that her hip bones protruded, and when we were together she spoke less and less. In spite of it all, I never softened in my determination to save Jacob first and heal Laurie later. I try to rationalize that merciless intransigence now: I was by then a master of internalizing dangerous emotions; my mind was overheated with the stress of that endless summer. It is all true and it is all bullshit too. The truth is, I was a fool. Laurie, I was a fool. I know that now.

I went to the Yoos' home around ten o'clock one morning. Derek's parents both worked, even during this pseudo-vacation week. I knew Derek would be home alone. He and Jacob were still texting regularly. They even spoke on the phone, though only during the day, when Derek's parents were not around to hear. I was convinced Derek would want to help his friend, he would want to talk to me, tell me the truth, but I was afraid he would not let me in anyway. He was a good kid. He would do as he had been told, as he always did, always had done. So I was prepared to talk my way into the house, even to force my way in to get to him. I remember feeling quite capable of that. I came to the house wearing baggy cargo shorts and a T-shirt that stuck to my sweaty back. I had gained some weight since this all began, and I recall that the shorts shimmied down my hips over and over, weighted down by my gut. I had to hike them up constantly. I had always been fit and trim. My sloppy new body made me ashamed, but I felt no inclination to fix it. Again, there would be time *after.*

Arriving at the Yoos' home, I did not

knock. I did not want to give the kid a chance to hide from me, to see me and refuse to answer the door, pretend he was not there. Instead I went around to the back, past the little flower garden, past a hydrangea shooting white conical bunches of flowers in every direction like fireworks, a blossoming that David Yoo waited all year for, I remembered.

The Yoos had built an extension off the back of their house. It contained a mud-room and a breakfast room. The walls were windowed all around. From the back deck I could see in through the kitchen to the little sitting area where Derek sprawled on a couch in front of the TV. There was patio furniture on this deck, an umbrellaed table and six chairs. If Derek had refused to let me in, I might have thrown one of those heavy patio chairs through the French door, like William Hurt in *Body Heat.* But the door was unlocked. I walked right into the house as if I owned it, as if I had just run out to the garage to take out the trash.

Inside, the house was cool, air-conditioned.

Derek scrambled to his feet but he did not come toward me. He stood with his skinny calves against the couch, in gym shorts and a black T-shirt with the Zildjian logo across the chest. His bare feet were long and bony. His toes pressed down into the carpet, arching like little caterpillars. Nerves. When I first met Derek, he was five years old and still pudgy. Now he was another scrawny, gangly, slightly spaced-out teenage kid like my own. He was just like Jacob in every way but one: there was no cloud on Derek's future, nothing to obstruct him. He would move through adolescence with the same zonked-out expression as Jacob, same crap clothes, same shambling, no-eye-contact manner, and he would pass right on into adulthood. He was the blameless kid Jacob might have been, and I thought briefly how nice it would be to have such an uncomplicated kid. I envied David Yoo even as I considered him, at the moment, an asshole without peer.

"Hello, Derek."

"Hi."

"What's wrong, Derek?"

"You're not supposed to be here."

"I've been here a hundred times."

"Yeah, but you're not supposed to be here now."

"I just want to talk. About Jacob."

"I'm not supposed to."

"Derek, what's wrong with you? You're all . . . flustered."

"No."

"Are you afraid of me?"

"No."

"Then why are you acting like this?"

"Like what? I'm not doing anything."

"You look like you just shit a brick."

"No. It's just, you're not supposed to be here."

"Relax, Derek. Sit down. I just want to know the truth, that's all. What on earth is going on here? What's *really* going on? I just wish someone would tell me."

I moved through the kitchen into the TV room cautiously, as if I were approaching a skittish animal.

"I don't care what your parents said, Derek. Your parents are wrong. Jacob deserves your help. He's your friend. Your *friend.* I am too. I'm your friend and this is what friends do, Derek. They help each other. That's all I want, is for you to be Jacob's friend, right now. He needs you."

I sat down.

"What did you tell Logiudice? What could

you possibly have told him that would make him believe my son is a murderer?"

"I didn't say Jake is a murderer."

"What did you tell him, then?"

"Why don't you ask Logiudice? I thought he had to tell you?"

"He's supposed to, Derek, but he's playing games. He's not a good guy, Derek. I know it might be hard for you to understand that. He didn't put you in front of the grand jury because then he would have to provide me with a transcript. He probably did not have you talk to a detective either, because then the cop would have written a report. So I need *you* to tell me, Derek. I need you to do the right thing. Tell me what you said to Logiudice that made him so sure Jacob is guilty."

"I told him the truth."

"Oh, I know, Derek. Everyone tells the truth. It's so tiresome. Because it's never the same truth. So I need to know *exactly* what you said."

"I'm not supposed to—"

"Dammit, Derek! What did you say!"

He recoiled then plunked down on the couch, as if the shout had blasted him backward.

I calmed myself. I said in a soft voice just short of despair, "Please, Derek. Please tell me."

"I just told him, you know, some things that have been going on in school."

"Like what?"

"Like Jake was getting picked on. Ben Rifkin was, like, the leader of this group of kids. Like slacker kids. They were kind of giving Jake a hard time."

"About what?"

"Like saying he was gay, that was the main thing. Just, like, rumors. Ben just made stuff up. And, you know, I don't even care if Jake *is* gay. I really don't. I wish he'd just say it if he was."

"Do you think he's gay?"

"I don't know. Maybe. But it doesn't matter, because he didn't do any of the things Ben said he did. Ben just made it up. He just liked tooling on Jake for some reason. Like it was a game for him or something. He was kind of a bully."

"What did Ben say?"

"I don't know. Just, like, starting rumors. Like he said Jake offered to blow a kid at this party—which he didn't. Or that he got a boner in the shower after track one day.

Or that one of the teachers went back into school during recess one day and caught Jake jerking off in one of the classrooms. It was all totally not true."

"Why did he say it, then?"

"'Cause Ben was a dick. There was just something about Jake that Ben didn't like, and that kind of got him excited, you know? It was like he couldn't help himself. If he saw Jake, he gave him a rash of shit. Every time. I guess he figured he could get away with it too. He was just a dick. To be honest? Nobody likes to say it because he got killed and everything? But Ben was a mean kid. Whoever did this—well, I don't know, I don't want to say—whatever. Ben was just a mean kid."

"But why was he mean to *Jacob*? I don't get that."

"He just didn't like him. Jake is like—I mean, I know Jake, okay? And I like him. But come on. I mean, you have to know Jake isn't, like, a normal kid?"

"Why not? Because kids thought he was gay?"

"No."

"Then what does 'normal' mean?"

He gave me a searching look. "Jake has

a mean streak of his own." Derek held his eyes on me.

I tried not to betray any emotion. Tried to stop my Adam's apple from bobbing down and up.

Derek said, "I think maybe Ben didn't know that. Ben kind of picked the wrong little freak to pick on. He had no clue."

"So that's why you went on Facebook and told everyone about the knife?"

"No. It was more than that. I mean, it was like, the whole reason he got the knife was he was afraid of Ben. He thought Ben was going to go after him someday and try to mess him up, and then Jake was going to have to defend himself. You never knew about any of this?"

"No."

"Jacob never told you about *any* of this?"

"No."

"Well, I told because I knew Jake got the knife and I knew it was because he was afraid Ben was going to try something. Maybe I shouldn't have said anything. I don't know. I don't know why I told."

"You told because it was the truth. You wanted to tell the truth."

"I guess."

"But that knife wasn't the murder weapon. The knife you saw, that Jacob had? It's not the one that killed Ben. They found another knife in Cold Spring Park. You know that, right?"

"Yeah, but who knows? They found a knife. . . ." Shrug. "Anyway, it was like, at the time everybody was still talking about 'Where's the knife?' And Jake always used to say, like, 'My dad's a DA and I know about the law,' like he knew what he could get away with. Like, if anyone ever accused him? You know?"

"Did he ever say that?"

"No. Not exactly."

"So is that what you told Logiudice?"

"No! 'Course not. 'Cause, like, this isn't stuff I really *know*, you know? This is just, like, what I think."

"So what exactly did you tell Logiudice?"

"Just that Jacob had a knife."

"The wrong knife."

"Well, if that's what you want to say, whatever. I just told Logiudice about the knife and that Ben was kind of bullying him. And that the morning it happened, Jake came into school with blood on him."

"Which Jacob admits. He found Ben.

He tried to help him. That's how he got the blood on him."

"I know, I know, An—Mr. Barber. I'm not saying anything about Jake. I'm just telling you what I told the DA. Jake came into school and I saw blood on him, and he told me he had to clean it up because people wouldn't understand. And he was right: they didn't."

"Derek, can I ask you something? Do you really think it's possible? I mean, is there anything else you're not telling me? Because what I'm hearing, it still doesn't make sense that Jacob did this. It just doesn't add up."

Derek squirmed. His body corkscrewed away from me.

"You think he did it, don't you, Derek?"

"No. I mean, there's like a one percent chance, you know? Just, like, a little bit of"—he held up his fingers a millimeter apart—"I don't know."

"Doubt."

"Yeah."

"Why? Why would you have even a little bit of doubt? You've known Jacob most of your life. You've been best friends."

"Because Jake—he's just kind of a dif-

ferent kid. You know, I'm not saying anything, all right? But he's just kind of—I said
he had, like, a mean streak but that isn't
really it. I don't know how to say it. It's not
like he has a temper or he gets mad or
anything. He doesn't get *mad,* you know?
He just—he's kind of mean. Not to me,
'cause I'm his friend. But to other kids sometimes? He just says weird things. Like rac-
ist stuff, just jokes. Or he calls fat girls fat
or he says inappropriate stuff about them,
like about their bodies. And he reads these
stories on the Net? Kind of porn, but about
torture. He calls it 'cutter,' like 'cutter porn.'
He'll say, like, 'Dude, I was up so late reading cutter on the Net last night.' He showed
me some of the stories? Like, on his iPod?
And I'm like, 'Dude, this is sick.' You know,
it's like stories about . . . you know, cutting
people? Like tying women up and cutting them and killing them and stuff? And
tying up men and cutting stuff off and"—he
grimaced—"you know, castrating them?
It's totally sick. He still does it."

"What do you mean he still does it?"

"He reads it."

"That's not true. I've been checking the
computer. I put a program on it that tells

me what Jacob does and where he goes on the Internet."

"He uses his iPod. That iPod Touch?"

For a moment I was the stupid, out-of-touch parent.

Derek said helpfully, "He finds them on these forums on the Net. This site called the Cutting Room. People trade stories, I guess. They write them and post them for other people to read."

"Derek, kids look at porn. I know that. You're sure that's not just what we're talking about?"

"I'm totally, totally sure. This is *not* porn. Anyway, it's not even just that. I mean, he can read whatever he wants. It's none of my business. But he just has this thing where he kind of doesn't care."

"Doesn't care about what?"

"About people, about animals, about anything." He shook his head.

I sat silent, waiting.

"One time we were out, a group of us, and we were just kind of sitting on this wall, like hanging out. It was the middle of the afternoon. And this guy goes by on the sidewalk and he has these, kind of like, crutches? Like, you know those kind that go up over your arm and there's like a ring that goes over your arm? And he couldn't really control his legs. He just sort of dragged them like he was paralyzed or he had some disease or something. And this guy goes by, and Jake just starts laughing. I mean, not like quiet laughing but really loud, like crazy laughing, like 'HA HA HA.' He wouldn't stop. The guy must have heard him; he went right past us, right in front of us. And we're all just kind of looking at Jacob like, 'Dude, what's wrong with you?' And he's like, 'Are you guys all blind? Didn't you even see that guy? He's a total freak show!' It was just . . . mean. I mean, I know you're Jacob's dad and all, and I don't like to say this, but Jake can be just mean. I don't like being around him when he's like that. I get a little scared of him, to tell you the truth."

Derek made a sad little grimace, as if he was making a difficult admission to himself for the first time. His friend Jake had let him down. He went on in a less disgusted, more mournful tone.

"Once—this was like last fall, I guess?— Jake found this dog. Just, like, a little mutt. He was lost, I guess, but he wasn't a stray because he had a collar on. Jake had him on, like, a string? You know, instead of a leash?"

"Jacob never had a dog," I said.

Derek nodded at me with that same sad expression, as if it was his duty to explain this to Jacob's poor, clueless father. He seemed to know, finally, how oblivious parents can be, and it disappointed him.

"I saw him later and I asked him about the dog, and Jake was like, 'I had to bury it.' So I was like, 'You mean, it died?' And he wouldn't really answer. He was just like, 'Dude, I had to bury it.' I didn't see Jake for a while after that, 'cause I sort of knew, you know? Like I knew it was bad. And there were these posters. Like the family that owned the dog, they put up these posters all over the place, like stapled on phone poles and trees, you know? Like with pictures of this dog? And I never said anything about it, and finally the family stopped putting up the posters, and I just kind of tried to forget about it."

A moment passed in silence. When I was sure he had nothing more to add, I said, "Derek, if you knew all this, how could you and Jacob still be friends?"

"We're not friends like we used to be, like when we were kids. We're just kind of *old* friends, you know? It's different."

"Old friends but still friends?"

"I don't know. Sometimes I think it's like he was never my real friend, you know? He was just kind of this kid I knew from school. I don't think he ever, like, *cared* about me. Not that he didn't *like* me or anything. He just didn't care either way, most of the time."

"And the rest of the time?"

Derek shrugged. His answer was a bit of a non sequitur but I'll put it down here just as he said it. "I always figured he'd get into trouble someday. I just figured it would be when we were grown up."

We sat there awhile, Derek and I, not saying anything. We both understood, I think, that there was no going back, no un-saying the things he had just said.

I drove home slowly through the town center, savoring the ride. Maybe it is only an error of hindsight, but it seems to me now that I knew what was coming, I knew this was the end of something, and it was a tiny pleasure to prolong the car ride, to be "normal" awhile longer.

At home, I continued to move in that deliberate way, up the stairs to my son's room.

His iPod Touch was on the bureau, a sleek glassy little slab that came alive in my hand. The iPod was password-protected, but Jacob had surrendered the password to us as a condition of keeping the iPod. I entered the four-digit password and opened the Web browser. Jacob kept only a handful of obvious sites bookmarked: Facebook, Gmail, a few blogs he liked about technology and video games and music. There was no trace of a site called the Cutting Room. I had to do a Google search to find it.

The Cutting Room was a message board, a place where visitors could post plain-text messages for others to read. The site was filled with stories that were essentially what Derek had described: extended sexual fantasies involving bondage and sadism, even mutilation, rape, murder. Some—a tiny fraction—seemed to have no sexual element; they described torture for its own sake, rather like the ultra-gory spatter-horror movies that fill the theaters now. The site had no images or video, only text, and even that was unformatted. From the stripped-down browser on the iPod, it was impossible to tell which of these stories Jacob had read or how long he had spent on the site. But the page did show that Jacob was a member of this message board: his screen name, Job, was displayed at the top of the page. I presume "Job" was a play on his first name or his initials (though Jacob's middle initial was not *O*), or maybe it was a sly reference to the trials he was enduring.

I clicked on the user name "Job" and a link took me to a page where Job's favorite stories on the site were saved. A dozen stories were listed. At the top of the list was a story called "A Walk in the Woods." It was dated April 19, over three months earlier. The fields for the author and up-loader both were blank.

It began, *"Jason Fears took a knife into the woods that morning because he figured he might need it. He kept the knife in his sweatshirt pocket and as he walked he curled his fingers around the grip and the knife in his fist sent a surge up his arm and through his shoulder and into his brain and lit up his solar plexus like a firework going off in the sky."*

The story went on in long, unfurling, purple sentences like that one. It was a lurid, barely fictionalized account of the murder of Ben Rifkin in Cold Spring Park. In the story the park was renamed "Rock River Park." Newton was called "Brooktown." Ben Rifkin became a shifty, villainous bully called "Brent Mallis."

I assumed Jacob wrote it, but there was no way to be certain. There was nothing in the story that gave away the writer's identity. The voice did sound like an adolescent, and Jacob was a bookish boy who had been lurking in the Cutting Room long enough to learn the genre. The author had at least a passing knowledge of Cold Spring Park, which was described pretty accurately. Still, the most I could say with certainty was that Jacob had read the story, which proved nothing, really.

So I got on with the business of lawyering away at the evidence. Minimizing it. Defending Jacob.

The story was no confession. There was nothing in it that I recognized as nonpublic information. The whole thing might have been pieced together out of newspaper clippings and a vivid imagination. Even the most chilling detail, when Ben— or "Brent Mallis"—cried, "Stop, you're hurting me," had been widely reported in the newspapers. As for the nonpublic information, how accurate was any of it? Even the investigators had no way of knowing whether Ben Rifkin really said "Hey, faggot" when he saw his killer in the woods that morning, as "Brent Mallis" said to "Jason Fears." Or whether, when the killer stabbed Ben in the chest, the knife slipped in with no resistance, no bump of bone, no sticking on skin or rubbery organs, "like he was stabbing into the air." These things were unwitnessed, unconfirmable.

Anyway, Jacob would have realized it was idiotic to write this trash whether or not he was actually guilty. Yes, he had posted the *Psycho* photo on Facebook, but surely he would not go this far.

Even if he had written it, or just read it, what did it prove? It would be stupid, yes, but kids do stupid things. The interior of a teenager's mind is an endless war between

Stupid and Clever; this was just a case of Stupid winning a battle. Considering the pressure Jake was under and the fact he'd been practically locked up in the house for months, and now the growing clamor as the trial approached, it was understandable. Could you really hold the kid responsible for every tasteless, tactless, brainless thing he said? What kid would not begin to act a little crazy in Jacob's situation? Anyway, who among us would be judged by the dumbest things we did as teenagers?

I told myself these things, I marshaled my arguments as I'd been trained to do, but I could not get that boy's cry out of my head: "Stop, you're hurting me." And something in me tore open. I don't know how else to put it. I still would not admit doubt into my thinking. I still believed in Jacob and, God knows, I still loved him, and there was no evidence—no real *proof*—of anything. The lawyer in me understood all this. But the part of me that was Jacob's father felt cut, wounded. An emotion is a thought, yes, an idea, but it is also a sensation, an ache in your body. Desire, love, hate, fear, repulsion—you *feel* these things in your muscle and bones, not just in your mind. That is how this little heartbreak felt: like a physical injury, deep inside my body, an internal bleeding, a nick that would continue to seep.

I read the story again, then I cleared it from the browser's memory. I put the iPod back on Jacob's bureau and I would have left it there and never said anything to him about it, certainly never would have said anything to Laurie either, but I worried there might be danger in the iPod. I was familiar enough with the Internet and with police work to know that digital footprints are not easily erased. Every click on the Web creates a record, on servers out in the ether and also on the hard drives of individual computers, and these records persist no matter how you try to delete them. What if the DA somehow found Jacob's iPod and scoured it for evidence? The iPod was dangerous in another way too, as a portal to the Web for Jacob that I could not police as easily as the family computers. The iPod was small and phone-like, and Jacob used it with the same expectation of privacy that he would if it were a phone. He was careless with it, and maybe sneaky too. The iPod was a leak. It was a danger.

I brought it down to the basement and laid it on my little worktable, glass side up, and I got a hammer and smashed it.

20 | One Son Was Here, the Other Was Gone

The market closest to our house was a Whole Foods, and we loathed it. The wastefulness of all those pyramids of immaculate fruit and vegetables which, we knew, could only be created by throwing away enormous amounts of cosmetically imperfect food. The bogus earthiness, an elaborate pretense that Whole Foods was something other than a luxury store. And of course the prices. We had always avoided shopping there because of the high prices. Now, with Jacob's case threatening to bankrupt us, the thought of it seemed particularly ludicrous. We had no business shopping there.

We were already ruined financially. We were not rich people to begin with. We had been able to live in this town only because we had bought in when prices were low and because we were leveraged up to our eyeballs. Now Jonathan's fee was already into six figures. We had spent all of Jacob's college money on it and begun dipping into retirement savings. Before the case was over, I was sure, we would be wiped out, borrowing against the house to pay the bills. I knew, also, that my career as a prosecutor was over. Even if the verdict was "not guilty," I would never be able to walk into a courtroom without trailing the stink of the accusation. Maybe after the case was ended Lynn Canavan would do the right thing and offer to keep me on the payroll, but I could not stay there, not as a charity case. Laurie might be able to go back to teaching, but we would not be able to pay the bills on her income alone. This is an aspect of crime stories I never fully appreciated until I became one: it is so ruinously expensive to mount a defense that, innocent or guilty, the accusation is itself a devastating punishment. Every defendant pays a price.

There was another reason for us to avoid Whole Foods as well. I was determined not to be seen around town, certainly not to do anything that might suggest we were taking the case lightly. It was a question of image. I wanted people to see our family as shattered, because we *were* shattered. When the jury pool filed into the courtroom, I did not want any of them to harbor some vague memory of the Barbers luxuriating in pricey shops while the Rifkin boy lay buried in the ground. An unflattering mention in the newspaper, a fanciful rumor, a baseless impression—these things could easily tip the jury against us.

But we went to Whole Foods one evening, all three of us, when time was short and we were sick of all the wariness and waiting, and we were hungry. It was just before Labor Day. The town had emptied out for the holiday.

And what a relief it was to be there. We were lulled by the wonderful, narcotic ordinariness of shopping at the market. We were so like our old selves—Laurie the competent shopper and meal-planner, me the bumbling husband grabbing the odd item here or there on a whim, Jacob the kid whimpering for something to eat right away, before we reached the register— that we forgot ourselves. We strolled up and down the aisles. We enjoyed the packages banked up around us, made little jokes about the organic foods on the shelves. At the cheese section Jacob made a joke about the smell of a potent Gruyère that they were offering customers to taste and the possible gastric consequences of eating too much of it, and we all laughed, all three of us, not because the joke was especially funny (though I am not above a good fart joke) but because Jacob had made a joke at all. Over the summer he had become so silent, such an enigma to us, that we celebrated just to see our little boy peeking out at us again. He smiled and it was impossible to believe he was the monster everyone seemed to think he was.

We were still smiling when we came out of this last aisle into the cash register area at the front of the store. All the aisles drained here, and the shoppers eddied around, sorting themselves into checkout lines. We took our place at the end of a short line with just a couple of people in front of us. Laurie stood with her hand on the push-bar of the cart. I stood beside her. Jacob was behind us.

Dan Rifkin guided his cart into the checkout line beside ours. He was five feet away, if that. For a moment he did not see us. His sunglasses rested on the top of his head, pillowed in his hair. He wore neatly pressed khaki shorts and a tucked-in polo shirt. His belt was canvas with a blue band on which was embroidered a pattern of little ships' anchors. He wore thin-soled loafers without socks. It was the sort of country-club-casual style that I have always thought looks ridiculous on a grown man. A naturally formal person often looks odd when he tries to dress down, just as a natural slob looks out of place in a suit. Dan Rifkin was not the sort of guy who looked at home in short pants.

I turned my back to him and whispered to Laurie that he was beside us.

Her hand went over her mouth. "Where?"

"Right behind me. Don't look."

She looked.

I turned back to find Rifkin's wife, Joan, had appeared beside him. She had some

of her husband's miniature, doll-like quality. She was small and slim and had a
lovely face. Her frosted blond hair was cut
in a pixie. She must have been very beautiful once—she still had the vivacious, actressy manner of a woman who knows how
to use her looks—but she was fading now.
Her face was gaunt and her eyes bugged
slightly, with years, with stress, with grief. I
had met her several times over the years,
before all this happened; she never remembered who I was.

Now the two of them stared at us. Dan
hardly moved. His keys dangled from his
hooked index finger without jangling. His
consternation or surprise or whatever he
was feeling barely registered on his face.

Joan's face was more animated. She
glared, offended by our presence here. No
one had to say anything. It was a matter of
numbers. We were three, they were two.
One son was here, the other gone. The
simple fact of Jacob's continued existence
must have seemed profane to them.

It was all so painfully obvious and awkward that the five of us stood there dumbstruck for a moment, gaping at each other while the commotion of the market went on around us.

I told Jacob, "Why don't you go wait in the car."

"Okay."

He began to move off.

The Rifkins still stared.

I had decided immediately not to say anything unless they initiated the conversation. It was impossible to imagine what I could say that would not be painful or tactless or provocative.

But Laurie wanted to speak. Her desire to walk over to them was palpable. With great effort, she was restraining herself. I find it touching and almost naive how complete is my wife's faith in communication and connection. To her, there is virtually no problem that does not benefit from a little talk-talk-talk. What is more, she genuinely believed that the case was somehow a shared misfortune, that our family was suffering also, that it was no easy thing to see your son wrongly accused of murder, to see his life ruined for no good reason. The tragedy of Ben Rifkin's murder did not lessen the tragedy of Jake's own victimization. I don't think Laurie meant to say any of this. She is much too empathetic. I think she just wanted to communicate her sympathy somehow, to connect, with the usual banality of "I'm so sorry for your loss" or some such.

Laurie said, "I—"

"Laurie," I cut her off, "go wait in the car with Jacob. I'll pay for the stuff."

It did not cross my mind simply to leave. We had a right to be there. We had a right to eat, surely.

Laurie moved past me toward Joan Rifkin. I made a halfhearted effort to stop her but there was never any way to talk my wife out of something once she decided to do it. She was a mule. A sweet, empathetic, brilliant, sensitive, lovely woman, but a mule just the same.

She walked right up to them and made a gesture with her hands, extending them palms up as if she wanted to take Joan's hands in hers, or maybe just signaling that she did not know exactly what to say, or that she carried no weapons.

Joan met this gesture by crossing her arms.

Dan raised his own arm slightly. He

looked like he was getting ready to hold Laurie off if for some reason she attacked.

Laurie said, "Joan—"

Joan spat in her face. She did it very suddenly, without bothering to work up the saliva in her mouth, and not much came out. It was more of a gesture, perhaps the gesture she thought was appropriate in the circumstances—but then, who could ever be prepared for circumstances like these?

Laurie covered her face with both hands, wiped the spit with her fingers.

"Murderers," Joan said.

I went to Laurie and put my hand on her shoulder. She was as still as stone.

Joan glowered up at me. If she were a man or if she was less genteel, maybe she would have gone after me. She quivered with hatred like a tuning fork. I could not hate her back. I could not be angry with her, could not find much feeling at all for her except sadness, sadness for all of us.

I said to Dan, "Sorry," as if there was no point in talking to Joan and it was up to us men to handle the emotions that our wives could not.

I took Laurie's hand and led her out of

the store with elaborate politeness, saying softly over and over "Excuse us . . . sorry . . . excuse us" as we squeezed past the other shoppers and their carts and out into the parking lot where no one recognized us and we were returned to the semi-anonymity that we still enjoyed in those last few weeks before the trial, before the deluge.

"We didn't get our things," Laurie said.

"It's okay. We don't need them."

21 | Beware the Fury of a Patient Man

It is the happy lot of defense lawyers to see the good in people. No matter how wicked or incomprehensible the crime, no matter how overwhelming the evidence of guilt, the defense lawyer never forgets his client is a human being like the rest of us. That, of course, is what makes every defendant worth defending. I cannot tell you how many times a lawyer has suggested to me that his baby-shaker or wife-beater "really isn't a bad guy." Even the swaggering mercenaries with their gold Rolexes and alligator briefcases harbor this tiny redeeming fleck of humanism:

every criminal is still a man, a complex of good and bad, fully deserving of our empathy and mercy. To cops and prosecutors, things are not so sunny. We have the opposite impulse. We are quick to see the stain, the worm, the latent criminality in even the best people. Experience tells us the nice man next door is capable of anything. The priest may be a pedophile, the cop a crook; the loving husband and father may harbor a filthy secret. Of course, we believe these things for the same reason the defender believes as he does: people are only human.

The more I watched Leonard Patz, the more I became convinced he was Ben Rifkin's killer. I followed him on his morning rounds, to Dunkin' Donuts then to work at Staples, and I was there when he came out of work too. His Staples uniform made him look ridiculous. The red polo shirt hugged his flabby torso too tightly. Khaki pants accentuated the sort of bulging pelvis that Jacob and his pals call a "front butt." I did not dare go into the store to see what they had Patz selling. Electronics, probably, computers, cell phones—he looked like the type. Of course it is the prosecutor's privilege to choose his defendant, but I simply could not understand why Logiudice preferred Jacob to this man. Maybe it is a parent's wishful thinking or a prosecutor's cynicism, but I still do not understand it, even now.

By August, I had been following Patz around for weeks, in the mornings and evenings, before and after his workday. Matt Magrath's information was proof positive, as far as I was concerned, but it would not fly in court. No jury would ever accept his word. I needed harder evidence, something that did not rely on that shifty kid. I do not know what exactly I was hoping to see by trailing Patz around like this. A stumble. A return to the scene, a late-night drive to dispose of evidence. Anything.

In the event, Patz did nothing especially suspicious. For that matter, he did not do very much at all. In his off hours, he seemed content to loaf in shops or hang out in his apartment near Cold Spring Park. He liked to eat at the McDonald's on Soldiers Field Road in Brighton, where he would order at the drive-through and eat in his plum-colored car while listening to the radio. Once, he went to the movies by himself. None of it was remotely significant. But nothing he did ever shook my certainty that Patz was the one. The outrageous possibility that my son would be sacrificed to save this man became an obsession. I grew more and more addled the longer I followed him, stared at him, the longer I dwelt on this idea. The dullness of his life, far from dispelling my suspicion, only infuriated me all the more. He was hiding, laying low, waiting for Logiudice to do his work for him.

On a sultry Wednesday evening in August, I followed directly behind Patz's car as he made his way home through Newton Centre, a shopping area and village green where several busy roads intersect. It was around five o'clock and still sunny. Traffic was lighter than usual (this is the sort of town that empties out in August) but still bumper-to-bumper. Most drivers had their car windows rolled up tight against the humid heat. A few, including Patz and me, kept our windows open and hung our left elbows out for a little relief. Even the ice-cream eaters on the sidewalk outside J.P. Licks had a limp, defeated look.

At a red light I nuzzled in behind Patz's car. I clenched the steering wheel tight.

Patz's brake lights flickered and his car lurched slightly.

I lifted my foot off the brake. I don't know why. I was not sure how far I intended to take it. But I was happy, for the first time in a long time, as my car rolled forward and bumped his with a satisfying *chunk.*

He looked at me in his rearview mirror and raised his hands. *What was that!*

I shrugged, backed the car up a few feet, then knocked his bumper again, a little harder this time. *Chunk.*

Through his rear window, I saw his shadowy shape put up its hands again in exasperation. I watched him shift the car into park, open the door, and hoist his bulk up out of the car.

And I became a different person. A different person, yet I moved and acted with a naturalness and fluency that was wild and unfamiliar, and thrilling.

I was out of the car and moving toward him before I was quite aware of my own motion, without ever actually deciding to confront him.

He raised his hands in front of his chest, palms forward, and his face registered surprise.

I gathered his shirt up in my hands and thrust him against his car, bending him backward. I buried my snout in his face and growled, "I know what you did."

He did not respond.

"I know what you did."

"What are you talking about? Who are you?"

"I know about the boy in Cold Spring Park."

"Oh my God, you're crazy."

"You have no idea."

"I don't know what you're talking about. Honest. You've got the wrong guy."

"Yeah? Do you remember going to meet Ben Rifkin in the park? Do you remember telling Matt Magrath you were going to do that?"

"Matt Magrath?"

"How long were you watching Ben Rifkin, how long were you stalking him? Did you ever talk to him? Did you bring your knife that day? What happened? Did you offer him the same deal you had with Matt, a hundred bucks for a feel? Did he turn you down? Did he make fun of you, call you names? Did he try to beat you up, push you around, scare you? What set you off, Leonard? What made you do it?"

"You're the father, aren't you?"

"No, I'm not Ben's father."

"No, the one that got charged. You're the father. They told me about you. The DA said you'd try to talk to me."

"What DA?"

"Logiudice."

"What did he say?"

"He said you had this idea in your head and you might try to talk to me someday, and I shouldn't talk to you. He said you were . . ."

"What?"

"He said you were crazy. He said you might be violent."

I let go of Patz and stepped back.

I was surprised to find I had lifted him off the ground. He slid down the side of his car, landing on his heels. His red Staples uniform shirt was pulled up out of his Dockers khakis, baring an expanse of round belly, but he did not dare straighten himself up yet. He eyed me cautiously.

"I know what you did," I assured him, coming back into myself. "No way my kid is going away because of you."

"But I didn't do anything."

"Yes, you did. Yes, you did. Matt told me all about it."

"Please just leave me alone. I didn't do anything. I'm just doing what the DA told me to do."

I nodded, feeling exposed and out of control. Embarrassed. "I know what you did," I said again, low and certain, as much to myself this time as to Patz. The phrase comforted me, like a little prayer.

Mr. Logiudice: And did you continue following Leonard Patz after that day?

Witness: Yes.

Mr. Logiudice: Why? What on earth did you hope to accomplish?

Witness: I was trying to solve the case, to prove Patz was the murderer.

Mr. Logiudice: You really believed that?

Witness: Yes. You made the wrong call, Neal. The evidence pointed at Patz, not Jacob. That was your best case. You were supposed to follow the evidence wherever it led. That was your job.

Mr. Logiudice: Boy, you don't give up, do you?

Witness: You don't have kids, do you, Neal?

Mr. Logiudice: No.

Witness: No, I didn't think so. If you did, you'd understand. Did you tell Patz not to talk to me?

Mr. Logiudice: Yes.

Witness: Because you knew if the jury heard the evidence against Patz, they never would have believed Jacob did it. You were loading the dice, isn't that right?

Mr. Logiudice: I was prosecuting my case. I was prosecuting the suspect I believed did it. That's my job.

Witness: Then why were you so afraid to let the jury hear about Patz?

Mr. Logiudice: Because he didn't do it! I was doing what I thought was right, based on the evidence I had at the time. Andy, look, you're not the one asking questions here. That's not your job anymore. It's mine.

Witness: It's just strange, isn't it? Telling a guy like that not to talk to the defense. It's burying exculpatory evidence, isn't it. But you had your reasons, didn't you, Neal?

Mr. Logiudice: Would you at least— Please. Call me Mr. Logiudice. I've earned that, at least.

Witness: Tell them, Neal. Go on, tell them how you knew Leonard Patz. Tell them what the jury never heard.

Mr. Logiudice: Let's move on.

22 | A Heart Two Sizes Too Small

Mr. Logiudice: Directing your attention to a document that's been marked Exhibit, um, 22, do you recognize this document?

Witness: Yes, it's a letter from Dr. Vogel to Jonathan Klein, our defense lawyer.

Mr. Logiudice: And the date?

Witness: It's dated October 2.

Mr. Logiudice: Two weeks before the trial.

Witness: Yes, give or take.

Mr. Logiudice: The bottom of the letter says, "CC: Mr. and Mrs. Andrew

Barber." Were you shown this letter at the time?

Witness: Yes, I was.

Mr. Logiudice: But your attorney never turned over this document in discovery, is that correct?

Witness: Not as far as I know.

Mr. Logiudice: Not as far as anyone knows.

Witness: Don't testify, Neal. Come on, ask a question.

Mr. Logiudice: All right. Why was this document never turned over to the prosecution?

Witness: Because it's privileged. It's a doctor-patient communication and it's work product, which means it was created by the defense team as part of its trial preparation. That makes it confidential. It's exempt from discovery.

Mr. Logiudice: But you've produced it now. And in response to an ordinary boilerplate discovery order. Why? Are you waiving the privilege?

Witness: The privilege isn't mine to waive. But it doesn't matter now, does it? The only thing that matters now is the truth.

Mr. Logiudice: Here we go. This is the part where you tell us how you believe in the system and all that.

Witness: The system is as good as the people running it, Neal.

Mr. Logiudice: Did you believe in Dr. Vogel?

Witness: Yes. Completely.

Mr. Logiudice: And you have confidence in her now? Nothing has happened to shake your faith in the doctor's observations?

Witness: I trust her. She's a good doctor.

Mr. Logiudice: So you don't dispute anything in this letter?

Witness: No.

Mr. Logiudice: And what was the purpose of this letter?

Witness: It was an opinion letter. It was meant to summarize the doctor's findings about Jacob so that Jonathan could make a decision about whether to call Dr. Vogel as a witness and whether he wanted to get into this whole subject at all, the subject of Jacob's mental health.

Mr. Logiudice: Would you read the second paragraph to the grand jury, please.

Witness: "The client presents as an articulate, intelligent, polite fourteen-year-old boy. His manner is shy and he is somewhat reticent in conversation, but nothing in his conduct suggests a compromised ability to perceive, recall, or relate the incidents involved in this case or to assist trial counsel in making informed, intelligent, well-reasoned decisions pertaining to his own legal defense."

Mr. Logiudice: What the doctor is saying there is that in her professional opinion Jacob was competent to stand trial, isn't that right?

Witness: That's a legal opinion, not a clinical one. But yes, obviously the doctor is aware of the standard.

Mr. Logiudice: And what about criminal responsibility? The doctor addresses that question in her letter as well, doesn't she? Look at paragraph three.

Witness: Yes.

Mr. Logiudice: Read it, please.

Witness: Quote: "There is insufficient evidence as yet to conclude definitively whether Jacob adequately perceives the distinction between right and wrong and can adequately govern his behavior to act according to that distinction. There may be sufficient evidence, however, to support a colorable argument relying on genetic and neurological evidence based on a theory of 'irresistible impulse.'" Unquote.

Mr. Logiudice: "There may be sufficient evidence," "a colorable argument"—that's a lot of hedging, isn't it?

Witness: It's understandable. People were bound to be skeptical about making excuses for

	murder. If the doctor took the stand and made that argument, she'd better be damn sure.
Mr. Logiudice:	But she did say, in fact, at least at this stage, that it was possible? It was a "colorable argument"?
Witness:	Yes.
Mr. Logiudice:	A murder gene?
Witness:	She never used that term.
Mr. Logiudice:	Would you read the paragraph labeled "Diagnosis Overview"? Page three, top of the page.
Witness:	Neal, do you want me to read the whole thing to them? The document is already in evidence. They can read it for themselves.
Mr. Logiudice:	Please. Humor me.
Witness:	Quote: "Jacob exhibits behavior and expresses thoughts and inclinations, both in private session and in his history outside direct clinical observation, that would support any or all of the following diagnoses in isolation or in combination: reactive

attachment disorder, narcissistic personality disorder"—look, if you're asking me to comment on a psychiatrist's clinical diagnosis—

Mr. Logiudice: Please, just one more. Page four, paragraph two, the sentence I've indicated with a sticky note.

Witness: Quote: "The best way to summarize this entire constellation of observations—lack of empathy, difficulties with impulse control, occasional cruelty—is to say that Jacob resembles the Grinch of Dr. Seuss: 'His heart is two sizes too small.'" Unquote.

Mr. Logiudice: You look upset. I'm sorry. Does that upset you?

Witness: Jesus, Neal. Jesus.

Mr. Logiudice: Is this how you felt when you first heard that your son had a heart that was two sizes too small?

[The witness did not respond.]

Mr. Logiudice: Is this how it felt?

Witness: Objection. Relevance.

Mr. Logiudice: Noted. Now answer the question, please. Is this how it felt?

Witness: Yes! How do you think I felt, for Christ's sake! I'm his father.

Mr. Logiudice: Exactly. How is it that you lived with a boy who had the capacity for this sort of violence all these years and you never even noticed it? Never suspected one thing was out of place? Never lifted a finger to address these psychological problems?

Witness: What do you want me to say, Neal?

Mr. Logiudice: That you knew. You knew, Andy. You knew.

Witness: No.

Mr. Logiudice: How is that possible, Andy? How could you not know? How is that even possible?

Witness: I don't know. I only know it's the truth.

Mr. Logiudice: Again with that. You sure do stick to your talking points,

	don't you? You keep saying "the truth, the truth, the truth," as if saying it makes it so.
Witness:	You don't have kids, Neal. I don't expect you to understand.
Mr. Logiudice:	Enlighten me. Enlighten all of us.
Witness:	You can't see your own kids straight. No one can. You love them too much, you're too close. If you had a son. If you had a son.
Mr. Logiudice:	Do you need a minute to gather yourself?
Witness:	No. Have you ever heard of confirmation bias? Confirmation bias is the tendency to see things in your environment that confirm your preconceived ideas and not see things that conflict with what you already believe. I think maybe something like that happens with kids. You see what you want to see.
Mr. Logiudice:	And what you don't want to see, you choose not to?

Witness: Not choose. You just don't see it.

Mr. Logiudice: But in order for that to be true, for it to be confirmation bias, you would have to genuinely believe in the thing. Because you're talking about an unconscious process. So you would have to genuinely believe in your heart of hearts that Jacob was an ordinary kid, that his heart was not two sizes too small, correct?

Witness: Yes.

Mr. Logiudice: But in this case, that couldn't be true, could it? Because you had reason to be on the lookout for signs of trouble, didn't you? Your whole life— your whole life, Andy—you've been aware of the possibility, isn't that true?

Witness: No, it is not.

Mr. Logiudice: No? Did you forget who your father was?

Witness: Yes. For thirty years or so, I forgot. I meant to forget, I purposely forgot, I was entitled to forget.

Mr. Logiudice: You were entitled?

Witness: Yes. It was a personal matter.

Mr. Logiudice: Was it, though? You never really believed that. You forgot who your father was? Forgot what your son might become if he turned out like Grandpa? Come on, you don't forget a thing like that. You knew. "Confirmation bias"!

Witness: Step back, Neal.

Mr. Logiudice: You knew.

Witness: Step back. Get out of my face. Act like a lawyer, for once.

Mr. Logiudice: Well, now. There's the Andy Barber we all know. Back in control of yourself. Master of self-control, master of self-delusion. Master actor. Let me ask you something: those thirty years when you forgot who you are, where you came from, you were telling yourself a story, weren't you? For that matter, you were telling everyone a story. In a word, you were lying.

Witness: I never said anything that was not true.

Mr. Logiudice: No, but you left a few things out, didn't you? You left a few things out.

[The witness did not respond.]

Mr. Logiudice: And yet now you want the grand jury to believe every word you say.

Witness: Yes.

Mr. Logiudice: All right, then. Go on with your story.

23 | Him

**Northern Correctional Institution,
Somers, Connecticut.**

The visiting booth at Northern seemed designed to disorient and isolate. A claustrophobic sealed white box, about five feet wide by eight feet deep, with a windowed door behind me and a plate-glass window in front. A beige dial-less phone on the wall at my right hand. A white counter to rest my arms on. The booth was designed to keep the prisoners caged in, of course: Northern was a level-five maximum security facility that permitted only no-contact visits. But it was I who felt entombed.

And when he appeared in the window—my father, Bloody Billy Barber—hands cuffed at his waist, a tangle of ash gray hair, smirking down at me—amused, I suppose, at his pissant kid showing up here finally—I was glad for the thick glass slab between us. Glad that he could see but not reach me. The leopard in the zoo wanders to the edge of his pen and, through the bars or across an unjumpable moat, he stares at you with contempt for your inferiority, for needing that barrier between you. There is a shared understanding in that moment, nonverbal but no less real: the leopard is predator and you are prey, and it is only the barrier that permits us humans to feel superior and secure. That feeling, standing at the leopard's cage, is edged with shame, at the animal's superior strength, at his hauteur, his low estimation of you. To my own surprise, what I felt in those first moments in my father's presence was precisely the zoo-goer's subtle shame. The surge of emotion took me by surprise. I had not expected to feel much of anything. Let's be honest: Billy

Barber was a stranger to me. I had not seen him in forty-five years or so, since I was a kid. But I could not have been more frozen by him. He held me as surely as if he had somehow materialized on my side of the glass and wrapped me in his arms.

He stood there framed in the window, a three-quarter-length portrait of an old con, his eyes on me. He gave a little snort.

I broke eye contact, and he sat down.

A guard stood several feet behind him, near the blank wall. (Everything was blank, every wall, every door, every surface. From what I could see, Northern C.I. seemed to be made up entirely of unbroken white plaster walls and gray concrete walls. The facility was new, completed only in 1995, so I assumed the lack of color was part of some crazy-making penal strategy. After all, it is no harder to paint a wall yellow or blue than white.)

My father picked up his phone—even as I write the words *my father* I feel a little thrill, and my mind reverses the film of my life back to 1961 when I last saw him, in the visiting room at the Whalley Avenue jail; that is the moment of divergence, the whole contingent, ramifying course of our two lives begins there—and I picked up my phone.

"Thanks for seeing me."

"They're not exactly standing in line."

On his wrist was the blue tattoo I had remembered for so many years. It was actually quite small and indistinct, a little fuzzy-edged crucifix that had darkened with age to plum purple, like a deep bruise. I had misremembered it. I had misremembered him: he was only average height, thin, more muscular now than I'd imagined. Ropy jail-house muscles, even at seventy-two. He had picked up a new tattoo as well, much more intricate and artful than the old one: a dragon that coiled itself around his neck so that its tail and snout met at the base of his throat like a necklace pendant.

"About time you come see me."

I sniffed. The risible suggestion that *his* feelings were hurt, that *he* was the victim here, pissed me off. What balls. Typical con, this guy was—always wheedling, angling, gaming.

"What's it been," he went on, "a whole life? A whole life I'm rotting away and you don't have time to come see your old man.

Not even once. What kind of kid are you? What kind of kid does that?"

"You practice that speech?"

"Don't smart-mouth me. What'd I ever do to you? Huh? Nothing. But a whole life you never come see me. Your own father. What kind of kid doesn't visit his own father for forty years?"

"I'm *your* son. That should explain it."

"My son? Not *my* son. I don't know you. Never laid eyes on you."

"Want to see my birth certificate?"

"Like I give a shit about a fuckin' birth certificate. You think that's what makes a son? One squirt fifty years ago, that's what you are to me. What'd you think? I'd be happy to see you? Did you think I'd be jumping up and down, whoop-dee-fuckin'-doo?"

"You could have said no. I wasn't on your visitor list."

"No one's on my fuckin' list. Whattaya think? Who would be on my fuckin' list? They don't let people visit here anyway. Just immediate family."

"You want me to leave?"

"No. Did you hear me say that?" He shook his head, frowned. "This fuckin' place. This place is the worst. I haven't been here the whole time, you know. They move me around. You do bad somewheres else, they send you here. It's a hole."

He seemed to lose interest in the subject and he fell silent.

I did not speak. I have found in any Q&A, in court, in witness interviews, wherever, often the best thing you can do is wait, say nothing. The witness will want to fill the awkward silence. He will feel a vague compulsion to keep talking, to prove he is not holding back, to prove he is smart and in the know, to earn your trust. In this case, I think, I waited just out of habit. Certainly I had no intention of leaving. Not until he said yes.

His mood shifted. He slumped. Almost visibly, he went from petulant to resigned, even self-pitying.

"Well," he said, "you came out big, at least. She must've fed you good."

"She did fine. With everything."

"How is she, your mother?"

"What do you give a shit?"

"I don't."

"So don't talk about her."

"Why shouldn't I?"

I shook my head.

"I knew her before you did," he said. He squirmed in his chair with a leer, wiggled his hips, mimed fucking her.

"Your grandson is in trouble. Did you know that?"

"Did I—? I didn't even know I had a grandson. What's his name?"

"Jacob."

"Jacob?"

"What's so funny?"

"The fuck kind of faggot name is Jacob?"

"It's a name!"

Bouncing with laughter, he sang in falsetto, "Jaaaacob!"

"Watch your mouth. He's a good kid."

"Yeah? Can't be that good or you wouldn't be here."

"I said watch your mouth."

"What's little Jacob in trouble for?"

"Murder."

"Murder? Murder. How old is he?"

"Fourteen."

My father lowered the phone to his lap and slumped back in his chair. When he sat back up again, he said, "Who'd he kill?"

"No one. He's innocent."

"Yeah, so am I."

"He's really innocent."

"Okay, okay."

"You never heard anything about this?"

"I never hear about anything in here. This place is a toilet."

"You must be the oldest con in here."

"One of 'em."

"I don't know how you survive it."

"You can't hurt steel." The handcuffs forced him to raise both arms as he held the phone in his left hand, and he flexed his unoccupied right arm. "You can't hurt steel." But then his bravado vanished. "This place is a hole," he said. "It's like living in a fuckin' cave."

He had a way of swinging between the two poles of hyper-machismo and self-pity. It was hard to tell which one was a put-on. Maybe neither was. On the street this sort of emotional volatility would have seemed crazy. In here, who knew? Maybe it was a natural reaction to this place.

"You put yourself in this place."

"I put myself in this place and I'm doing my bid and I'm not complaining. You hear me complaining?"

I did not answer.

"So what d'you want outa me? You want

me to do something for poor innocent little Jacob?"

"I may want you to testify."

"Testify to what?"

"Let me ask you something. When you killed that girl, what did it feel like? Not physically. I mean, what was in your mind, what were you thinking about?"

"What do you mean, what was I thinking about?"

"Why did you do it?"

"What do you want me to say? You tell me."

"I just want you to tell the truth."

"Yeah, right. Nobody wants that. Especially the people who tell you they want the truth—trust me, they don't want the truth. You tell me what you want me to say to help the kid out and I'll say it. I don't give a shit. What do I give a shit?"

"Let me put it this way. When it happened, were you thinking anything? Anything at all? Or was it kind of an irresistible impulse?"

The corner of his mouth curled upward. "An irresistible impulse?"

"Just answer."

"Is that what you're going for?"

"Never mind what I'm going for. I'm not going for anything. Just tell me what you felt."

"I felt an irresistible impulse."

I exhaled loud and long. "You know, if you were a better liar, you might not be in here."

"If you weren't such a good liar, you might not be out there." He eyed me. "You want me to help get the kid off, I'll help you. He's my grandkid. Just tell me what you need."

I had already decided Bloody Billy Barber was not going to come within ten miles of the witness stand. He was worse than a liar—he was a bad liar.

"All right," I said, "you want to know what I came for? This is what I came for." I held up a little packet: a sterile swab and a plastic envelope to hold it. "I need to wipe your gums with this. For DNA."

"The guards won't let you."

"Let me worry about the guards. I need you to let me."

"What do you need my DNA for?"

"We're testing for a certain mutation. It's called MAOA Knockout."

"What in the fuck is MAOA Knockout?"

"It's a genetic mutation. They think it might code your body to be more aggressive in certain environments."

"Who thinks that?"

"Scientists."

His eyes narrowed. You could practically read his thoughts, the selfish opportunism of a career con: maybe here was an argument to flip his own conviction.

"The more you talk, the more I think maybe Jacob isn't so innocent."

"I didn't come here to hear your opinion. I came to get your spit on this Q-tip. If you say no, I'll go get a court order and come back and we'll take it the hard way."

"Why would I say no?"

"Why would you do anything? Guys like you I don't understand."

"What's to understand? I'm the same as anyone else. Same as you."

"Yeah, okay, whatever."

"Don't give me 'okay, whatever.' Did you ever stop to think that without me you wouldn't exist?"

"Every day."

"See? There."

"It's not a happy thought."

"Well, I'm still your old man, kiddo,

whether you like it or not. It don't have to make you happy."

"It don't."

After some negotiation and a call to the deputy warden, a deal was struck. I would not be allowed to swab my father's mouth personally, which would have been the best method because it would create the cleanest chain of custody: I could testify that the sample was genuine because the Q-tip never left my possession. Not at Northern. "No contact" meant no contact. At length, I was allowed to give the kit to a guard, who passed it to my father.

I talked him through the procedure step by step on the phone in the visiting booth. "All you have to do is break open the package and wipe the Q-tip around your cheek a little. Just so it soaks up a little spit. Swallow first. Then wipe it on the inside of your cheek near the back of your mouth, back where your jaws meet. Then I want you to put the Q-tip in that plastic bottle there, without touching the tip to anything else, then screw the top on. Then I want you to put that label across the top, and sign and date the label. And I need to be able to watch you do all that, so don't block me."

With his hands still cuffed, he ripped open the paper package holding the swab. It was a long wooden stick, longer than an ordinary Q-tip. He put the swab straight into his mouth like a lollipop and he pretended to bite it. Then, looking at me through the window, he bared his teeth and wiped the cotton tip across his upper front gums. Then he swirled it around at the back of his mouth, in the pocket of his cheek. He held the stick up to the window.

"Now you."

Part
THREE

"I have in mind an experiment. Take an infant—regardless of ancestry, race, talent, or predilection, so long as he is essentially healthy—and I will make of him whatever you like. I will produce an artist, soldier, doctor, lawyer, priest; or I will raise him to be a thief. You may decide. The infant is equally capable of all these things. All that is required is training, time, and a properly controlled environmment."

—JOHN F. WATKINS,
Principles of Behaviorism (1913)

24 | It's Different for Mothers

For years I never expected to lose in court. In practice, I did lose, of course. Every lawyer loses, just as every baseball player makes an out seventy percent of the time he goes to bat. But I was never intimidated, and I spat on prosecutors who were—the politicians and wheeler-dealers who were afraid to try a case that was not a sure thing, who would not risk a not-guilty. To a prosecutor, there is no dishonor in a not-guilty, not when the alternative is a sleazy deal. We are not measured by simple won-lost records. The truth is, the best won-lost records are not built on great trial work. They are built on cherry-picking only the strongest cases for trial and pleading out the rest, regardless of the right and wrong of it. That was Logiudice's way, not mine. Better to fight and lose than sell out your victim.

That is one reason I loved homicides. You cannot plead guilty to murder in Massachusetts. Every case must go to trial. The rule is a remnant of the days when murder was punishable by death in this state. In a capital case, no shortcuts were permitted, no deals. The stakes were simply too high. So to this day every homicide case, no matter how lopsided, must be tried. Prosecutors cannot cherry-pick the sure winners for trial and the long shots to dump. *Well,* I liked to think, *so much the better. Then the difference will be me. I will win even with the weaker case.* That was how I saw it. But then, we all tell ourselves stories about ourselves. The money man tells himself that by getting rich he is actually enriching others, the artist tells himself that his creations are things of deathless beauty, the soldier tells himself he is on the side of the angels. Me, I told myself that in court I could make things turn out right—

that when I won, justice was served. You can get drunk on such thinking, and in Jacob's case I was.

As the trial approached, I felt a familiar battlefield euphoria. It never crossed my mind that we would lose. I was energized, optimistic, confident, pugnacious. All of it in hindsight seems strangely disconnected from reality. But it is not so strange, if you think about it. Treat a man like an anvil and he will long to hit back.

The trial began in mid-October 2007, at the height of leaf season. Soon the trees would release their leaves all at once, but for the moment the foliage was in its final brilliant efflorescence of red, orange, and mustard.

On the eve of the trial, a Tuesday night, the air was unseasonably warm. The overnight temperature did not fall much below sixty degrees, and the air was dense, humid, agitated. I woke up in the middle of the night, sensing something wrong in the atmosphere, as I always do when Laurie cannot sleep.

She was lying on her side, up on one elbow, head propped in her hand.

"What's wrong?" I whispered to her.

"Listen."

"To what?"

"*Sh.* Just wait, listen."

Outside, the night rustled.

There was a loud screech. It began as an animal's yelp then quickly rose into a piercing high-pitched shriek, like the *screel* of a train's brakes.

"What on earth is that?" she said.

"I don't know. A cat? A bird maybe? Something is killing it."

"What would be killing a cat?"

"A fox, a coyote. Raccoon, maybe."

"It's like we live in the woods, all of a sudden. This is the city! I've lived here all my life. We never had foxes and coyotes. And those huge wild turkeys we get in the yard? We never had any of that."

"There's a lot of new development. The town's getting built up. Their natural habitats are disappearing. They're getting flushed out into the open."

"Listen to that sound, Andy. I can't even tell what direction it's coming from or how far away it is. It's like it's right next to us. It must be one of the neighbors' cats."

We listened. It came again. This time the

dying animal's screeches definitely sounded like a cat. The cry began recognizably as a cat's mewling before the wild, electrified shrieks began.

"Why is it taking so long?"

"Maybe it's toying with its prey. Cats do that with mice, I know."

"It's awful."

"It's nature."

"To be cruel? To torture your prey before you kill it? How is that natural? What evolutionary advantage does cruelty give?"

"I don't know, Laurie. It's just the way it is. Whatever would attack a cat like that— some starving coyote or wild dog or whatever—I'm sure it's desperate. It can't be easy to hunt around here."

"If he's desperate, then he should kill it and eat it already."

"Why don't we try to get some sleep. We've got a big day tomorrow."

"How can I sleep with that?"

"You want one of my Ambien?"

"No. They knock me out all the next morning. I want to be alert tomorrow. I don't know how you take those things."

"Are you kidding? I eat them like Tic Tacs. They don't knock me out *enough*."

"I don't need pills, Andy. I just want that sound to stop."

"Come on, lie down."

She let her head down. I folded my body against her back, and she seated herself against me.

"You're just nervous, Laurie. It's understandable."

"I don't know if I can do this, Andy. Really, I don't have the strength."

"We'll get through it."

"It's easier for you. You've seen the whole process before. And you're not a mother. Not that this is *easy* for you. I know it's not. But it's different for me. I just can't do it. I'm not going to make it."

"I wish I could make it go away for you, Laurie, but I can't."

"No. This helps, anyway, what you're doing now. We'll just lie here. It has to stop soon."

The shrieks went on for another fifteen minutes or so. Neither of us slept much even after they stopped.

When we emerged from our house at eight o'clock the next morning, a Fox 25 news van idled across the street, smoke wisping from the tailpipe. A cameraman filmed us as we walked to the car. He was faceless behind his shoulder-held camera. Or rather, the camera was his face, his one-eyed insect head.

Outside the courthouse in Cambridge, we made our way to the front entrance on Thorndike Street, where reporters swarmed. Again they bumbled against one another as we came up the block. Again the cameras jostled for a clear shot, again the microphones probed the air in front of us. The crush of reporters was much easier to deal with this time, having been through it once before at the arraignment. Jacob's presence excited them most, but I was oddly thankful that Jacob had to run this gauntlet. I had a theory that it was always better for a defendant to be bailed and out on the street than to be held in the pretrial lockup, as most of my own murder defendants had been. Defendants who did not make bail seemed to leave the building only one way, via the prisoners' exit—heading for Concord, not home. Those prisoner-defendants moved down through the courthouse, like meat through a grinder or like the steel balls that bounce down a pachinko machine: from the jail on the top floors, down through the various courtrooms, finally out through the basement-level garage, where the sheriff's vans carted them off to the various prisons. Better that Jacob walk in through the front door, better that he retain his freedom and dignity as long as possible. Once this building caught you in its gears, it did not like to let go.

25 | The Schoolteacher, Glasses Girl, the Fat Somerville Guy, Urkel, the Recording Studio Guy, the Housewife, Braces Woman, and Other Oracles of Truth

In Middlesex County, judges were ostensibly assigned to trials at random. No one actually believed such a lottery existed. The same few judges were assigned high-profile cases over and over, and the judges who kept drawing the winning lottery tickets tended to be prima donnas—just the sort who would lobby for the gig behind the scenes. But no one ever complained. Bucking the entrenched routines of that courthouse was generally an exercise in pissing upwind, and anyway the self-selection of egomaniacal judges probably was for the best. It takes a healthy dose of ego to keep command of a contentious courtroom. That and it made for a better show: big cases need big personalities.

So it came as no surprise that the judge assigned to Jacob's trial was Burton French. Everyone knew he would be. The hairnetted cafeteria ladies, the mental-patient janitors, even the mice that scratched around behind the ceiling tiles all knew that, if a TV camera was going to be in the courtroom, the judge on the bench would be Burt French. He was very likely the only judge whose face the public recognized, as he appeared often on the local news shows to dilate on matters legal. The camera loved him. In person he had a slightly laughable Colonel Blimp appearance—a wine-cask body supported uncertainly by two wiry legs—but as a talking head on the TV screen he projected the sort of reassuring gravity we like to see in our judges. He spoke in definitive declarations, none of the "on the one hand, on the other hand" that journalists rely on. At the same time he was never bombastic; he never seemed to be faking or provoking, manufacturing the "heat" that TV loves. Rather, he had a way of using his square, serious face, of tucking in his chin and leveling his eyes at the camera and saying things like "The Law does not permit [this or that]." You could hardly blame viewers for thinking, *If The Law could talk, this is what it would sound like.*

What made all this so unbearable to the lawyers who gathered to gossip before the First Session every morning or over lunch at the Cinnabon in the Galleria food court was that Judge French's gruff no-bullshit attitude was itself pure bullshit. The man who presented himself in public as the embodiment of The Law, they thought, was in reality a publicity seeker, an intellectual lightweight, and in the courtroom a petty tyrant. Which made him the perfect embodiment of The Law, when you really thought about it.

Of course by the time Jake's trial began I did not give a rat's ass about Judge French's failings. All that mattered was the game, and Burt French was an advantage to us. He was essentially conservative, not the sort of judge to go out on a limb for a novel legal theory like the Murder Gene. Equally important, he was the sort of judge who liked to test the lawyers who appeared before him. He had a bully's instinct for weakness or uncertainty, and he loved to torment bumbling, unprepared lawyers. Throwing Neal Logiudice in front of a guy like that was chumming the water, and Lynn Canavan made a mistake by doing it in such an important case. But then, what choice did she have? She could not send me anymore.

So it began.

But it began—as is often the case with an event you have anticipated too eagerly for too long—with a sense of anticlimax. We waited in the crowded gallery of courtroom 12B as the clock spun past nine o'clock, nine-fifteen, nine-thirty. Jonathan sat beside us, unfazed by the delay. He checked in with the judge's clerk a few times, only to be told each time that there were delays in setting up the pool camera whose video feed the news stations, including Court TV, were to share. Then we waited awhile longer while the larger-than-usual jury pool which we had reserved was being organized. Jonathan reported these things to us, then opened up his *New York Times* and read peacefully.

At the front of the courtroom, Judge French's clerk, a woman named Mary Mc- Quade, fiddled with some papers; then, satisfied, she stood and surveyed the chamber with crossed arms. I always got along with Mary. I made it my business to. The court clerks were gatekeepers to the judges and therefore influential. Mary in particular seemed to enjoy the secondhand prestige of her position, the nearness to power. And the truth is, she did her job well, brokering between Judge French's bluster- ing and the lawyers' constant jockeying for advantage. The word *bureaucrat* has a negative connotation, but we do need bu- reaucracies, after all, and it is good bureau- crats that make them go. Mary certainly made no apologies for her place in the system. She wore expensive, stylish eye- glasses and decent suits, as if to separate herself from the hacks in the other court- rooms.

In a chair along the far wall was the court officer, an enormous fat man named Ernie Zinelli. Ernie was sixty-odd years old and three hundred–odd pounds, and if there was ever actually trouble in the court- room, the poor guy would probably keel over of a heart attack. His presence as the judge's enforcer was purely symbolic, like the gavel. But I loved Ernie. Over the years he had grown increasingly open with me about his opinions of defendants, which were generally unfavorable in the extreme, and about judges and lawyers, which were only slightly more positive.

That morning, these two old colleagues of mine barely acknowledged me. Mary glanced in my direction occasionally but gave no sign she had ever seen me before. Ernie risked a little grin. They seemed afraid someone might think that any friendly gestures were directed at Jacob, who sat beside me. I wondered if they had been instructed to ignore me. Probably they just figured I had joined the other team.

When the judge finally did take the bench a little before ten, we were stiff from sitting.

Everyone stood at Ernie's recital of the familiar "Oyez, oyez, oyez, the Superior Court of the Commonwealth of Massachusetts is now in session," and Jacob fidgeted right through to the end: "All ye having business before this court come forward and ye shall be heard." His mother and I both put a hand on Jacob's back to reassure him.

The case was called, Jonathan gestured to Jacob, and the two of them crossed the bar and took their seats at the defense table, as they would every morning for the next two weeks.

This would be Laurie's view of the entire trial. From the front row of the gallery benches, she would sit impassively for hour after hour, day after day, staring at the back of Jacob's head. Poised on that bench, my wife looked very pale and thin among the spectators, as if Jacob's case was a cancer that she had to endure, a physical struggle. And yet, no matter how she withered, I could not help seeing in Laurie the ghost of her younger self, the teenaged girl with a lovely, full, heart-shaped face. I have an idea that this is what enduring love really means. Your memories of a girl at seventeen become as real and vivid as the middle-aged woman sitting in front of you. It is a happy sort of double vision, this seeing and remembering. To be seen this way is to be known.

Laurie was miserable sitting there. The

parents of young defendants have been consigned to a peculiar purgatory in these trials. We were expected to be present but silent. We were implicated in Jacob's crime as both victims and perpetrators. We were pitied, since we had done nothing wrong. We had just been unlucky, lost the pregnancy lottery, and been stuck with a rogue child. Sperm + egg = murderer—something like that. Can't be helped. At the same time we were despised: *somebody* had to be responsible for Jacob, and we had created the boy and raised him—we must have done *something* wrong. Even worse, now we had the gall to support the killer; we actually wanted to see him get away with it, which only confirmed our antisocial nature, our bone-deep badness. Of course, the public view of us was so contradictory and jumped-up with emotion that there was no way to answer it, no right way to act. People would think what they wanted, they would imagine for us whatever sinister or suffering interior life they chose. And for the next two weeks Laurie would play her part. She would sit there at the back of the courtroom as still and expressionless as a marble statue. She would watch the back of her son's head, trying to interpret the tiniest micromovements. She would react to nothing. It did not matter that once she had held that baby boy in her arms and whispered in his ear, "Sh, sh." At this point, nobody gave a shit.

When he finally took the bench, Judge French scanned the room as the clerk read out the case: "Number oh-eight-dash-four-four-oh-seven, Commonwealth v. Jacob Michael Barber, a single count of murder in the first degree. For the defendant, Jonathan Klein. For the Commonwealth, Assistant District Attorney Neal Logiudice." The judge's handsome, grave face settled briefly on each of the players, Jacob, the lawyers, even us, conferring on each a momentary significance while we were in his gaze, which vanished as soon as his eyes swept on.

Over the years I had tried many cases before Judge French, and although I thought he was a bit of an empty suit, I liked him well enough. He had been a football player at Harvard, a defensive lineman. In his senior year he had fallen on a fumble in the end zone against Yale, and this singular brilliant moment had stuck with him. He kept a framed picture of it on his office wall, big Burt French in his crimson and gold uniform lying on his side on the ground, cuddling the precious egg he'd found. I suspect the picture struck me differently than it did Judge French. To me, he was the sort of guy such things happened to. Rich and good-looking and all the rest, no doubt opportunities had always presented themselves like so many footballs lying in his way and he had merely to fall on them, all the while presuming his good fortune was the natural product of his talent. One wonders how a charmed man like him would have been affected by a father like Bloody Billy Barber. All that ease, all that naturalness, all that credulous self-confidence. For years I had studied men like Burt French, despised them, copied them.

"Mr. Klein," the judge said, slipping on a pair of half-glasses, "any preliminary motions before we begin the voir dire?"

Jonathan stood. "A couple of things, Your Honor. First, the defendant's father, Andrew Barber, would like to enter an appearance in the case on the defendant's behalf. With the court's permission, he is going to second-chair me at the trial."

Jonathan went to the clerk and handed her the motion, a single sheet announcing that I would be part of the defense team. The clerk handed the sheet to the judge, who frowned at it.

"It's not really my decision, Mr. Klein, but I'm not sure it's wise either."

"It's the family's wish," Jonathan said, distancing himself from the decision.

The judge scribbled his name on the sheet, allowing the motion. "Mr. Barber, you can come forward."

I came around the bar and sat down at the defense table beside Jacob.

"Anything else?"

"Your Honor, I have filed a motion *in limine* to exclude scientific evidence based on an alleged genetic predisposition to violence."

"Yes. I have read your motion and I am inclined to allow it. Do you wish to be heard further before I rule? As I understand it, your position is that the science has not been established and, even if it was, there

is no specific evidence of a violent propensity, genetic or otherwise, in this case.
Is that the gist of it?"

"Yes, Your Honor, that's the gist."

"Mr. Logiudice? Do you want to be heard
or will you rest on your brief? It seems to
me the defense is entitled to a hearing on
that sort of evidence before it comes in.
Mind you, I am not excluding such evidence
definitively. I am merely ruling that, if you
choose to offer evidence of a genetic tendency to violence, we will hold a hearing
at that time, outside the jury's presence, to
decide whether it will be admitted or not."

"Yes, Your Honor, I would like to be heard
on that."

The judge blinked at him. His face read
plain as day, *Sit down and shut up.*

Logiudice stood and buttoned his suit
coat, a slim three-button number that, when
buttoned up this way, did not fit him properly. Logiudice's neck craned forward
slightly while the jacket stayed erect, which
caused the coat collar to float an inch or
two away from his neck like a monk's cowl.

"Your Honor, the Commonwealth's
position—and we are prepared to offer expert evidence on this point—is that the sci-

ence of behavioral genetics has made great strides and continues to advance every day, and it is already mature enough by far and away to be admitted here. We would submit that this is even the extreme case where to exclude such evidence would be improper—"

"The motion is allowed."

Logiudice stood there a moment, unsure if his pocket had just been picked.

"Mr. Logiudice," the judge explained as he signed the motion, *Allowed. French, J.,* "I have not excluded the evidence. My ruling is simply that, if you want to offer it, you will have to provide notice to the defense and we will have a hearing on its admissibility before you offer it to the jury. Understood?"

"Understood, Your Honor."

"Let me be crystal clear: not a word of it until I rule it's coming in."

"Understood, Your Honor."

"We're not going to turn this into a circus." The judge sighed. "All right, anything else before I bring in the jury venire?"

The lawyers shook their heads.

With a series of nods—the judge to the clerk, the clerk to the court officer—the potential jurors were fetched from one of the lower floors. They shuffled in, rubbernecking the courtroom like tourists wandering through Versailles. The chamber must have disappointed them. It was a grungy courtroom in the modern style: high boxy ceilings, minimalist furnishings of maple wood and black laminate, muted indirect lighting. Two flags drooped from listing flagpoles, an American flag to the judge's right and the flag of Massachusetts to his left. The American flag at least had its original vivid colors; the state flag, once pure white, had faded to a dingy ivory. Otherwise there was nothing, no statue, no chiseled Latin inscription, no portrait of a forgotten judge, nothing to relieve the Scandinavian austerity of the design. I had been in this courtroom a thousand times, but the jurors' disappointment made me look at it, finally, and realize how exhausted it all appeared.

The jury pool filled the entire gallery at the back of the courtroom, leaving only the two benches that had been reserved for the defendant's family, reporters, and a few others whose courthouse connections entitled them to remain. The potential jurors were a mix of working people and housewives, kids and retirees. Jury pools usually skewed slightly blue-collar and underemployed, since these were the people more likely to respond to a summons. But this jury pool had a vaguely professional look to it, I thought. Lots of good haircuts, new shoes, BlackBerry holsters, pens sticking out of pockets. This too was good for us, I decided. We wanted smart, coolheaded jurors, people with the brains to understand a technical defense or the limitations of scientific evidence, and the balls to say *Not guilty.*

We began the process of voir dire, the question-and-answer process by which juries are chosen. Jonathan and I each had our jury seating charts, a table of two rows, six columns—twelve places in all, plus two extra boxes on the right side of the sheet—matching the chairs in the jury box. Twelve jurors, plus two alternates who would hear all the evidence but would not take part in the deliberations unless one of the jurors dropped out. Fourteen candidates were called forward, fourteen chairs were filled, we scribbled the names plus a few notes in the boxes on our scorecards, and the process began.

Jonathan and I conferred on each potential juror. We had six peremptory challenges, which we could use to eliminate a juror without stating a reason, and an unlimited number of challenges "for cause," meaning challenges based on some explicit reason to think the juror would be biased. For all the strategizing, jury selection has always been something of a shot in the dark. There are pricey experts who claim to remove some of the guesswork using focus groups, psychological profiling, statistics, and so on—the scientific method—but predicting how a stranger will judge your case, especially based on the very limited information in a jury questionnaire, is frankly more art than science, the more so in Massachusetts where the rules severely limit how extensively jurors may be questioned. And yet, we tried to sort them. We looked for education; for suburbanites who might sympathize with Jacob and not hold his comfortable background against him; for dispassionate professions like accountant, engineer, programmer. Logiudice tried to load up on working folks, parents, anyone who might be outraged at the crime and who would have little problem believing a boy could kill even on scant provocation.

Jurors came forward, sat, were dismissed, and new candidates came forward and sat, and we scribbled details about them in our seating charts—

And two hours later we had our jury.

We gave each juror a nickname so we could remember them. They were: the Schoolteacher (forewoman), Glasses Girl, Grandpa, Fat Somerville Guy, Recording Studio Guy, Urkel, the Canal (a woman born in Panama), Waltham Mom, the Waitress, Construction Guy (properly a wood-floor installer, a surly squinty-eyed piece of work whom we worried about from the start), Concord Housewife, Truck Driver (actually a delivery guy for a commercial food-supply company), Braces Woman (alternate), and the Bartender (alternate). They had nothing in common except their glaring lack of qualifications for the job. It was almost comical how ignorant they were of the law, of how trials worked, even of this case, which had been splashed all over the newspapers and evening news. They were chosen for their perfect ignorance of these things. That is how the system works. In the end, the lawyers and judges happily step aside and hand the entire process over to a dozen complete amateurs. It would be funny if it were not so perverse. How futile the whole project is. Surely Jacob must have realized it as he looked at those fourteen blank faces. The towering lie of the criminal justice system—that we can reliably determine the truth, that we can know "beyond a reasonable doubt" who is guilty and who is not—is built on this whopper of an admission: after a thousand years or so of refining the process, judges and lawyers are no more able to say what is true than a dozen knuckleheads selected at random off the street. Jacob must have shivered at the thought.

26 | Someone Is Watching

That night, over dinner, in the safety of our kitchen, we chattered excitedly. Words came tumbling, grumbles, boasts, fears. We were working off nervous energy more than anything else.

Laurie did her best to keep all the talk going. She was evidently exhausted from a sleepless night and a long day, but she always believed that the more we talked, the better off we would all be. So she posed questions and confessed her own fears and kept passing dishes of food, inviting us to talk and talk. In these light moments,

I glimpsed the old effervescent Laurie—or rather, I heard her, for her voice never aged. In every other way Laurie withered during Jacob's crisis: her eyes looked sunken and haunted, her peaches-and-cream complexion became sallow and cracked. But her voice was gloriously untouched. When she opened her mouth, out came the same teenage girl's voice I had first heard nearly thirty-five years before. It was like a phone call from 1974.

At one point Jacob said of the jury, "I don't think they liked me, just the way they were looking at me."

"Jacob, they've only been in the box one day. Give them a chance. Besides, so far all they know about you is that you've been accused of murder. What do you expect them to think?"

"They're not supposed to think anything yet."

"They're human, Jake. Just don't give them any reason to dislike you, that's all you can do. Stay cool. No reactions. None of your faces."

"What faces?"

"You have a face you make when you're not paying attention. You scowl."

"I don't scowl!"

"You do."

"Mom, do I scowl?"

"I haven't noticed it. Sometimes your father gets carried away with the strategy."

"You do, Jake. It's like—" I made the scowling face.

"Dad, that's not a scowl. You just look constipated."

"Hey, I'm serious. That's what you look like when you're not paying attention. It makes you look angry. Don't let the jury see that face."

"That's my face! What can I do?"

"Just be your handsome self, Jacob, " Laurie said sweetly. She gave him a broken little smile. Her sweatshirt was on backward. She seemed unaware of it, though the tag rubbed against her throat.

"Hey, speaking of my handsome self, did you guys know there's a Twitter hashtag about me?"

Laurie: "What does that mean?"

"It's a way for people to talk about me on Twitter. And what they're saying? It's all like: *Jacob Barber is gorgeous. I want to have his baby. Jacob Barber is innocent.*"

Me: "Yeah, what else are they saying?"

"All right, there's *some* bad things, but mostly it's positive. Like seventy percent."

"Seventy percent positive?"

"About."

"You've been following it that closely?"

"It only happened today. But yeah, of course I read it. You've got to check it out, Dad. Just go to Twitter and search for 'pound sign Jacob Barber,' no spaces." He wrote it on his paper napkin: *#jacobbarber.* "I was a trending topic! Do you know what that means? Usually that's like Kobe Bryant or Justin Timberlake or people like that."

"That's, um, great, Jacob." I gave a skeptical look to the boy's mother.

This was not the first time our son's Internet celebrity had come up. Someone— probably a school friend—had put together a website, JacobBarber.com, to support him. The site featured a message board where people could declare Jacob's innocence or wish him well or expound on his saintly character. Negative messages were filtered out. There was a Facebook group supporting him too. The consensus online was that Jacob was a little odd, possibly homicidal, definitely attractive, conclusions that were not unrelated. He also got occasional text messages on his cell phone from strangers. Most were vicious, but not all. Some were from girls who told him he was cute or made sexual propositions. He claimed these messages ran about two to one negative versus positive, and this seemed to be enough for him. He knew he was innocent, after all. Anyway, he did not want to change his cell phone number.

Laurie: "Maybe you should stay off Facebook and all that, Jacob. At least until this is over."

"I just read, Mom. I never write anything. I'm a lurker."

"A lurker? Don't use that word. Do me a favor, just stay away from the Internet for a while, will you? You could get hurt."

"Jacob, I think what your mother is saying is that the next couple of weeks may go easier if we just try to stay on an even keel. So maybe we should all just close our ears a little bit."

"I'll miss my fifteen minutes of fame," he said. He grinned, oblivious and blithely brave, as only a kid can be.

Laurie looked horrified.

"That'd be a real shame," I grumbled.

"Jacob, let's hope you have your fifteen minutes of fame for something else."

We all went quiet. Silverware clinked on plates.

Laurie said, "I wish that guy would turn off his engine."

"What guy?"

"That guy." She gestured with her knife toward the window. "Don't you hear him? There's a guy sitting in his car out there with the engine running. It's giving me a headache. It's like this buzz in my ear that won't go away. What's the word for that, when you get a buzz in your ear?"

"Tinnitus," I said.

She made a face.

"Crossword puzzles," I explained.

I got up to look out the window, more curious than concerned. It was a big sedan. I couldn't make out precisely what model. Some oversized end-of-the-American-auto-industry crap four-door, maybe a Lincoln. It was parked across the street, two houses down, in a dark area between streetlights where I could not see the driver at all, even in silhouette. Inside there was a dot of amber light like a star as the driver took a drag from a cigarette, then the little star winked out.

"Probably just waiting for someone."

"So let him wait with the engine off. Hasn't this guy heard of global warming?"

"Probably an older guy." I was inferring from the cigarette, the idling engine, the aircraft-carrier-sized car—all habits that belonged to an older generation, I thought.

"Asshole's probably a reporter," Jacob said.

"Jake!"

"Sorry, Mom."

"Laurie, why don't I go talk to him? I'll tell him to turn it off."

"No. Who knows what he wants? Whatever he's up to, it can't be good. Just stay put."

"Honey, you're being paranoid." I never used words like *honey* or *sweetie* or *dear,* but the gentle tone seemed necessary. "It's probably just some old geezer smoking a butt, listening to the radio. He probably doesn't realize he's bothering anyone leaving the engine running."

She frowned skeptically. "You're the one who keeps saying we have to keep our heads down, stay out of trouble. Maybe he wants you to come out there and try something. Maybe he's trying to bait you into it."

"Laurie, come on. It's just a car."

"Just a car, huh?"

"Just a car."

But it was not just a car.

Around nine I took out the garbage: one plastic barrel of trash, one awkward rectangular green bucket of recycling. The recycling bucket was sized in such a way that it could not quite be carried in one hand comfortably. Your fingers always began to cramp halfway up the driveway, so that carrying both items to the sidewalk in one trip involved a fast-waddling race-walk out to the street before the recycling spilled all over. It was not until I had put the barrel and the recycling bucket down and arranged them neatly side by side that I noticed the same car again. It had moved. This time it was parked a few houses away from ours in the other direction, again across the street. The engine was off. No firefly of a burning cigarette inside. The car might even have been empty. It was impossible to tell in the dark.

I peered into the dark to make out some details about the car.

The engine came on, then the head-lights. The car had no front license plate.

I began to pace toward it, curious.

The car backed away from me slowly, like an animal sensing a threat, then it backed away fast. At the first cross street, it did a quick, expert turnaround and drove off. I never got closer than twenty yards. In the dark, I could not make out anything about the car, not even the color or the make. It was reckless driving on such a small street. Reckless and good.

Later still, after Laurie had sensibly gone to sleep, I sat watching Jon Stewart with Jacob in the living room. I had spread my-self across the couch with my right foot propped on the cushion and my right arm dangled over the backrest. I felt an itch, a faint sensation of being watched, and I lifted the blind to peek out again.

The car was back.

I went out the back door, through the neighbor's backyard, and emerged behind the car. It was a Lincoln Town Car, license plate 75K S82. The interior was dark.

I walked up slowly alongside the driver's door. I felt ready to knock on the glass, to open the door, pull the guy out of the car, to pin him down on the sidewalk and warn him to stay away from us.

But the car was empty. I looked around briefly for the driver, a man with a cigarette. But I was being a fool. Laurie was making me paranoid too. It was just a parked car. Probably the driver was in one of the adjacent houses sound asleep or screwing his wife or watching the tube or doing any of the things normal people do, the things we used to do. What had I really seen, after all?

Still, better safe than sorry. I called Paul Duffy.

"Counselor," he answered in his old laconic way, as if he was pleased to hear from me, pleased and not surprised, even after months of silence, at eleven-thirty on the eve of opening statements.

"Duff, sorry to bother you."

"No bother. What's wrong?"

"It's probably nothing. I think there might be someone watching us. He's been parked outside all night."

"It's a man?"

"I'm not sure. I didn't see him. Just the car."

"You said 'him.'"

"I'm assuming."

"What was he doing?"

"It was just a car parked out front of the house with his engine running. This was around six, dinnertime. Then I saw him again around nine o'clock. But as soon as I started to walk toward him, he turned around and took off."

"Has he threatened you in any way?"

"No."

"Have you ever seen the car before?"

"No. I don't think so."

Deep breath into the phone. "Andy, can I give you a piece of advice?"

"I wish somebody would."

"Go to bed. Tomorrow's a big day for you. You're all under a lot of pressure."

"You think it's just a parked car."

"Sounds to me like it's just a parked car."

"Would you do me a favor and run the plate? Just to be sure. Laurie's really stressed. It'd make her feel better."

"Just between you and me?"

"Of course, Duff."

"Okay, give it to me."

"It's Mass. plate number 75K S82. It's a Lincoln Town Car."

"All right, hold on."

There was a long silence as he called it in. I watched Steven Colbert with the sound muted.

When he came back, he said, "That plate belongs on a Honda Accord."

"Shit. It's stolen."

"No. It hasn't been reported stolen, at least."

"So what's it doing on a Lincoln?"

"Probably just borrowed it, in case somebody noticed him and reported the plate to the cops. All you need is a screwdriver."

"Shit."

"Andy, you need to call this in to Newton P. D. It's still probably nothing, but file a report and at least get it on the record."

"I don't want to do that right now. The trial starts tomorrow. If I report it, it'll find its way into the news. I can't have that. It's important we seem normal and stable right now. I want that jury to see a regular family, just like them. Because we *are* just like them."

"Andy, if someone's threatening you . . ."

"No. No one's threatened us. No one's actually done anything. You said yourself, it looks like just a parked car."

"But you were worried enough that you called me."

"Doesn't matter. I'll deal with it. If the jury hears about it, half of them would think we're full of shit. They'd think we're faking it to drum up sympathy, like we're trying to play the victim in all this. No drama. Anything that makes us look odd, untrustworthy, phony, *strange,* makes it harder to get them to say *not guilty.*"

"So what do you want to do?"

"Maybe you could send a cruiser by without filing a report? Just move him along, scare him off. Just so I can tell Laurie she doesn't have to worry."

"I better do it myself, otherwise there'll have to be a report."

"I appreciate it. There's no way I can ever pay you back."

"Just get your kid home safe, Andy."

"You mean that?"

A pause.

"I don't know. This whole thing just doesn't feel right. Maybe it's just seeing you and Jacob at the defense table. I've known that kid since he was born."

"Paul, he didn't do it. I guarantee it."

He grunted, unconvinced. "Andy, who would be watching your house?"

"The victim's family? Maybe some kid who knew Ben Rifkin? Some nut who read about the case in the paper? Could be anyone. Did you guys ever follow up on Patz?"

"Who knows? Andy, I have no idea what's going on over there. They've got me in a friggin' public relations unit. Next thing, they'll have me riding up and down the turnpike giving speeding tickets. They pulled me off the case as soon as Jacob got indicted. I half expected them to investigate *me,* like I was in some kind of cover-up with you. So I don't have much information. But there was no reason for them to keep going after Patz once they charged someone else. The case was already solved."

We both considered that in silence a moment.

"All right," he said, "I'll be by. Tell Laurie it's okay."

"I already told her it's okay. She doesn't believe me."

"She won't believe me either. Whatever. You go get some sleep too. You two won't make it like this. It's only the first night."

I thanked him and went upstairs to climb in bed with Laurie.

She lay curled up like a cat, her back to me. "Who was that?" she murmured into her pillow.

"Paul."

"What'd he say?"

"He said it's probably just a parked car. Everything's okay."

She groaned.

"He said you wouldn't believe him."

"He was right."

27 | Openings

What was Neal Logiudice think-
ing when he stood up to deliver his opening statement to the jury? He was keenly
aware of the two unmanned cameras on
him. That much was clear as he meticulously buttoned the top two buttons of his
coat. It was apparently a second new suit,
not the same one he had worn the day before, though today's suit was the same hip
three-button style. (The shopping spree
was a mistake. He tended to preen in his
new costumes.) He must have imagined
himself as a hero. Ambitious, sure, but his
goals matched the public's—what was

good for Neal was good for everyone, except Jacob of course—so no harm in that.
There must have been a rightness too in
seeing me at the defense table, literally
displaced. I don't mean to suggest there
was any sense of Oedipal payback in Logiudice's head that day. Anyway, he gave
no outward sign of it. As he arranged his
new coat and stood for a moment plump-
ing for the jury—the two juries, I should
say, one in court, one on the other side of
the TV cameras—I saw only a young man's
vanity. I could not hate him or even begrudge him a little self-satisfaction. He had
graduated, grown up, he was finally The
Man. We all have felt such things at one
time or another. Oedipal or not, it is a pleasure after long years to stand in our fathers'
place, and it is a perfectly innocent pleasure. Anyway, why blame Oedipus? He was
a victim. Poor Oedipus never meant to hurt
anybody.

Logiudice nodded toward the judge
(*Show the jury you are respectful . . .*).
He glared balefully at Jacob as he passed
(*. . . and that you are not afraid of the defendant, because if you do not have the
courage to look him in the eye and say*

"guilty," how can you expect the jury to do it?). He stood directly in front of the jury with his fingertips resting on the front rail of the jury box (*Close up the space between you; make them feel you are one of them*).

"A teenage boy," he said, "found dead. In a forest called Cold Spring Park. Early on a spring morning. A fourteen-year-old boy stabbed three times in a line across the chest and tossed down an embankment slick with mud and wet leaves, and left to die facedown less than a quarter mile from the school he'd been walking to, a quarter mile from the home he'd left only minutes before."

His eyes roamed across the jury box.

"And the whole thing—the decision to do this, the choice—to take a life, to take this boy's life—it only takes a second."

He let the phrase hang there.

"One split second and"—he snapped his fingers—"snap. It only takes a second to lose your temper. And that is all you need, a second, an instant, to form the intention to murder. In this courtroom it is called *malice aforethought.* The conscious decision to kill, however quickly the intention forms, however briefly it is in the murderer's mind. First-degree murder can happen just . . . like . . . that."

He began to pace the length of the jury box, lingering to make eye contact with each juror as he passed.

"Let's think about the defendant a moment. This is a case about a boy who had everything: good family, good grades, beautiful home in a wealthy suburb. He had it all, more than most, anyway, much more. But the defendant had something else too: he had a lethal temper. And when he was pushed—not too hard, just teased, just messed around with, the sort of thing that must go on every day in every school in the country—but when he was pushed a little too far and he decided he'd had enough, that lethal temper finally just . . . snapped."

You must tell the jury the "story of the case," the tale that led to the final act. Facts are not enough; you must weave them into a story. The jury must be able to answer the question "What is this case about?" Answer that question for them and you win. Distill the case down to a single phrase for them, a theme, even a single word. Embed that

phrase in their minds. Let them take it back into the jury room with them, so that when they open their mouths to discuss the case, your words come tumbling out.

"The defendant snapped." He snapped his fingers again.

He came to the defense table, stood too close, purposely disrespecting us by invading our space. He leveled his finger at Jacob, who looked down at his lap to avoid it. Logiudice was entirely full of shit but his technique was magnificent.

"But this wasn't just any boy from a good home in a good suburb. And he wasn't just any boy with a quick temper. This defendant had something else that set him apart."

Logiudice's finger slid from Jacob to me.

"He had a father who was an assistant district attorney. And not just any assistant district attorney either. No, the defendant's father, Andrew Barber, was the First Assistant, the top man, in the very office where I work, right here in this building."

In that moment I could have reached out and grabbed that fucking finger and torn it off Logiudice's pale freckled hand. I looked him in the eye, showed nothing.

"This defendant—"

He withdrew his finger, raised it above his shoulder as if he were testing the wind, then he wagged it in the air as he moved back to the jury box.

"This defendant—"

Do not refer to the defendant by name. Call him only "the defendant." A name humanizes him, makes the jury see him as a person worthy of sympathy, even mercy.

"This defendant wasn't some clueless kid. No, no. He'd watched for years as his father prosecuted every major murder in this county. He'd listened to the dinner table conversations, overheard the phone calls, the shop talk. He grew up in a home where murder was the family business."

Jonathan dropped his pen on his notepad, emitted an exasperated hissing sigh, and shook his head. The suggestion that "murder was the family business" came awfully close to the argument Logiudice had been barred from making. But Jonathan did not object. He could not appear to be obstructing the prosecution with technical, legalistic defenses. His defense would not be technical: Jacob did not do it. Jonathan did not want to muddy that message.

I understood all this. Still, it was infuriating to watch such contemptible bullshit go unchallenged.

The judge eyed Logiudice.

Logiudice: "At least, murder *trials* were the family business. The business of proving a murderer guilty, what we're doing right here right now—this was something the defendant knew a little about, and not from watching TV shows. So when he snapped— when the moment came, the last deadly provocation, and he went after one of his own classmates with a hunting knife—he had already laid the groundwork, just in case. And when it was over, he covered his tracks like an expert. Because in a way he was an expert.

"There was only one problem: even experts make mistakes. And over the next few days we're going to uncover the tracks that led right back to him. And only to him. And when you've seen all the evidence, you'll know beyond a reasonable doubt, beyond *any* doubt, that this defendant is guilty."

A pause.

"But why? You're asking, Why would he kill a boy in his eighth-grade class? Why would any child do this to another child?"

He made a perplexed gesture: eyebrows raised, big shrug.

"Well, we've all been in school."

His lips began to curl up into a smirk, conspiratorial. *Let's be naughty together and have a laugh in the courtroom.*

"Come on, we've all been there, some of us more recently than others."

He gave a crocodile smile which was, to my amazement, returned with little knowing grins from the jurors.

"That's right, we've all been there. And we all know how kids can be. Let's face it: school can be difficult. Kids can be mean. They tease, they horse around, they poke fun. You're going to hear testimony that the victim in this case, a fourteen-year-old boy named Ben Rifkin, teased the defendant. Nothing especially shocking, nothing that would be a big deal to most kids. Nothing you wouldn't hear on any playground in any town if you left this courtroom right now and drove around a bit.

"Let me be clear about something: it is

not necessary to make a saint out of Ben
Rifkin, the victim in this case. You're going
to hear some things about Ben Rifkin that
maybe aren't too flattering. But I want you
to remember this: Ben Rifkin was a boy
like any other boy. He was not perfect. He
was a regular kid with all the flaws and all
the growing pains of an ordinary teenager.
He was fourteen years old—fourteen!—
with his whole life stretched out in front of
him. Not a saint, not a saint. But who among
us would want to be judged only by the first
fourteen years of our lives? Who among us
was complete and . . . and . . . and *finished*
at fourteen?

"Ben Rifkin was everything the defendant wanted to be. He was handsome,
cool, popular. The defendant, on the other
hand, was an outsider among his own
classmates. Quiet, lonely, sensitive, odd.
An outcast.

"But Ben made a fatal mistake in teasing this strange boy. He didn't know about
that temper, about the defendant's hidden
capacity—even desire—to kill."

"Objection!"

"Sustained. The jury will disregard the

remark about the defendant's desire, which is complete speculation."

Logiudice did not look away from the jury. He stood stone-still, shirked the objection, pretended he had not even heard it. *The judge and the defense are trying to keep it from you, but we know the truth.*

"The defendant made his plans. He got a knife. And not a kid's knife, not a whittling knife, not a Swiss Army knife—a hunting knife, a knife designed for killing. You will hear about that knife from the defendant's own best friend, who saw it in the defendant's hand, who heard the defendant say he meant to use it against Ben Rifkin.

"You will hear that the defendant thought it all out; he planned the murder. He even described the murder several weeks later in a story that he wrote and even brazenly posted on the Internet—a story in which he describes how the murder was conceived, planned in detail, and executed. Now, the defendant may try to explain away this story, which includes a detailed description of Ben Rifkin's murder, including details known only to the actual murderer. He may tell you, 'I was only fantasizing.' To which I say, as no doubt you will, What sort of kid fantasizes about a friend's murder?"

He paced, allowing the question to hang.

"Here is what we know: when the defendant left his house and set off for Cold Spring Park the morning of April 12, 2007, as he walked off into the woods, he took with him a knife in his pocket and an idea in his head. He was ready. From that point, all that remained was the trigger, the spark that made the defendant . . . snap.

"So what was that trigger? What was it that converted a fantasy of murder into the real thing?"

He paused. It was the central question to be answered, the riddle Logiudice simply had to solve: how does a normal boy with no history of violence suddenly do something so brutal? Motive is an element of every case, not legally but in the head of each and every juror. That is why motiveless (or undermotivated) crimes are so hard to prove. Jurors want to understand what happened; they want to know *why.* They demand a logical answer. Apparently Logi-

udice had none. He could only offer theories, guesses, probabilities, "murder genes."

"We may never know," he admitted, doing his best to shrug off the gaping hole in
his case, the very strangeness of the crime,
its apparent inexplicability. "Did Ben call him
a name? Did he call him *faggot* or *pussy,*
as he had in the past? Or *geek* or *loser*?
Did he push him, threaten him, bully him
somehow? Probably."

I shook my head. *Probably?*

"Whatever it was that set the defendant
off, when he met Ben Rifkin in Cold Spring
Park that fateful morning, April 12, 2007,
around eight-twenty A.M.—where he knew
Ben would be, because the two of them
had been walking to school through those
woods for years—he chose to put his plan
into action. He stabbed Ben three times. He
punched the knife into his chest"—he demonstrated with three swordfighter thrusts of
his right arm—"*one, two, three.* Three neat,
evenly spaced wounds in a line across the
chest. Even the pattern of the wounds suggests premeditation, coolness, self-control."

Logiudice paused, a little uncertainly this
time.

The jurors appeared unsure also. They watched him with expressions of concern. His opening statement, which had started so strong, had foundered on this all-important question of *why.* He seemed to want it both ways: at one moment Logiudice was suggesting Jacob had snapped, lost his temper, and murdered his classmate in a sudden rage. A moment later, he was suggesting Jacob had planned the murder for weeks, deliberated coolly over the details, used the lawyerly expertise of a prosecutor's son, then waited for his opportunity. The trouble, obviously, was that Logiudice himself had never quite been able to answer the question of motive, no matter how many theories he threw at it. The murder of Ben Rifkin just did not make sense. Even now, after months of investigation, we were asking, *Why?* I was sure the jury would sense Logiudice's problem.

"When it was done, the defendant disposed of the knife. And he went off to school. He pretended to know nothing, even when the school was put in a lockdown and the police were frantically trying to solve the case. He kept his cool.

"Ah, but the defendant ought to have

known, this son of a prosecutor, from his own long apprenticeship, that murder always leaves a trace. There is no such thing as an immaculate murder. Murder is messy, bloody, filthy work. Blood sprays and spatters. In the excitement of killing, mistakes are made.

"The defendant had left a fingerprint on the victim's sweatshirt, pressed into the victim's own wet blood—a print that could only have been made in the immediate aftermath of the murder.

"And then the lies begin to pile up. When the fingerprint is finally identified, weeks after the murder, the defendant switches his story. After denying for weeks that he knew anything about the murder, now he claims he was there but only *after* the murder."

A skeptical look.

"A motive: an outcast schoolboy with a grudge against a classmate who had been teasing him.

"A weapon: the knife.

"A plan: detailed in a description of the murder written by the defendant himself.

"The physical evidence: the fingerprint on the victim's body, in the victim's own blood.

"Ladies and gentlemen, the evidence is

overwhelming. This is a mountain of evidence. It leaves no room for doubt. When this trial is over and I have proved all the things I have just described to you, I am going to stand right here before you again, this time to ask you to do your part, to say what it obviously true, to draw the only conclusion you can: guilty. That word, *guilty*, will be hard to say, I promise you. It is hard for anyone to judge another. All our lives we are taught not to. 'Judge not,' the Bible tells us. It is especially hard when the defendant is a child. We believe fervently in the innocence of our children. We want to believe in it; we want our children to be innocent. But this child is not innocent. No. When you look at all the evidence against him, you will know in your heart of hearts there is only one just verdict in this case: guilty. *Verdict,* from the Latin for 'say the truth.' That is all I am going to ask you to do, say the truth: guilty. Guilty. Guilty. Guilty. Guilty."

He gave them a look that was determined, righteous, imploring.

"Guilty," he said again.

He bowed his head mournfully, then returned to his chair, where he slumped down, apparently drained or lost in thought or grieving the dead boy, Ben Rifkin.

Behind me, a woman in the audience whimpered. There were sounds of footsteps and the swinging door as she rushed out of the courtroom. I did not dare turn around to look.

My sense was that Logiudice's opening had been quite good. It was by far the best I had ever seen him deliver. But it was not the home run he needed. There was still room for doubt. *Why did he do it?* The jurors must have sensed the weakness in his case, the doughnut hole at its center. That was a real problem for the prosecution, since there is no time in a trial when the state's case looks stronger than in the opening statement, where the story is pristine and uncontradicted, before the evidence has been dinged up by the realities of a trial, bumbling friendly witnesses, expert hostile witnesses, cross-examination, and all the rest. My impression was that he had left us an opportunity.

"Defense?" the judge said.

Jonathan stood up. It struck me at the time—and still does now, when I see him—that he was one of those men whom it is easy to imagine as a boy, even in his gray-haired sixties. His hair was perpetually mussed, his coat unbuttoned, his tie and collar always a little askew, as if the whole getup were a boys' school uniform that he wore only because the rules required it. He stood before the jury box and scratched the back of his head and his face became perplexed as he thought it all over. For all anyone knew, he had not prepared a thing to say and needed a moment to compose his thoughts. After Logiudice's long open-ing, which somehow managed to seem both rehearsed and rambling, Jonathan's rumpled spontaneity was a breath of fresh air. Now, I admire Jonathan and I like him too, so I may be placing a thumb on the scale for him, but it seemed to me, even before he opened his mouth to speak, that he was the more likeable of the two law-yers, which is no small thing. Compared with Logiudice, who seemed unable to draw a breath without calculating how it would be seen by others, Jonathan was all natu-ralness, all ease. Slouching in the court-room in his lousy suit, distracted by his own thoughts, he looked as at home as a man in his pajamas in his own kitchen eating over the sink.

"You know," he began, "I think about one thing he said, the lawyer for the government." He waved his arm behind him in the general direction of Logiudice. "The death of a young man like Ben Rifkin is awful. Even among all the crimes, all the murders, all the terrible things we see here, it's just tragic. He was just a boy. And all the years this boy had in front of him, all the things he might have become, the great doctor, great artist, the wise leader, it's all lost. All lost.

"When you see a tragedy as enormous as that, you want to make it right, you want to fix it somehow. You want to see justice done. Maybe you feel angry; you want to see someone pay. We all feel these things, we're all only human.

"But Jacob Barber is innocent. I want to say that again so there's no misunderstanding: Jacob Barber is completely innocent. He did nothing at all, he had nothing to do with this murder. This is the wrong man.

"The evidence you just heard about, it all turns out to be nothing. The moment you scratch the surface, the moment you look at it, you understand what really happened, and the state's case blows away like smoke. That fingerprint, for example, which the government lawyer made so much of. You will hear how that fingerprint got there, just as Jacob told the policeman who arrested him, the moment he was asked. He found his classmate lying on the ground wounded, and he did what any good person would do: he tried to help. He rolled Ben over to check on him, to see if he was okay, to help him. And when he saw Ben was dead, he did the exact same thing many of us would do: he got scared. He did not want to get involved. He worried that if he told anyone he'd seen the body, let alone touched it, he would become a suspect, he might be accused of something he did not do. Was that the right reaction? Of course not. Does he wish he had been braver and told the truth right from the start? Of course he does. But he is a boy, he is human, and he made a mistake. There's no more to it than that.

"Don't—"

He stopped, looked down, considered his next sentence.

"Don't let it happen twice. One boy is dead. Don't destroy another innocent boy to make up for it. Don't let this case become a second tragedy. We've had enough tragedy already."

The first witness was Paula Giannetto, the jogger who discovered the body. I did not know this woman but I recognized her from around town, from the market or Starbucks or the dry cleaner. Newton is not a small town, but it is divided into several "villages" and within these neighborhoods the same faces keep popping up. Oddly, I did not remember seeing her jogging in Cold Spring Park, though apparently we both ran there often around the time of the murder.

Logiudice led her through her testimony, which dragged on too long. He was over-thorough, anxious to get from her every last ounce of detail and pathos there was to be got. Ordinarily, for the prosecutor a funny transformation takes place with the first witness: after standing center-stage for his opening statement, the prosecutor now steps out of the spotlight. The focus shifts to the witness, and the rules require the prosecutor to be almost passive in his questions. He steers the witness or prods her along with neutral questions like "What happened next?" or "What did you see then?" But Logiudice was quite picky about the details he wanted from Paula Giannetto. He kept stopping her to probe about this or that. Jonathan never objected to any of this, since none of the testimony tied Jacob to the murder even remotely. But again I sensed Logiudice fumbling his case, not by some grand strategic blunder but inch by inch, in a thousand little ways. (Was this wishful thinking? Maybe. I do not pretend to be objective.) Giannetto was on the stand for the better part of an hour relating her story, which was essentially unchanged since she first told it the day of the murder.

It had been a cool, damp spring morning. She was running along a hilly section of trail through Cold Spring Park when she saw what seemed to be a boy lying facedown on a leaf-strewn embankment, which sloped down to a tiny algae-skinned pond. The boy wore jeans, sneakers, and a sweatshirt. His backpack had tumbled down the hill near him. Giannetto was jogging by herself and she did not see anyone else near the body. She had passed a couple of other joggers and kids walking to school (the park was a common route to the McCormick School, which abutted it), but she saw no one near the body. She had not heard anything either, no cries or sounds of a struggle, since she had been listening to music on her iPod, which she wore in a holder strapped to her upper arm. She was even able to name the song that was playing when she saw the body: "This Is the Day" by a group called The The.

Giannetto stopped, removed the earbuds of her iPod, and looked down at the boy from the trail above. From just a few feet away, she saw the bottoms of his sneakers, his body foreshortened. She said, "Are you okay? Do you need help?" When she got no response, she went down to check on him, sidestepping carefully down the hill because of the slippery leaves. She was a mother, she said, and she could not imagine not checking on the boy, as she would expect others to do for her kids. She had it in her head that the boy had passed out, maybe from some sickness or allergy, maybe even from drugs or who knew what. So she got down on her knees beside him and jostled his shoulder, then jostled both shoulders, then rolled him over by his shoulders.

That is when she saw the blood that soaked his chest and the reddened leaves under him and all around him, still wet and glistening, draining out of the three vent-holes in his chest. The boy's skin was gray but there were small splotches of pink on his face, she said. She had a vague recollection that his skin was cold to the touch but she had no specific memory of touching it. Perhaps the body had shifted in her hands so that its skin brushed her hand. The head fell back heavily, the mouth gawped open.

It took her a moment to process the surreal fact that the boy in her arms was dead. She dropped the body, which she had been holding under the shoulders. She screamed. She slid away from it on her butt, then turned and managed to scramble over the leaves on all fours back up the hill to the trail.

For a moment, she said, nothing happened. She stood there, alone in the woods, staring at the body. She could hear the music still playing faintly in her earbuds, still playing "This Is the Day." The whole thing had not even lasted the three minutes it takes to get through a pop song.

It took a ludicrously long time to bring out this simple story. After such a lengthy direct examination, Jonathan's cross was brief almost to the point of comedy.

"You never saw the defendant, Jacob Barber, in the park that morning, did you?"

"No."

"No further questions."

With the next witness, Logiudice mis-stepped. No, more than that. He stepped in shit. The witness was the Newton P. D. detective who had headed up the investigation for the local department. This was a standard, *pro forma* sort of witness. Logiudice had to begin by running a few witnesses up there to establish the essential facts and the timetable of that first day, when the murder was discovered. The first-responding cop is often called to testify about the state of the murder scene and the critical early moments of the investigation, before the case is joined—and taken over—by the State Police CPAC unit. So this was a witness Logiudice had to call, really. He was just following the playbook. I'd have done the same thing. The trouble was, he did not know his witness as well as I did.

Lieutenant Detective Nils Peterson joined the force in Newton just a few years before I started at the DA's office, fresh out of law school. Which is to say, I had known Nils since 1984—when Neal Logiudice was in high school struggling to maintain a busy schedule of A.P. classes, band, and compulsive masturbation. (I am speculating. I cannot say for sure that he was in the band.) Nils had been handsome when we were younger. He had the sandy blond hair you might imagine based on his name. Now, in his early fifties, his hair had darkened, his back was a little stooped, his belly thickened. But he had an attractive soft-spoken demeanor on the stand, with none of the abrasive, cocksure bluster some cops exude. Juries swooned for him.

Logiudice took him through the basic facts. The body had been found lying on its back, face up to the sky, having been flipped over by the jogger who discovered it. The pattern of the three stab wounds.

The lack of obvious motive or suspects. No signs of struggle or defensive wounds, suggesting a sudden or surprise attack. Photos of the body and the surrounding area were entered into evidence. In the first minutes and hours of the investigation, the park had been sealed and searched, with no results. Several footprints were found in the park but none in the immediate area of the body and none that were ever matched to a suspect. In any case it was a public park—there were probably thousands of footprint traces, if you cared to look for them.

And then this.

Logiudice: "Is it the usual procedure that an assistant district attorney is assigned to direct homicide investigations right away?"

"Yes."

"Who was the assistant district attorney assigned to the case that day?"

"Objection!"

Judge French: "I'll see counsel at sidebar."

Logiudice and Jonathan went to the far side of the judge's bench where they talked in low murmurs. Judge French stood tall above them, as was his habit. Most judges wheeled their chairs over to the rail or leaned in close, the better to whisper with the lawyers. Not Burt French.

The sidebar conference took place out of the jury's hearing and mine. The next few paragraphs I have cut and pasted from the trial transcript.

The judge: "Where are you going with this?"

Logiudice: "Your Honor, the jury is entitled to know the defendant's own father was in charge of the early stages of the investigation, particularly if the defense is going to suggest anything was handled improperly, as I suspect they will have to."

"Counselor?"

Jonathan: "Well, our objection is two-fold. First, it is irrelevant. It is guilt by association. Even if the defendant's father should not have taken the case and even if he mishandled it in some way—and I'm not suggesting that either is true—it still doesn't say a damn thing about the defendant himself. Unless Mr. Logiudice means to suggest the son was involved in a conspiracy with his father to cover up evidence of the crime, then there is no way to con-

strue evidence against the father as having anything to do with the son's guilt or
innocence. If Mr. Logiudice wants to indict
the father for obstruction of justice or some
such thing, then he should go ahead and
do it and we'll all come back here someday and we'll have a trial on that. But that's
not the case we're trying here today.

"The second objection is that it is improperly prejudicial. It is guilt by insinuation. He is trying to poison the jury with the
suggestion that the father must have known
the son was involved and therefore he must
have been up to something improper. But
there's no evidence either that the father
suspected his son—which he certainly did
not—or that he did anything improper when
he was leading the investigation. Let's be
honest: the prosecutor wants to toss a stink
bomb into this courtroom to distract the jury
from the fact that there is virtually no direct
evidence against the defendant. It's—"

"Okay, okay, I got it."

Logiudice: "Your Honor, how important
it is, that's for the jury to decide. But they
have a right to know. The defendant can't
have it both ways: he can't argue that the

cops screwed up and then conveniently leave out the fact that the cop in charge was the defendant's own father."

The judge: "I'm going to allow it. But Mr. Logiudice, I'm warning you, if this trial gets sidetracked into a discussion of whether the father screwed up, intentionally or not, I'm going to cut it off. The defense has a point: that's not the case we're here to try. If you want to indict the father, do it."

The transcript does not record Logiudice's reaction, but I remember it well. He looked across the courtroom directly at me.

Returning to the little lectern near the jury box, he faced Nils Peterson and resumed his questions. "Detective, I'll repeat the question. Who was the assistant DA assigned to the case that day?"

"Andrew Barber."

"Do you see Andrew Barber in the courtroom here today?"

"Yes, he's right there, beside the defendant."

"And did you know Mr. Barber when he was an assistant DA? Did the two of you ever work together?"

"Sure, I knew him. We worked together many times."

"Were you friendly with Mr. Barber?"

"Yes, I'd say so."

"Did it occur to you at the time that it was odd Mr. Barber was handling a case involving his own son's school, a class-mate, a boy he might even have known something about?"

"No, not really."

"Well, did it seem strange to you that Mr. Barber's son might well become a wit-ness in the case?"

"No, I didn't think about that."

"But, when he was leading the case, the defendant's father pushed for a sus-pect who turned out not to be involved, a man who lived near the park who had a record as a sexual offender?"

"Yes. His name was Leonard Patz. He had a record for indecent A&Bs on kids, things like that."

"And Mr. Barber—Andrew Barber, the father—wanted to pursue this man as a suspect, did he not?"

"Objection. Relevance."

"Sustained."

Logiudice: "Detective, while the defendant's father was leading the investigation, did you consider Leonard Patz as a suspect?"

"Yes."

"And Patz was later cleared when the defendant's own son was charged?"

"Objection."

"Overruled."

Peterson hesitated here, seeing the trap. If he went too far to help his friend, he would necessarily help the defense. He tried to find a middle way. "Patz was not charged."

"And when Mr. Barber's son was charged, were you surprised at that point by Mr. Barber's earlier involvement in the case?"

"Objection."

"Overruled."

"I thought it was surprising, yes, in the sense—"

"Have you ever heard of a prosecutor or a cop becoming involved in an investigation of his own son?"

Cornered, Peterson drew a deep breath. "No."

"It would be a conflict of interest, wouldn't it?"

"Objection."

"Sustained. Move on, Mr. Logiudice."

Logiudice asked a few more desultory, halfhearted questions, relishing the afterglow of a victory. When he sat down, he had the dopey, flushed face of a man who just got laid, and he kept his head down until he could overmaster it.

On cross, Jonathan again did not bother to attack much of anything Peterson had said about the crime scene, because again there was virtually nothing in his rendition that pointed to Jacob. There was so little trace of antagonism between these two soft-spoken guys, in fact, and the questions were all so inconsequential, that it might have been a defense witness Jonathan was questioning.

"The body was lying in a twisted position when you arrived at the scene, is that right, Detective?"

"Yes."

"So, given the fact the body had been moved, some evidence had been lost even before you arrived. For example, the position of the body can often help you reconstruct the attack itself, isn't that right?"

"Yes, it is."

"And when the body is flipped over, the

effect of lividity—or the blood settling with gravity—is also reversed. It's like turning over a sand timer: the blood starts to flow the other way, and the inferences you usually draw from lividity are lost, isn't that right?"

"Yes. I'm not a forensics expert, but yes."

"Understood, but you *are* a homicide detective."

"Yes."

"And it's fair to say that, as a general rule, at a murder scene when the body is disturbed or moved, evidence is often lost."

"Generally true, yes. In this case, there's no way of knowing if anything was actually lost."

"Was the murder weapon found?"

"Not that day, no."

"Was it ever found?"

"No."

"And besides the single fingerprint on the victim's sweatshirt, there was nothing at all that pointed to a particular defendant?"

"Correct."

"And of course the fingerprint was not identified until much later, right?"

"Yes."

"So the crime scene itself, on that first day, did not yield any evidence that pointed to a particular suspect?"

"No. Just the unidentified fingerprint."

"So it's fair to say that at the beginning of the investigation you didn't have any obvious suspects?"

"Yes."

"So in that situation, as an investigator, wouldn't you want to know, wouldn't it be relevant information that a known, convicted pedophile lived adjacent to that park? A man with a record of sexual assaults on young boys of about the victim's age?"

"It would."

I could feel the jury's eyes on me as they seemed to understand, finally, where Jonathan was going—that he was not simply settling for a series of small hits.

"So it didn't seem improper or unusual or the slightest bit odd to you when Andy Barber, the defendant's father, focused his attention on this man, this Leonard Patz?"

"No, it didn't."

"In fact, based on what you knew at the time, he wouldn't be doing his job if he *didn't* check out this man, would he?"

"No, I don't think so."

"And, in fact, you learned in your subsequent investigation that Patz was indeed known to walk in that park in the mornings, isn't that true?"

"Yes."

"Objection." There was not much conviction in Logiudice's voice.

"Overruled." Plenty of conviction in the judge's voice. "You opened the door, Counselor."

I had always disliked Judge French's tendency to let his sympathies show. He was a ham, and generally his emoting favored the defense. His courtroom always felt like a home game for the defendant. Now that I was on the defendant's side, of course, I was delighted to see the judge so openly cheerleading for us. It was an easy ruling, anyway. Logiudice had opened this subject. He could not now prevent the defense from exploring it.

I gestured to Jonathan and he came over to accept a piece of paper from me. When he read it, his eyebrows rose. I had written three questions on the paper. He folded the paper neatly and moved closer to the witness stand.

"Detective, did you ever disagree with any of the decisions Andy Barber made when he was leading the investigation?"

"No."

"And, in fact, isn't it true that you also wanted to pursue the investigation against this man, Patz, at the beginning of the investigation?"

"Yes."

A juror—Fat Somerville Guy, in chair number seven—actually snorted and shook his head.

Jonathan heard that guffaw over his shoulder from the jury box, and he looked like he was about to sit down.

I gave him a look that said, *Go on.*

He frowned. Outside of TV shows, you do not go for the kill on cross-examination. You land a few shots then sit your ass down. The witness, remember, has all the power, not you. Plus, the third line on that page was the archetypal Question You Never Ask On Cross: open-ended, subjective, the sort of question that invites a long, unpredictable answer. To a veteran lawyer, the feeling was like the moment in a horror movie when the babysitter hears a noise in the basement and opens the creaky door to go down and investigate. *Don't do it!* the audience says.

Do it, my expression insisted.

"Detective," he began, "I know this is awkward for you. I'm not asking you to express any opinion about the defendant himself. I understand you have a job to do on that score. But limiting our discussion to the defendant's father, Andy Barber, whose judgment and integrity has been called into question here—"

"Objection."

"Overruled."

"How long have you known the older Mr. Barber?"

"A long time."

"How long?"

"Twenty years. More, probably."

"And having known him over twenty years, what is your opinion of him as a prosecutor, with respect to his ability, his integrity, his judgment?"

"We're not talking about the son? Only the father?"

"That's right."

Peterson looked directly at me. "He's the best they've got. The best they used to have, anyway."

"No further questions."

No further questions meaning *Fuck you.* Logiudice would never again focus quite so explicitly on my role in the investigation, though it was a note he touched on a few times in the course of the trial. No doubt, that first day he successfully planted the idea in the jurors' minds. For the time being, that may have been all he needed to accomplish.

Still, we walked out of the courtroom that afternoon feeling victorious.

It didn't last.

28 | A Verdict

Dr. Vogel informed us grimly, "I'm afraid I have some rather difficult things to say."

We had all been feeling drained. The stress of a full day in court leaves you bone-tired and muscle-sore. But the doctor's gloom put us on red alert. Laurie focused on her with an intent expression, Jonathan with his usual owlish curiosity.

Me: "I promise you, we're used to bad news. At this point, we're bulletproof."

Dr. Vogel avoided my eyes.

In hindsight I hear how ridiculous I must have sounded. We parents often talk with ridiculous bravado when it comes to our kids. We swear that we can take any abuse, beat any challenge. No test is too great. Anything for our kids. But no one is bullet-proof, parents least of all. Our kids make us vulnerable.

In hindsight I see too that this meeting was exquisitely timed to break us. Only an hour or so had passed since court had ad-journed for the day, and as the adrenaline receded, so did our sense of triumph, leav-ing us doped, punch-drunk. We were in no shape for bad news.

The scene was Jonathan's office near Harvard Square. We were seated around the circular oak table in his book-walled li-brary, just the four of us, Laurie and me, Jonathan and Dr. Vogel. Jacob was out in the waiting room with Jonathan's young as-sociate, Ellen.

When Dr. Vogel turned away from me, when she could not look me in the eye, she must have been thinking, *You think you're bulletproof? Just wait.*

"How about you, Laurie?" the shrink said in her solicitous, therapeutic voice. "Do you think you can handle this right now?"

"Absolutely."

Dr. Vogel's eyes moved over Laurie: her hair, which kinked up like stretched springs, and her complexion, which now looked jaundiced, with dark bags under her eyes. She had lost so much weight, the skin sagged and pouched on her face and her clothes drooped on her bony shoulders. I thought: when did all this deterioration happen? All at once, with the strain of this case? Or gradually, over the years, without my noticing? This was not my Laurie anymore, the brave girl who invented me and who, it now seemed, I had invented for myself. She looked so wasted, in fact, it occurred to me that she was dying before our eyes. The case was consuming her. She was never built for this sort of fight. She had never been hard. She had never had to be. Life never hardened her. It was not her fault, of course, but to me— who felt unbreakable, even this late in the events—Laurie's fragility was impossibly poignant. I was prepared to be hard for both of us, for all three of us, but there was nothing I could do to protect Laurie from the stress. You see, I could not stop loving her, and I still cannot. Because it is easy to be hard if you have a stony nature. But imagine what it cost Laurie that day as she sat bolt upright at the edge of her chair, gamely focused on the doctor, ready for yet another blow. She never stopped defending Jacob, never stopped analyzing the chessboard, calculating every move and countermove. She never stopped protecting him, even in the end.

Dr. Vogel said, "Why don't I just explain my conclusions a little bit, then afterward I'll answer your questions if you have any, okay? I know it's very, very hard to hear difficult news about Jacob, but brace yourselves for just a few minutes, okay? Just listen, then we can talk."

We nodded.

Jonathan said, "For the record, none of this is discoverable by the prosecution. You don't have to worry. Everything we discuss here and everything Dr. Vogel tells you now is privileged. This conversation is absolutely confidential. It never leaves this room. So you can speak frankly, as can the doctor, okay?"

More nodding.

"I don't understand why we have to do

this," I said. "Jonathan, why do we even have to get into this if our defense is that Jacob didn't do it at all?"

Jonathan made a V of his hand and stroked his short white beard. "I hope you're right. I hope the case goes well and we never have to raise this issue."

"Then why do this?"

Jonathan turned away slightly, dismissing me.

"Why do this, Jonathan?"

"Because Jacob looks guilty."

Laurie gasped.

"I don't mean that he *is* guilty, only that there is a lot of evidence against him. The Commonwealth has not put up their strongest witnesses yet. This is going to get harder for us. A lot harder. And when it does, I want to be prepared. Andy, you of all people should understand that."

"All right," the doctor said, wading in. "I've just given Jonathan my report. Really, it's an opinion letter, a summary of my conclusions, what I would say if I was ever called to testify and what I think you could expect if this issue ever came up at trial. Now, I wanted to speak with you two alone first, without Jacob. I have not shared my conclusions with Jacob. When this case is over, depending on how it goes, we can have a more meaningful conversation about how to deal with some of these issues in a clinical setting. But for now our concern is not therapy, it is the trial. I was engaged for a specific purpose, as an expert for the defense. So that's why Jacob is not in the room now. He will have a lot more work to do when the trial is over. But for now we need to speak candidly about him, which may be easier if he's out of the room.

"There are two disorders that Jacob exhibits pretty clearly, narcissistic personality disorder and reactive attachment disorder. There is some suggestion of an antisocial personality disorder as well, which is a not uncommon comorbidity, but because I'm not as certain of the diagnosis, I haven't included it in my report.

"It is important to realize that not all the behaviors I'm going to describe are necessarily pathological, even in combination. To some extent every teenager is a narcissist, every adolescent is dealing with attachment issues. It is a matter of degree. We are not talking about a monster here. We're talking about an ordinary kid—only more so. So I don't want you to hear this as a condemnation. I want you to *use* the things I'm telling you, not be overwhelmed by them. I want to give you the tools, the vocabulary, to help your son. The point is to understand Jacob better, okay? Laurie? Andy?"

We agreed, obediently, dishonestly.

"Good. Okay, narcissistic personality disorder. This is the one you probably know something about. Its primary characteristics are grandiosity and lack of empathy. In Jacob's case, the grandiosity does not come across as dramatic or boastful, arrogant, haughty, which is what people commonly associate with it. Jacob's grandiosity is quieter. It shows up as an inflated sense of self-importance, a conviction he is special, exceptional. Rules that might apply to others do not apply to him. He feels he is not understood by his peers, especially the other kids at school, with a few select exceptions whom Jacob identifies as special like him, usually based on their intelligence.

"The other key aspect of NPD, especially in the context of a criminal case, is lack of empathy. Jacob exhibits an unusual coldness toward others, even—and this surprised me, given the context—even for Ben Rifkin and his family. When I asked Jacob about it in one of our sessions, his response was that people die every day by the millions; that car crashes are statistically more significant than murder; that soldiers kill thousands more and get medals for it—so why should we worry about one murdered boy? Even when I tried to lead him back to the Rifkins and prodded him to express some sort of feeling for them or for Ben, he couldn't or wouldn't do it. All of which fits a pattern of incidents you have described throughout Jacob's childhood in which other children have been injured around him, children flying off jungle gyms and being knocked off bicycles and so forth.

"He seems to regard other people not just as less significant than himself, but as less human. He cannot see himself mirrored in others in any way. He cannot seem to imagine that others have the same universal human feelings that he does—pain, sadness, loneliness—which is a sensitivity that ordinary adolescents have no trouble understanding at this age. I won't belabor the point. The relevance of these feelings in a forensic context is obvious. Without empathy, anything is permitted. Morality becomes very subjective and flexible.

"The good news is that NPD is not a chemical imbalance. And it is not genetic. It is a complex of behaviors, a deeply ingrained habit. Which means it can be unlearned, over time."

The doctor went on with barely a pause.

"The other disorder is actually the more disturbing one. Reactive attachment disorder is a relatively new diagnosis. And because it is new, we don't know much about it. There hasn't been much study done. It is uncommon, it is difficult to diagnose, and it is difficult to treat.

"The critical aspect of RAD is that it stems from a disruption of ordinary childhood emotional attachments in infancy. The theory is that ordinarily infants attach to a single, reliable caregiver, and from that secure base they explore the world. They know that their basic emotional and physical needs will be met by that one person. Where that reliable caregiver is not present or where the caregiver changes too often, children may relate to others in inappropriate ways, sometimes grossly inappropriate ways: aggression, rage, lying, defiance, lack of remorse, cruelty; or overfamiliarity, hyperactivity, self-endangerment.

"The definition of this disorder requires some sort of disruption in early caregiving— 'pathogenic care,' usually mistreatment or neglect by the parent or caregiver. But there is some controversy about exactly what that means. I am not suggesting either of you were deficient in any way. This is not about your parenting. But recent research suggests the disorder can arise even without deficient caregiving. Some children just seem temperamentally vulnerable to attachment disorders, so that even minor disruptions—day care, for example, or being passed from one caregiver to the next too often—can be enough to trigger an attachment disorder."

"Day care?" Laurie.

"Only in exceptional cases."

"Jacob was in day care from the time he was three months old. We both worked. I stopped teaching when he was four."

"Laurie, we don't know enough to presume a cause and effect. You have to resist the urge to blame yourself. There is no reason to think neglect is the cause here.

Jacob may just have been one of these vulnerable, hypersensitive children. This is all a very new area. We researchers are struggling to understand it ourselves."

Dr. Vogel gave Laurie a reassuring look, but there was a hint in her voice of protesting too much, and I could see Laurie was not mollified.

Unable to help, Dr. Vogel simply plowed on. She seemed to think that the best way to get across all this devastating information was to do it quickly and get it over with.

"In Jacob's case, whatever the trigger, there is evidence of atypical attachment as an infant. You've reported that as a child he seemed guarded and hypervigilant at times, or erratic and prone to excessive anger and lashing out at other times."

Me: "But *all* kids are 'erratic' and 'prone to excessive anger.' Lots of kids go to day care and don't—"

"It would be very unusual to see RAD"—she pronounced it as a rhyme for *bad*—"in the absence of some sort of neglect, but we simply don't know."

"Enough!" Laurie raised both hands in a stop sign. "Just stop it!" She stood and pushed her chair away, retreated to the far corner of the room. "You think he did it."

"I didn't say that," Dr. Vogel demurred.

"You didn't have to say it."

"No, Laurie, really, I don't have any way to know whether he did it. That's not my job. It's not what I set out to determine."

Me: "Laurie, this is psychobabble. She said herself, you could say these things about any kid—narcissistic, self-centered. Find me a teenager who *isn't* like that. It's garbage. I don't believe a word of it."

"Of course you don't! You never see these things. You're so determined to be normal and for *us all* to be normal that you just close your eyes and ignore anything that doesn't fit."

"We *are* normal."

"Oh my God. Do you think this is normal, Andy?"

"This situation? No. But do I think Jacob is normal? Yes! Is that so crazy?"

"Andy. You're not seeing things right. I feel like I have to think for both of us because you just can't see."

I went over to her to comfort her, to lay my hand on her crossed arms. "Laurie, this is our son."

She flailed her hands, batting mine away. "Andy, stop it. We are not normal."

"Of course we are. What are you talking about?"

"You've been pretending. For years. All this time you've been pretending."

"No. Not about the important things."

"The important things! Andy, you didn't tell the truth. All this time you never told the truth."

"I never lied."

"Every day you didn't tell, you were lying. Every day. Every day."

She shoved past me to confront Dr. Vogel again. "You think Jacob did it."

"Laurie, please sit down. You're upset."

"Just say it. Don't sit there and read me your report and recite the *DSM* to me. I can read the *DSM* too. Just say what you mean: he did it."

"I can't tell you he did or didn't do it. I just don't know."

"So you're saying he *might* have done it. You think it's actually possible."

"Laurie, please sit down."

"I don't want to sit down! Answer me!"

"I see certain traits and behaviors in Jacob that disturb me, yes, but that's a very different thing—"

"And it's our fault? Excuse me: it *could* be our fault, it's *possible* that it *might just be* our fault, because we're such bad parents, because we had the nerve, the . . . the cruelty to put him in day care like every other kid in this town. Every other kid!"

"No. I would not say that, Laurie. It is positively *not* your fault in any way. Put that thought right out of your head."

"And the gene, this mutation you tested for. What do you call it? Knockout whatever."

"MAOA Knockout."

"Does Jacob have it?"

"The gene is not what you're suggesting. I've explained, at the most it creates a predisposition—"

"Doctor. Does. Jacob. Have it?"

"Yes."

"And my husband?"

"Yes."

"And my—I don't even know what to call him—my father-in-law?"

"Yes."

"Well, there you go. Of course he does.

And what you said earlier, about Jacob's heart being two sizes too small, like the Grinch?"

"I should not have phrased it like that. That was a foolish thing to say. I'm sorry."

"Never mind how you phrased it. Do you still believe it? Is my son's heart two sizes too small?"

"We need to work on building an emotional vocabulary for Jacob. It's not about the size of his heart. His emotional maturity is not at the same level as his peers."

"What level is it at? His emotional maturity?"

Deep breath. "Jacob presents some of the characteristics of a boy half his age."

"Seven! My son has the emotional maturity of a seven-year-old! That's what you're saying!"

"That's not the way I'd put it."

"So what do I do? What do I do?"

No answer.

"What am I supposed to do?"

"Shh," I said, "he'll hear you."

29 | The Burning Monk

Day three of the trial.

Beside me at the defense table, Jacob picked at a gristly nubbin of skin on his right thumb, near the nail. He had been scraping away at this area of his thumb for a while, nervously, absently, and had opened a little crack that extended from the cuticle down about a quarter inch toward the knuckle. He did not chew the cuticle, as kids often do. His method involved scratching the skin with a fingernail, lifting little peels and shavings until he succeeded in scooping up a substantial sliver, whereupon he would bear down and set about

removing the rubbery protrusion by a bat-
tery of wiggles, tugs, and, when all else
failed, slicing it with the dull edge of a fingernail. The area of these excavations never
had a chance to heal. After a particularly
aggressive excision, blood would seep from
the wound, and he would have to squeeze
his thumb with a Kleenex, if he had one, or
stick the whole thing in his mouth to slurp
it clean. He seemed to believe, against all
logic, that no one could be bothered by
this nauseating little drama.

I took the hand Jacob was punishing
and moved it down into his lap, out of the
jurors' sight, then rested my arm protec-
tively on the back of his chair.

On the stand, a woman was testifying.
Ruthann Something-or-other. She was fifty
years old or so. Likeable face. Short, plain
haircut. More gray hair than dark, a fact she
made no effort to conceal. No jewelry except a watch and wedding ring. She wore
black clogs. She was one of the neighbors
who walked their dogs along the trails in
Cold Spring Park every morning. Logiudice had called her to testify that she passed
a boy who roughly resembled Jacob near

the murder scene that morning. It would have been a worthwhile bit of evidence if only this woman could deliver on it, but she was obviously suffering on the stand. She washed her hands over and over in her lap. She weighed every question before answering. Before long, her anxiety became more compelling than her actual testimony, which did not amount to much.

Logiudice: "Could you describe this boy?"

"He was average, I guess. Five nine, five ten. Skinny. He was wearing jeans and sneakers. Dark hair."

This was not a boy she was describing, it was a shadow. Half the kids in Newton fit the description, and she was not done yet. She hedged and hedged, until Logiudice was reduced to prompting his own witness by sneaking into his questions little reminders, like cue cards, of what she had said in her initial answers to the police on the day of the murder. The prosecutor's constant prompting got Jonathan up on his feet to object over and over, and the whole thing became increasingly ridiculous, with the witness getting ready to recant the ID, and Logiudice too dense to get her off the stand before she made it official, and Jonathan jumping up and down to object to the leading—

and somehow it all faded into the background for me. I could not focus on it, let alone care about it. I had a sinking sense that this whole trial did not matter. It was already too late. Dr. Vogel's verdict mattered at least as much as this one would.

Next to me was Jacob, this riddle Laurie and I had made. His size, his resemblance to me, the likelihood that he would fill out and come to resemble me even more—all this shattered me. Every father knows the disconcerting moment when you see your child as a weird, distorted double of yourself. It is as if for a moment your identities overlap. You see an idea, a conception of your boyish inner self, stand right up in front of you, made real and flesh. He is you and not you, familiar and strange. He is you restarted, rewound; at the same time he is as foreign and unknowable as any other person. In the push/pull of this confusion, with my arm on the back of his chair, I touched his shoulder.

Guiltily he laid his hands flat on his lap, where he had gone back to picking the raw skin on his right thumb and had managed to pry up a new sliver.

Directly behind me, Laurie sat alone on the front bench. She sat alone every day of the trial. We were friendless in Newton, of course. I wanted to enlist Laurie's parents to sit with her in the courtroom. I am sure they would have done it. But Laurie would not allow it. She was being a bit of a martyr here. She had brought down catastrophe on her own family by marrying into mine; now she was determined to pay the price alone. In court, people tended to leave a foot or so on either side of her. Whenever I turned, she was alone in that zone of isolation on the bench, distracted, her arms half folded, her chin resting in one hand, listening, looking down at the floor rather than at the witness. The night before, Laurie had been so shaken by Dr. Vogel's diagnosis that she begged one of my Ambiens and still could not sleep. Lying in bed in the dark, she said, "If he *is* guilty, Andy, what do we do?" I told her there was nothing to do at the moment but wait until the jury decided if he was guilty or not. I tried to snuggle with her to comfort her, which seemed like the husbandly thing to do, but my touch rattled her even more and she wriggled away from me to the very edge of the bed, where she lay as still as she could but quite obviously awake, her sniffles and little movements betraying her. Back in her teaching days, Laurie had been (to me) a miraculous sleeper. She turned off the light as early as nine o'clock because she had to wake up so early, and she was asleep as soon as her head hit the pillow. But that was another Laurie.

Meanwhile, in the courtroom Logiudice apparently had decided to ride it out to the end with this witness, even as she gave every sign of imploding. It is hard to justify Logiudice's decision in strategic terms, so I imagine he just wanted to prevent Jonathan from having the honor of eliciting her final recantation. Or maybe he still hoped, desperately, that she would come around in the end. But he would not give up, the stubborn bastard. It was actually sort of noble, in a weird way, like a captain going down with his ship or a monk dousing himself with gasoline and setting himself on fire. By the time Logiudice got to his last question—he had scripted the whole examination on his yellow legal pad and stuck to the script even as the witness improvised freely—Jonathan had put down his pen and was watching through his fingers.

Question: "Is the boy you saw in Cold Spring Park that morning sitting here in the courtroom today?"

Answer: "I can't be sure."

"Well, do you see a boy matching the description you gave of the boy from the park?"

Answer: "I don't—I'm really not sure anymore. It was a kid. That's all I know for sure. It was a long time ago. The more I think about it, I just don't want to say. I don't want to send some kid to prison for life if there's a chance I might be wrong. I couldn't live with myself if I did that."

Judge French blew out a long, droll sigh. He arched his eyebrows and removed his glasses. "Mr. Klein, I take it you have no questions?"

"No, Your Honor."

"I didn't think so."

Things did not improve much for Logiudice the rest of that day. He had organized his witnesses into logical groups, and today was devoted to the civilian witnesses.

They were passersby. None had seen anything especially damning from Jacob's point
of view. But then, it was a weak case, and
Logiudice was right to throw everything he
had into the pot. So we heard from two
more people, a man and a woman, who
each testified they saw Jacob in the park,
albeit not near the murder scene. Another
witness saw a figure running from the general area of the murder. She could not say
anything about this person's age or identity, but the clothes roughly matched what
Jacob was wearing that day, even if jeans
and a light jacket were not exactly a distinctive uniform, especially in a park filled
with kids walking to school.

Logiudice did end on a harrowing note.
His last witness was a man named Sam
Studnitzer who was walking his dog through
the park that morning. Studnitzer had a very
short haircut, narrow shoulders, a gentle
manner.

"Where were you going?" Logiudice
asked.

"There is a field where dogs can run
around off the leash. I take my dog most
mornings."

"What kind of dog is he?"

"A black Lab. His name is Bo."

"What time was it?"

"Around eight-twenty. I'm usually earlier."

"Where in the park were you and Bo?"

"We were on one of the paths through the woods. The dog had gone on ahead, sniffing around."

"And what happened?"

Studnitzer hesitated.

The Rifkins were in the courtroom, on the front bench behind the prosecution table.

"I heard a little boy's voice."

"What did the little boy say?"

"He said, 'Stop, you're hurting me.'"

"Did he say anything else?"

Studnitzer slumped, frowned. Quietly: "No."

"Just 'Stop, you're hurting me'?"

Studnitzer did not answer, but clamped fingers over his temples, covering his eyes.

Logiudice waited.

The courtroom was so dead quiet, Studnitzer's sniffly breathing was clearly audible. He took his hand away from his face. "No. That's all I heard."

"Did you see anyone else around you?"

"No. I couldn't see very far. The sight lines are limited. That part of the park is hilly. The trees grow thick. We were coming down a little slope. I couldn't see anyone."

"Could you tell which direction the cry came from?"

"No."

"Did you look around, did you investigate? Did you try to help the little boy in any way?"

"No. I didn't know. I thought it was just kids. I didn't know. I didn't think anything of it. There are so many kids in that park every morning, laughing, fooling around. It sounded like just . . . roughhousing." His eyes fell.

"What did the boy's voice sound like?"

"Like he was hurt. He was in pain."

"Were there any other sounds after the cry? Pushing, sounds of a struggle, anything at all?"

"No. I didn't hear anything like that."

"What happened next?"

"The dog was alert, hyper, strange. I didn't know what his problem was. I kind of pushed him along, and we kept on walking through the park."

"Did you see anyone as you were walking?"

"No."

"Did you observe anything else unusual that morning?"

"No, not until after, when I heard the sirens and cops started streaming into the park. That's when I found out what happened."

Logiudice sat down.

Everyone in the courtroom was hearing those words in a loop in their heads: *Stop, you're hurting me. Stop, you're hurting me.* I have not gotten them out of my head yet. I doubt I ever will. But the truth is, even this detail did not point to Jacob.

To underscore that fact, Jonathan stood up on cross to ask a single perfunctory question: "Mr. Studnitzer, you never saw this boy, Jacob Barber, in the park that morning, did you?"

"No."

Jonathan took a moment to shake his head in front of the jury and say, "Terrible, terrible," to demonstrate that we too were on the side of the angels.

There it stood. Despite everything—Dr. Vogel's awful diagnosis and Laurie's shell shock and the hauntingly ordinary words of the boy as he was stabbed—after three days we were still up, way up. If this were a Little League game, we might be talking about the mercy rule. As it turned out, it was our last good day.

Mr. Logiudice: Let me stop you there for just a moment. I understand your wife was upset.

Witness: We were all upset.

Mr. Logiudice: But Laurie in particular was struggling.

Witness: Yes, she was having a hard time handling the pressure.

Mr. Logiudice: More than that. She was clearly having her doubts about Jacob's innocence, especially after you all spoke with Dr. Vogel and got the full diagnosis in some detail. She even asked you point-blank what you two ought to do if he was guilty, didn't she?

Witness: Yes. A little later. But she was very upset at that moment. You have no idea what this sort of pressure is like.

Mr. Logiudice: What about you? Weren't you upset too?

Witness: Of course I was. I was terrified.

Mr. Logiudice: Terrified because you were finally beginning to consider the possibility Jacob might be guilty?

Witness: No, terrified because the jury might convict him whether he was actually guilty or not.

Mr. Logiudice: It still hadn't crossed your mind that Jacob might actually have done it?

Witness: No.

Mr. Logiudice: Not once? Not for a single second?

Witness: Not once.

Mr. Logiudice: "Confirmation bias," is that it, Andy?

Witness: Fuck you, Neal. Heartless prick.

Mr. Logiudice: Don't lose your temper.

Witness: You've never seen me lose my temper.

Mr. Logiudice: No. I can just imagine.

[The witness did not respond.]

Mr. Logiudice: All right, let's continue.

30 | The Third Rail

Trial day four.

Paul Duffy on the stand. He wore a blue blazer, rep tie, and gray flannel pants, which was about as formal as he ever managed to dress. Like Jonathan, he was one of those men it is easy to imagine as boys, men whose appearance almost forces you to see the boy inside. It was nothing particular about his physical features, but a boyish quality in his manner. Maybe it was just the effect of my long friendship with him. To me, Paul remained twenty-seven years old forever, his age when I met him.

For Logiudice, of course, that friendship

made Duffy a slippery witness. At the start, Logiudice's manner was tentative, his questions overly cautious. If he had asked, I could have told him that Paul Duffy was not going to lie, even for me. It just wasn't in him. (I would have told him also to put down his ridiculous yellow pad. He looked like a goddamn amateur.)

"Would you state your name for the record, please?"

"Paul Michael Duffy."

"What do you do for work?"

"I'm a lieutenant detective with the Massachusetts State Police."

"How long have you been employed by the state police?"

"Twenty-six years."

"And what is your current assignment?"

"I am in a public relations unit."

"Directing your attention to April 12, 2007, what was your assignment on that date?"

"I was in charge of a special unit of detectives assigned to the Middlesex District Attorney's Office. The unit is called CPAC, for Crime Prevention and Control. It consists of fifteen to twenty detectives at any given time, all with the special training and experience required to assist the ADAs and local departments in the investigation and prosecution of complex cases of various kinds, particularly homicides." Duffy recited this little speech in a drone, from rote memory.

"And had you participated in many homicide investigations prior to April 12, 2007?"

"Yes."

"Approximately how many?"

"Over a hundred, though I was not in charge of all of them."

"Okay, on April 12, 2007, did you receive a phone call about a murder in Newton?"

"Yes. Around nine-fifteen A.M. I got a call from a Lieutenant Foley in Newton informing me there had been a homicide involving a child in Cold Spring Park."

"And what was the first thing you did?"

"I called the district attorney's office to inform them."

"Is that standard procedure?"

"Yes. The local department is required by law to inform the state police of all homicides or unnatural deaths, then we inform the DA immediately."

"Who specifically did you call?"

"Andy Barber."

"Why Andy Barber?"

"He was the First Assistant, which means he was the second in command to the district attorney herself."

"What was your understanding about what Mr. Barber would do with that information?"

"He would assign an ADA to run the investigation for their office."

"Might he keep the case for himself?"

"He might. He handled a lot of homicides himself."

"Did you have any expectations that morning as to whether Mr. Barber would keep the case for himself?"

Jonathan lifted his butt six inches from his chair. "Objection."

"Overruled."

"Detective Duffy, what did you think Mr. Barber would do with the case at that point?"

"I did not know. I suppose I figured he might keep it. It looked like it might be a big case right from the get-go. He kept those sorts of cases a lot. But if he put someone else on it, that would not have surprised me either. There were other good people there besides Mr. Barber. To be honest, I did not really think about it much. I had my own job to do. I let him worry about the DA's office. My job was to run CPAC."

"Do you know whether the district attorney, Lynn Canavan, was informed right away?"

"I don't know. I presume so."

"All right, after telephoning Mr. Barber, what did you do next?"

"I went to the location."

"What time did you arrive there?"

"Nine thirty-five in the morning."

"Describe the scene when you first arrived."

"The entrance to Cold Spring Park is on Beacon Street. There is a parking lot at the front of the park. Behind that there are tennis courts and playing fields. Then behind the fields it is all woods, and there are trails leading off into the woods. There were a lot of police vehicles in the parking lot and on the street out front. Lots of cops around."

"What did you do?"

"I parked on Beacon Street and approached the location on foot. I was met by Detective Peterson of the Newton Police and by Mr. Barber."

"Again, was there anything unusual

about Mr. Barber's presence at the homicide scene?"

"No. He lived pretty close to the location,
and he generally went to homicide scenes
even if he didn't intend to keep the case."

"How did you know Mr. Barber lived
near Cold Spring Park?"

"Because I've known him for years."

"In fact, you two are personal friends."

"Yes."

"Close friends?"

"Yes. We were."

"And now?"

There was a hitch before he answered.
"I can't speak for him. I still consider him a
friend."

"Do you two still see each other socially?"

"No. Not since Jacob was indicted."

"When was the last time you and Mr.
Barber spoke?"

"Before the indictment."

A lie, but a white lie. The truth would
have been misleading to the jury. It would
have suggested, wrongly, that Duffy
could not be trusted. Duffy was biased but
honest about the big questions. He did not
flinch as he delivered the statement. I did

not flinch at it either. The point of a trial is to reach the right result, which requires constant recalibration along the way, like a sailboat tacking upwind.

"All right, you get to the park, you meet Detective Peterson and Mr. Barber. What happens next?"

"They explained the basic situation to me, that the victim had already been identified as Benjamin Rifkin, and they walked me through the park to the actual scene of the homicide."

"What did you see when you got there?"

"The perimeter of the area was already taped off. The M.E. and crime-scene-services technicians had not arrived at the location yet. There was a photographer from the local police there taking pictures. The victim was still lying on the ground, the body, with nothing much around it. Basically they froze the scene when they got there, to preserve it."

"Could you actually see the body?"
"Yes."

"Could you describe the position of the body when you first saw it?"

"The victim was lying on a hill with the head at the lower end and the feet farther up the hill. It was twisted so the head was looking up toward the sky and the bottom half of the body and the legs were on its side."

"What did you do next?"

"I approached the body with Detective Peterson and Mr. Barber. Detective Peterson was showing me details about the scene."

"What was he showing you?"

"At the top of the hill, near the trail there was a good deal of blood on the ground, cast-off blood. I saw a number of droplets that were quite small, less than an inch in diameter. There were also a few larger stains that appeared to be what is called contact smears. These were on the leaves."

"What is a contact smear?"

"It's when a surface with wet blood contacts another surface and the blood transfers. It leaves a stain."

"Describe the contact smears."

"They were farther down the hill. There were several. They were several inches long at first, and as you went farther down the hill they became thicker and longer, more blood."

"Now, I understand that you are not a

criminalist, but did you form any impressions at the time, or theories, about what this blood evidence suggested?"

"Yes, I did. It looked like the homicide had taken place near the trail, where there were blood drops that had fallen, then the body fell or was pushed down the side of the hill, causing it to slide on its stomach, leaving the long contact smears of blood on the leaves."

"All right, so having formed this theory, what did you do next?"

"I went down and inspected the body."

"What did you see?"

"It had three wounds across the chest. It was a little difficult to see because the front of the body was soaked in blood, the victim's shirt. There was also quite a bit of blood around the body where it had apparently been draining out of these wounds."

"Was there anything unusual about those bloodstains, the pooled blood around the body?"

"Yes. There were some molded prints, shoe prints and other impressions, in the blood, meaning someone had stepped in the wet blood and left a print in it, like a mold."

"What did you conclude from those molded shoe prints?"

"Obviously someone had stood or knelt beside the body soon after the murder, while the blood was still wet enough to take the impression."

"Were you aware of the jogger, Paula Giannetto, who discovered the body?"

"Yes, I was."

"How did that figure in your thinking about the molded prints?"

"I thought she might have left them, but I could not be sure."

"What else did you conclude?"

"Well, there was quite a bit of blood that had been cast off during the attack. It had sprayed and also been smeared. I did not know how the attacker might have been standing, but I figured from the position of the wounds on the victim's chest that he was probably standing right in front of him. So I figured the person we were looking for might have some blood on him. He might also have a weapon, although a knife is small and pretty easy to dispose of. But the blood was the big thing. It was a reasonably messy scene."

"Did you make any other observations

about the victim, particularly about his hands?"

"Yes, they were not cut or injured."

"What did that suggest to you?"

"The absence of defensive wounds suggested he did not struggle or fight back against his assailant, which suggested he was either surprised or never saw the attack coming and did not have a chance to get his hands up to block the blows."

"Suggesting he may have known his assailant?"

Jonathan levitated his butt a few inches above his chair again. "Objection. Speculation."

"Sustained."

"All right, what did you do next?"

"Well, the murder was still relatively fresh. The park had been sealed, and we immediately searched it to ascertain if there were any individuals in it. That search had begun before I got there."

"And did you find anyone?"

"We found a few people who were pretty far away from the scene. No one seemed particularly suspicious. There was no indication that any of them were connected with the homicide in any way."

"No blood on them?"

"No."

"No knives?"

"No."

"So it's fair to say that in the early hours of the investigation you had no obvious suspects?"

"We had no suspects at all."

"And over the next few days, how many suspects were you able to identify and develop?"

"None."

"What did you do next? How did you continue the investigation?"

"Well, we interviewed everyone we could who had any information. The victim's family and friends, anyone who might have seen anything the morning of the murder."

"Did this include the victim's classmates?"

"No."

"Why not?"

"There was some delay in getting into the school. The parents in the town were concerned about us interviewing the kids. There was some discussion about whether the kids needed to have a lawyer present at the interviews and whether we could go into the school without a warrant, into the lockers and things. There was also some discussion about whether it was appropriate to use the school building for the interviews and which students we would be allowed to interview."

"What was your reaction to all this delay?"

"Objection."

"Overruled."

"I was angry, to be honest. The colder a case gets, the harder it is to solve."

"And who was running the case with you for the district attorney's office?"

"Mr. Barber."

"Andrew Barber, the defendant's father?"

"Yes."

"Did it strike you by this time that there was something inappropriate about Andy Barber working this case when his son's school was involved?"

"Not really. I mean, I was aware of it. But it wasn't like a Columbine thing: we didn't necessarily have a kid-on-kid murder. We did not have any real reason to believe any of the kids at the school were involved, let alone Jacob."

"So you never questioned Mr. Barber's

judgment in this regard, even in your own mind?"

"No, never."

"Did you ever discuss it with him?"

"Once."

"And would you describe that conversation?"

"I just said to Andy that, you know, just to cover your . . . derriere, you might want to pass this one off."

"Because you saw a conflict of interest?"

"I saw that his kid's school might be involved, and you never know. Why not just keep your distance?"

"And what did he say?"

"He said there was no conflict, because if his kid was ever in danger from a murderer, then that was all the *more* reason he would want to see the case solved. Plus, he said he felt some responsibility because he lived in the town and there weren't many homicides there, so he figured people would be especially upset. He wanted to do the right thing for them."

Logiudice paused at that last phrase and glared at Duffy for just an instant.

"Did Mr. Barber, the defendant's father,

ever suggest that you pursue a theory that one of Ben Rifkin's classmates might have murdered him?"

"No. He never suggested that or ruled it out."

"But he did not actively pursue a theory that Ben was killed by a classmate?"

"No. But you don't 'actively pursue'—"

"Did he try to steer the investigation in any other direction?"

"I don't understand, 'steer' it?"

"Did he have any other suspects in mind?"

"Yes. There was a man named Leonard Patz who lived near the park, and there was some circumstantial indication he might be involved. Andy wanted to pursue that suspect."

"In fact, wasn't Andy Barber the only one pushing Patz as a suspect?"

"Objection. Leading."

"Sustained. This is your witness, Mr. Logiudice."

"Withdraw the question. You did ultimately interview the children, Ben's classmates at the McCormick School?"

"Yes."

"And what did you learn?"

"Well, we learned at some length—

because the kids were not very forthcoming—that there was an ongoing beef between Ben and the defendant, between Ben and Jacob. Ben had been bullying Jacob. That led us to begin considering Jacob as a suspect."

"Even while his father ran the investigation?"

"Certain aspects of the investigation had to be carried out without Mr. Barber knowing."

This came as a hammer blow to me. I had not heard it before. I had assumed something like it, but not that Duffy himself was involved. He must have seen my face fall, because a helpless look crossed his face.

"And how did this come about? Was another assistant DA appointed to investigate the case without Mr. Barber's knowledge?"

"Yes. You."

"And this was done on whose approval?"

"The district attorney, Lynn Canavan."

"And what did this investigation reveal?"

"Evidence developed against the defendant to the effect that he had a knife consistent with the wounds, he had sufficient motive, and most important he had stated his intention to defend himself with the knife if the victim continued to bully him. The defendant had also come to school with a small amount of blood on his right hand that morning, blood drops. We learned these things from the defendant's friend, Derek Yoo."

"The defendant had blood on his right hand?"

"According to his friend Derek Yoo, yes."

"And he had announced his intention to use the knife on Ben Rifkin?"

"That's what Derek Yoo informed us."

"At some point did you become aware of a story on a website called the Cutting Room?"

"Yes. Derek Yoo described that to us as well."

"And did you investigate this website, the Cutting Room?"

"Yes. It is a site where people post fantasy stories that are mostly about sex and violence, including some very disturbing—"

"Objection."

"Sustained."

"Did you find a story on the Cutting Room website that related to this case?"

"Yes, we did. We found a story that described the murder essentially from the murderer's point of view. The names were changed and some of the details were a little off, but the situation was the same. It was obviously the same case."

"Who wrote that story?"

"The defendant did."

"How do you know that?"

"Derek Yoo informed us the defendant had told him."

"Were you able to confirm that in any other way?"

"No. We were able to determine the ISP of the computer the story was originally uploaded from, which is like a fingerprint identifying where the computer is located. It came back to the Peet's coffee shop in Newton Centre."

"Were you able to identify the actual machine that was used to upload the story?"

"No. It was someone who linked to the coffee shop's wireless network. That was as far as we could trace it. Peet's does not keep records of which computers jump on and off that network, and it does not require users to sign on to the network with a name or a credit card or anything. So we could not trace it any further."

"But you had Derek Yoo's word that the defendant had admitted writing it?"

"Correct."

"And what was it about the story that made it so compelling, that convinced you only the murderer could have written it?"

"Every detail was there. The clincher for me was that it described the angle of the knife wounds. The story said the stabs were planned to enter the chest at an angle that would allow the knife blade to penetrate between the ribs to maximize the damage to internal organs. I didn't think anyone would know about the knife angle. It wasn't public information. And it would not be an easy detail to guess because it requires the attacker hold the knife at an unnatural angle, horizontally, so it slips between the ribs. Also the level of detail, the planning—it was essentially a written confession. I knew we had probable cause to arrest at that point."

"But you did not arrest the defendant immediately?"

"No. We still wanted to find the knife and any other evidence that the defendant might have hidden in the house."

"So what did you do?"

"We got the warrant and hit the house."

"And what did you find?"

"Nothing."

"Did you take the defendant's computer?"

"Yes."

"What sort of computer was it?"

"It was an Apple laptop, white in color."

"And did you have the computer searched by specialists trained in uncovering material from hard drives of this kind?"

"Yes. They were not able to find anything directly incriminating."

"Did they find anything at all that was relevant to the case?"

"They found a software program called Disk Scraper. The program erases from the hard drive traces of old or deleted documents or programs. Jacob is very good with computers. So it's still possible the story was deleted from the computer even though we couldn't find it."

"Objection. Speculation."

"Sustained. The jury is instructed to disregard the last sentence."

Logiudice: "Were they able to find pornography?"

"Objection."

"Overruled."

"Were they able to find pornography?"

"Yes."

"Any other violent stories or anything connected to the murder?"

"No."

"Were you able to corroborate Derek Yoo's claim that Jacob had a knife in any way? Was there any paperwork from the purchase of the knife, for example?"

"No."

"Was the actual murder weapon ever found?"

"No."

"But a knife *was* found in Cold Spring Park at some point?"

"Yes. We continued to search the park for some time after the murder. We felt that the perpetrator must have ditched the knife somewhere in the park to avoid detection. We did finally find a knife in a shallow pond. The knife was about the right size, but subsequent forensic analysis showed it was not the knife used in the murder."

"How was that determined?"

"The blade of this knife was larger than the wounds would indicate, and it did not have a serrated blade consistent with the torn edges of the victim's wounds."

"So what did you conclude from the fact

that the knife had been thrown in the pond there?"

"I thought it was put there to throw us off, to send us down the wrong path. Probably by someone who did not have access to the forensic reports describing the wounds and the likely characteristics of the weapon."

"Any guesses about who might have planted that knife?"

"Objection. Calls for speculation."

"Sustained."

Logiudice considered a moment. He took a deep, satisfied breath, relieved finally to have a professional witness to work with. That Duffy knew and liked me—that he was somewhat biased in Jacob's favor and visibly conflicted about being on the stand—only made his testimony the more damning. *Finally,* Logiudice evidently felt, *finally.*

"No further questions," he said.

Jonathan bounced up and went to a spot at the far end of the jury box, where he leaned against the rail. If he could have climbed into the jury box itself to ask his questions, he would have.

"Or the knife might have just been dropped there for no reason at all?" he said.

"It's possible."

"Because things are tossed away in parks all the time?"

"True."

"So when you say the knife may have been planted there to deceive you, that's a guess, isn't it?"

"An educated guess, yes."

"A wild guess, I'd say."

"Objection."

"Sustained."

"Let's go back a little, Lieutenant. You testified that there was a lot of blood found at the scene, cast-off blood, spatters, contact smears, and of course the victim's shirt was soaked in blood."

"Yes."

"There was so much blood, in fact, you testified that when you went off to search the park for suspects, you were looking for someone with blood on him. Isn't that what you said?"

"Looking for someone who *might* have blood on him, yes."

"A lot of blood on him?"

"I was not certain of that."

"Oh, come on now. You testified that, based on the pattern of the wounds, Ben

Rifkin's attacker was probably standing right in front of him, correct?"

"Yes."

"And you testified there was cast-off blood."

"Yes."

"'Cast-off' meaning it was thrown, projected, it shot out?"

"Yes, but—"

"In fact, in a case with so much blood, with wounds this grievous, you would have to think the attacker would have quite a bit of blood on him because the wounds would spurt?"

"Not necessarily."

"Not necessarily but very likely, isn't it, Detective?"

"It's likely."

"And of course in a stabbing, the attacker has to stand quite close to the victim, within arm's length, obviously?"

"Yes."

"Where it would be impossible to avoid the spray?"

"I didn't use the word *spray.*"

"Where it would be impossible to avoid the cast-off blood?"

"I can't say that for sure."

"And the description of Jacob with blood on him as he arrived at school that morning—you heard this from his friend Derek Yoo, isn't that right?"

"Yes."

"And what Derek Yoo described was that Jacob had some small amounts of blood on his right hand, isn't that right?"

"Yes."

"None on his clothes?"

"No."

"None on his face or anywhere else on his body?"

"No."

"On his shoes?"

"No."

"All of which is perfectly consistent with the explanation Jacob gave his friend Derek Yoo, isn't it, that he discovered the body *after* the attack and *then* he touched it with his right hand?"

"It is consistent, yes, but not the only possible explanation."

"And of course Jacob did go to school that morning?"

"Yes."

"He was in school just minutes after the murder, we know that, right?"

"Yes."

"When does school start at the McCormick?"

"Eight thirty-five."

"And when was the time of the murder, according to the M.E., if you know?"

"Sometime between eight and eight-thirty."

"But Jacob was in his seat in school at eight thirty-five with no blood on him at all?"

"Yes."

"And if I were to suggest to you, hypothetically, that the story Jacob wrote that impressed you so much—that you described as virtually a written confession—if I were to show you evidence that Jacob did not make up the facts in that story, that all the details in the story were already well known among the students at the McCormick School, would that affect your thinking about how important it was as evidence?"

"Yes."

"Yes, of course!"

Duffy looked at him poker-faced. His job here was to say as little as possible, to pare away every extra word. Volunteering details could only help the defense.

"Now, on this question of Andy Barber's role in the investigation, are you suggesting that your friend Andy did anything wrong or inappropriate here?"

"No."

"Can you point to any errors or suspicious decisions he made?"

"No."

"Anything you questioned then or now?"

"No."

"There was some mention of this man Leonard Patz. Even knowing what we know now, does it seem inappropriate to you that Patz was once considered a legitimate suspect?"

"No."

"No, because in the early stages of an investigation, you pursue every reasonable lead, you cast your net as wide as possible, isn't that right?"

"Yes."

"In fact, if I told you that Andy Barber still believes that Patz was the real killer in this case, would that surprise you, Lieutenant?"

Duffy made a little frown. "No. That's what he always believed."

"Isn't it also true that you were the detective who brought Leonard Patz to Mr. Barber's attention in the first place?"

"Yes, but—"

"And was Andy Barber's judgment about homicide investigations generally reliable?"

"Yes."

"Did it seem odd to you in any way that Andy Barber wanted to pursue an investigation of Leonard Patz for Ben Rifkin's murder?"

"Odd? No. It made sense, based on the limited information we had at the time."

"And yet the investigation of Patz was never seriously pursued, was it?"

"It was stopped once the decision was made to indict Jacob Barber, yes."

"And who made that decision, to stop focusing on Patz?"

"The district attorney, Lynn Canavan."

"Did she make that decision alone?"

"No, I believe she was advised by Mr. Logiudice."

"Was there any evidence at the time that excluded Leonard Patz as a suspect?"

"No."

"Has any evidence ever come up that clears him directly?"

"No."

"No. Because that angle was simply dropped, wasn't it?"

"I suppose."

"It was dropped because Mr. Logiudice wanted it dropped, no?"

"There was a discussion among all the investigators, including the district attorney and Mr. Logiudice—"

"It was dropped because in that discussion Mr. Logiudice pushed to have it dropped, isn't that right?"

"Well, we're here now, so obviously yes." There was a trace of exasperation in Duffy's voice.

"So, even knowing what we know now, do you have any doubts about your friend Andrew Barber's integrity?"

"No." Duffy thought about it, or pretended to. "No, I don't think Andy ever had any suspicions about Jacob."

"You don't think Andy suspected anything?"

"No."

"The boy's own father, who lived with him his whole life? He did not know anything?"

Duffy shrugged. "I can't say for sure. But I don't think so."

"How is it possible to live with a child for fourteen years and know so little about him?"

"I can't say for sure."

"No. In fact, you've known Jacob all his life too, haven't you?"

"Yes."

"And initially you had no suspicions about Jacob either, did you?"

"No."

"In all those years, it never seemed to you there was anything dangerous about Jacob? You had no reason to suspect him, did you?"

"No."

"No, of course not."

"Objection. Request that Mr. Klein not add his own commentary to the witness's answers."

"Sustained."

"My apologies," Jonathan said with a great show of insincerity. "Nothing further."

The judge: "Mr. Logiudice. Redirect?"

Logiudice considered. He might have left it there. Certainly he had enough to argue to the jury that I was crooked and had hijacked the investigation to cover for my crazy kid. Hell, he did not even have to argue it; the jury had heard it intimated several times in testimony. In any event, I was not the one on trial here. He could have just taken his winnings and moved on. But he was puffed up from his newfound momentum. You could see in his face that he felt himself in the grip of a grand inspiration. He seemed to believe the kill shot was right there within reach. Another little boy in a grown-up's body, unable to resist the cookie jar in front of him.

"Yes, Your Honor," he said, and went to a spot directly in front of the witness stand.

A little rustle in the courtroom.

"Detective Duffy, you say you have no reservations at all about the way Andrew Barber conducted this case?"

"That's right."

"Because he didn't know anything, isn't that right?"

"Yes."

"Objection. Leading. This is a prosecution witness."

"He can have it."

"And how long would you say you've known Andy Barber, how many years?"

"Objection. Relevance."

"Overruled."

"I guess I've known Andy over twenty years."

"So you know him pretty well?"

"Yes."

"Inside and out?"

"Sure."

"When did you learn that his father is a murderer?"

Boom.

Jonathan and I both shot out of our seats, jostling the table. "Objection!"

"Sustained! The witness is instructed not to answer that question and the jury is to disregard it! Give it no weight. Treat the question as if it was never asked." Judge French turned to the lawyers. "I'll see counsel at sidebar right now."

I did not go with Jonathan to the sidebar conference so, again, I am quoting the judge's whispered comments from the trial transcript. But I did watch the judge as he spoke, and I can tell you he was obviously furious. Red-faced, he put his hands on the edge of the judge's bench and leaned over to hiss at Logiudice.

"I am shocked, I'm stunned you did that.

I explicitly told you in no uncertain terms not to go there or I would declare a mistrial. What do you have to say, Mr. Logiudice?"

"It was defense counsel who chose to cross on this question of the character of the defendant's father and the integrity of the investigation. If he chooses to make that an issue, the prosecution is perfectly entitled to argue its side of the case. I was just following up on Mr. Klein's line of questioning. He specifically raised the issue of whether the defendant's father had any reason to suspect his son."

"Mr. Klein, I presume you are going to move for a mistrial."

"Yup."

"Step back."

The lawyers went back to their respective tables.

Judge French remained standing to address the jury, as was his habit. He even unzipped his robe a bit and gripped the edge of its collar as if he were posing for a statue. "Ladies and gentlemen, I am instructing you to ignore that last question. Strike it from your minds entirely. There is a saying in the law that 'you cannot unring the bell,' but I'm going to ask you to do just that. The question was improper and the prosecutor should not have asked it, and I want you to be aware of that. Now, I am going to dismiss you for the day while the court attends to other business. The sequestration order remains in place. I remind you not to talk about this case with anybody at all. Do not listen to media reports about it or read about it in the newspapers. Turn off your radios and TVs. Block yourself off from it entirely. All right, the jury is dismissed. We'll see you tomorrow morning, nine o'clock sharp."

The jury filed out, exchanging looks with each other. A few of them stole glances at Logiudice.

When they were gone, the judge said, "Mr. Klein."

Jonathan stood. "Your Honor, the defendant moves for a mistrial. This issue was the subject of extensive pretrial discussion, the upshot of which was that the issue is so volatile and so prejudicial that mentioning it would result in a mistrial. This was the third rail that the prosecution was explicitly told not to touch. Now he has."

The judge massaged his forehead.

Jonathan continued, "If the court is not

inclined to declare a mistrial, the defendant will move to expand its witness list by two: Leonard Patz and William Barber."

"William Barber is the defendant's grandfather?"

"Correct. I may need a governor's warrant to get him transported here. But if the prosecution insists on this bizarre insinuation that the defendant somehow is guilty by inheritance, that he is a member of a criminal family, born a murderer, then we have a right to rebut that."

The judge stood there a moment, grinding his molars. "I'll take it under advisement. I'll give you my decision in the morning. Court is adjourned till nine o'clock tomorrow."

Mr. Logiudice: Before we move on, Mr. Barber, about that knife, the one that was thrown in the lake to throw off the investigators. Do you have any idea who might have planted that knife?

Witness: Of course. I knew from the start.

Mr. Logiudice: Did you? And how's that?

Witness: The knife was missing from our kitchen.

Mr. Logiudice: An identical knife?

Witness: A knife that matched the description I'd been given. I've since seen the knife that was recovered from the pond, when we were shown the state's evidence. It's our knife. It was old, pretty distinctive. It did not match the set. I recognized it.

Mr. Logiudice: Then it was thrown in the pond by someone in your family?

Witness: Of course.

Mr. Logiudice: Jacob? To deflect any inference of guilt from the actual knife he owned?

Witness: No. Jake was too smart for that. And I was too. I knew what the wounds looked like; I'd talked to the forensics people. I knew that knife couldn't have made Ben Rifkin's wounds.

Mr. Logiudice: Laurie, then? Why?

Witness: Because we believed in our son. He told us he didn't do it.

We didn't want to see his life ruined just because he'd been foolish enough to buy a knife. We knew people would see that knife and jump to the wrong conclusion. We talked about the danger of it. So Laurie decided to give the cops another knife. The only problem was, she was the least sophisticated among the three of us about these things and she was also the most upset. She was not careful enough. She chose the wrong sort of knife. She left a loose end.

Mr. Logiudice: Did she talk to you before she did this?

Witness: Before, no.

Mr. Logiudice: After, then?

Witness: I confronted her. She did not deny it.

Mr. Logiudice: And what did you say to this person who'd just interfered with a homicide investigation?

Witness: What did I say? I said I wished she'd talked to me first. I would have given her the right knife to throw.

Mr. Logiudice: Is that really how you feel now, Andy? That this is all a joke? Do you really have so little respect for what we do here?

Witness: When I said that to my wife, I assure you I wasn't joking. Let's leave it at that.

Mr. Logiudice: All right. Continue with your story.

When we got back to our car in the garage a block from the courthouse, there was a white piece of paper tucked under the windshield wiper. It was quarter-folded. Opening it, I read,

JUDGMENT DAY IS COMING
MURDERER, YOU DIE

Jonathan was still with us, making it a group of four. He frowned at the note and slipped it into his briefcase. "I'll take care of this. I'll file a report with the Cambridge police. You all go home."

Laurie said, "That's all we can do?"

"We should let the Newton police know too, just in case," I suggested. "Maybe it's time we had a cruiser camped out by our house. The world's full of lunatics."

I was distracted by a figure standing in the corner of the garage, quite a distance away but obviously watching us. He was an older man, near seventy probably. He wore a jacket, golf shirt, and scally cap. Looked like a million guys around Boston. Some old mick tough. He was lighting a cigarette—it was the flare of his lighter that caught my eye—and the glowing tip of the cigarette linked him with the car that had been parked outside our house a few nights before, the interior blacked out except for the little glowing firefly of a cigarette tip in the car window. And wasn't he just the sort of dinosaur to drive a Lincoln frickin' Town Car?

Our eyes met for a moment. He thrust his lighter into his pants pocket and continued walking, out through a doorway to a staircase, and he was gone. Had he been walking before I saw him? He seemed to have been standing and staring, but I had only just glanced over. Maybe he had just stopped a moment before to light the cigarette.

"Did you see that guy?"

Jonathan: "What guy?"

"That guy who was just over there looking at us."

"Didn't see him. Who was he?"

"I don't know. Never seen him before."

"You think he had something to do with the note?"

"Don't know. I don't even know if he was looking at us. But he seemed to be, you know?"

"Come on," Jonathan encouraged us toward the car, "there are a lot of people looking at us lately. It'll be over soon."

31 | Hanging Up

Around six that night, as the three of us finished our dinner—Jacob and I indulging ourselves in a little cautious optimism, spitting on Logiudice and his desperate tactics; Laurie trying to keep up the appearance of confidence and normalcy, even as she had become vaguely suspicious of the both of us—the phone rang.

I answered. An operator informed me that she had a collect call. Would I accept the charges? It came as a surprise that people still made collect calls. Was this a prank? Were there any phone booths left to make a collect call from? Only in prisons.

"Collect call from who?"

"Bill Barber."

"Jesus. No, I won't accept. Wait a minute, hang on." I held the phone against my chest, as if my heart would speak to him directly. Then: "All right, I'll accept the charges."

"Thank you. Please hold while I connect you. Have a nice day."

A click.

"Hallo?"

"What is it?"

"What is it? I thought you was gonna come down and visit me again."

"I've been a little busy."

He mimicked me, *"Oh, I been a little busy.* Relax, would ya? I'm just shittin' ya, you dope. Wha'd ya think? *Hey, come on down, junior, I'll take ya out fishin'!* I'll take you fishin'—you know for what? For fishes!" I had no idea what this meant. Some prison slang, presumably. Whatever it meant, the joke was funny to him. He roared into the phone.

"Jesus Christ, you talk a lot."

"No shit, 'cause I got no one to talk to in this fuckin' place. My kid never visits me."

"Was there something you wanted? Or did you just call to chat?"

"I want to know how the kid's trial is going."

"What do you care?"

"He's my grandson. I want to know."

"His whole life you never even knew his name."

"Whose fault is that?"

"Yours."

"Yeah, I'm sure you think that."

A pause.

"I heard my name came up in court today. We're following the whole thing here. It's like the World Series for cons."

"Yeah, your name came up. See, even sitting in prison, you're still screwing your family over."

"Oh, junior, don't be such a pisser. The kid's gonna get off."

"You think so? You figure you're a pretty good lawyer, Mister Life-Without-Parole?"

"I know a few things."

"You know a few things. *Pff.* Do me a favor, Clarence Darrow: don't call here and tell me my business. I've already got a lawyer."

"Nobody's telling you your business, junior. But when your lawyer talks about bringing me in to testify, that makes it my business, now, don't it?"

"It isn't going to happen. That's all we need is you on the stand. Turn the whole thing into a circus."

"You got a better strategy?"

"Yeah, we do."

"What is it?"

"We're not even going to put on a case. We'll put the Commonwealth to its burden. They have— What am I even talking to you about this for?"

"Because you want to. When the chips are down, a kid needs his old man."

"Is that a joke?"

"No! I'm still your father."

"No, you're not."

"I'm not?"

"No."

"Then who is?"

"Me."

"You don't have a father? What are you, a tree?"

"That's right, I don't have one. And I don't need one now."

"Everybody needs a father, everybody needs a father. You need me now more than ever. How else are you gonna prove that 'irresistible impulse' thing?"

"We don't need to prove it."

"No? Why not?"

"Because Logiudice can't prove his case. That's obvious. So our defense is simple: Jacob didn't do it."

"What if that changes?"

"It won't."

"So why'd you come all the way down here and ask me about it? And test my spit? What was that all about?"

"Just covering my bases."

"Just covering your bases. So the kid didn't do it but just in case he did."

"Something like that."

"So what's your lawyer want me to say, then?"

"He doesn't want you to say anything. He shouldn't have said that in court today. It was a mistake. He was probably thinking he'd run you up there to testify that you never had anything to do with your grandson. But I already told you, you're not coming anywhere near that courtroom."

"You better talk with your lawyer about that."

"Listen to me, Bloody Billy. I'm going to say this for the last time: you don't exist. You're just a bad dream I used to have when I was a kid."

"Hey, junior, you want to hurt my feelings? Kick me in the balls."

"What's that supposed to mean?"

"It means don't bother calling me names. It don't bother me. I'm the kid's grandfather no matter what you say. Nothing you can do about it. You can deny me all you want, pretend I don't exist. Doesn't matter. Doesn't change the truth."

I sat down, suddenly unsteady.

"Who's this guy Patz your cop friend testified about?"

I was pissed and confused, agitated, so I did not stop to consider. I blurted, "He's the guy who did it."

"That killed this kid?"

"Yeah."

"You sure?"

"Yes."

"How do you know?"

"I've got a witness."

"And you're gonna let my grandson take the hit for it?"

"*Let* him? No."

"Then do something, junior. Tell me about this guy Patz."

"What do you want to know? He likes little boys."

"He's a child molester?"

"Sort of."

"Sort of? Either he is or he isn't. How can you be sort of a child molester?"

"Same way you were a murderer before you actually murdered someone."

"Oh, stop it, junior. I told you, you can't hurt my feelings."

"Would you stop calling me that, 'junior'?"

"Does it bother ya?"

"Yes."

"What should I call ya?"

"Don't call me anything."

"*Pssh.* I got to call you something. How else am I gonna talk to ya?"

"You're not."

"Junior, you got a lot of anger, you know that?"

"Was there anything else you wanted?"

"Wanted? I don't want anything outa you."

"I figured maybe you want a cake with a file in it."

"Funny guy. A file in it. I get it. 'Cause I'm in prison."

"That's right."

"Listen to me, junior, I don't need no cake with a file in it, all right? You know why? I'll tell you why. 'Cause I'm not in prison."

"No. Did they let you out?"

"They don't have to let me out."

"They don't? Let me give you a tip, crazy old man. That big building with the bars? The one they never let you out of? That's called a prison, and you are definitely in it."

"No. See, now you're the one that doesn't get it, junior. All they got locked up in this hole is my body. That's all they got, my body, not me. I'm everywhere, see? Everywhere you look, junior, everywhere you go. Okay? Now, you just keep my grandkid out of this place. You got that, junior?"

"Why don't you do it? You're everywhere."

"Maybe I will. Maybe I'll fly right up there—"

"Look, I got to go, all right? I'm hanging up."

"No. We're not done—"

I hung up on him. But he was right, he

was right there with me, because his voice kept right on rattling in my ears. I picked the phone up and smashed it down in its cradle again—one two three times—until I could not hear him anymore.

Jacob and Laurie both were staring at me with wide eyes.

"That was your grandfather."

"I caught that."

"Jake, I don't want you to ever talk to him, all right? I'm serious."

"Okay."

"You're never to speak to him, even if he calls you. You just hang up the phone. You got it?"

"Okay, okay."

Laurie glared. "That goes for you too, Andy. I don't want that man calling my house. He's poison. Next time he calls, you hang up the phone, got it?"

I nodded.

"Are you all right, husband?"

"I don't know."

32 | The Absence of Evidence

Trial day five.

At the stroke of nine, Judge French stormed the bench and announced in a clenched way that the defendant's motion for mistrial was denied. He said—as the stenographer repeated his words into a cone-shaped microphone which she held over her face like an oxygen mask— "Defendant's objection to the mention of the defendant's grandfather is noted for the record and the issue is preserved for appeal. I have given the jury a curative instruction. I think that's enough. The prosecutor is cautioned not to mention the issue any further, and that's all we're going to hear about it. Now, absent any other objections, Court Officer, bring in the jury and let's get started."

I can't say I was surprised. Mistrials are rare. The judge was not going to flush away the state's enormous investment in seeing this trial through to the end, not if he could help it. He might have been embarrassed by a mistrial too. It might look like he had lost control of his courtroom. Logiudice knew all this, of course. He may have crossed the line intentionally, betting that the high stakes in this case made a mistrial particularly unlikely. But that is unkind.

The trial swept on.

"What is your name, please?"

"Karen Rakowski. R-A-K-O-W-S-K-I."

"What is your occupation and your current assignment?"

"I am a criminalist with the Massachusetts State Police. I'm currently assigned to the State Police Crime Lab."

"What is a criminalist, exactly?"

"A criminalist is someone who applies the principles of the natural and physical sciences to identify, preserve, and analyze

evidence at a crime scene. She later testi-
fies to her findings in a court of law."

"How long have you been a criminalist
with the state police?"

"Eleven years."

"Approximately how many crime scenes
would you say you've investigated over
the course of your career?"

"Approximately five hundred."

"Are you a member of any professional
organizations?"

Rakowski proceeded to rattle off the
names of a half dozen organizations, then
her degrees and a teaching position and a
few publications, all of which went swiftly
by like a freight train: difficult to distinguish
in detail but impressive in its length. The
truth was, no one listened to Rakowski's
information dump because no one really
questioned her qualifications. She was well
known and respected. It should be pointed
out that the job of "criminalist" has become
a lot more professional and rigorous than
it was when I started out. It has even become fashionable. Forensic science has
become a lot more complex, particularly
with respect to DNA evidence. No doubt

the job has been glamorized by shows like *CSI* too. Whatever the reason, the job attracts more and better candidates now, and Karen Rakowski was among the first wave of criminalists in our county who were not just cops moonlighting as amateur scientists. She was the real thing. It was a lot easier to picture her in a white lab coat than in the jodhpurs and jackboots of the state police. I was glad she had been assigned the case. I knew she would give us a fair shake.

"On April 12, 2007, at around ten A.M., did you get a phone call about a murder in Cold Spring Park in Newton?"

"Yes, I did."

"What did you do in response?"

"I went to the location, where I was met by Lieutenant Duffy, who gave me a briefing about what he had at the crime scene and what he wanted me to do. He brought me to the location where the body was lying."

"Had the body been moved, as far as you know?"

"I was told it had not been disturbed since the police arrived there."

"Had the medical examiner arrived yet?"

"No."

"Is it preferable for the criminalist to arrive before the medical examiner?"

"Yes. The M.E. can't process the body without moving it. Once the body is moved, obviously you can't draw any inferences from its position."

"Now, in this case you knew that the body had already been moved by the jogger who discovered it."

"I did."

"Were you able to draw any conclusions from the position of the body and from the surrounding scene nonetheless, when you first saw it?"

"Yes. It was apparent that the attack had taken place at the top of the hill by a walking trail and that the body had slid down the hill afterward. That was evidenced by a trail of blood leading down the hillside to the final resting position of the body."

"These are the contact smears of blood we heard about yesterday?"

"Yes. When I arrived, the body itself had been rolled over face up, and I could see that the victim's T-shirt was soaked with what appeared to be wet blood."

"What significance did you attach, if any,

to the large amount of blood on the victim's body?"

"At the time, none. Obviously, the wounds were significant and fatal, but I knew that before I arrived."

"But doesn't the large amount of blood at the scene suggest a bloody struggle?"

"Not necessarily. Blood circulates through our bodies constantly. It is a hydraulic system: it is being pumped around and around. It moves through the circulatory system, through the veins, under pressure. When a person is killed, the blood is no longer under the pressure of a pump and its movement is then controlled by the ordinary laws of physics. So a lot of the blood that was apparent at the scene, both on the victim himself and on the ground underneath and around him, might have simply drained out of him because of gravity, because of the way the body was lying: feet above head, facedown. So the blood on the body might have been postmortem bleeding. I could not tell yet."

"Okay, so what did you do next?"

"I examined the scene more closely. I observed some blood spatters near the top of the hill, at what seemed to be the point of the attack. There were only a few spatters here."

"Let me stop you there. Is there a discipline in the forensic sciences of blood spatter analysis?"

"Yes. It is the study of the patterns of blood spatters, which can yield useful information."

"Were you able to get any useful information from the blood spatters in this case?"

"Yes. As I was saying, at the point of attack there were a few very small blood spatters, less than an inch in size, and it was apparent from their size that they had fallen more or less straight down to the ground, spattering evenly in all directions. That is called a low-velocity drop or sometimes 'passive bleeding.'"

Logiudice: "Now, yesterday we heard some discussion by the defense about whether you could expect to find blood on the attacker's body or on his clothes after an attack like this one. Based on your observations of the blood spatters, do you have an opinion about this?"

"Yes. It is not *necessarily* true that the attacker here would have blood on him. Going back to the circulatory system that pumps blood through the body: remember that once blood is ejected from the body out into the air, it is subject to the ordinary laws of physics just like anything else. Now, it's true, if an artery is cut, depending where it is on the body, you would expect the blood to gush out. That's called 'arterial gushing.' Same with a vein. But if it's a capillary, you might see just dripping like this. I did not see any spatters at the scene that seemed to have been cast off with force. That sort of cast-off blood would land at an angle and spatter unevenly, like this." She demonstrated by sliding her fist along the length of her forearm to show how the blood drop would spread across the surface at impact. "It is also possible that the assailant stood behind the victim when he stabbed him, which would put him out of the trajectory of any spraying blood. And of course it is possible the assailant changed his clothes after the attack. All of which is simply to say that you cannot automatically assume that the assailant in this case would be covered in blood after the attack despite the large amount of blood found at the scene."

"Are you familiar with the saying 'The

absence of evidence is not evidence of absence'?"

"Objection. Leading."

"He can have it. You can answer the question."

"Yes."

"What does that saying mean?"

"It means that, just because there is no physical evidence proving a person's presence at a particular time and place, you cannot necessarily conclude that he was not actually there. It's probably easier to understand if I put it this way: a person can be present at a crime and leave no physical evidence there."

Rakowski's testimony went on for some time. It was a critical part of Logiudice's case and he took his time putting it in. She testified in detail that the blood found at the scene was all the victim's. There was no physical evidence found in the immediate vicinity of the body that could be linked to any other person—no finger-, hand-, or shoe prints, no hairs or fibers, no blood or other organic material—with the single exception of that damn fingerprint.

"Where precisely was the fingerprint located?"

"The victim was wearing a zippered sweatshirt with the zipper open. On the inside of that sweatshirt, about here"—she indicated a spot on the inside of her own jacket, on the left side of the lining where an interior pocket is often located—"there was a plastic tag with the manufacturer's name. The print was found on that tag."

"Does the surface on which a fingerprint is found affect its value?"

"Well, some surfaces take a print better. This was a flat surface. It had been wetted with blood, almost like an inked pad, and it showed the fingerprint very clearly."

"So this was a clean print?"

"Yes."

"And after studying this fingerprint, whose print did you determine it was?"

"The defendant, Jacob Barber's."

Jonathan stood and said with a shrug in his voice, "We'll stipulate it's the defendant's fingerprint."

The judge said, "Without objection," and he turned to the jury: "The meaning of a stipulation is that the defense concedes that a fact is true without the prosecutor having to prove it. Both parties agree to the truth of this fact, therefore you may take it as true and proven. Okay, Mr. Logiudice."

"What significance, if any, did you assign to the fact that the fingerprint was in the victim's own blood?"

"Obviously the blood had to be on that tag first in order for the defendant's finger to be pressed into it. So the significance is that the fingerprint was put there after the attack had begun, or at least after the victim had been cut at least once, and soon enough after the attack that the blood on that tag was still wet, since dry blood would not have taken the print the same way, if at all. So that print was put there during or very soon after the attack."

"How big a window are we talking about? How soon before the blood on that tag is too dry to take the fingerprint?"

"There are a lot of factors involved. But not more than fifteen minutes on the outside."

"Even sooner, is it likely?"

"Impossible to say."

Good girl, Karen. Don't take the bait.

The only sparring took place when Logiudice tried to enter into evidence a knife,

a sleek and wicked thing called a Spyderco Civilian, which was the knife Jacob
specifically named in his story imagining
the Rifkin murder. Jonathan vehemently
objected to this knife being shown to the
jury since there was no evidence that Jacob ever owned such a knife. I had dumped
Jacob's knife long before the cops searched
his room, but I blanched at the sight of the
Spyderco Civilian. It looked very similar to
Jacob's. I didn't dare turn around to look at
Laurie, so I can only report what she later
told me: "I died when I saw it." Judge French
ultimately did not allow Logiudice to enter
the knife in evidence. Its physical appearance, he said, was "inflammatory" given
how weakly the government had linked the
knife to Jacob. Which was Judge French's
way of saying he was not about to let Logiudice start waving a lethal-looking knife
around the courtroom as a way to work
the jury up into a lynch mob—not until the
government offered a witness who could
say Jacob had such a knife. But he would
allow the expert to testify about the knife
in general terms.

    "Is that knife consistent with the victim's
wounds?"

"Yes. We examined the size and shape of the blade relative to the wounds and they were consistent. The blade on that particular knife is curved and has a serrated edge, which would account for the ragged tears at the edge of the wounds. It is a knife designed for slashing at an opponent, as you would in a knife fight. A knife intended to make a neat slice will typically have a smooth, very sharp edge, like a scalpel."

"So the killer might have used exactly that sort of knife?"

"Objection."

"Overruled."

"He might have, yes."

"Could you tell from the angle of the wounds and the design of the knife how the killer might have inflicted the fatal wounds, what sort of motion he might have used?"

"Based on the fact that the wounds enter the body essentially straight, that is, on a horizontal plane, it would seem that the assailant most likely stood directly in front of the victim, was of about equal height, and stabbed straight ahead in three thrusts holding his arm roughly level."

"Would you demonstrate the motion you mean, please?"

"Objection."

"Overruled."

Rakowski stood up and thrust her right arm ahead three times. She sat back down.

Logiudice said nothing for a few seconds. The courtroom was silent enough in those moments that I heard someone behind me in the gallery emit a long breath, *whoo.*

Jonathan fought gallantly on cross. He did not attack Rakowski directly. She was obviously competent and playing it straight, and there was nothing to be gained by savaging her. He kept the focus on the physical evidence and how thin it really was.

"The government mentioned the phrase 'The absence of evidence is not evidence of absence.' Do you remember that?"

"Yes."

"Isn't it also true that the absence of evidence is precisely that: an absence of evidence?"

"Yes."

Jonathan showed a wry smile to the jury. "In this case, we have a fairly substantial absence of evidence, don't we? There is no blood evidence against the defendant?"

"No."

"Genetic evidence? DNA?"

"No."

"Hairs?"

"No."

"Fibers?"

"No."

"Anything at all that puts the defendant at the scene besides that fingerprint?"

"No."

"Handprints? Fingerprints? Shoe prints? All missing?"

"That's true."

"Well! Now, that's what I call an absence of evidence!"

The jury laughed. Jacob and I laughed, more with relief than anything else. Logiudice jumped up to object and the objection was sustained, but it hardly mattered.

"And the fingerprint that was found, Jacob's fingerprint on the victim's sweatshirt. Isn't it true that fingerprint evidence has one huge limitation: you can't tell *when* the print was put there?"

"That's true, except for the inference to be drawn from the fact the blood was still wet when the defendant's finger touched it."

"Yes, the wet blood. Exactly. May I pose

a hypothetical to you, Ms. Rakowski? Let's suppose, hypothetically, that the defendant, Jacob, came upon the victim, his friend and classmate, lying on the ground in the park as he, Jacob, walked to school. Suppose, again for our hypothetical, suppose it was only minutes after the attack. And suppose finally that he held the victim by his sweatshirt in an attempt to help him or to be sure he was okay. Wouldn't that be perfectly consistent with finding the fingerprint where you did?"

"Yes."

"And finally, with regard to the knife we heard about, the—what was it?—the Spyderco Civilian. Isn't it true that there are many knives that could have created those wounds?"

"Yes. I presume so."

"Because all you have to judge by is the characteristics of those wounds, the size and shape, the depth of penetration, and so on, isn't that right?"

"Yes."

"And all you know, therefore, is that the murder weapon seemed to have a jagged edge and a blade of a certain size, isn't that right?"

"Yes."

"Did you make any effort to determine how many knives out there fit that description?"

"No. I was asked by the DA only to determine whether that particular knife was consistent with the victim's wounds. I was not given any other knives to compare."

"Well, that's putting the rabbit into the hat, then, isn't it?"

"Objection."

"Sustained."

"The investigators made no effort to determine how many knives could have made those wounds?"

"I was not asked about other models, no."

"Do you have any idea, roughly? How many knives would leave a wound about two inches wide and penetrate three or four inches?"

"I don't know. I would be speculating."

"A thousand? Come on, it must be at least that many."

"I couldn't say. It would be a large number. You have to remember, a small knife can create an opening larger than the blade itself, because the attacker can use it to slice the wound open. A scalpel is quite small but obviously it can create a very large incision. So when we talk about the size of the wound relative to the blade, what we're talking about is the maximum size of the blade, the outer limit, because obviously the blade cannot be larger than the opening it was inserted into, at least if we're talking about a penetration wound as we are here. Below that limit, the size of the wound alone cannot tell you precisely how big the knife was. So I can't answer your question."

Jonathan cocked his head. He was not buying it. "Five hundred?"

"I don't know."

"One hundred?"

"It's possible."

"Ah, it's possible. So our chances are one in a hundred?"

"Objection."

"Sustained."

"Why were the investigators interested in that particular knife, Ms. Rakowski, the Spyderco Civilian? Why did they ask you to compare that model with the wounds?"

"Because it was mentioned in an account of the murder that the defendant wrote—"

"According to Derek Yoo."

"Correct. And the same witness apparently saw a similar knife in the defendant's possession."

"Derek Yoo again?"

"I believe so."

"So the only thing connecting that knife to Jacob is this one mixed-up boy, Derek Yoo?"

She did not answer. Logiudice objected too quickly. It did not matter.

"Nothing further, Your Honor."

33 | Father O'Leary

The case was becoming a close thing, it seemed to me, but I still felt optimistic. Logiudice was hoping to draw an inside straight—to assemble a winning combination out of a messy hand of deuce-three-five-six. He had no choice, really. He had crap cards. No ace, no piece of evidence so damning it *required* the jury to convict. His last hope was a cohort of witnesses culled from Jacob's classmates. I could not imagine any of the McCormick kids commanding that much respect from the jury.

Jacob felt as I did, and we had a fine

old time ridiculing Logiudice's case, reassuring ourselves that every card he laid
down was a deuce or a three. Jonathan's
bit about the "absence of evidence" and
the dressing-down Logiudice got for allud-
ing to the murder-gene issue particularly
delighted us. I do not mean to suggest Jacob was not scared shitless. He was. We
all were. Jacob's anxiety just took the form
of beating his chest a little. Mine too. I felt
aggressive, all adrenaline and testosterone.
I was a fast-idling engine. The nearness of
such an enormous catastrophe as a guilty
verdict sharpened every sensation.

Laurie was a lot more gloomy. She assumed that in a close case, the jury would
feel it was their duty to convict. They would
take no chances. Just lock up this boy-
monster, protect everyone else's innocent
babes, and be done with it. She also figured the jury would want to see someone
swing for the murder of Ben Rifkin. Anything less and justice would not have been
done. If the neck in the noose happened to
be Jacob's, they would take it. In all Laurie's
doomsaying, I heard intimations of something darker, but I did not dare challenge
her on it. Some feelings it is better not to

surface. Some things a mother should never be forced to say about her son, even if she believes them.

So we declared a truce that night. We resolved to stop the endless rehashing of the forensic testimony we had heard that day. No more talk about the nuances of blood spatters and angles of knife entry and all that. Instead we sat on the couch and watched TV in contented silence. When Laurie went upstairs around ten, I had a vague idea that I might follow her. Once, I would have. My libido would have pulled me up the stairs like a Great Dane on a leash. But that was over now. Laurie's interest in sex had vanished, and I could not imagine going to sleep beside her or going to sleep at all. Anyway, someone needed to turn off the TV and tell Jacob to go to bed when the time came, otherwise the kid would be up until two.

Just after eleven—Jon Stewart was just coming on—Jake said, "He's here again."

"Who?"

"The guy with the cigarette."

I peered through the wood shutters in our living room.

Across the street was the Lincoln Town

Car. It was parked, brazenly, right across the street from our house, under a street-light. The window was open a crack so the driver could flick his cigarette ashes out onto the street.

Jacob said, "Should we call the cops?"

"No. I'll take care of it myself."

I went to the coat closet in the front hall and rummaged out a baseball bat that had been there for years, stuck in among the umbrellas and boots where Jacob must have left it after Little League one day. It was aluminum, red, a kid-sized Louisville Slugger.

"Maybe this isn't such a good idea, Dad."

"It's a fantastic idea, trust me."

I concede, looking back, that this was, in fact, not a fantastic idea. I was not unaware of the harm I could do to the public's perception of us, even of Jacob. I think I had some vague notion I would throw a scare into Cigarette Man without doing any real harm. More to the point, I felt like I could run through a wall, and I wanted to do *something* finally. I'm not sure how far I meant to take it, honestly. In the event, I never got the chance to find out.

As I reached the sidewalk in front of my

own house, an unmarked police cruiser—a black Interceptor—raced up between us. It seemed to come out of nowhere, its wigwags and blue flashers lighting up the street. The cruiser parked at an angle to the front of the Lincoln, blocking it from leaving.

Out popped Paul Duffy, in plain clothes except for a state police windbreaker and a badge clipped to his belt. He looked at me—I think by now I had dropped the bat to my side, at least, though I must have looked ridiculous anyway—and he raised his eyebrows. "Get back in the house, Babe Ruth."

I did not move. I was so shocked, and my feelings about Duffy were so mixed at this point, that I could not really listen to him anyway.

Duffy ignored me and went to the Lincoln.

The driver's window opened with an electric hum and the driver asked, "Is there a problem?"

"License and registration, please."

"What did I do?"

"License and registration, please."

"I have a right to sit in my car, don't I?"

"Sir, are you refusing to provide identification?"

"I'm not refusing anything. I just want to know what you're bothering me for. I'm just sitting here minding my own business on a public street."

The driver relented, though. He popped his cigarette into his mouth and leaned far over so he could wiggle his wallet out from under his ass. When Duffy took the license and went back to his cruiser, the guy looked at me from under the brim of his scally cap and said, "How ya doin', pal?"

I did not answer.

"Everything okay with you and your family?"

More staring.

"It's good to have a family."

I did not answer again, and the guy went back to smoking his cigarette with theatrical nonchalance.

Duffy came out of the cruiser again and handed the guy his license and registration.

Duffy: "Were you parked here the other night?"

"No, sir. I don't know anything about that."

"Why don't you move on, Mr. O'Leary. Have a good night. Don't come back here again."

"It's a public street, isn't it?"

"Not for you."

"All right, Officer." He leaned way over again and grunted as he wedged his wallet into his back pocket. "Sorry. I move a little slow. Getting old. Happens to everyone, right?" He grinned up at Duffy then at me. "You gentlemen have a nice evening." He pulled his seat belt across his chest and made a show of clicking it. "Click it or ticket," he said. "Officer, I'm afraid you'll have to move your car. You're blocking me."

Duffy went to his cruiser and backed it up a few feet.

"G'night, Mr. Barber," the man said, and he cruised off slowly.

Duffy came up to stand beside me.

I said, "You want to tell me what that was all about?"

"I think we better talk."

"You want to come in?"

"Look, Andy, I understand if you don't want to have me around, in the house, whatever. It's okay. We can just talk here."

"No. It's all right. Just come in."

"I'd rather—"

"I said it's okay, Duff."

He frowned. "Is Laurie up?"

"You afraid to face her?"

"Yes."

"But you're not afraid to face me?"

"I'm not thrilled about it, to be honest."

"Well, don't worry. I think she's asleep."

"You mind if I take that?"

I handed him the bat.

"Were you really gonna use it?"

"I have the right to remain silent."

"Probably a good time to do that."

He tossed the bat into his cruiser and followed me inside.

Laurie stood at the top of the stairs in flannel pajama bottoms and a sweatshirt with her arms crossed. She said nothing.

Duffy said, "Hi, Laurie."

She turned away, went back to bed.

"Hi, Jacob."

"Hi," Jacob said, constrained by manners and habit from expressing any sense of anger or betrayal.

In the kitchen I asked what he had been doing outside our house.

"Your lawyer called me. He said he wasn't getting any traction in Newton or Cambridge."

"So he called you? I thought you were in public relations now."

"Yeah, well, I did this as kind of a personal project."

I nodded. I don't know how I felt about Paul Duffy at that moment. I suppose I understood that he did what he had to do in testifying against Jacob. I could not think of him as my enemy. But we would never be friends again either. If my kid wound up in Walpole doing life without parole, it would be Duffy who put him there. We both knew that. Neither of us had the words to address any of this directly, so we ignored it. This is the best thing about men's friendships: most any awkwardness can be ignored by mutual agreement and, true connection being unimaginable, you can get on with the easier business of parallel living.

"So who is he?"

"His name is James O'Leary. They call him Father O'Leary. Born February 1943, so sixty-four years old."

"Grandfather O'Leary, more like."

"He's no joke. He's an old gangster. His

record goes back fifty years and it reads like a statute book. It's all there. Weapons, drugs, violence. The feds had him up on a RICO charge with a bunch of other guys back in the eighties but he beat it. He used to be a muscle guy, that's what I was told. A leg-breaker. Now he's too old for that."

"So what does he do now?"

"He's a fixer. Hires himself out, but it's just small-time stuff. He makes problems go away. Whatever you need, collections, evictions, shutting people up."

"Father O'Leary. So what's he got against Jacob?"

"Nothing, I'm sure. The question is who is paying him and for what."

"And?"

Duffy shrugged. "I have no idea. Must be somebody who's got a beef with Jacob. That's a big group at the moment: anybody who knew Ben Rifkin, anybody who's ticked off about this case—hell, anybody with basic cable."

"Great. So what do I do if I see him again?"

"Cross the street. Then call me."

"You'll send the public relations department?"

"I'll send the Eighty-Second Airborne if I have to."

I smiled.

"I still got a few friends," he assured me.

"Are they going to let you go back to CPAC?"

"Depends. We'll see if Rasputin lets them when he becomes DA."

"He still needs one big hook before he runs for DA."

"Yeah, that's the other thing: he's not going to get it."

"No?"

"No. I've been looking into your friend Patz."

"Because you got crossed on it?"

"That and I remember you asking about Patz and Logiudice and whether there was any connection between them. Why would Logiudice not want to look at him for this murder?"

"And?"

"Well, maybe it's nothing but there is a connection there. Logiudice had a case with him when he was in the Child Abuse Unit. It was a rape. Logiudice broke it down to indecent A&B and pleaded it out."

"So?"

"It might be nothing. Maybe the victim was reluctant or could not go through with it for whatever reason, and Logiudice did the right thing. Or maybe he dumped the wrong case, and Patz went off and committed a murder. Not the kind of thing you put on a campaign poster." He shrugged. "I don't have access to the DA's files. That's as far as I could get without calling attention to what I was doing. Hey, it's not much, but it's something."

"Thanks."

"Yeah, we'll see," he murmured. "It kind of doesn't matter if it's true, does it? If you just mention something like that in court, kick up a little dust in people's eyes, know what I mean?"

"Yeah, I know what you mean, Perry Mason."

"And if Logiudice takes it on the chin, that's just a bonus, right?"

I smiled. "Yeah."

"Andy, I am sorry, you know."

"I know you are."

"This job sucks sometimes."

We stood looking at each other a few seconds.

"All right," he said, "well, I'll let you get to

sleep. Big day tomorrow. You want me to sit out there awhile in case your friend comes back?"

"No. Thanks. We'll be okay, I think."

"Okay. So, see you later, I guess."

Before I got into bed twenty minutes later, I raised the bedroom shade to peek out at the street. The black cruiser was still there, as I knew it would be.

34 | Jacob Was Mad

Trial day six.

Father O'Leary was in the audience at the back of the courtroom when the trial resumed next morning.

Laurie, looking gray and depleted, was at her lonely post in the front row of the gallery.

Logiudice, his confidence buoyed by the performances of a series of professional witnesses, moved with a little strut. It is a peculiarity of trials that, though the witness is ostensibly the star, the lawyer who is asking the questions is the only one in the courtroom who is free to move around as he pleases. Good lawyers tend not to move much, since they want the jurors' eyes to remain on the witness. But Logiudice could not seem to find a comfortable perch as he flitted from the witness stand to the jury box to the prosecution table and various points in between before finally coming to roost at the lectern. I suspect he was on edge about the day's slate of civilian witnesses, Jacob's classmates, determined not to let these amateur witnesses run away with his case the way the last ones had.

On the stand was Derek Yoo. Derek who had eaten in our kitchen a thousand times. Who had lounged on our couch watching football games and scattering Doritos on the carpet. Derek who had jumped around the living room playing GameCube and Wii with Jacob. Derek who had blissfully nodded his head for hours, probably stoned, to the pounding bass beat of his iPod while Jacob did the same beside him—the music so loud we could hear it murmuring in his headphones; it was like hearing their thoughts. Now, seeing this same Derek Yoo on the stand, I would happily have skinned him alive, with his limp brush-proof garage-band hair and sleepy slacker expression, who now threatened to send my son to Walpole forever. For the event, Derek wore a tweed sport coat that hung off his narrow shoulders. His shirt collar was too big. Cinched under his tie, it bunched and twisted, and dangled from his skinny neck like a waiting noose.

"How long have you known the defendant, Derek?"

"Since kindergarten, I guess."

"You went to elementary school together?"

"Yes."

"Where was that?"

"Mason-Rice in Newton."

"And you've been friendly ever since?"

"Yes."

"Best friends?"

"I guess so. Sometimes."

"You've been to each other's houses?"

"Yeah."

"Hung out together after school and on weekends?"

"Yeah."

"Have you been in the same homeroom?"

"Sometimes."

"When was the last time?"

"Not last year. This year Jake is not in school. I guess he has a tutor. So I guess two years ago."

"But even in years when you weren't in the same homeroom, you remained close friends?"

"Yeah."

"So how many years is it that you and the defendant have been close friends?"

"Eight."

"Eight. And you're how old?"

"I'm fifteen now."

"Is it fair to say that, as of the day Ben Rifkin was murdered, April 12, 2007, Jacob Barber was your best friend?"

Derek's voice went quiet. The thought made him either sad or embarrassed. "Yeah."

"Okay. Directing your attention to the morning of April 12, 2007, do you remember where you were that morning?"

"In school."

"About what time did you get to school?"

"Eight-thirty."

"How did you get to school that day?"

"Walked."

"Did your route take you through Cold Spring Park?"

"No, I come from the other direction."

"Okay. When you got to school, where did you go?"

"I stopped at my locker to put my stuff away, then I went to homeroom."

"And the defendant was not in your homeroom that year, correct?"

"Yes."

"Did you see him before homeroom that morning?"

"Yeah, I saw him at the lockers."

"What was he doing?"

"He was just putting his stuff in his locker."

"Was there anything unusual about his appearance?"

"No."

"About his clothes?"

"No."

"Was there anything on his hand?"

"There was a big spot. It looked like blood."

"Describe the spot."

"It was just, like, a red spot, like the size of a quarter."

"Did you ask him about it?"

"Yes. I said, 'Dude, what did you do to your hand?' And he was like, 'Oh, it's nothing. Just a scratch.'"

"Did you see the defendant try to remove the blood?"

"Not right then."

"Did he deny that the spot on his hand was blood?"

"No."

"Okay, what happened next?"

"I went off to homeroom."

"Was Ben Rifkin in your homeroom that year?"

"Yes."

"But he wasn't in homeroom that morning."

"No."

"Did that seem strange to you?"

"No. I don't know if I even noticed. I guess I would have figured he was just out sick."

"So what happened in homeroom?"

"Nothing. Just the usual: attendance, some announcements, then we went off to class."

"What was your first class that day?"

"English."

"Did you go?"

"Yeah."

"Was the defendant in your English class?"

"Yeah."

"Did you see him in the classroom that morning?"

"Yes."

"Did you speak to him?"

"We just said hello, that's all."

"Was there anything unusual about the defendant's manner or anything he said?"

"No, not really."

"He didn't seem upset."

"No."

"Anything unusual about his appearance?"

"No."

"No blood on his clothes, nothing like that?"

"Objection."

"Sustained."

"Would you describe the defendant's appearance when you saw him in English class that morning?"

"I think he was just wearing, like, regular clothes: jeans, sneakers, whatever. There was no blood on his clothes, if that's what you mean."

"What about on his hands?"

"The spot was gone."

"He'd washed his hands?"

"I guess."

"Were there any cuts or scratches on his hands? Any reason he might have been bleeding?"

"Not that I remember. I wasn't really paying attention. It didn't matter then."

"Okay, what happened next?"

"We had English class for like fifteen minutes, then there was an announcement that the school was being put in a lockdown."

"What is a lockdown?"

"It's when you have to go back to your homeroom and they take attendance and lock all the doors and keep everyone there."

"Do you know why the school gets put in a lockdown?"

"Because there's some kind of danger."

"What did you think when you heard the school was going into a lockdown?"

"Columbine."

"You thought somebody was at the school with a gun?"

"Yeah."

"Did you have any idea who?"

"No."

"Were you afraid?"

"Yeah, of course. Everybody was."

"Do you remember how the defendant reacted when the principal announced the lockdown?"

"He didn't say anything. He just kind of smiled. There wasn't much time. We just heard it and everybody ran."

"Did the defendant seem nervous or frightened?"

"No."

"At the time, did anybody know what the lockdown was about?"

"No."

"Did anyone connect it to Ben Rifkin?"

"No. I mean, later that morning they told us, but not at the start."

"What happened next?"

"We just stayed in our homerooms with the doors locked. They came on the intercom and they told us we weren't in any danger, there were no guns or anything, so the teachers unlocked the door and we just kind of waited there. It was like a drill or something."

"You had practiced lockdowns before?"

"Yeah."

"What happened next?"

"We stayed there. They told us to take

out our books and read or do homework or whatever. Then they canceled school for the rest of the day and we went home around eleven."

"Nobody ever questioned you or the other students?"

"Not that day, no."

"Nobody ever searched the school or the lockers or any of the students?"

"Not that I saw."

"So when school got out and they finally let you leave the room, what did you see?"

"There were just a lot of parents waiting outside the school to get their kids. All the parents came to the school."

"When did you see the defendant next?"

"We were texting that afternoon, I guess?"

"By texting, you mean you were exchanging text messages on your cell phones?"

"Yes."

"What did you talk about?"

"Well, at that point all we knew was that Ben got killed. We didn't know, like, exactly what happened or anything. So we were just both like, Did you hear anything? What did you hear? What's going on?"

"And what did the defendant say to you?"

"Well, I was just like, Dude, isn't that the way you go to school? Did you see anything? And Jake just said no."

"He said no?"

"That's right."

"He didn't say that he'd seen Ben lying on the ground and he tried to revive him or see if he was okay?"

"No."

"What else did he say while you were texting?"

"Well, we were just kind of joking because Ben had been kind of picking on Jacob for a while. So we were all like, 'Couldn't happen to a nicer guy' and 'Your wishes came true' and stuff like that. I know that sounds really bad now but it was just, like, joking."

"When you say Ben Rifkin had been picking on Jacob, describe what you mean. What exactly had been going on between those two?"

"Ben was just like, he was in a different group. He was just—I don't want to say not-nice things about him after what happened and everything—but he was not very nice to Jake or to me, or to anyone in our group."

"Who is in your group?"

"It was pretty much me, Jake, and this other kid, Dylan."

"And what was your group like? What was your reputation in school?"

"We were geeks." Derek said this without embarrassment or bitterness. Did not bother him. Just the way it was.

"And Ben, what was he like?"

"I don't know. He was handsome."

"He was handsome?"

Derek flushed. "I don't know. He was just in a different group than us."

"Were you friends with Ben Rifkin?"

"No. I mean, I knew him, like, to say hello, but we weren't friends."

"But he never picked on you?"

"I don't know. He probably called me a fag or whatever. I wouldn't call it bullying or anything. Somebody calls you a fag, it's just like, whatever. It was no big deal."

"Did Ben call other people names?"

"Yes."

"Like what?"

"I don't know, fag, geek, slut, bitch, loser, whatever. It was just the way he was, it was kind of the way he talked."

"To everyone?"

"No, not everyone. Just kids he didn't like. Kids he didn't think were cool."

"Was Jacob cool?"

Shy smile. "No. None of us were."

"Did Ben like Jacob?"

"No. Definitely not."

"Why not?"

"Just didn't."

"For no reason? Was there some kind of beef between them? Anything specific?"

"No. It was just like, Ben didn't think Jake was cool. None of us were. He said stuff to all of us."

"But it was worse for Jacob than for you or Dylan?"

"Yes."

"Why?"

"I think he just kind of saw that it got to Jake. Like I said, for me, if somebody calls you a fag or a geek or whatever, what can you do? I just kind of didn't fight back. But Jake got all bent out of shape, so Ben just kept on doing it."

"Doing what?"

"Calling him names."

"What names?"

" 'Fag' mostly. Some other things, worse things."

"What worse things? Go ahead. You can say them."

"It was mostly about being gay. He would keep asking Jacob whether he'd done different gay stuff. He just kept saying it over and over and over."

"Saying what?"

Derek took a deep breath. "I don't know if I can use the words."

"It's all right. Go ahead."

"He'd say, like, 'Did you suck anyone's—' I don't really want to say it. It was just stuff like that. He just wouldn't stop."

"Did anyone at school think Jacob actually was gay?"

"Objection."

"Overruled."

"No. I mean, I don't think so. It's not like anyone cared anyway. *I* don't care." He looked at Jacob. "I still don't care."

"Did Jacob ever say anything to you about being gay, either way?"

"He said he wasn't."

"In what context? Why did he say that to you?"

"I was just, like, telling him to ignore Ben.

I was like, 'Hey, Jake, it's not like you're gay anyway, so what do you care?' So he said he wasn't, and he said it wasn't about whether he was gay; it was about Ben giving him shit—giving him grief, I mean—and how long was it going to go on before anyone did anything to stop it? He just knew it was wrong and no one was doing anything to stop it."

"So Jacob was upset about it?"

"Yes."

"He felt he was being bullied?"

"He *was* being bullied."

"Did you ever intervene to try to stop Ben from bullying your friend?"

"No."

"Why not?"

"Because it wouldn't have mattered. Ben wouldn't have listened. It doesn't work that way."

"Was the bullying just verbal? Or did it ever become physical?"

"Sometimes Ben would push him or like jostle him as he went by, like knock him with his shoulder. Sometimes he took Jake's stuff, like stuff from his backpack or his lunch or whatever."

"Now, the defendant looks like a big kid.

How could Ben get away with picking on him?"

"Ben was big too, and he was kind of tougher. And he had more friends. I think we all—like Jake and Dylan and me—we kind of knew we weren't important kids. I mean, I don't know, it's weird. It's kind of hard to explain. But if it got to be a real fight with Ben, we would have just been cut out."

"Socially, you mean."

"Yeah. And then what would school be like if we were just, like, alone?"

"Did Ben do this to other kids too, or just Jacob?"

"Just Jacob."

"Any idea why?"

"'Cause he knew it made Jake mad."

"You could see it made him mad?"

"Everyone could."

"Did Jacob get mad a lot?"

"At Ben? Of course."

"At other things too?"

"Yeah, a little."

"Tell us about Jacob's temper."

"Objection."

"Overruled."

"Go ahead, Derek, tell us about the defendant's temper."

"He just, like, got really upset about stuff. He kind of stewed about it and he couldn't let it go. He'd get himself all worked up on the inside and then sometimes he would kind of go off over some little thing. He'd always feel bad afterward and he'd be embarrassed because it was like he was always overreacting, because it was never just about whatever made him go off. It was all the other stuff he'd be thinking about."

"And you know this how?"

"Because he'd tell me."

"Did he ever lose his temper with you?"

"No."

"Did he ever lose his temper in front of you?"

"Yeah, sometimes he could be a little schizo."

"Objection."

"Sustained. The jury will ignore that last comment."

"Derek, would you describe a time you saw the defendant lose his temper?"

"Objection, relevance."

"Sustained."

"Derek, would you tell the court what happened when the defendant found a stray dog?"

"Objection, relevance."

"Sustained. Move on, Mr. Logiudice."

Logiudice puckered his mouth. He flipped a page of his yellow pad, a page of questions he would set aside. Like a bird rustled from his perch, he began to move nervously around the courtroom again as he asked his questions until, at length, he settled back into his place at the lectern near the jury box.

"For whatever reason, in the days after Ben Rifkin's murder, you became concerned about your friend Jacob's role in it?"

"Objection."

"Overruled."

"You can answer, Derek."

"Yes."

"Was there anything in particular, besides his temper, that made you suspicious of Jacob?"

"Yes. He had a knife. It was like kind of an army knife, like a combat knife. It had this really really sharp blade with all these . . . *teeth.* It was a really scary knife."

"You saw this knife yourself?"

"Yeah. Jake showed it to me. He even brought it to school once."

"Why did he bring it to school?"

"Objection."

"Sustained."

"Did he show you the knife once at school?"

"Yeah, he showed me."

"Did he say why he was showing it to you?"

"No."

"Did he tell you why he wanted a knife at all?"

"I think he just thought it was cool."

"And how did you react when you saw the knife?"

"I was like, 'Dude, that's cool.'"

"You weren't bothered by it?"

"No."

"Concerned?"

"No, not then."

"Was Ben Rifkin around when Jacob produced the knife that day?"

"No. Nobody knew Jake had the knife. That's the thing. He was just walking around with it. It was like Jake had this secret."

"Where did he carry the knife?"

"In his backpack or his pocket."

"Did he ever show it to anyone else or threaten anyone with it?"

"No."

"All right, so Jacob had a knife. Was there anything else that made you suspicious of your friend Jacob in the hours and days after Ben Rifkin was murdered?"

"Well, like I said, at the very beginning nobody knew what happened. Then it kind of came out that Ben got killed with a knife in Cold Spring Park, and I just kind of knew."

"Knew what?"

"Knew—I mean, I felt like he probably did it."

"Objection."

"Sustained. The jury will disregard the last answer."

"How did you know Jacob—"

"Objection."

"Sustained. Move on, Mr. Logiudice."

Logiudice pursed his lips, regrouped. "Did Jacob ever talk about a website called the Cutting Room?"

"Yes."

"Would you tell the jury, what is the Cutting Room?"

"It's like a porn site, kind of, only it's just stories and anyone can write stories and post them there."

"What kind of stories?"

"Like S&M, I guess. I don't really know. It's, like, sex and violence."

"Did Jacob talk about the site often?"

"Yeah. He liked it, I guess. He used to go there a lot."

"Did you go there?"

Sheepish, blushing. "No. I didn't like it."

"Did it bother you that Jacob went there?"

"No. It's his business."

"Did Jacob ever show you a story on the Cutting Room that described Ben Rifkin's murder?"

"Yes."

"When did Jacob show you this story?"

"Like late April, I think."

"After the murder?"

"Yeah, a few days after."

"What did he tell you about it?"

"He just said he had this story he wrote and he posted it on this message board."

"You mean he posted it online for other people to read?"

"Yeah."

"And did you read the story?"

"Yes."

"How did you find it?"

"Jacob sent me a link."

"How? Email? Facebook?"

"Facebook? No! Anyone could have seen it. I think it was email. So I went to the site and I read it."

"And what did you think of the story when you read it the first time?"

"I don't know. I thought it was weird that he wrote it, but it was kind of interesting, I guess. Jacob was always a really good writer."

"Did he write other stories like this one?"

"No, not exactly. He wrote some that were, like—"

"Objection."

"Sustained. Next question."

Logiudice produced a document, laser-printed, thick with text on both sides. He laid it on the witness stand in front of Derek.

"Is that the story the defendant told you he wrote?"

"Yes."

"Is that printout an accurate record of the story precisely as you read it that day?"

"Yeah, I guess."

"Move the document be admitted in evidence."

"The document is admitted and marked Commonwealth's Exhibit . . . Mary?"

"Twenty-six."

"Commonwealth's exhibit twenty-six."

"How do you know for sure that the defendant wrote this story?"

"Why would he say it if it wasn't true?"

"And what was it about the story that made you so concerned about Jacob and the Rifkin murder?"

"It was just, like, a total description, every little detail. He described the knife, the stabs in the chest, the whole thing. Even the character, the kid that got stabbed—in the story Jake calls him 'Brent Mallis,' but it's obviously Ben Rifkin. Anyone who knew Ben would know. It wasn't like totally fiction. It was just obvious."

"Do you and your friends sometimes exchange messages on Facebook?"

"Sure."

"And three days after Ben Rifkin was murdered, on April 15, 2007, did you post a message on Facebook saying, 'Jake, everyone knows you did it. You have a knife. I've seen it.'"

"Yes."

"Why did you post that message?"

"I just didn't want to be the only one who knew about the knife. It was like, I didn't want to be alone knowing that."

"When you posted that message on Facebook accusing your friend of the murder, did he ever respond?"

"I wasn't really accusing him. It was just something I wanted to say."

"Did the defendant respond in any way?"

"I'm not sure what you mean. I mean, he posted on Facebook, but not really responding to that."

"Well, did he ever deny that he murdered Ben Rifkin?"

"No."

"After you published your accusation on Facebook in front of his whole class?"

"I didn't *publish* it. I just put it on Facebook."

"Did he ever deny the accusation?"

"No."

"Did you ever accuse him directly, to his face?"

"No."

"Before you saw that story on the Cutting Room, did you ever report your suspicions about Jacob to the police?"

"Not exactly."

"Why not?"

"Because I wasn't totally sure. Plus, the cop in charge of the case was Jacob's dad."

"And what did you think when you realized that it was Jacob's dad who was running the case?"

"Ob-*jec*-tion." Jonathan's voice was disgusted.

"Sustained."

"Derek, one last question. It was you that sought out the police to share this information, isn't that right? Nobody had to come ask you?"

"That's right."

"You felt you had to turn in your own best friend?"

"Yeah."

"No further questions."

Jonathan stood up. He seemed for all the world to be unfazed by what he had just heard. And he would conduct a gallant cross, I knew. But something had obviously changed in the courtroom. The atmosphere was electric. It was as if we had all just decided something. You could read it in the faces of the jurors and Judge French, you could hear it in the supreme quiet of the crowd: Jacob was not going to walk out of that courtroom, not out the front door anyway. The excitement was a mix of relief—everyone's doubts were resolved at last, about whether Jacob did it and whether he would get away with it—and palpable eagerness for revenge. The rest of the trial would be only details, formalities, tying up loose ends. Even my friend Ernie the court officer looked at Jacob with a wary eye, assessing how he would react to the handcuffs. But Jonathan seemed not to notice the drop in air pressure. He moved to the lectern and slipped on the half-glasses he wore on a chain around his neck and began to take it apart piece by piece.

"These things you've told us about, they bothered you, but not so much that you broke off your friendship with Jacob?"

"No."

"In fact, you two continued to be friends for days and even weeks after the murder, isn't that right?"

"Yes."

"Isn't it true that you even went to Jacob's house after the murder?"

"Yes."

"So it's fair to say that you weren't too sure at the time that Jacob really was the murderer?"

"Yeah, that's right."

"Because you wouldn't want to remain friends with a murderer, of course?"

"No, I guess not."

"Even after you posted that message on Facebook where you accused Jacob of the murder, you *still* remained friends with him? You still remained in contact, still hung around?"

"Yes."

"Were you ever afraid of Jacob?"

"No."

"Did he ever threaten or intimidate you in any way? Or lose his temper at you?"

"No."

"Isn't it true that it was your parents who told you you couldn't stay with friends with Jacob, that you *never* decided to stop being friends with Jacob?"

"Kind of."

Jonathan backed off, sensing Derek beginning to hedge, and he moved to a new topic. "The day of the murder, you said you saw Jacob before school and again in English class right after school started?"

"Yes."

"But there was no indication that he had been involved in any kind of struggle?"

"No."

"No blood?"

"Just the little spot on his hand."

"No scratches, no torn clothes, nothing like that? No mud?"

"No."

"In fact, it never even occurred to you, looking at Jacob in English class that morning, that he might have been involved in anything on the way to school?"

"No."

"When you later came to the conclusion that Jacob might have committed the murder, as you've suggested here, did you take that into account? That after a bloody, fatal knife attack, Jacob somehow emerged without a drop of blood on him, without so much as a scratch? Did you think about that, Derek?"

"Kind of."

"Kind of?"

"Yes."

"You said Ben Rifkin was a bigger kid than Jacob, bigger and tougher?"

"Yes."

"But still Jacob came out of this struggle without a mark on him?"

Derek did not answer.

"Now, you said something about Jacob grinning when the lockdown was announced. Did other kids grin? Is it natural enough for a kid to grin when there's excitement, when you're nervous?"

"Probably."

"It's just something kids do sometimes."

"I guess."

"Now, the knife you saw, Jacob's knife. Just to be clear, you have no idea whether that was the knife that was used in the murder?"

"No."

"And Jacob never said anything to you about *intending* to use the knife on Ben Rifkin, because of the bullying?"

"Intending? No, he didn't say that."

"And when he showed the knife to you, it never occurred to you that he planned to kill Ben Rifkin? Because if it did, you would have done something about it, right?"

"I guess."

"So, as far as you knew, Jacob never had a *plan* to kill Ben Rifkin?"

"A plan? No."

"Never talked about when or how he was going to kill Ben Rifkin?"

"No."

"Then, later, he just sent you the story?"

"Yeah."

"He sent you a link by email, you said?"

"Yes."

"Did you save that email?"

"No."

"Why not?"

"It didn't seem smart. I mean, for Jake—from Jacob's point of view."

"So you deleted the email because you were protecting him?"

"I guess."

"Can you tell me, of all the details in that story, was there anything that was new to you, anything you didn't already know either from the Web or from news stories or from other kids talking?"

"No, not really."

"The knife, the park, the three stab wounds—that was all well known by then, wasn't it?"

"Yes."

"Hardly a confession, then, is it?"

"I don't know."

"And did he say in the email that he'd written the story? Or just found it?"

"I don't remember exactly what the email said. I think it was just, like, 'Dude, check this out' or something like that."

"But you're sure Jacob told you he wrote the story, not that he just read it?"

"Pretty sure."

"*Pretty* sure?"

"Pretty sure, yeah."

Jonathan went on in this way for some time, doing what he could, shaving away and shaving away at Derek Yoo's testimony, scoring what points he could. Who knows what the jurors were really making of it. All I can tell you is that the half dozen jurors who were furiously taking notes during Derek's direct testimony had put down their pens now. Some were no longer even looking at him; they had dropped their eyes to their laps. Maybe Jonathan had won the day and they had decided to discount Derek's testimony entirely. But it did not seem that way. It seemed like I had been fooling myself, and for the first time I began to imagine in realistic terms what it would be like when Jacob was in Concord prison.

35 | Argentina

Driving home from court that day I was morose, and my sadness infected Jacob and Laurie. From the start, I had been the steady one. It upset them, I think, to see me lose hope. I tried to lie for them. I said all the usual things about not feeling too up on a good day or too down on a bad day; about how the prosecution's evidence always looks worse on first sight than it does later, in the context of the whole case; about how juries are impossible to anticipate and we should not read too much into their every little gesture. But my tone gave me away. I thought we had probably lost the case that day. At a minimum, the damage was enough that we would have to present a real defense. It would be foolish to rely on "reasonable doubt" at this point: the story Jacob had written about the murder read like a confession, and try as he might, Jonathan could not disprove Derek's testimony that Jacob wrote it. I did not admit any of this. There was nothing to gain by telling the truth, so I didn't. All I said to them was that "It wasn't a good day." But that was enough.

Father O'Leary did not appear to watch over us that night, or anyone else. We Barbers were left in complete isolation. If we had been shot out into space, we could not have felt more alone. We ordered Chinese food, as we had a thousand times the last few months, because China City delivers and the driver speaks so little English that we did not have to feel self-conscious opening the door for him. We ate our boneless spare ribs and General Gao's chicken in near silence, then slunk off to opposite corners of the house for the evening. We were too sick of the case to talk about it anymore but too obsessed with it to talk about anything else. We were too gloomy for the idiocies of TV—suddenly our lives seemed finite, and much too short to waste—and too distracted to read.

Around ten, I went into Jacob's room to check on him. He lay on his back on the bed.

"You okay, Jacob?"

"Not really."

I went over and sat on the side of the bed. He hoisted his butt over to make room, but Jake was getting so big there was hardly enough space for both of us. (He used to lie right on my chest for naps when he was a baby. He had been no bigger than a loaf of bread.)

He rolled onto his side and propped his head on his hand. "Dad, can I ask you something? If you thought things were looking bad, like the case was about to go the wrong way, would you tell me?"

"Why?"

"No, not 'why'; just, would you tell me?"

"Yeah, I guess so."

"Because it wouldn't make sense to— well, if I took off, what would happen to you and Mom?"

"We'd lose all our money."

"They'd take away the house?"

"Eventually. We put it up as security on your bail."

He considered this.

"It's just a house," I told him. "I wouldn't miss it. It doesn't matter as much as you."

"Yeah, but still. Where would you guys live?"

"Is this what you've been lying here thinking about?"

"A little bit."

Laurie came to the door. She folded her arms and leaned on the doorpost.

I said, "Where would you go?"

"Buenos Aires."

"Buenos Aires? Why there?"

"It just sounds like a cool place."

"Says who?"

"There was an article about it in the *Times.* It's the Paris of South America."

"Hm. I didn't know South America had a Paris."

"It is in South America, right?"

"Yeah, it's in Argentina. You may want to do a little more research before you run off there."

"Is there a—whaddaya call it?—a treaty, like a fugitive treaty?"

"An extradition treaty? I don't know. I guess that'd be another thing you'd want to check out first."

"Yeah. I guess so."

"How would you pay for the ticket?"

"I wouldn't. You would."

"And a passport? You surrendered yours, remember?"

"I'd get a new one somehow."

"Just like that? How?"

Laurie came and sat on the floor beside the bed and stroked his hair. "He'd sneak across the border into Canada and he'd get a Canadian passport."

"Hm. Not sure it's actually that easy, but okay. So what would you do once you got to Buenos Aires, which we know is in Argentina?"

Laurie said, "He'd dance the tango." Her eyes were wet.

"Do you know how to dance the tango, Jacob?"

"Not exactly."

"Not exactly, he says."

"Not exactly, like, meaning not at all." He laughed.

"Well, you can get tango lessons in Buenos Aires, I would think."

Laurie said, "In Buenos Aires, everybody knows the tango."

"You'll need someone to dance the tango *with,* won't you?"

He smiled shyly.

Laurie said, "Buenos Aires is filled with beautiful women who dance the tango. Beautiful, mysterious women. Jacob will have his pick."

"Is that true, Dad? Lots of beautiful women in Buenos Aires?"

"That's what I hear."

He lay back and laced his fingers behind his head. "This is sounding better and better."

"What will you do there when you get done dancing the tango, Jake?"

"Go to school, I guess."

"I pay for that too?"

"Of course."

"And after school?"

"I don't know. Maybe I'll be a lawyer like you."

"Don't you think you'll want to keep a low profile? You know, being a fugitive and all?"

Laurie answered for him. "No. They're going to forget all about him and he's going to have a long, happy, wonderful life in Argentina with a beautiful woman who dances the tango, and Jacob will be a great man." She got up on her knees so she could look at his face and continue to stroke his hair as he lay there. "He'll have children, and his children will have children, and he'll bring so much happiness to so many people that no one will ever believe that once upon a time in America people said horrible things about him."

Jacob closed his eyes. "I don't know if I can go to court tomorrow. I just don't want to do it anymore."

"I know, Jake." I laid my palm on his chest. "It's almost over."

"That's what I'm afraid of."

Laurie: "I don't think I can do it anymore either."

"It'll be over soon. We just have to hang in there. I promise."

"Dad, you'll tell me, right? Like you said? If it's time for me to . . . ?" He cocked his head toward the door.

I suppose I could have told him the truth. *It's not like that, Jake. There's nowhere to go.* But I didn't. I said, "It's not going to happen. We're going to win."

"But *if.*"

"If. Yeah, definitely I'll tell you, Jacob." I tousled his hair. "Let's try to get some sleep."

Laurie kissed his forehead, and I did the same.

He said, "Maybe you guys'll come to Buenos Aires too. We can all go."

"Can we still order from China City there?"

"Sure, Dad." He grinned. "We'll fly it in."

"Okay, then. For a second, I didn't think it was a realistic plan. Now get some sleep. Another big day tomorrow."

"Let's hope not," he said.

When Laurie and I got into bed, she said in a pillow-talk murmur, "When we were talking about Buenos Aires, that was the first time I've felt happy in I don't know how long. I don't remember the last time I smiled."

But her confidence must have faltered, because only a few seconds later, as she lay on her side facing me, she whispered, "What if he went to Buenos Aires and killed someone there?"

"Laurie, he's not going to Buenos Aires and he's not going to kill anyone. He didn't kill anyone *here.*"

"I'm not so sure."

"Don't say that."

She looked away.

"Laurie?"

"Andy, what if we're the ones who are wrong? What if he gets off and then, God forbid, he does it again? Don't we have some responsibility?"

"Laurie, it's late, you're exhausted. We'll have this conversation some other time. For now, you need to stop thinking that way. You're making yourself crazy."

"No." She gave me an imploring look, like *I* was the one who was not making sense. "Andy, we need to be honest with each other. This is something we need to think about."

"Why? The trial isn't over yet. You're quitting too soon."

"We need to think about it because he's our son. He needs our support."

"Laurie, we're doing our job. We're supporting him, we're helping him get through the trial."

"Is that our job?"

"Yes! What else is there?"

"What if he needs something else, Andy?"

"There *is* nothing else. What are you

talking about? There's nothing more we can do. We're already doing everything humanly possible."

"Andy, what if he's guilty?"

"He won't be."

Her breathy whispering became intense, pointed. "I don't mean the verdict. I mean the truth. What if he really is guilty?"

"He isn't."

"Andy, is that what you really think? He didn't do it? Simple as that? You have no doubt at all?"

I did not answer. I could not bear to.

"Andy, I can't read you anymore. You need to talk to me, you need to tell me. I'm never sure what's going on inside you anymore."

"Nothing's going on inside me," I said, and the statement felt even truer than I'd intended.

"Andy, sometimes I just want to grab you by the lapels and *make* you tell the truth."

"Oh, the thing with my father again."

"No, it's not that. I'm talking about Jacob. I need you to be absolutely honest here, for *me.* I need to know. Even if *you* don't, *I* need to know: do you think Jacob did it?"

"I think there are things a parent should never think about a child."

"That's not what I asked."

"Laurie, he's my son."

"He's *our* son. We're responsible for him."

"Exactly. We're responsible for him. We need to stick with him." I put my hand on her head, stroked her hair.

She swiped it away. "No! Andy, do you understand what I'm saying to you? If he's guilty, then we're guilty too. That's just the way it is. We're implicated. We made him— you and me. We created him and we sent him out into the world. And if he really did this—can you handle that? Can you handle that possibility?"

"If I have to."

"Really, Andy? Could you?"

"Yes. Look, if he's guilty, if we lose, then we'll have to face that somehow. I mean, I *get* that. We'll still be his parents. You can't resign from this job."

"Andy, you are the most infuriating, dishonest man."

"Why?"

"Because I need you to be here with me right now, and you're not."

"I am!"

"No. You're managing me. You're talking in platitudes. You're in there behind those handsome brown eyes and I don't know what you're really thinking. I can't tell."

I sighed, shook my head. "Sometimes I can't tell either, Laurie. I don't know what I'm thinking. I'm trying not to think at all."

"Andy, please, you *have* to think. Look inside yourself. You're his father. You can't avoid this. Did he do it? It's a yes-or-no question."

She was pushing me toward it, this towering black idea, Jacob the Murderer. I brushed against it, touched the hem of its robe—and I could not go any further. The danger was too great.

I said, "I don't know."

"Then you think he might have."

"I don't know."

"But it's possible, at least."

"I said I don't know, Laurie."

She scrutinized my face, my eyes, searching for something she could trust, for bedrock. I tried to put on a mask of resolve for her, so she would find in my expression whatever it was she needed—reassurance, love, connection, whatever. But the truth?

Certainty? I did not have those. They were not mine to give.

A couple of hours later, around one A.M., there was a siren in the distance. This was unusual; in our quiet suburb the cops and fire engines generally do not use them. Flashers only. The siren lasted only five seconds or so, then resonated in the quiet, suspended like a flare. Behind me Laurie was asleep in the same position as before, with her back to me. I went to the window and looked out but there was nothing to see. I would not find out until the next morning what that siren was and how, unknown to us, everything had already changed. We were already in Argentina.

36 | Helluva Show

The phone rang at five-thirty the next morning, my cell phone, and I answered it automatically, conditioned over the years to receive these emergency calls at crazy hours. I even answered in my old commanding voice, "Andy Barber!," to convince people that I had not actually been sleeping, no matter what the hour.

When I hung up, Laurie said, "Who was that?"

"Jonathan."

"What's wrong?"

"Nothing."

"So what was it?"

I felt a grin spread over my face and a dreamy, bewildered happiness embraced me.

"Andy?"

"It's over."

"What do you mean, it's over?"

"He confessed."

"What? Who confessed?"

"Patz."

"What!"

"Jonathan did what he said he would in court: he had him served. Patz got the subpoena and last night he killed himself. He left a note with a full confession. Jonathan said they've been at his apartment all night. They confirmed the handwriting; the note is legit. Patz confessed."

"He confessed? Just like that? Is that possible?"

"It doesn't seem real, does it?"

"How did he kill himself?"

"Hung himself."

"Oh my God."

"Jonathan says he's going to move for dismissal as soon as court opens."

Laurie's hands covered her mouth. She was already crying. We embraced, then we ran into Jacob's room as if it were

Christmas morning—or Easter, given that this miracle was more in the nature of a resurrection—and we shook him awake and hugged him and shared the incredible news.

And everything was different. Just like that, everything was different. We got dressed in our trial clothes and we bided our time till we could drive to the courthouse. We watched the news on TV and checked Boston.com for mention of Patz's suicide but there was none, so we sat there grinning at one another and shaking our heads in disbelief.

It was better than a not-guilty from the jury. We kept saying this: *not guilty* is merely a failure of proof. Jacob had actually been proven *innocent.* It was as if the entire horrific episode was erased. I do not believe in God or miracles, but this was a miracle. I cannot explain the feeling any other way. It felt as if we had been saved by some sort of divine intervention—by a real miracle. The only limit on our joy was the fact we could not quite believe it and we did not want to celebrate until the case was officially dismissed. It was at least conceivable, after all, that Logiudice would continue his prosecution even in the face of Patz's confession.

In the event, Jonathan did not get the chance to move for dismissal. Before the judge even took the bench, Logiudice filed a nol pros—a nolle prosequi, which announced the government's decision to drop the charges.

At nine sharp, the judge bounded out to the bench with a little grin. He read over the nol pros with a theatrical flourish and, with a palm-up motion of his hand, he asked Jacob to stand. "Mr. Barber, I see from your face and from your dad's face that you've already heard the news. So let me be the first to tell you the words I'm sure you've longed to hear: Jacob Barber, you are a free man." There was a cheer—a cheer!—and Jacob and I hugged.

The judge banged his gavel but he did so with an indulgent smile. When the courtroom was relatively quiet again, he gestured to the clerk, who read in a monotone—apparently only she was not happy for the result—"Jacob Michael Barber, in the matter of indictment number oh-eight-dash-four-four-oh-seven, the Commonwealth having nolle prosequi the within indictment,

it is ordered by the court that you be dis-
charged of this indictment and go without
day insofar as this indictment is concerned.
The bail previously posted may be returned
to the surety. Case dismissed."

Go without day. The awkward legal for-
mulation that is the defendant's ticket out.
It means, You may go without any more
court days scheduled—go and not come
back.

Mary rubber-stamped the indictment,
slipped the paper into her file, and tossed
the file into her out-box with such bureaucratic efficiency that you might have thought
she had a stack of cases to get through
before lunch.

And it was over.

Or almost over. We made our way
through the crowd of reporters, jostling now
to congratulate us and get their video in
time for the morning shows, and we wound
up literally running down Thorndike Street
to the garage where we were parked. Running, laughing—free!

We made it to our car and for an awkward moment we were preoccupied with
trying to find the words to thank Jonathan,
who graciously declined the credit because,

he said, truthfully, he had not actually done anything. We thanked him anyway. Thanked him and thanked him. I pumped his arm up and down, and Laurie hugged him. "You would have won," I told him. "I'm sure of it."

In all of this, it was Jacob who saw them coming. "Uh-oh," he said.

There were two of them. Dan Rifkin came first. He was wearing a tan trench coat, fancier than most, over-designed, with a profusion of buttons, pockets, and epaulettes. He still had that doll-like immobile face, so it was impossible to know exactly what he intended. Apologizing to us, perhaps?

A few feet behind him was Father O'Leary, a giant by comparison with Rifkin, ambling along with his hands in his pockets and his scally cap pulled low over his eyes.

We turned slowly to meet them. We must all have had the same expression, puzzled but pleased to see this man who should naturally have been our friend now, despite the pain he had been through, graciously coming to welcome us back into his world, into the real world. But his expression was strange. Hard.

Laurie said, "Dan?"

He did not respond. He took from one of the deep pockets of his trench coat a knife, an ordinary kitchen knife, which I recognized, absurd as this sounds, as a Wüsthof Classic steak knife because we have the same set of knives in a knife block on our kitchen counter. But I did not have time to fully fathom the sublime weirdness of being stabbed with such a knife because almost immediately, before Dan Rifkin got within a few feet of us, Father O'Leary grabbed Rifkin by the arm. He banged Rifkin's hand once on the hood of the car, which caused the knife to clatter down to the concrete garage floor. Then he flipped Rifkin's arm behind the little man's back and easily— so easily he might have been manipulating a mannequin—he bent him over the hood of the car. He said to Rifkin, "Easy there, champ."

He did all this with expert, graceful professionalism. The whole transaction could not have lasted more than a few seconds, and we were left gaping at the two men.

"Who *are* you?" I said finally.

"Friend of your father's. He asked me to look out for you."

"My father? How do you know my father? No, wait, don't tell me. I don't want to know."

"What do you want me to do with this guy?"

"Let him go! What's wrong with you?"

He did.

Rifkin straightened himself up. He had tears in his eyes. He looked at us with helpless impotence—apparently he still believed Jacob had killed his son, but he could not do anything about it—and he staggered off, to what torments I cannot imagine.

Father O'Leary went to Jacob and extended his hand. "Congratulations, kid. That was something in there this morning. Did you see the expression on that asshole DA's face? Priceless!"

Jacob shook his hand with a bewildered expression.

"Helluva show," Father O'Leary said. "Helluva show." He laughed. "And you're Billy Barber's kid?"

"Yeah." I had never been proud to say that. I'm not sure I had ever actually said it out loud in public before. But it gave me a connection to Father O'Leary and it seemed to amuse him, so we both smiled at it.

"You're bigger than him, that's for sure.

You could fit two of that little shit inside a you."

I did not know what to do with that comment so I just stood there.

"Tell your old man I said hello, all right?" Father O'Leary said. "Jesus, I could tell you stories about him."

"Don't. Please."

Finally to Jacob: "It's your lucky day, kid." He laughed again and ambled away and I have never seen Father O'Leary again to this day.

Part
FOUR

"Precisely how the electrical signals and chemical reactions occurring second by second in the human body make the leap to thought, motivation, impulse—where the physical machinery of man stops and the ghost in the machine, consciousness, begins—is not truly a scientific question, for the simple reason that we cannot design an experiment to capture, measure or duplicate it. For all we have learned, the fact remains that we do not understand in any meaningful way why people do what they do, and likely never will."

—PAUL HEITZ,
"Neurocriminology and Its Discontents,"
American Journal of Criminology and Public Policy, Fall 2008

37 | After-Life

Life goes on, probably too long if we're being honest about it. In a long life there are thirty or thirty-five thousand days to be got through, but only a few dozen that really matter, Big Days when Something Momentous Happens. The rest—the vast majority, tens of thousands of days—are unremarkable, repetitive, even monotonous. We glide through them then instantly forget them. We tend not to think about this arithmetic when we look back on our lives. We remember the handful of Big Days and throw away the rest. We organize our long, shapeless lives into tidy little stories, as I am doing here. But our lives are mostly made up of junk, of ordinary, forgettable days, and "The End" is never the end.

The day Jacob was exonerated, of course, was a Big Day. But after it, remarkably, the little days just kept on coming.

We did not return to "normal"; we had, all three of us, forgotten what normal was. At least, we had no illusions that we would ever get back to it. But in the days and weeks after Jacob's release, as the euphoria of our vindication receded, we did fall into a routine, if a barren one. We went out very little. Never to restaurants or other public places where we felt leered at. I took over the grocery shopping, since Laurie would not risk running into the Rifkins at the market again, and I picked up the wifely habit of planning the week's dinner menus in my head as I shopped (pasta Monday, chicken Tuesday, hamburgers Wednesday . . .). We went to a few movies, usually midweek when the theaters were less crowded, and even then we made a point of slipping in just as the lights went down. Mostly we loafed around the house. We surfed the Web incessantly, entranced, glassy-eyed. We exercised on the tread-

mill in the basement rather than jog outside. We upped our Netflix plan so that we
had as many DVDs on hand as possible.
It sounds dismal, looking back on it, but at
the time it felt wonderful. We were free, or
something like it.

We considered moving—not to Buenos
Aires, alas, but to more prosaic places
where we might start again: Florida, California, Wyoming, anywhere we imagined
people went to reinvent themselves. For a
while I was preoccupied with the little town
of Bisbee, Arizona, where I was told it is
easy to get lost and stay lost. There was
always the possibility of leaving the country too, which had a certain glamor. We
got into interminable discussions about all
this. Laurie doubted we could outrun the
publicity the case had received, no matter
how far we moved. Anyway, she said, her
whole life was in Boston. For my part, I was
eager to move somewhere else. I did not
belong to any place to begin with; my home
was wherever Laurie was. But I never was
able to make much headway with her.

In Newton bad feelings lingered. Most
of our neighbors had reached their own
verdict: not guilty, but not exactly innocent

either. Jacob may not have murdered Ben Rifkin, but they had heard enough to be disturbed by him. His knife, his violent fantasies, his wicked bloodline. To some, the abrupt end of the trial seemed fishy too. The kid's continued presence in town worried and irritated people. Even the kind ones were not anxious to have Jacob in their children's lives. Why take a chance? Even if they were ninety-nine percent sure of his innocence, who would risk being wrong when the stakes were so high? And who would risk the stigma of being seen with him? He was a pariah, whether he was actually guilty or not.

With all this, we did not dare send Jacob back to school in Newton. When he had first been indicted and promptly suspended from school, the town had been obliged to hire a home tutor for him, Mrs. McGowan, and we rehired her now to continue homeschooling him. Mrs. McGowan was the only regular visitor to our house, virtually the only one who ever saw the way we actually lived. When she walked in, a bit dowdy and heavy-hipped, her eyes would dance around, taking in the piles of dirty laundry, the unwashed dishes in the kitchen sink, Jacob's dirty hair. We must have seemed a little crazy to her. But she continued to show up every morning at nine to sit with Jacob at the kitchen table, reviewing his lessons, drubbing him for not doing his homework. "No one's going to feel sorry for you," she told him forthrightly. Laurie took an active part in Jacob's lessons too. She was a remarkable teacher, I thought, patient, kind. I had never actually seen her teach before, but watching her work with Jacob, I thought: she *should* go back to teaching. She should have been doing it all along.

As the weeks went by, Jacob was quite content in his new solitary life. He was a natural hermit. He did not miss school or his friends, he said. In fact, homeschooling might have suited him best from the start. It gave him the best part of school, the "content" (his word), without the myriad complications of girls, sex, sports, bullies, peer pressure, cliques—the complication of other kids, basically. Jake was just happier alone. After what he'd been through, who could blame him? When we discussed moving, it was always Jacob who was most enthusiastically in favor. The farther, the remoter, the better. Bisbee, Arizona, would suit him fine, he thought. That was Jacob—that equanimity, that poise, half serene, half oblivious. It will sound weird, I know, but Jacob, who always had the most at stake in this case, never broke down and cried, never lost it. Sometimes he would get angry or sullen or introverted, occasionally self-pitying, as all kids do, but he never came apart. Now that the case was over, he was that same even-tempered kid. It was not hard to imagine why his classmates might find his eerie composure a little off-putting. Personally, I found it admirable.

I did not have to work, at least for a while. I was still technically on paid leave from the district attorney's office. My full salary continued to be direct-deposited to my checking account, as it had been throughout this entire episode. No doubt this was a tricky problem for Lynn Canavan. She had backed the wrong horse. Now she had no excuse to fire me since I had done nothing wrong, but she could not very well bring me back as First Assistant either. Eventually she would have to offer me a position and I would have to refuse it, and that would be the end of it. But in the near term she seemed willing to keep me on the payroll in return for my keeping my mouth shut, which seemed like a small price to pay. I would have kept my mouth shut anyway; I liked her.

Meanwhile, Canavan had bigger fish to fry. She had to figure out what to do about Logiudice, the Rasputin in her court, whose professional implosion had surely ended his own political hopes and, if she was not careful, might end hers too. But, again, she could not fire a prosecutor merely for losing a case, otherwise who would ever be willing to go to work for her? The general view was that Canavan would run for attorney general or even governor soon and leave the whole mess behind for the next DA to clean up. But for the time being, all she could do was watch and wait. Maybe Logiudice could resurrect his reputation somehow. Hey, you never know.

I did not worry much about my own career for the time being. Certainly I was done as a prosecutor. The snickering would have been too much. I suppose I might have gone on as some other kind of lawyer. There was always criminal defense, where the link to Jacob's case might even have been a badge of honor—the drama of an innocent boy wrongly accused, who had stood up to The Man, or whatever. But it was a little late in the day to be switching sides. I was not sure I could bring myself to defend the same scumbags I had spent a lifetime locking up. Where that left me I had no idea. In limbo, I suppose, like the rest of my family.

Of the three of us, Laurie was the most beaten up by the trial. In the weeks that followed she did recover a little, but she never did return to what she was Before. She never put back on the weight she had lost, and her face would always look drawn to me. It was as if she'd aged ten years in just a few months. But the real change was inside. In those first weeks after Jacob's trouble, there was a cool, guarded quality about Laurie. She was wary. To me, this new, more cautious manner was under-standable. She had been victimized, and she responded the way victims do. It did alter the dynamics of our family—no more Mom warmly imploring Jacob and me, the family involutes, to share our feelings and jabber about our problems and generally turn ourselves inside out for her. She had withdrawn from all that, for a while at least. She watched us from a distance now. I could hardly begrudge her any of this. Damaged at last, my wife had become a little like me, a little harder. Damage hardens us all. It will harden you too, when it finds you—and it will find you.

38 | The Policeman's Dilemma

Northern Correctional Institution, Somers, Connecticut.

In the visiting booth again. Sealed up in my white-walled compartment, thick glass window in front of me. Steady background noise: murmuring in the adjacent booths, in the distance muted shouts and prison racket, announcements over an intercom.

Bloody Billy shuffled into the window frame, his hands cuffed to a waist chain, a second chain running from his waist down to his cuffed ankles. No matter: he came into the room like a tyrannical king, chin thrust forward, badass sneer, gray hair combed back over his head in a crazy-old-man pompadour.

Two guards piloted him to the chair but without laying a hand on him. One of them released the handcuffs from his waist while the other watched, then they both backed away, out of the window frame.

My father picked up the phone and, with his hands joined at his chin as if in prayer, he said, "Junior!" His tone said, *What a pleasant surprise!*

"Why did you do it?"

"Do what?"

"Patz."

His eyes traveled from my face to the phone on the wall and back, reminding me to watch what I said on a monitored line.

"Junior, what are you talking about? I've been here the whole time. Maybe you haven't heard: I don't get out much."

I unfolded a Triple-I record, a multistate criminal record. It was several pages long. I palmed it smooth and pressed the front page against the glass with five fingertips for him to read the name: *James Michael O'Leary, a.k.a. Jimmy, Jimmy-O, Father O'Leary, DOB 2/18/43.*

He leaned forward and squinted at the document. "Never heard of him."

"Never heard of him? Really?"

"Never heard of him."

"You did a bid with him right here."

"A lot of guys come through here."

"Six years you were here together. Six years!"

He shrugged. "I don't socialize. It's jail, not Yale. Maybe if you had a picture or something?" Mischievous wink. "But I never heard of this guy."

"Well, he's heard of you."

Shrug. "Lot of people have heard of me. I'm a legend."

"He said you asked him to look out for us, to look out for Jacob."

"Bullshit."

"To protect us."

"Bullshit."

"You sent someone to protect us? You think I need you to protect my kid?"

"Hey, I never said any of that. This is all you talkin'. Like I said, I never heard of this guy. I don't know what the hell you're talking about."

Now, spend enough time in a courthouse and you become a connoisseur of lying. You learn to recognize the various types of bullshit, as Eskimos are said to distinguish different types of snow. The sort of winking denial Billy was indulging here—in which the words *I didn't do it* were delivered in a way that announced *Of course I did it, but we both know you can't prove it*—must be every criminal's special delight. To laugh in a cop's face! Certainly my dirtbag father was enjoying the hell out of it. From the cop's point of view, there is no sense fighting this sort of confession-denial. You learn to accept this situation. It is part of the game. It is the policeman's dilemma: sometimes you can't prove the case without a confession, but you can't get a confession unless you already have proof.

So I just took the paper down from the glass and dropped it on the little melamine counter in front of me. I sat back and rubbed my forehead. "You fool. You stupid old fool. Do you know what you've done?"

"Fool? What are you, calling me a fool? I didn't do shit."

"Jacob was innocent! You stupid, stupid old man."

"Watch your mouth, junior. I don't have to stay here talking to you."

"We didn't need your help."

"No? Could've fooled me."

"We would have won."

"And if you didn't? What then? You want the kid to rot in a place like this? You know what this place is, junior? This is a grave. It's a garbage dump. It's a big hole in the ground where they throw the trash nobody wants to see anymore. Anyways, you're the one who told me that night on the phone, you were going to lose."

"Look, you can't—you can't just—"

"Jesus, junior, keep your dress on, would you? This is fuckin' embarrassing. Look, I'm not saying anything about what happened, okay? 'Cause I don't know. Whatever happened to this guy—what's his name? Patz?—whatever happened to this guy, I don't know. I'm stuck here in this pit. What the hell do I know? But if you're asking me to boohoo because some kiddy-raper child-molester piece of shit got killed, or killed himself, or whatever? Forget about it. Good riddance. One less piece of shit in the world. Fuck him. He's gone." He held a fist to his mouth and blew into it then blossomed open his fingers, like a magician making a coin disappear. *Gone.* "One less asshole in the world, that's all it is. Guy like that, the world's a better place without him."

"But *with* you?"

He glared. "Hey, I'm still here." He puffed his chest. "It don't matter what you think of me. I'm still here, junior, whether you like it or not. You can't get rid of me."

"Like cockroaches."

"That's right, I'm a tough old cockroach. Proud of it."

"So what did you do? Call in a favor? Or just reach out to an old friend?"

"I told you, I don't know what you're talking about."

"You know, the thing is, it actually took me a while to figure it out. I've got a cop friend who told me this guy Father O'Leary was an old leg-breaker and he was still working as a fixer, and when I asked what that meant, a 'fixer,' he said, 'He makes problems go away.' So that's what you did, isn't it? You called an old friend and you made the problem go away."

No answer. Why should he help me by talking? Bloody Billy understood the policeman's dilemma as well as I did. No confession, no case; no case, no confession.

But we both knew what went down. We were thinking the exact same thing, I'm sure: Father O'Leary goes over there one night, after a particularly bad day for Jacob in court, and he puts a scare into this fat kid, waves a gun in his face, makes him sign a confession. The kid probably shit his pants before Father O'Leary strung him up.

"Do you know what you've done to Jacob?"

"Yeah, I saved his life."

"No. You took away his day in court. You took away his chance to hear the jury say 'not guilty.' From now on, there'll always be a little doubt. There'll always be people convinced Jacob is a murderer."

He laughed. Not a little laugh but a roar. "His day in court? And I'm the fool? Junior, you know what? You're not as smart as I thought you were." He laughed some more. Big, crazy, gusting belly laughs. He mimicked me in a high, prissy voice, "'Oh, his day in court!' Jesus, junior! It's a wonder you're out there and I'm in here. How the fuck does that happen? You dumb gavoon."

"It's a crazy world. Imagine, them putting a guy like you in prison."

He ignored me. He leaned forward as if he meant to whisper a secret in my ear through the inch-thick slab of glass. "Listen," he confided, "you want to get all Dudley Do-Right here? You want to throw your kid back in the shit? Is that what you want, junior? Call the cops. Go ahead, call the cops and tell them this whole crazy story you've got about Patz and this guy O'Leary I supposedly know. What do I give a shit? I'm in here for life anyway. You won't be hurting me. Go on. He's your kid. Do what you want with him. Like you said, maybe the kid'll get off. Take your chances."

"They can't try Jacob again anyway. Jeopardy's attached."

"So? Even better. Sounds like you think this guy O'Leary committed a murder. If I was you, I'd go report it right away. Is that what you're going to do, Mr. DA Man? Or maybe that won't look so good for the kid, will it?"

He looked me square in the eyes for a few seconds until I became aware of my own blinking.

"No," he said, "I didn't think so. We through here?"

"Yeah."

"Good. Hey, guard! Guard!"

Two guards ambled over with skeptical faces.

"Me and my son are all done visiting. You guys ever met my son?"

The guards did not answer, did not even glance at me. They seemed to think it was a trick to get them to look away for a second and they were not about to fall for it. Their job was to get the wild animal back into its cage. That was dangerous enough. There was no percentage in breaking protocol.

"All right," my father said as one of the guards fished around for the key to reattach the cuffs to his harness. "You come back soon, junior. Remember, I'm still your father. I'll always be your father." The guards began to rustle him out of the chair but he went right on talking. "Hey," he said to the guards, "you should get to know this guy. He's a lawyer. Maybe you guys'll need a lawyer somed—"

One of the guards pulled the phone from his hand and hung it up. He stood the prisoner up, reattached the handcuffs to his waist chain, then tugged the whole arrangement of chains to make sure he was properly trussed. Billy's eyes were on me the whole time, even as the guards jostled him. What he saw when he looked at me is anybody's guess. Probably just a stranger in a window frame.

Mr. Logiudice: I'm going to ask you again. And I'm going to remind you, Mr. Barber, you are under oath.

Witness: I'm aware of that.

Mr. Logiudice: And you are aware we are talking about a murder here.

Witness: The M.E. ruled it a suicide.

Mr. Logiudice: Leonard Patz was murdered and you know it!

Witness: I don't know how anyone could know that.

Mr. Logiudice: And you have nothing to add?

Witness: No.

Mr. Logiudice: You have no idea what happened to Leonard Patz on October 25, 2007?

Witness: None.

Mr. Logiudice: Any theories?
Witness: No.
Mr. Logiudice: Do you know anything at all
                    about James Michael O'Leary,
                    also known as Father O'Leary?
Witness: Never heard of him.
Mr. Logiudice: Really? You've never even
                    heard the name.
Witness: Never heard of him.

I remember Neal Logiudice standing there with his arms crossed, smoldering. Once upon a time, I might have patted him on the back, told him, "Witnesses lie. Nothing you can do. Go have a beer, just let it go. All crime is local, Neal—these guys all come back sooner or later." But Logiudice was not the type to shrug off an insolent witness. Probably he did not give a shit about the Patz murder, anyway. This was not about Leonard Patz.

It was already late afternoon when Logiudice finally forced me into a little harmless perjury. I had been testifying all day, and I was tired. It was April. The days were beginning to get longer. The daylight was just beginning to dim when I said, "Never heard of him."

By then Logiudice must have known he was not going to restore his own reputation here, least of all by asking for my help. He resigned from the DA's office soon after. He is a defense lawyer in Boston now. I have no doubt he will make a great defense lawyer too, right up until the day he is disbarred. But for now, I console myself with that image of him in the grand jury room doing a slow burn as his case, and his career, collapsed before his eyes. I like to think of it as the last lesson I ever taught him, my former protégé. It's the policeman's dilemma, Neal. After a while you get used to it.

39 | Paradise

It turns out, you can get used to most anything. What one day seems a shocking, unbearable outrage over time comes to seem ordinary, unremarkable.

As those first few months passed, the insult of Jacob's trial gradually lost its power to enrage us. We had done all we could. This grotesque thing had happened to our family. We would always be known for it. It would be the first sentence in all our obituaries. And we would always be shaped by the experience, in ways we could not guess at the time. All this began to seem normal, permanent, hardly worth commenting on.

And when it did—when we started to get used to our new life as a notorious family, when we finally began to look forward, not back—our family gradually reemerged.

Laurie was the first of us to reawaken. She renewed her friendship with Toby Lanzman. Toby had not reached out to us during the trial, but she was the first of our Newton friends to reconnect with us afterward. Still her old fit, commanding self—same lean runner's face, same springy, high-rumped body—Toby guided Laurie in a fearsome exercise program that included long, cold jogs along Commonwealth Avenue. Laurie wanted to get stronger, she said. Soon Laurie was driving herself through grueling workouts even without Toby. She would come back from increasingly long runs, red-faced and glistening with sweat in the dead of winter. "Have to get stronger."

Recovering her role as family captain, Laurie threw herself into the great project of reviving Jacob and me as well. She cooked tremendous breakfasts of waffles or omelettes or hot cereal, and now that we had no jobs to rush off to, we lingered over the newspapers, which Jacob read on his MacBook while Laurie and I shared the newsprint versions of the *Globe* and the *Times.* She organized family movie nights and even allowed me to pick the gangster pictures I love, then she suffered good-naturedly as Jacob and I repeated our favorite lines over and over: "Say hello to my leetle friend" and "I didn't know until this day that it was Barzini all along." She said that my Brando sounded like Elmer Fudd, which required a trip to YouTube to show Jacob who Elmer Fudd was. How strange to hear ourselves laughing again.

And when all this was not working fast enough, when Jacob and I could not seem to shake the gloom of the last year, Laurie decided that stronger medicine was needed.

"Why don't we go away for a while?" she said brightly at dinner one night. "We could take a family vacation like we used to."

It was one of those blindingly obvious ideas that hits you like a revelation. Of course! The moment she suggested it, we knew that *of course* we had to go. Why had it taken us so long to think of it? Just talking about the idea made us a little giddy.

"That's brilliant," I said. "Clear our heads!"

"Push the reset button!" Jacob.

Laurie raised her fists and wiggled them, she was so excited. "I am so *sick* of all this. I hate this house. I hate this town. I hate the way I feel all day—trapped. I just really want to be someplace else."

My memory is that the three of us went right to the computer and chose our destination that same night. We picked a resort in Jamaica called Waves. None of us had ever heard of Waves or been to Jamaica. We based the decision on nothing more than the resort's own website, which dazzled us with fantastically Photoshopped images: palm trees, white-sand beaches, aquamarine ocean. It was all so perfect and so obviously fraudulent that we could not resist it. It was travel porn. There were laughing couples, she toned and tan in her bikini and wrap, he gray at the temples but sporting a full rack of bodybuilder's abs—the soccer mom and middle manager transformed at Waves into their true inner minx and stud. There was a hotel complex festooned with shutters and verandas, the exteriors brightly painted to evoke a fantasy Caribbean village. The hotel overlooked a network of cerulean swimming pools with fountains and swim-up bars. The Waves logo shimmered on every pool floor. The blue pools spilled from one down to the next until the water reached the edge of a low cliff, and over the edge an elevator descended to a horseshoe-shaped beach and a pristine little cay and, off in the distance, the blue of the ocean stretched all the way out into the endless blue of the sky with no clear horizon line, which would have spoiled the illusion that Waves inhabited the same round planet as everyplace else. It was just the sort of dreamworld we longed to escape into. We did not want to go anyplace "real"; you cannot be in a place like Paris or Rome without thinking, and we wanted most of all not to think. At Waves, happily, it seemed no thought could survive for long. Nothing would be allowed to spoil the fun.

The remarkable thing about all this emotional manipulation was that it actually worked. We actually achieved the traveler's fantasy of leaving our old selves and all our troubles behind. We were transported, in both senses. Not all at once, of course, but little by little. We felt the weight begin to lift the moment we booked the trip, a nice long two-week stay. Then we felt lighter still when the plane lifted off from Boston, and even more so when we stepped out into the glare and the warm tropical breeze on the tarmac at the little airport in Montego Bay. Already we were different. We were strangely, miraculously, deliriously happy. We looked at one another with surprise, as if to say, *Could this be true? Are we really . . . happy?* You will say that we were deluding ourselves; our troubles were no less real. And of course that is true, but so what? We had earned a vacation.

At the airport, Jacob grinned. Laurie held my hand. "It's paradise!" she beamed.

We made our way through the terminal and out to a small shuttle bus, where a driver held a clipboard with the Waves logo and a list of guests he was supposed to pick up. He looked a little bedraggled in a T-shirt, shorts, and shower sandals. But he grinned at us and he peppered his sentences with *"Ya, mahn!"* and generally he made a good show of it. "Ya, man!" he said over and over, until we were saying it too. Obviously he had performed this happy-native routine a thousand times. The pasty vacationers ate it up, us included. *Ya, man!*

The bus ride lasted nearly two hours. We bounced over a crumbling road that roughly followed the north coast of the island. To our right were lush green mountains, to the left, the sea. The poverty of the island was hard to miss. We passed little tumbledown houses and shanties knocked together from scrap wood and corrugated tin. Ragged women and scrawny kids walked along the sides of the road. The vacationers in the bus were subdued during the ride. The natives' poverty was a bummer and they wanted to be sensitive to it; at the same time they had come for a good time and it wasn't *their* fault the island was poor.

Jacob found himself seated on the wide bench at the back of the bus next to a girl about his age. She was pretty in a debate-team way, and the two kids chatted cautiously. Jacob kept his answers short, as if every word was a stick of dynamite. He wore a dumb grin. Here was a girl who did not know anything about the murder, did not even seem aware that Jacob was a geek who could not quite bring himself to look a girl in the eye. (He was proving himself quite capable of looking this girl in the chest, however.) It was all so wonderfully normal, Laurie and I made a point of not staring lest *we* screw it up for him.

I whispered, "And I figured *I'd* get laid on this trip before Jacob."

"My money's still on you," she said.

When the bus finally arrived at Waves, we passed through a grand gate, past lush manicured beds of red hibiscus and yellow impatiens, and stopped under a portico at the main entrance to the hotel. Grinning bellmen unpacked the bags. They wore uniforms that combined British military bits—pith helmets blancoed to a dazzling whiteness, black pants with a thick red stripe down the side—and bright flower-print shirts. It was a delirious combination, just right for the army of Paradise, the good-time army.

In the lobby, we checked in. We exchanged our money for the in-house currency of Waves, little silver coins called "sand dollars." A good-time soldier in a pith helmet served a complimentary rum punch, about which I can tell you only that it contained grenadine (it was bright red) and rum, and I immediately had another, feeling it was my patriotic duty to the pseudonation of Waves. I tipped the soldier, Lord knew how much since the exchange rate for sand dollars was a nebulous thing, but the tip must have been generous because he pocketed the coin and said, "Ya, man," illogically but happily. From there, my memory of the first day gets a little fuzzy.

And the second.

I apologize for the silly tone, but the truth is we were damn happy. And relieved. With the strain of the previous year finally removed, we got a little silly. I know this story is all a very solemn business. Ben Rifkin had still been murdered, even if it had not been by Jacob. And Jacob had only been saved by the intervention of a second murder arranged by a deus ex prison—a secret only I was aware of. And of course, as the accused, we were still widely presumed guilty of *something* and so we had no right to be happy anyway. We had taken to heart Jonathan's very strict instructions never to laugh or smile in public, lest anyone think we were not treating the situation with the proper gravity, lest they think we were anything less than shattered. Now, finally, we exhaled and, in our exhaustion, we felt intoxicated even when we weren't. We did not feel like murderers at all.

We spent our first few mornings at the beach, afternoons at one of the many pools. Every evening the resort offered some sort of entertainment. This might be a musical show or karaoke or a talent contest for the guests. Whatever the format, the staff exhorted us to have the most extroverted sort of fun. They would call from the stage in lilting island accents, "Come on, ev-ry-bah-dy, make some noise!" and we guests would clap and cheer with maximum gusto. Afterward there would be dancing. A good dose of Waves punch was required to get through it.

We ate ravenously. Meals were all-you-can-eat buffets, and we made up for months of undereating. Laurie and I spent our sand dollars on beers and piña coladas. Jacob even tried his first beer. "Good," he pronounced it manfully, though he did not finish it.

Jacob spent most of his time with his new girlfriend, whose name—brace yourself—was Hope. He was content to be with us too, but more and more the two of them went off together. Later we found out that Jacob had given her a false last name. Jacob Gold, he called himself, borrowing Laurie's maiden name, which is why Hope never found out about the case. We did not know about Jacob's little subterfuge at the time, so we were left to wonder what it meant, exactly, that this girl was flirting with Jacob. Was she so oblivious that it never occurred to her to do a simple Google search on him? If she had Googled "Jacob Barber," she would have come up with about three hundred thousand results. (The number has grown since then.) Or maybe she did know and got some weird thrill out of dating this dangerous pariah. Jacob told us Hope had no idea about the case, and we did not dare question her directly for fear of spoiling the first good thing that had happened to Jacob in a very long time. We did not see much of Hope, anyway, in the few days we knew her. She and Jake preferred to be by themselves. Even if we were all at the pool together, the two of them would come over to say hello, then they would go sit at a little distance from us. Once we glimpsed them holding hands furtively as they lay on adjacent chaises.

I want to say—it is important you

know—we liked Hope, not least because she made our son happy. Jacob brightened whenever she was around. She had a warm way about her. She was courteous and polite, with blond hair and a wonderful soft Virginia accent that seemed lovely to us Bostonians. She was a little pudgy but comfortable in her body, comfortable enough to wear bikinis every day, and we liked her for that too, for the easy way she carried herself, free of the usual morbid teenage insecurities. Even her unlikely name added to the fairy-tale symmetry of her sudden appearance on stage. "Finally we have Hope," I would say to Laurie.

The truth is, we were not entirely focused on Jacob and Hope. Laurie and I had our own relationship to work on. We had to relearn each other, reestablish the old patterns. We even resumed our sex life, not frantically but slowly, tentatively. Probably we were as clumsy as Jacob and Hope, who no doubt were fumbling over each other at the same time, in secret corners and thrust up against palm trees. Laurie got very brown very quickly, as she always has. To my middle-aged eyes she looked insanely sexy, and I began to wonder if the website did not have it right, after all: she looked more and more like the hot soccer mom in the ad. She was still the best-looking woman I ever saw. It was a miracle that I got her in the first place and a miracle that she stayed with me as long as she did.

I think that, sometime in that first week, Laurie began to forgive herself for the primal sin—as she saw it—of losing faith in her own son, of doubting his innocence during the trial. You could see it in the way she began to loosen up around him. This was an internal struggle for her; she had nothing to reconcile with Jacob, since he never knew about her doubts, let alone that she had actually been afraid of him. Only Laurie could forgive herself. Personally, I did not see it as such a big deal. As betrayals go, this was a small one, and understandable in the circumstances. Maybe you have to be a mother to know why she took it so hard. All I can say is that, as Laurie began to feel better, our whole family began to return to its normal rhythm. Our family orbited around Laurie. Always had.

We quickly settled into a few routines, as people must, even in dreamworlds like Waves. My favorite ritual was to watch the sunset from the beach as a family. Every evening, we brought beers down with us and dragged three beach chairs to the water's edge so we could sit with our feet in the water. Hope joined us to watch the sunset once, seating herself tactfully beside Laurie like a lady-in-waiting attending her queen. But generally it was just us three Barbers. Around us in the dimming light, little children would play in the sand and the shallow water, toddlers, even a few babies and their young parents. Gradually the beach would get quieter as the other guests left to get ready for dinner. The lifeguards would drag the empty beach chairs across the sand and stack them for the night, making a clatter, and finally the lifeguards themselves would leave, and only a few sunset gazers would linger on the beach. We would look out into the distance, where two arms of land reached out to encircle the little bay, and the horizon would burn yellow then red then indigo.

Looking back on it now, I picture my happy family of three sitting on that beach at sunset and I want to freeze the story there. We must have looked so normal, Laurie and Jacob and me, so much like all the other partyers and suburbanites at that resort. We must have seemed just like everyone else, which, when you get down to it, is all I ever really wanted.

Mr. Logiudice: And then?
Witness: And then—
Mr. Logiudice: Then what happened,
                       Mr. Barber?
Witness: The girl disappeared.

40 | No Way Out

Evening was coming on now. Outside, daylight was withdrawing, the sky going dull, the familiar sunless gray sky of a cold spring in New England. The grand-jury room, no longer flooded with clear sunlight, went yellow under the fluorescent lights.

The jurors' attention had come and gone the last few hours, but now they sat up attentively. They knew what was coming.

I had been in the chair testifying all day. I must have looked a little haggard. Logiudice circled me excitedly, like a boxer sizing up a woozy opponent.

Mr. Logiudice: Do you have any information about what happened to Hope Connors?

Witness: No.

Mr. Logiudice: When did you learn she had vanished?

Witness: I don't recall exactly. I remember how it began. We got a call in our room at the resort around dinnertime. It was Hope's mother, asking if she was with Jacob. They had not heard from her all afternoon.

Mr. Logiudice: What did you tell her?

Witness: That we hadn't seen her.

Mr. Logiudice: And Jacob? What did he say about it?

Witness: Jake was with us. I asked him if he knew where Hope was. He said no.

Mr. Logiudice: Was there anything unusual about Jacob's reaction when you asked him that question?

Witness: No. He just shrugged. There was no reason to worry. We all figured she'd probably just gone off to explore. Probably she lost track of time. There was no cell phone reception there, so the kids were constantly disappearing. But the resort was very safe. It was completely fenced in. No one could get in to harm her. Hope's mom wasn't panicked either. I told her not to worry, Hope would probably be back any minute.

Mr. Logiudice: But Hope Connors never did come back.

Witness: No.

Mr. Logiudice: In fact, her body was not found for several weeks, isn't that right?

Witness: Seven weeks.

Mr. Logiudice: And when it was found?

Witness: The body was washed up on the shore several miles away from the resort. She drowned, apparently.

Mr. Logiudice: Apparently?

Witness: When a body is in the water that long— It had deteriorated. My understanding is that it had also been fed on by marine life.

I don't know for certain; I was not privy to that investigation. Suffice it to say, the body did not yield much evidence.

Mr. Logiudice: The case is considered an unsolved homicide?

Witness: I don't know. It shouldn't be. There's no evidence to support that. The evidence suggests only that she went swimming and drowned.

Mr. Logiudice: Well, that's not quite true, is it? There is some evidence that Hope Connors's windpipe was crushed before she went into the water.

Witness: That inference is not supported by the evidence. The body was badly degraded. The cops down there—there was so much pressure, so much media. That investigation was not conducted properly.

Mr. Logiudice: That happened quite a bit around Jacob, didn't it? A murder, a botched investigation. He must have been the unluckiest boy.

Witness: Is that a question?

Mr. Logiudice: We'll move on. Your son's name has been widely linked to the case, hasn't it?

Witness: In the tabloids and some sleazy websites. They'll say anything for money. There's no profit in saying Jacob was innocent.

Mr. Logiudice: How did Jacob react to the girl's disappearance?

Witness: He was concerned, of course. Hope was someone he cared about.

Mr. Logiudice: And your wife?

Witness: She was also very, very concerned.

Mr. Logiudice: That's all, "very, very concerned"?

Witness: Yes.

Mr. Logiudice: Isn't it fair to say she concluded Jacob had something to do with that girl's disappearance?

Witness: Yes.

Mr. Logiudice: Was there anything in particular that convinced her of this?

Witness: There was something that happened at the beach. It was the day the girl disappeared.

Jacob got there—this was late afternoon, to watch the sunset—and he sat on my right. Laurie was on my left. We said, "Where's Hope?" Jacob said, "With her family, I guess. I haven't seen her." So we made some kind of joke—I think it was Laurie who asked—if everything was all right between them, if they'd had a fight. He said no, he just hadn't seen her for a few hours. I—

Mr. Logiudice: Andy? Are you all right?

Witness: Yeah. Sorry, yes. Jake—he had these spots on his bathing suit, these little red spots.

Mr. Logiudice: Describe the spots.

Witness: They were spatters.

Mr. Logiudice: What color?

Witness: Brownish red.

Mr. Logiudice: Blood spatters?

Witness: I don't know. I didn't think so. I asked him what it was, what did he do to his bathing suit? He said he must have dripped something he'd been eating, ketchup or something.

Mr. Logiudice: And your wife? What did she think of the red spatters?

Witness: She didn't think anything at the time. It was nothing, because we didn't know the girl was missing yet. I told him to just go jump in the water and swim around until the bathing suit was clean.

Mr. Logiudice: And how did Jacob react?

Witness: He didn't react at all. He just got up and he walked out on the dock—it was an H-shaped dock; he walked out the right-hand dock-and he dove in.

Mr. Logiudice: Interesting that it was you who told him to wash the bloodstains off his bathing suit.

Witness: I had no idea if they were bloodstains. I still don't know if that's true.

Mr. Logiudice: You still don't know? Really? Then why were you so quick to tell him to jump in the water?

Witness: Laurie said something to him about how the bathing suit was expensive and Jacob should take better care of his things.

He was so careless, such a slob. I didn't want him to get in trouble with his mother. We were all having such a good time. That's all it was.

Mr. Logiudice: But this was why Laurie was upset when Hope Connors first went missing?

Witness: Partly, yes. It was the whole situation, everything we'd been through.

Mr. Logiudice: Laurie wanted to go home immediately, isn't that right?

Witness: Yes.

Mr. Logiudice: But you refused.

Witness: Yes.

Mr. Logiudice: Why?

Witness: Because I knew what people would say: that Jacob was guilty and he was running away before the cops could pick him up. They would call him a killer. I wasn't going to let anyone say that about him.

Mr. Logiudice: In fact, the authorities in Jamaica did question Jacob, didn't they?

Witness: Yes.

Mr. Logiudice: But they never arrested him?

Witness: No. There was no reason to arrest him. He didn't do anything.

Mr. Logiudice: Jesus, Andy, how can you be so damn sure? How can you be sure of that?

Witness: How can anyone be sure of anything? I trust my kid. I have to.

Mr. Logiudice: You have to why?

Witness: Because I'm his father. I owe him that.

Mr. Logiudice: That's it?

Witness: Yes.

Mr. Logiudice: What about Hope Connors? What did you owe her?

Witness: Jacob did not kill that girl.

Mr. Logiudice: Kids just kept dying around him, is that it?

Witness: That's an improper question.

Mr. Logiudice: I'll withdraw it. Andy, do you honestly think you're a reliable witness? Do you honestly think you see your son right?

Witness: I think I'm reliable, yes, generally. I don't think any parent can be completely objective about his kid, I'll concede that.

Mr. Logiudice: And yet Laurie had no trouble seeing Jacob for what he was, did she?

Witness: You'll have to ask her.

Mr. Logiudice: Laurie had no trouble believing Jacob had something to do with that girl's vanishing?

Witness: As I said, Laurie was very shaken by the whole thing. She was not herself. She came to her own conclusions.

Mr. Logiudice: Did she ever discuss her suspicions with you?

Witness: No.

Mr. Logiudice: I'll repeat the question. Did your wife ever discuss her suspicions about Jacob?

Witness: No, she did not.

Mr. Logiudice: Your own wife never confided in you?

Witness: She did not feel that she could. Not about this. We'd talked about the Rifkin case, of course. I think she knew there were some things I just could not discuss; there were some places I just could not go. Those things she would just have to handle by herself.

Mr. Logiudice: So after two weeks in Jamaica?

Witness: We came home.

Mr. Logiudice: And when you got home, at that point did Laurie finally voice her suspicions about Jacob?

Witness: Not really.

Mr. Logiudice: "Not really"—what does that mean?

Witness: When we got home from Jamaica, Laurie was very, very quiet. She wouldn't discuss anything at all with me, really. She was very wary, very upset. She was scared. I tried to talk to her, draw her out, but she didn't trust me, I think.

Mr. Logiudice: Did she ever discuss what you two ought to do, morally, as parents?

Witness: No.

Mr. Logiudice: If she had asked you, what would you have said? What do

	you think your moral obligation was as parents of a murderer?
Witness:	It's a hypothetical question. I don't believe we were parents of a murderer.
Mr. Logiudice:	All right, hypothetically then: If Jacob was guilty, what should you and your wife have done about it?
Witness:	You can ask the question as many ways as you like, Neal. I won't answer it. It never happened.

What happened then I can honestly say was the most genuine, spontaneous reaction I ever saw out of Neal Logiudice. He flung his yellow pad in frustration. It fluttered like a shotgunned bird tumbling out of the sky, settling in the far corner of the room.

An older woman on the grand jury gasped.

I thought for a moment it was one of Logiudice's phony gestures—a cue to the jury: *Can't you see he's lying?*—the better because it would not show up in the transcript. But Logiudice just stood there, hands on hips, looking at his shoes, faintly shaking his head.

After a moment he collected himself. He folded his arms and took a deep breath. *Back to it. Lure, trap, fuck.*

He raised his eyes to me and saw— what? A criminal? A victim? In any event, a disappointment. I rather doubt he had the sense to see the truth: that there are wounds worse than fatal, which the law's little binary distinctions—guilty/innocent, criminal/victim—cannot fathom, let alone fix. The law is a hammer, not a scalpel.

Mr. Logiudice: You understand this grand jury is investigating your wife, Laurie Barber?

Witness: Of course.

Mr. Logiudice: We've been here all day talking about her, about why she did this.

Witness: Yes.

Mr. Logiudice: I don't give a damn about Jacob.

Witness: If you say so.

Mr. Logiudice: And you know that you're not under any suspicion, of anything at all?

Witness: If you say so.

Mr. Logiudice: But you are under oath. I don't need to remind you of that?

Witness: Yes, I know the rules, Neal.

Mr. Logiudice: What your wife did, Andy—I don't understand why you won't help us. This was your family.

Witness: Pose a question, Neal. Don't make speeches.

Mr. Logiudice: What Laurie did—doesn't it bother y—

Witness: Objection! Pose a proper question!

Mr. Logiudice: She should be indicted!

Witness: Next question.

Mr. Logiudice: She should be indicted and brought to trial and locked up, and you know it!

Witness: Next question!

Mr. Logiudice: On the date of offense, March 19, 2008, did you receive news about the defendant, Laurie Barber?

Witness: Yes.

Mr. Logiudice: How?

Witness: Around nine A.M. the doorbell rang. It was Paul Duffy.

Mr. Logiudice: What did Lieutenant Duffy say?

Witness: He asked if he could come inside and sit down. He said he had terrible news. I told him, Just say it, whatever it was, just tell me right there at the door. He said there'd been an accident. Laurie and Jacob were in the car, on the pike, and it went off the road. He said Jacob was dead. Laurie was banged up pretty bad but she would make it.

Mr. Logiudice: Go on.

[The witness did not respond.]

Mr. Logiudice: What happened next, Mr. Barber?

[The witness did not respond.]

Mr. Logiudice: Andy?

Witness: I, um—I felt my knees begin to buckle, I started to fall straight down. Paul reached out to grab me. He held me up. He helped me into the living room to a chair.

Mr. Logiudice: What else did he tell you?

Witness: He said—

Mr. Logiudice: Do you need to take a break?

Witness: No. Sorry. I'm all right.

Mr. Logiudice: What else did Lieutenant Duffy tell you?

Witness: He said there were no other cars involved. There were witnesses, other drivers, who saw the car aim directly at a bridge abutment. She did not put on the brakes or try to steer away from it. The witnesses said she accelerated as she headed for the collision. She actually accelerated. The witnesses thought the driver must have passed out or had a heart attack or something.

Mr. Logiudice: It was murder, Andy. She murdered your son.

[The witness did not respond.]

Mr. Logiudice: This grand jury wants to indict her. Look at them. They want to do the right thing. We all do. But you have to help us. You have to tell us the truth. What happened to your son?

[The witness did not respond.]

Mr. Logiudice: What happened to Jacob?

[The witness did not respond.]
Mr. Logiudice: This can still come out right,
             Andy.
Witness: Can it?

Outside the courthouse, a hard wind jetted down Thorndike Street. Another architectural flaw: the high, flat walls on all four sides created a tornado wind around the base of the building. On a raw April evening like this, with the wind swirling around it, the courthouse could be hard even to reach. There might as well have been a moat around it. I pulled my coat around me and made my way down Thorndike toward the garage with the wind jostling my back. It was the last time I was ever in that courthouse. I leaned back against the wind like a man holding a door closed.

Of course, some things are impossible to put behind you. I have imagined those last moments over and over. I relive the last few seconds of Jacob's life every day, and when I sleep I dream of it. It does not matter that I was not there. I cannot keep my mind from seeing it.

With less than one minute remaining in his life, Jacob lolled in the middle row of the minivan with his long legs stretched out in front of him. He always sat in the second row, like a little kid, even when he and his mom were the only ones in the car. He was not wearing his seat belt. He was often careless about it. Ordinarily Laurie would have hassled him to put it on. That morning she did not.

Jacob and Laurie had not spoken much during the ride. There was not much to say. Jacob's mom had been quiet and saturnine since we had come back from Jamaica a few weeks earlier. He was smart enough to give her some space. Deep down, he must have known he had lost his mother—lost her trust, not her love. It was hard for them to be together. So, after exchanging a few labored words as they drove up Route 128, they both fell silent once they reached the turnpike, heading west off the ramp. The minivan merged into traffic and picked up speed, and mother and son settled in for the long dull ride.

There was another reason for Jacob's silence. He was going to an interview at a private school in Natick. We did not think any school would admit him, honestly. What school would risk the legal liability, even if it was willing to brave the notoriety of having bloody Jacob Barber on campus? We expected Jacob would be homeschooled for the rest of his high school years. But we had been instructed that the town would not cover the costs of homeschooling under a special-ed plan unless we had exhausted all other options, so a few perfunctory interviews had been arranged. The whole process was difficult for Jacob—he had to prove he was not wanted by being rejected over and over—and this morning the need for another pointless interview made him sullen. The schools granted him interviews, he thought, just to get a glimpse of him, to see what the monster looked like up close.

He asked his mom to turn on the radio. She put on WBUR, the NPR news station, but turned it off quickly. It was painful to be reminded that the great world continued to turn, unnoticing.

After a few minutes on the highway, there were tears on Laurie's face. She clenched the wheel.

Jacob did not notice. He was lost in his own thoughts. His eyes were fixed on the view ahead of him, between the two front seats. Through the windshield: the crowd of cars speeding in formation down the track.

Laurie signaled and moved into the right lane, where the traffic was sparse, and she began to pick up speed, 76, 77, 78, 79, 80. She unclipped her seat belt and handed it back over her left shoulder.

Jacob would have grown, of course. In a couple of years his voice would have deepened. There would have been new friends. In his twenties he would have looked more and more like his father. His dark stare would have relaxed, with time, into a gentler expression as he set down the worries and sorrows of adolescence. His rawboned frame would have filled out. He would not have been as big as his hulking father, just a little taller, a little broader in the shoulders than most. He would have considered law school. All kids imagine themselves in their parents' occupations, however briefly, however un-comfortably. But he would not have be-come a lawyer. He would have considered the work too extroverted, too theatrical, too pedantic for his reticent personality.

He would have spent a long time searching, a long time laboring in jobs that did not suit him.

As the minivan crossed 85 miles per hour, Jacob said, without any real concern, "Going a little fast there, aren't you, Mom?"

"Am I?"

He would have met his grandfather. He was curious already. And given his own legal problems, he would have wanted to confront the whole issue of his patrimony, of what it meant to be the grandson of Bloody Billy Barber. He would have gone to meet the man and been disappointed. The legend—the nickname, the fearsome reputation, the murder that was literally unspeakable to so many—was much bigger than the withered old man behind it, who in the end was just a thug, albeit a well-bred thug. Jacob would have come to terms with it somehow. He would not have done it the way I did, by erasing it, ignoring it, willing it away. He was too thoughtful to fool himself that way. But he would have made his peace with it. He would have passed from son to father, and only then would he have seen how little the whole thing really meant.

Later, after some wandering, he would have settled somewhere far away, somewhere no one had ever heard of the Barbers, or at least where no one knew enough about the story to bother with it. Somewhere out west, I think. Bisbee, Arizona, maybe. Or California. Who knows? And in one of those places, one day he would have held his own son in his arms and looked down into that baby's eyes—as I did with Jacob many times—and wondered, *Who are you? What are you thinking?*

"Are you all right, Mom?"

"Of course."

"What are you doing? This is dangerous."

88, 89, 90. The minivan, a Honda Odyssey, was actually quite heavy—not mini at all, its name notwithstanding—and had a powerful engine. It was easy to speed. It felt very stable at high speeds. Driving it, I was often surprised to glance down at the speedometer and discover I was doing 80 or 85 miles an hour. But above 90, it began to shudder a little and the wheels began to lose contact with the road.

"Mom?"

"I love you, Jacob."

Jacob pressed himself back against

his seat. His hands scrabbled for the seat belt but it was already too late. There were only a few seconds left. He still did not understand what was going on. His mind grasped at explanations for the speed, for Mom's bizarre calm: a jammed accelerator, a rush to avoid being late for the interview, or maybe her attention had just wandered.

"I love you and your father both."

The minivan began to slip into the breakdown lane on the right side of the road, first the right wheels stepping over the line, then the left—only seconds remaining now—and continued to pick up speed as the road went down a little hill, assisting the engine, which was beginning to top out as the vehicle hit 96, 97, 98.

"Mom! Stop!"

She launched the minivan directly at a bridge abutment. It was a molded-concrete wall built into the side of a hill. The abutment was guarded by a Jersey barrier, which ought to have guided the minivan away from a direct impact. But the vehicle was going too fast and the angle of approach was too direct, so that when Laurie edged into it the Jersey barrier lifted the right-side wheels, causing the vehicle to skitter up the wall and, disastrously, to flip. Laurie lost control of the car immediately but she never let go of the steering wheel. The van scraped and skidded up the Jersey barrier and vaulted off the top of it, its momentum catapulting it up into the air as it rolled three-quarters of the way to upside down, like a ship capsizing to its port side.

With the minivan in the air, rolling counterclockwise, the engine racing, Laurie screaming—a fraction of a second, that's all—Jacob would have thought of me—who had held him, my own baby, looked down into *his* eyes—and he would have understood I loved him, no matter what, to the very end—as he saw the concrete wall flying forward to meet him.

About the Author

WILLIAM LANDAY is the author of two other novels: *Mission Flats,* which won the Dagger Award for best debut crime novel, and *The Strangler,* which was nominated for the Strand Magazine Critics Award for best crime novel of the year. He lives in Boston.

www.williamlanday.com